WHAT REMAINS
BEHIND

A Novel by Teny Jacobs

For Merrit
Happy Hanukkah!

Chapter 1
Mitch

I can't believe that I was ever so naive. Having been born and raised in New York City, Brooklyn if you want to be technical about it, I have always considered myself to be more sophisticated than most people, but the events of the last half year have convinced me that it was merely a self-created illusion with which I stroked my own ego.

I suppose I could try to blame it on youth and inexperience, but I would not exactly consider myself young when forty is beckoning from a year and a half away, and after fifteen years in the corporate world, I should hardly be a novice at the way big stakes games are played.

The only defense I have is that I didn't want to see the facts that were so clearly before me. I didn't want to believe that people with whom I had chosen to cast my lot would behave in such a manner. I may not have wanted to believe it, but the bottom line is that I've seen and heard enough over the years to have handled things far more intelligently. The brutal truth is that I don't know why I behaved the way I did.

That may not be as honest as it sounds either. The fact is, the status quo was pretty pleasing where I was concerned. I had a comfortable job with a company that provided excellent benefits, a salary that many would envy and my future looked rosy, if not as secure as that of some of those who had been there longer. I had just celebrated my third wedding anniversary with the woman of my dreams. We had a beautiful home, savings in the bank, and a nice little portfolio that my stockbroker wife had created for us. Aside from being beautiful and charming, she is a genius at her career. What sane person would want to rock that boat? Besides, the possibilities that swam through my conscious from time to time sounded so ludicrous and far-fetched, it seemed more credible that it was paranoia than the truth.

I know that even if they didn't come out and say it, there were people who thought that I led a charmed life. I have always been able to find a job that interests me, having qualities that make me highly employable, including a resume detailing several promotions. I am reasonably good-looking, and am fortunate enough to have a wife who is more than easy on the eyes. We have been told on many occasions that we are a dashing-looking couple, a study in contrasts. I am tall, a little over six foot two and athletic of build; Astrid, my wife, at five foot seven is also tall but willowy. Her Swedish blood is apparent in her straight ash blonde hair, fine facial features and light blue eyes. My dark wavy hair, dark eyes and nose that's a bit too generous for the rest of my face are a badge of my Jewish ancestry. Still, we fit together in perfect harmony like pieces of an abstract jigsaw puzzle. Surrounded by our eclectic collection of friends of different size, shape and color, we are hardly conspicuous.

But back to the heart of the matter. About a year and a half ago, I was hired as a design engineer by the Businetex corporation of Rochester, New York. They are not as large as Kodak or Xerox but are a major producer of office equipment and report quarterly earnings in millions. Actually, I had no burning desire to change jobs at that point in my career, having enjoyed my tenure as a design engineer for a far smaller company in Connecticut. Astrid was working as a stockbroker in Manhattan, we had a nice house in an affluent suburb, and life was good.

Then, the roof fell in on us. Astrid's father, who had never been to a doctor in his adult life, had a massive heart attack. All the long-lived Swedes on his family tree were of no help. He was gone before we could arrange a flight to his bedside. Astrid was beside herself. Despite everyone's assurances that there was no warning, that there was nothing she could have done, I don't think even God himself could have convinced her of that truth.

Astrid is an only child, and she and her parents were always very close. Had they not urged her to pursue her career in New York, she would not have left home, and we would never have met. I liked her parents. I did from the first time we met, and they seemed to like me. It was not as generous as it sounded that I suggested to Astrid that we invite her mother to live with us. Our home was more than ample size, and her mother is a terrific cook.

Inga Lindstrom in not your classic meddling mother-in-law either. The one time that Astrid asked her advice about how to settle an argument we were having, she later confided that her mother had responded, "That is for you and Mitchell to work out." When you see Inga, it is obvious where Astrid got her sensational looks. Inga looks like a mature version of Princess Grace without the extra pounds. There is only one major character flaw in the woman of which I am aware. She is independent to a fault.

When we urged Inga to relocate to Connecticut, after Gus Lindstrom's death, she would not even consider that option.

"I'm comfortable in my own home, my life and job are in Rochester, and I see no reason to leave." she declared.

"But Mom, you'll be all alone," worried Astrid.

"I don't mind being on my own," she reassured us, "and I have friends here, if I choose not to be."

You could not win an argument with Inga. She always had a logical answer for every point you tried to make. She made it very clear that she was completely self-reliant. Even later on, when we were living only twenty minutes away, when Inga cut herself on a broken canning jar one Saturday evening, she bandaged her own hand and drove herself to the emergency room, where she received nineteen stitches.

"Mom, you should have called us," chided Astrid, worriedly studying the bandage between her mother's right thumb and index finger. "We would have driven you to the hospital, waited with you, offered moral support."

"Nonsense," replied Inga. "It was unpleasant enough for me to wait in that noisy, dirty place without ruining your evening as well."

When, on a whim, I applied for the job I now hold, was offered it on my terms, and Astrid found a job in Rochester that she was willing to take, her mother urged us not to make the move unless we were doing it for ourselves. I would never say this to Astrid because it is her home, but I didn't want to live in or near Rochester. It's not that it's a bad place; it isn't. It just seemed like a wannabe of what we could have, did have when we were living in Connecticut.

If I felt so strongly about it, why did we move to Rochester? That's the simplest question thus far. Because I love Astrid so much that I would do anything for her, and that I would tell her. I did it for her, and I'm not sorry because Perinton, where we lived, was a nice suburb and, generally, our life was good; spending an occasional day with Inga could hardly be construed as punishment.

Had it been my mother, it would have been a whole different story. It's not that I don't love her; I do, very much. It's just far easier to love her from a distance. Rifka is the opposite of Inga in so many ways. She doesn't consider what she does to be interfering; she would call it guidance. Of course, she's had so much more practice at life, and knows so much more about what's best for everyone, that she feels that her adult children should just sit back and allow her to run our lives. My sister and I don't exactly see it that way.

My sister Marilyn married at twenty, probably having seen it as a chance to escape my parents' home. It didn't exactly work the way she'd envisioned but that's a long story. I, on the other hand, was a bachelor until the age of thirty-five. My mother thought that bachelorhood was fine until I was approaching thirty with no prospects in sight. When I left for college, my mother had taken me aside for a heart to heart talk.

"I want you to know that your father and I will accept nothing but a nice Jewish girl for a daughter-in-law," she warned me earnestly.

Actually, my father was an easygoing sort, who probably would have accepted whatever I chose to do with my life with relative good humor, but my mother made up in intensity for what he lacked. Never wanting to admit that she was asking for something for herself, Rifka always prefaced a request with, "For myself, I don't care so much but it would kill your father if you...." You fill in the blank. Anything she didn't approve of would have killed my father.

When I was thirty-two, Rifka said, "If you get married, the girl doesn't have to be Jewish, as long as she's white."

I was amused that she had lowered her standards.

On my thirty-fourth birthday, after we had eaten cake for dessert, my mother took me aside. "I want you to know that any nice girl will do; as long as you aren't a fairy, your father and I will be happy."

I had laughed. "I'm glad you've finally found your way to liberalism," I teased.

I put off introducing Astrid to my family for as long as I could. I was sure that she and Marilyn would love each other, and Bert, my brother-in-law, has never been a problem; we've always been buddies. I was only afraid that Marilyn would warn Astrid to escape while there was still time. Now, don't get me wrong. Marilyn and I are as close as a brother and sister three years apart can be. Oh, sure, we went through our fair share of squabbles and sibling rivalry as kids, but once she graduated from high school and I was a sophomore, we were more allies than sparring partners. It's just that Rifka as a mother-in-law is the stuff of which nightmares are made.

I need not have worried. My parents were instantly charmed by Astrid, particularly my father. No one could breathe a bad word about her in his presence; she was a goddess in his eyes. Dad died of cancer six months after we were married, but I always felt that the happiest moments of his last days were spent with Astrid.

My primary reason for moving to Rochester was for us to be closer to Astrid's mother but my motives were not as selfless as I have inferred My best friend Artie lived in Rochester and I would be lying if I said that I wasn't anxious for us to live in the same city once again.

Artie was recruited to work for Kodak right out of college, and he had moved over to Businetex about three years before I joined them, so he was a long-time Rochestarian. He passionately loved his work, and that's saying something, because his supervisor, Jerry Fallow, made my supervisor, Bob, look like a prince among men.

When he heard that I was even considering the possibility of moving here, he was delighted.

"Rochester is the ideal place for you and Astrid to look for jobs," he enthused. "There's a lot of tech, and because it's so highly white collar, the people have a lot of disposable income. There are always opportunities for engineers, and Astrid will be brilliant at convincing them to invest some of that extra money."

Astrid had actually worked for her present employer before, and they were delighted to have her back. Artie's enthusiasm for working at Businetex was contagious enough to convince me to apply for a job that was available, they wanted me, and the rest is history.

Artie and I had been friends almost all our lives, since we were four. In fact, the day Artie moved onto the block was the only time in my life that I can remember my father spanking me, for crossing the street by myself. The Kornfelds lived diagonally across the street from us, and Artie and I had spotted each other from opposite curbs.

"Come on over," I'd invited.

"I'm not allowed to cross the street by myself," he'd replied.

I wasn't allowed either, but no one was around so I looked both ways, as Marilyn had taught me, and I didn't see any cars. This was my first major foray into disobedience, and I had expected the asphalt to part and a giant bolt of lightning to emerge from the sky, but there had been no cataclysmic reaction, no screeching brakes, no loud scream in my mother's voice.

We had so much in common that our meeting seemed almost a cosmic event.

"How old are you?" I had asked immediately, before even learning his name.

"I'll be five in January. How old are you?"

"I'll be five in March."

Artie nodded knowingly. "I'm tall for my age but you look about the same size."

"I think you're bigger," I conceded.

"You'll catch up. I'm Arthur Louis Kornfeld but everyone calls me Artie. What's your name?"

"Mitch. Mitchell Goldblatt. I don't have a middle name.

"I don't know what you'd need one for," he said, with wisdom well beyond his nearly five years. "I'm glad I met you."

I too was glad we met. His family was also Jewish, so I knew my parents would approve of our friendship. We discovered that he had two sisters to my one, and we both loved sports. Artie and I became so involved in getting acquainted that I forgot where I was and how I got there. When my father called me for lunch, I didn't hear him. When he spotted me, I had to think fast.

"How did you get across the street?" he asked.

I lied without missing a beat. "Mrs. Nowicki crossed me. She was sweeping the sidewalk and I asked her to take me across."

My father had responded with two "potches," the first for crossing the street by myself, and the second for lying.

Apparently, everyone on the block knew that Mrs. Nowicki had been in the hospital all week with "female troubles." Everyone but me, that is.

Anyway, Artie and I had been best friends ever since, keeping in touch from different colleges, and later, different cities as each of us followed separate courses. We had always been able to talk about anything, and after Astrid and I came to Rochester, we saw a lot of each other. Astrid and I usually had dinner with him once a week, and he and I played tennis three times a week. I felt as if some invisible benefactor had given me a gift.

Life for Astrid and me would have been damn near perfect, in fact, had it not been for my tendency to procrastinate when it came to things that I didn't consider to be high priority. In my own defense, I believe that this is something that is beyond my control, and I can provide evidence to support my case.

I noticed very early on that Astrid had an inordinately large collection of shoes.

"Is there a particular reason why you have so many pairs?" I asked her, studying her closet one day while we were still dating.

"I need the right shoes to go with my clothes," she explained matter-of-factly.

I accepted that for quite a while. I had a pair of black dress shoes, brown shoes that I wore to work and my sneakers. However, soon after we moved to Rochester, when she excitedly showed me her newest acquisition, I began to wonder.

"You already have black shoes," I protested, studying the shiny high-heeled sandals that she offered for my inspection.

"They aren't like these. I have flat sandals, open-toed wedges, loafers and mid-heeled pumps but no dressy high-heeled sandals. These are perfect." She slipped the left shoe on her foot and wiggled her polished toes at me. "Aren't they cute?"

I admired every part of my wife, down to her feet. "They look great on you," I replied truthfully.

"And black is a great color for dressy shoes," she said. "They go with so much of my wardrobe."

"A practical acquisition," I said, still mystified.

"Yes," she replied, "and they were on sale. I'm quite proud of myself!"

I came to conclude that women are born with a "shoe gene." They can never have too many pairs, are attracted to colors that no self-respecting man would consider and they can smell a sale miles away. These are traits basic to their nature; they cannot be held accountable.

When I worked up the courage to tell Astrid my theory, I was surprised by her reaction. "Don't you think that's a little sexist?"

"Maybe," I conceded, "but I've never met a straight man who had more than four pairs of shoes, not counting football cleats and golf shoes. Do you know a woman who has less than ten pairs?"

"I don't ask every woman I know how many pairs of shoes she owns."

"But you've seen every woman you know in more than ten different pairs, haven't you?" I wondered.

"What are you getting at?"

"I'm not accusing you of anything. I'm merely suggesting that acquiring many pairs of shoes is instinctive, like a bird knowing how to build a nest. It's the 'shoe gene' that's responsible."

"And men don't have it?"

"None that I know."

"If that's the case, there must be a parallel equivalent," she said. "Nature favors symmetry."

"Maybe," I conceded, "but I can't think of any one that applies across the board. Maybe there is a variety to choose from for the male of the species."

"And what gene were you born with?" she asked, raising her eyebrows.

"I don't know," I admitted.

"Possibly, the 'procrastination gene,'" she said.

"Maybe that's the explanation," I agreed.

She was annoyed at me for putting off something I had promised to do and I really couldn't blame her. After a storm, we had noticed some shingles from the roof of our house on the driveway.

"Do you think we need a new roof?" she had asked worriedly as we tried to assess the damage from the ground.

"I doubt it," I said. "The roof on this house is only eight years old; it should still be sound. Besides, there aren't any leaks from the ceilings."

"What should we do?" she wondered.

"We need to get a roofer to come and take a look. If he seals anything that's open, nails down the loose shingles and replaces what blew off, we should be fine," I said decisively.

"Do you want me to find someone?" she offered.

This was sexist, but I hardly considered the roof to be her bailiwick. "No, I'll take care of it," I promised. "Bob McCann lives in an old house, and he mentioned having a reliable roofer."

"Your boss talks about his roofer at work?" asked Astrid incredulously.

"Not usually," I replied. "He said that he wished that we were as dependable as his roofer. He was putting us down for not coming up with a fix for the J-6 quickly enough. He said if the roofer came up with the wrong fix as often as we did, he would have leaks all over his house. I'll find out who this roofing genius is and give him a call."

I meant to take care of the roof; it's just that we had an unusually long stretch of nice weather after that, and the roof was not foremost in my thoughts. When a sudden thunderstorm blew up one night a week and a half later, Astrid began to think about it.

"Did you ever speak to that roofer?" she asked.

"I've been busy," I protested. "I'll ask Bob tomorrow."

I meant to ask Bob, but when I came into his office, he immediately presented me with a list of problems requiring immediate attention.

"This needs to be handled today, Mitch," he warned.

"There's nothing major here," I said, examining the list. "It's a matter of crossing the t's and dotting the i's; I'll take care of it."

"See that you do," he said, as if all of this was my fault when, in fact, this was the first I'd been told of these issues.

A week later, I came home from work to find Astrid in one of the spare bedrooms, strategically placing empty pots on the floor and furniture.

"What's up?" I asked.

"You never called that roofer and now, the roof is leaking!"

"I'm sorry," I said. "I've been busy. I'll take care of it tomorrow."

"Don't bother," she replied, sounding annoyed. "I've already called someone. He recommended someone else to repair the damage to the ceiling in here too. He's coming tomorrow afternoon at four, and I've arranged to be home early, to meet him."

"I'm sorry," I replied.

"Yes, I know," sighed Astrid. "You're always sorry, but that doesn't solve the problems that arise when you continually put things off."

I can't say that all men procrastinate. Artie never did, and he was always on my case about my bad habit. I remember one time, when we were fifteen, we were doing a science project together.

"I know what our project is going to be," he declared on the way home from school, "and if I do say so myself, it is brilliant."

You might think that I would have resented his making that kind of decision without consulting me, but in our long friendship, I had learned that his grand schemes were always superior to my mere ideas.

"What?" I asked.

"We're going to build a windmill to generate electric power," he said.

"Those are pretty large to take in to school," I protested.

"A miniature windmill," he said.

"What if there's no wind that day?"

"We'll use an electric fan to simulate wind," he decided. "That way, there's no chance for failure. We don't even have to leave the building for it to work."

"I like it," I agreed.

We were both really excited about this science fair. The winner would be entered in the citywide science fair, and the winner of that competition would be sent to Washington, DC to enter the national science fair.

"I love it," said Artie. "I think we have a good chance to win."

"How do we do this?" I wondered.

"There have to be books about it in the school library," decided Artie. "We can't make it too complicated. We should have it light a lamp."

"How about that old sign your father has in the basement?" I suggested, thinking of an illuminated advertisement for some unheard of remedy that Julius had picked up at a rummage sale. "That would be kind of cool!"

"I'll ask him," agreed Artie. "In fact, I'll get all the materials together that we're going to need. You go to the library tomorrow and look up windmills. Then, check out the books you find that tell you how to build one, and we'll get started."

I had every intention of getting those books and, in fact, I was on my way to the library during my lunch hour when I ran into Mary Ann Murray, a girl in my English class on whom I'd had a serious crush for a while.

"Hi, Mitch," she said in that perky voice that I found so charming.

"Hi, Mary Ann," I replied. "Where are you off to?"

"Library," she replied. "I'm trying to figure out this math assignment, and I'm totally lost."

"What is it?" I asked, walking along beside her.

"Slide rules," she said miserably. "All I can get mine to do is fall apart!"

"I know how to use one," I replied. "I'd be happy to show you."

"Oh, Mitch, you're a lifesaver!"

Artie was, as usual for him, brimming with enthusiasm as we walked home after school. "Dad says that we may use the sign," he informed me, "and my mother doesn't think they'll miss the fan for a week or so. I found some scraps of lumber in the basement, and Dad thinks the roll of bell wire he has is heavy enough, but we can buy more if the books call for something different. Did you have time to look them over?"

"I didn't get them," I confessed sheepishly.

Artie glared at me. "That was your part of the assignment," he reminded me. "I can never count on you to remember what's important."

"I meant to do it," I said. "In fact, I was on my way to the library when I ran into Mary Ann Murray. I offered to show her how to use a slide rule, and by the time we were done, I was late for gym."

"And you were so distracted, staring at her breasts, that you forgot all about our winning entry to the science fair."

I tried to diffuse his anger. "I was engaged in a scientific pursuit," I said. "I was trying to decide if they were real or not."

"What difference does it make? You're never going to get close enough to her to find out."

"I don't know," I mused. "She was pretty attentive while I was explaining how to use a slide rule."

"She's a shiksa-your parents will never go for it."

"For heaven sake, Artie, I'm not going to marry her. I just want to spend time with a pretty girl. Is that so wrong?"

"I'm glad to hear that you're not seriously interested in her," he said.

"I wouldn't say that I'm not interested. She got my attention, if you know what I mean."

"Really, Mitch, we're fifteen. Every female gets our attention, but you've got to know that we're not going to get any for a long time!"

"How can you be so sure?"

"We're too young for sex," declared Artie.

"How old do we have to be?"

"I don't know, but have you met any fifteen year olds who claim to have scored?"

"None I can think of," I admitted.

"And tell me that you believe that they wouldn't be bragging if they had," smirked Artie.

"My dad claims that he wakes up stiff in the morning. Do you think that's what he means?" I looked at Artie out of the corner of my eye, sure that I would get a rise out of him.

"No," he replied, completely deadpan, "I'm sure it isn't what he means, but he probably does; I think all males do."

"That's too gross to even think about!" I replied.

"Well, think about that the next time you see Mary Ann. That should keep you calm enough to remember to get those books tomorrow!"

Looking back on my life now, I sincerely wish that I had less of a tendency to procrastinate and that I paid more attention to things that didn't seem important, but needed my attention nonetheless.

One of those things seemed so minor that I didn't pay any attention to it until it had created major harm. I remember that day so clearly, which is strange because it was such an ordinary day. I'd had the usual abundance of meetings, which accomplished little and prevented the participants from getting any real work done. I'd given a presentation, and for once, had received no argument from Bob, my supervisor, a rare event. I always felt a little bit sorry for his wife, Roberta or Bobbie as she prefers, because giving people a hard time was something at which he excelled. I think part of the reason that their marriage had endured for over twenty years was that he was rarely home.

I even remember that I'd eaten Manhattan clam chowder and a tuna sub, my favorites, for lunch, because when I walked in the door and smelled lasagna in the oven, my stomach growled, and I remember thinking that after such a big lunch, I shouldn't have been hungry.

I knew that Astrid was already at home because her Saab was in the garage. I've always hated that car. The seats are uncomfortable, the lines don't excite me, and the brakes feel like I'm going to have to put my foot out to stop it in time, but Astrid has always driven a Saab, from the day she got her license. She calls the car Sven - it's a male because it has a stick shift - and she insists that they understand each other. The paint is black, the color I like least for a car, and it's practically new; I bought it for her last April, for her thirty-second birthday. I told you I would do anything for that woman. I am perfectly happy with my three year old Subaru.

Astrid was prancing barefoot around the kitchen, assembling the makings of a salad. She offered her cheek absently for my kiss.

"There's a letter that came for you today," she related, before I had even put my briefcase away. "It looks like it might be important."

We had agreed early in our marriage that the person who picked up the mail opened all but personal-looking correspondence.

"What's it about?" I asked.

"It's from Businetex."

I picked up the mail. There was an electric bill, two offers for pre-approved credit cards, a postcard from our neighbors, who were in Hawaii for their tenth anniversary, and the letter from Businetex. I pulled the letter out and popped a piece of carrot from the salad into my mouth as I read.

"So?" I said, when I had finished.

"What do you think about that?"

"Not much," I shrugged.

"I think you should turn them down."

"Why?"

I could read in her expression that she was exasperated that I didn't see her point without her having to verbalize it. "It seems like exploitation to me."

"It says in the letter that the practice is routine. They claim it makes the company more secure. We should probably be flattered that they chose to include me."

"How can an intelligent man like you be so gullible, Mitch? It's apparent what's in it for them, but what's in it for you? Tell me that."

"I don't know; until five minutes ago, I hadn't given it any thought at all.

"It seems underhanded, at best, and I wonder if it is even legal. It's a negative option."

"What do you mean?"

"Unless you notify the attorneys representing them in this matter otherwise by the date specified, you are automatically a participant. They take your silence as an affirmative."

"If you have a problem about this, I'll tell them no," I offered.

"I don't want you to do it for me; I want you to do it because you agree that it's wrong."

"Look, honey, Businetex has occupied enough of my time for one day," I said, pulling silverware from the drawer to put on the table. "I'll take care of it tomorrow, on their time. When do we eat?"

She looked like she was going to say something else but changed her mind. "Another ten minutes," she replied.

I took the offending letter, slipped it into my briefcase, and tried to put it out of my mind, but not before I made a mental note to ask Artie about it the next time I saw him.

It was out of my mind before I had finished setting the table that night but now, with the holidays approaching, it is forever with me. When I think of how my life has changed in the past half year, I realize more and more that I should have paid a lot more attention to details, and to my wife's excellent intuition.

Chapter 2
Artie

There isn't a day that passes that I don't think about Artie. Saying that he was my best friend seems to minimize what he really meant to me. He was my mentor, my teacher, in some ways my idol. I am not referring only to our relationship as adults; it began within weeks of our first meeting and continued through the entire thirty-four years that our friendship endured.

Everyone who knew Artie quickly realized that he was special. I couldn't deny that many thought that he and his family were weird, but he was probably the most intelligent human being I have ever known, and I am not alone in that assessment.

Artie's parents were both teachers; his mother taught junior high school math, and his father taught high school science. They revered learning and allowed their children a great deal more leeway in the pursuit of self-discovery than most parents would have permitted. His mother, Alice, was by far the most serene Jewish mother I have ever encountered. When her children did something that would have evoked a blood-curdling shriek from Rifka, Alice quietly tried to reason with them about why that particular activity was unwise. They didn't always see things her way, but she considered their disobedience a manifestation of their personalities, rather than a punishable offense. My mother referred to her as "the anarchist."

Julius Kornfeld was a putterer. He was always coming up with clever ideas to make their lives more interesting and their house more livable. For the first six months that they lived on my street, Mr. Kornfeld spent every spare moment of his time working on his remodeling projects. He lined wall after wall with shelves to hold the family's numerous books and collectibles. He set up aquariums in his children's rooms, with a master control area for filters and heaters in their basement. He built a racquetball court in an unused area of the basement. Going to their house was like being in an amusement park. I thought it was fabulous. My mother responded with a contemptuous sniff every time I mentioned going over there. She did not try to stop me, because she could not provide a compelling reason for her opposition, but it was obvious that their life-style did not meet strict Goldblatt standards, and she did little to mask her disapproval.

Artie and I had much in common but we were very different in many ways. I had always wanted a pet: a dog, a cat, a bird, some fish; I wasn't real fussy.

Rifka's answer was always the same: "What does this look like; a zoo?"

I have to admit that my first introduction to Artie's family's idea of a pet shocked me, although I don't think I had even turned five at the time. A short time after we met, Artie and I charged into the Kornfeld kitchen for a drink of water.

"Your father wants to talk to you for a few minutes," said Alice as she handed us each a glass of bottled water.

"Am I in trouble?" asked Artie.

"No, I don't think so," replied his mother. "He wanted to talk to you about that boa."

"What's a boa?" I asked as we made our way down the basement stairs toward the sounds of hammering.

"A boa constrictor, a snake," replied Artie.

"A real one?" I asked, wide-eyed.

"Yeah," he said. "We're going to get a pet snake. We can't have anything with fur or feathers; my dad's allergic."

"Snakes are scary," I declared.

"No," said Artie, shaking his head. "We had a python before we moved here, and he was neat."

"Why didn't you bring him?" I asked.

"He was too big," said Artie. "We lived in an apartment and we didn't know we would get a house so soon, so my dad traded him to another teacher for a lizard."

"You have a lizard?" I asked, even more incredulous.

"Not anymore," said Artie. "He was mean. Denise hated him; he bit her twice, and my dad gave him away."

"Boys, come here for a minute," said Julius Kornfeld, looking up and seeing us making our way down the stairs. He was a tall man, with hair a faded version of Artie's but the identical piercing blue eyes. "I want to see if you can reach these shelves with the step stool."

Artie jumped energetically onto the stool and put up his hand. "All but the top," he said.

Julius nodded. "In another year, you'll reach that too. I think they're fine."

"Mom said you wanted to talk to me," said Artie.

"I did," said Julius. "I don't think that boa is going to work out. He's pretty aggressive."

"Aggressive?" repeated Artie.

"He isn't used to being handled," replied Julius. "That was the problem with the monitor lizard."

"Couldn't we teach him?" asked Artie hopefully.

"No, I don't think so. He's bigger than they said and he's very strong. I don't think he's right for us, but there's a skink we can get instead."

"What's a skink?" I asked.

"Another lizard," said Artie, his nose wrinkled distastefully.

"He's not like the monitor," said Julius. "I think you would like him; he looks like a snake with legs. He's only a foot long and he's used to kids. The owner's daughter sits on their terrace with him, and he suns himself on her head."

"If he's so nice, why are they giving him away?" wondered Artie.

"Their landlord found out about the lizard and said that if he isn't gone in a week, they will get thrown our of their apartment."

"They should get a house," said Artie.

"Son, not everyone is lucky enough to be able to afford their own house."

"I guess not," agreed Artie. "So we're going to get this lizard?"

"I told him I would talk to the family."

"Denise won't want it."

"If we take him on a trial basis, she might agree," said Julius with a smile.

"Is it a boy?" asked Artie.

"I don't know," admitted Julius. "Does it make a difference?"

"I guess not," shrugged Artie. "Sure, it sounds okay to me, as long as we can get a snake too."

"You know I promised that we would," replied Julius. "As soon as we find the right snake for our family, we will."

"And we can keep the skink too, if we like him?"

"As long as you kids take good care of him, I don't see why not."

"All right!" beamed Artie as we ran back out to the yard to resume his version of an archeological dig.

Artie's parents thought that having a pet was the best way for a child to learn responsibility and sensitivity to the ways of other creatures. Because of Mr. Kornfeld's allergies, they couldn't choose the conventional types of animals. For most of the summer, he suffered constantly. I can remember walking by their house one evening, when Julius was having a particularly severe sneezing fit. The noises the man made were unlike anything I'd ever heard.

"What do they have in that house?" my father had asked. "Farm animals?"

The neighbors, my parents among them, would have had a fit had they known exactly what was in residence on their street at any given time, but they never knew. The animals were kept in aquariums, well cared for, and they never escaped. I learned much later what those types of animals usually eat, but the Kornfelds had managed to train them to live on chicken innards. I don't know what happened to all the lizards. The last I heard, Artie's older sister, Robyn, still had Monty, their last python, and at that time about five years ago, he was twenty feet long.

There were sometimes casualties in the menagerie. I remember a few salamanders that, for some unexplained reason, did not survive, and Artie regularly lost fish from his aquarium over the years. When Samson, the hermit crab, died it was like a member of the family had been lost.

When there was a death, Artie had a ritual that he followed faithfully. I remember my initiation to this custom vividly, although I couldn't have been more than six at the time. We came in from a day of playing with some other kids on our street, and Alice Kornfeld was standing by the kitchen sink, looking grim.

"Gabriel is dead," she said to Artie.

"Are you sure?"

"Yes," she replied softly. "I went to feed them and he was floating on the top of the tank."

"He seemed fine earlier," protested Artie.

"These things happen with fish," explained Alice. "Maybe conditions weren't perfect in the tank or possibly, he was sick and we didn't realize it. It would have been difficult for him to let us know that there was something wrong in time for us to help him."

"Where is he?" asked Artie.

Alice removed a margarine tub from the sink and allowed us to peer in. Gabriel was floating inertly in an inch of water.

"Are there any empty boxes?" asked Artie.

"No," replied Alice. "Take the Jell-O out and I'll put it in a plastic bag."

We proceeded to the backyard, and I was assigned the important task of holding Gabriel in his Jell-O box, while Artie went into the garage to get garden trowels. Together, we dug a hole about six inches square and a foot deep. Carefully, Artie lowered Gabriel into his final resting place and we methodically covered the hole.

Neither Artie nor I had ever been to an actual funeral, but we improvised. Artie said a few words about Gabriel, that he was a beautiful angelfish and an accomplished swimmer. It sounds silly now, but it was kind of touching at the time.

"Do you think the twenty-third psalm is right?" he asked.

I had no idea but didn't want to admit my ignorance, so I nodded mutely in agreement. I was amazed to discover that, although the words were familiar to me, Artie knew every one of them by heart.

Through the years, we practiced variations on this same ritual many times over. We would bury the remains, Artie would say a few words about the deceased and, usually, read an appropriate poem or passage from a book. He was a voracious reader and could usually think of a quote to fit the occasion. Later on, Artie read about the ancient Celts marking their graves with cairns, so we would gather pebbles from the yard and build them into small mounds over the newly dug earth. They always disappeared after a while, but we knew the area of the flower bed where the graveyard was located. I never mentioned our funerals to anyone else. I know my parents would have thought this behavior bizarre, at best. Looking back on it, I think it may have been good training for what we would face later on in life, but it was easier not have to justify what we did to those whom I was certain would not understand.

Artie and I had a custom that we never broke. Every Sunday, during the years that we were not living in the same city, we would engage in a marathon phone conversation. During one of our more memorable chats, I asked him if it bothered him that his family did many things that people regarded as weird.

"What did we do that anyone could possibly consider weird?" he wondered.

"Oh, I don't know," I replied sarcastically. "Your choices in pets were not exactly mainstream."

"It wasn't like we took them outside or anything," he protested. "They never made too much noise or defecated on anyone's lawn or bit the neighbor's kid. How many people on our block who had dogs or cats can say that?"

"Probably no one," I conceded.

"Beside, I don't think anyone but you knew they were there."

"My parents certainly didn't," I agreed, "or I never would have been allowed to set foot in your house."

"I'm sure other people do things in their homes that others consider odd. Remember when we saw Mrs. Kovak vacuuming her blinds, while she was buck naked?"

"It's etched indelibly in my brain," I admitted. "She had to be close to eighty."

"More like ninety," countered Artie, and I could hear that he was smiling. "That was stranger than anything my family did. We were almost mainstream."

"Far from it," I laughed. "How many people do you know who became vegetarians at ten?"

"It was just an experiment. I guess Mom figured that if Denise was going to do it, it was easier to cook that way for everyone. Anyway, tofu is a great low-fat source of protein."

"If you can stand the taste," I said, wrinkling my nose in distaste even though he couldn't see me.

"You mean lack of taste," he corrected authoritatively. "The beauty of tofu is its blandness. You use the flavors you like to give it personality."

"Spoken like a true vegetarian," I laughed.

"Tofu is trendy now, but you'll be happy to know that the rest of my family never touches it. All of them quickly reverted to omnivore status. Having learned that I can lead a healthy lifestyle without animal products, I will always be a vegetarian."

I had no reason to doubt him; Artie was nothing if not a man of his word.

"Anyway," he continued, "since we spent most of our time together, until we went away to school, you've done your share of weird things too."

"I suppose that's true," I conceded.

When the Kornfelds first moved onto our street, they could not find a nursery school for Artie that would keep him for the full day, and both of his parents were working full time. At that time, preschools were not commonplace, the way they are now. I happened to be playing near the front door one afternoon when Alice Kornfeld approached my mother.

"Rifka, do you have a moment?" she said.

My mother looked up from the newspaper she had been reading on our front stoop. I know that to the unindoctrinated, it looks like an ordinary concrete stairway to the front door but the stoop is an integral part of Brooklyn social life.

"What is it, Alice?" asked my mother warily.

I was only four and I could hear the disdain in her voice, so I'm sure Alice sensed it as well, but if she did, she didn't let on.

"I've encountered a problem," she said. "I haven't been able to find suitable childcare for Artie. Julius and I are both gone for the entire school day. I was wondering if you knew of someone trustworthy."

"I'm home with Mitch," replied my mother. "I've never had occasion to need anyone."

"You're very fortunate," said Alice. "I thought it was at least worth asking."

She turned and started to walk away when I heard Rifka call out to her. My mother thought his parents were odd, but she had a soft spot for Artie. He was bright, funny and cute with his flaming red hair and freckles.

"Alice?"

"Yes, Rifka?"

"Since I'm here anyway, it wouldn't be any trouble for me to keep an eye on Artie while you're working. Mitch will enjoy having him to play with."

"Rifka, I couldn't ask so great a favor," protested Alice. "I'm sure I'll find someone. I asked for your recommendation because I know that you are a good parent; we all love Mitch."

"We're fond of Artie too," said my mother. "Bring him here and don't worry about it."

"If you're sure," said Alice.

"I'm sure," replied my mother.

"Of course, I'll pay you the going rate," Alice assured her.

"Don't be silly," replied my mother. "You're a neighbor; I couldn't take your money."

"Of course you can," protested Alice. "We can all use a few dollars here and there for the extras."

"No!" said my mother sharply. "If you mention money again, I won't do it. I might need a favor sometime, a dependable person to watch my children."

"It would be my great pleasure," Alice assured her.

"Some of the stuff we learned together was very useful," he insisted in our conversation, more than twenty years later. "People thought it was weird that we both knew how to read before we started kindergarten."

"My mother didn't; she thought it was an inspired idea of yours to teach me, and I will concede that it came in handy. Still does."

"Well, you owe me one."

"I'm sure I owe you many, if we were keeping score," I agreed.

"Come to think of it, you probably do," he said. "You probably wouldn't have learned to ride a bike until you were at least fifty, if had been up to Rifka."

"More like sixty," I chuckled.

Artie and I were both quite pleased with the arrangement between our mothers. When we began going to school full time, my mother got a job as a receptionist and bookkeeper in a beauty parlor. Marilyn and I would be getting home before Ma was done with work, so the Kornfelds agreed that Artie's sister Denise, who was thirteen, would keep an eye on all the kids until the parents came home. Marilyn was the same age as Robyn so they hung out together, although they never became close friends.

We only had about an hour from the time we got home from school until Rifka returned around four-thirty, but Artie and I always made the best of that time. There were books all over the Kornfeld house, and when either of us wanted to know something, Artie could always figure out how to look it up. When she watched us after school, Denise didn't really care what we did, as long as we stayed out of her way. We fooled around with Artie's chemistry set, invented our own games, or played racquetball in the basement undisturbed.

Artie was appalled when he learned that I didn't know how to ride a bike.

"I'll teach you," he declared.

"My mother won't let me," I lamented.

"We don't have to ask her," replied Artie. "You can learn on my bike and when you can ride, you'll show her and convince her to buy you a bike of your own."

"How can you teach me?" I wondered. "You aren't big enough to hold the bike up."

"That's simple," declared the six year old expert. "First, you sit on the seat with the kick stand down; you won't fall off that way. You put your legs out to the side and make the bike straight."

"Like this?" I asked, wondering how sitting on a bike supported by my legs was going to get me anywhere.

"That's good," nodded Artie. "Now, you have to pick your feet up a little bit while you sit straight in the middle, so the bike doesn't fall over.

That wasn't as easy as it sounded, but in less than a day, I could feel that the bike was staying upright for a few seconds before it started to fall over.

"Now, we're ready for he next step," he informed me.

I was doubtful that putting up the kick stand and trying to coast along, propelled by my feet, was going to work, but Artie was so sure that I could do it that I too became convinced. He held on to the back of the seat and ran alongside the bike, as I tentatively tried to coast down the block. I made it past two houses before the bike toppled over, and I found myself lying on the Schaeffer's front lawn.

"It didn't work," I protested, lying on my side in the grass. Fortunately, I wasn't hurt.

"Sure it did," protested Artie. "You made it all the way here. You need to go a little faster to keep the bike up. It's in one of my father's books; it has something to do with physics. I don't understand all of it yet, but if you go faster, it will work."

I didn't want to get back on that bike. I was the one who had wound up lying in the grass, but I hated the idea that Artie could effortlessly ride a bike and I couldn't. I brushed myself off and straddled the bike again.

"You did it!" said Artie triumphantly as I put my feet down four houses later, to prevent the bike from falling.

"I guess I did," I agreed incredulously.

"Now, all you have to do is start to pedal."

"If I do that, how will I keep the bike from falling?" I wondered.

"The bike won't fall if you pedal," explained Artie. "You felt that you were balanced when you came here from the Schaeffer's."

"I thought so," I agreed, "but if I hadn't put my feet down, I would have fallen."

"You can still put your feet down," said Artie. "It will just be a little farther, from the pedals."

It's unbelievable to me now that I had such great faith in him that I defied gravity in the way that he suggested. I began to coast, the way I had before, and when I felt myself balance, I put my feet on the pedals, and I was riding. I made it halfway to the corner before I panicked, forgot to put my feet down, and fell off the bike.

"You did it!" shrieked Artie, jumping up and down excitedly as he made his way toward me.

I had not landed on the lawn this time. I stared at my skinned elbow. "I fell," I protested.

"Before you fell, you were doing it just like everyone else does," insisted Artie. "The next time, you'll remember to put your feet down. You can ride a bike!"

"This will be the last time, after my mother sees my elbow."

"Don't show it to her," shrugged Artie. "There's some Bactine our bathroom. We'll clean it off, and it will be fine."

"She'll see it," I protested.

"We'll spill something on your shirt. She'll make you change when you get home. Put on a shirt with sleeves that cover it."

As usual, Artie was right. A dollop of strawberry jam in the center of my shirt resulted in my being sent up to my room to change. My mother never did see my scraped elbow. The next time I tried Artie's bike, it was as if I really knew how to ride. When I felt confident that I could do it, it was time to approach my mother about getting a bike of my own.

Rifka consistently had one reaction to my request to do anything athletic.

"What, are you crazy? You're liable to hurt yourself!"

She would not even discuss getting me a bicycle until I demonstrated on Artie's that I could actually ride it without falling off. She wouldn't commit at once but promised to give it some thought, and to discuss it with my father. I'm sure he had some influence in convincing her to give in. There was one condition to my having a bike on which she would not budge.

"If you ride a bike, you're going to wear a helmet," she announced.

"Oh, Ma!" I protested. "All the other kids will laugh."

"Let them laugh," she replied. "You'll have the last laugh when you fall and don't get hurt."

"I'll look like a weirdo."

"Those are my terms."

I hated that helmet, but I dutifully wore it, despite the sneers of my peers. Artie's parents thought it was an inspired idea and bought him one too, which he proudly wore. I would never admit it to Rifka, but in this instance, she was really ahead of her time.

"On reflection, I suppose we're even on the bicycle thing," said Artie during our adult conversation. "If your mother hadn't come up with the idea of our wearing helmets, I probably would not be the magnificent specimen I am today."

"I'm sure you would have thought of the helmet on your own," I said. "You were always ten paces ahead of everyone I know."

"You were no slouch yourself," he said as we signed off. "I miss you, Mitch," he added, ending his conversation as he always did.

"Yeah, me too," I agreed, ending as I always did. I suppose I should have thought more about why I never said it first.

It was true that Artie excelled at everything he tried. He did very well in school, and some of it must have rubbed off on me, because we both got excellent grades. Artie taught me all sorts of things over the years, not all of them intellectual pursuits.

I suppose our childhood was never far from either of our thoughts. I remember meeting Artie for a beer after my first day at Businetex. I think he was more nervous than I was when he left me in the lobby that morning, although he tried to sound casual when he told me to meet him for a beer that afternoon. He had arrived first at the small neighborhood bar down the street from Businetex and had ordered a Miller for each of us.

"You're still drinking that? I thought you would have found something more high tech and trendy by now," I teased as I slid into the darkened booth opposite him. "Tofu beer, something healthy."

"Tastes lousy," he grinned, and I wasn't sure whether he was kidding or not. "Besides, every healthy adult needs one vice; this is mine. This takes me back to our misspent youth; don't forget, you are the one who got me started."

"Me?" I asked incredulously, almost choking on my first sip of beer. "How do you figure that?"

"My first beer was from the refrigerator in your parents' basement."

"You suggested it," I protested.

"My parents were into clean living," smiled Artie. "In our house, all you would find was juice, milk, bottled water and seltzer. We'd been doing that for ages; we had to keep it fresh and exciting. We needed something to make us pee a lot, something that would work quickly."

"As with most things, I didn't know beer would do that until you told me," I said. "In fact, at twelve, I didn't know what beer tasted like, until we had it together that time."

"I didn't either," confessed Artie, taking a long swallow, "but I'd done some reading and learned that alcohol is a diuretic. Beer was taking our contests to the next level. It's not enough to only have ideas; you have to tweak them, always take them one step beyond."

"You never had mere ideas," I said. "Everything you did was an intricate master plan."

"Wasn't it convenient that I mapped it out for both of us?"

"Usually," I agreed, "but the peeing contests were pretty lowbrow."

"I disagree," said Artie, placing his bottle on the table and looking at me earnestly. "We had an intricate set of rules that we had to follow. We had to agree on when it was time to rush into the bathroom, we both had to start before the sand in the egg timer ran out, and the last one to finish was the winner. There was no room for cheating: we were both there at the same time. It was as legitimate a game as Monopoly or Scrabble, although a lot more creative."

"But you always won," I protested.

"That was strategy," smiled Artie, with that self-satisfied grin I knew so well. "I knew I had to pace myself. You were so relieved that we got there in time that you rushed it."

"We didn't always get there in time," I reminded him. "Remember that time when Denise got into the bathroom at your house and wouldn't come out?"

"It was hitting my socks by the time I told you to tell her that Ronald Schwartz was on the phone," grinned Artie.

"But you still won. I don't think I ever beat you, not once."

"You didn't," he declared authoritatively, "because I never lost sight of my objective."

"That's been true of you in almost everything," I agreed.

"It's served me well in my life, and particularly in my career."

"Speaking of careers, aren't you going to ask me how my first day of work went?"

"No, I don't think so," he replied. "I can see that you survived. You're sitting here drinking a beer with me, and you seem none the worse for wear. I'd say that it went as well as a first day on any job will."

I was exasperated. "Is there anything you don't know?" I asked sarcastically.

"There are many things I don't know, but I intend to find all of them out before I'm finished. I'll be sure to enlighten you about the interesting ones."

"You do that; I'm counting on it," I said, punching his arm affectionately as I stood to leave the bar.

That was just Artie, how he was, and if I was perfectly honest, I think it was part of his charm.

After spending such an extensive portion of my childhood with him, I had assumed that Artie and I would always be together, so you can imagine what a shock it was when we began applying to colleges and discovered that we were not interested in the same schools.

"I'm going to major in English and creative writing," protested Artie when I showed him the science curriculum for the SUNY school I was considering, because they were one of two that had an engineering program.

His father was a science teacher and his mother taught math; I assumed that he would naturally gravitate toward some type of science, but I was wrong.

"How do your parents feel about that?" I wondered.

"They're fine with it," he replied. "They say it's my decision."

Artie chose a small, private college in central New York, while I was given a choice by my parents of the State University or one of the city colleges. Marilyn had gone to

Brooklyn College, and my parents continued to treat her like she was in high school, so I was smart enough to learn from her mistake. Artie and I went our separate ways.

That is not to say that we weren't in touch. We spoke on the phone at least once a week and spent all our time at home together. We were supposed to write, but Artie was better at that and more committed to it than I was. It was in one of these letters that I learned of Artie's first major decision of his college career, and I did not take it well.

Artie was one of the few freshman on his campus to have a car. When he had taken a driver education course during his senior year of high school, his father had allowed him to buy an old junker with some of his savings. Every weekend, the two of them, usually with my help, would work on the car. By the time he passed his road test, it was roadworthy and more presentable than I had ever thought it could be. Artie had joined a fraternity and volunteered through one of their service projects to provide rides to other students who needed transportation. Mass for Catholic students was held at a small church off campus, and he was assigned the dubious honor of arising early on Sunday mornings to provide rides for those who wanted to go. Instead of waiting in the car, Artie attended Mass along with the others. He did some reading about Catholicism and decided to convert.

His parents, who had accepted every other odd decision any of the children had ever made with complete aplomb, went crazy. Apparently, individuality did not extend to matters of faith for them. They insisted that it was merely a phase he was going through, and he would return to Judaism when he tired of the novelty. They should have known Artie better; I did.

That is not to say that I accepted his decision with any more grace than they did. We had suffered through Hebrew school at East Midwood Jewish Center together, had our Bar Mitzvahs a month apart, and I could not accept that he would become a Catholic.

"What's the punch line?" I asked sarcastically, after he reaffirmed in person the news that I had chosen to ignore in his letter."

"There is no punch line; I'm absolutely serious. I did a lot of reading, serious research, and I have decided that the Catholic religion more closely fits what I believe than Judaism does."

"In what way?" I demanded. "Convince me."

"No," said Artie softly. "Religion is a personal thing; what's right for me isn't necessarily right for you."

"You're just rebelling," I accused, sounding a lot more like my parents than I ever wanted to. "You finally found a way to get a rise from your unflappable family, and you're milking it to the fullest."

"It's not about what they believe," he insisted. "It's about who I am, spiritually."

Artie never tried to convert me, but he was unshakable in his faith. Much later, I came to accept that he was sincere in his beliefs, and his conversion had been for his own sake rather than that of anyone else, although I still do not understand exactly why. Had it been exclusively up to me, I am ashamed to say that I don't think our friendship would have endured. Although I was never very religious and have lapsed even further into apathy over the years, I took Artie's rejection of Judaism as a rejection of our youth together. It was personal for me. Over the years, I have known many practicing Catholics, born into the church, who have more questions and doubts than Artie did. Maybe his certainty that his new faith was the true one was because it was something he chose on his own, but it was a wound between us. Although we found our way back to each other, the scar remained.

I had assumed that once we finished school, we would both get jobs in the city, and we would be together again, but those were not Artie's plans.

"I've got a job!" I informed him happily when I was hired by a firm in New York City.

"That's great news!" he replied enthusiastically.

"It is, but you're going to have to find something soon," I continued. "The rents here are outrageous. I won't be able to afford a place on my own, but I think on both our salaries, we can manage something."

"That isn't going to work," he said. "I already have three offers. The big decision now is whether I prefer Syracuse, Buffalo or Rochester."

"What's wrong with New York?" I demanded.

"Nothing; it's a great city, but it's not where I want to live."

"Why not?"

"I like the slower pace of upstate. It's near enough for me to visit New York, when I feel that I need some cultural stimulation, but it's far enough away that I don't have to move my car between eleven and two every Tuesday and Thursday."

"You don't need a car in New York," I protested. "You can get around on the subway."

"I like having a car," he replied.

Artie ended up accepting a job with Eastman Kodak in Rochester. He had visited that city a few times with one of his frat brothers, and decided that it wouldn't be a bad place to live.

The only apartment I could afford on my own was a studio in Queens, so I joined the army of daily subway commuters. Housing is a lot cheaper in Rochester; Artie had a large one bedroom to himself on the second floor of a house in a tree-lined upscale city neighborhood.

I visited him on several occasions. He had joined a health club that had indoor tennis courts, and when we played, it felt close to old times. Tennis was my game, although Artie preferred racquetball. I could even win an occasional set from him at tennis. When we were on the court, our differences did not seem so great, and we managed to find our old closeness. Artie was working as a technical writer, and he loved what he was doing. I was employed as a systems engineer, and I liked the paycheck.

"You've got to find a job you like," he insisted, any time he could get me to listen. "You will be far more productive if you enjoy what you are doing."

He was constantly sending me job listings, the majority of them in or around Rochester. I finally took his advice and did change jobs, but the company I went to work for was located in Connecticut.

Over the years, I had a long succession of girlfriends. Artie used to get a photo and the rundown on each one, and he would rate them by drawing little foxes in the margins of his letters, one to four depending on his impression of the flame of the moment. Once, when I started seeing someone on the rebound, he picked up on that and drew a tiny pig in the margin with my name on its side; he was right of course.

When I started seeing Astrid, he gave her four little foxes and a fifth big one wearing a wedding veil. When he met her, he told me that he had underestimated her in the ratings. I was never quite sure if one of those foxes wasn't just for the fact alone that she was a Rochester girl. Astrid and I kept trying to think of someone we knew who we thought would be right to introduce to Artie, but we could never quite come up with an acceptable candidate.

I almost succeeded in ending my friendship with Artie right before Astrid's and my wedding. Astrid had been married before so she didn't want any type of big affair. We decided to have just our families and a few close friends join us for dinner at an elegant country inn, after a very brief ceremony in a gazebo near a lake on the grounds. Artie was to stand up for me, of course, and he came to stay with us for a few days before the wedding. Astrid had gone to have her hair, make-up and nails done as a trial run before the main event, so Artie and I were alone.

"Artie, why haven't you ever married?" I asked casually.

"I've been waiting to find a girl like Astrid," he replied. "Does she have a sister?"

"She's an only child, but maybe we can see about having her cloned," I'd thrown back.

"They haven't made much progress on that in higher animals," he countered.

"Artie, have you ever had a serious girlfriend?" I persisted.

"No one special," he shrugged. "Why?"

I should have let it drop, but I was wound up about the wedding, and my brain was not really paying close attention to my mouth. "I was wondering if there could be another reason why you don't date."

"And what would that be?"

"Is it possible that you're gay?"

Artie studied me silently for several moments. "Have I ever given you any reason to believe that I am gay?"

I shook my head.

"Then what made you say that?"

"I don't know. You've never mentioned a girlfriend, I've never known you to go out on a date; I've known you most of my life, and I've never seen you with a woman. I thought maybe there was a reason that I didn't know about."

"I'm not gay," said Artie softly. "I don't relate well to women; I don't know why."

I should have accepted what he said and let it drop, but for some reason, I couldn't. "Have you ever let yourself consider the possibility?"

"Is it mandatory?" he asked, his annoyance unmasked. "If I were gay, I think I'd know about it."

"Not if you've never let yourself consider the idea," I had persisted.

"Thank you, Dr. Freud. I'm going out for some air," he'd added curtly as he walked out the door.

I tried to apologize later, after he returned.

"Don't worry about it, Mitch," he said. "You spoke your mind; I expect no less from you. No apology is necessary."

"But you're angry."

"No, I'm not angry. I guess I was taken by surprise that you thought that I might be gay, and this is the first you've mentioned it."

"It's not something that I've given a lot of thought," I said. "Neither of us is young anymore, and I suppose I was wondering if there was a reason you have waited even longer than I have to marry."

"There's no sinister reason, other than I haven't met anyone I want to spend serious time with, let alone the rest of my life."

"I didn't think it was an offensive question," I protested, still worried about his hurt feelings. "I have nothing against gay people; I believe we are who we are."

"As do I," agreed Artie. "I guess the reason I reacted the way I did was that I was surprised. I have known you for most of my life, and I probably love you more than any other human being I have met."

I will always regret that I didn't tell him right then that I felt the same way, but I couldn't.

"Has our relationship ever involved anything sexual?" he asked.

"No, of course not," I replied.

Artie nodded. "Don't you think that if I were inclined in that direction, you would have known?"

"Not necessarily," I replied. "I assumed that you felt that after I handled your conversion to Catholicism so well, there was no way you would dare to even broach the subject."

"I wouldn't have had a choice," said Artie. "If I were gay, I would have discussed it with you first, because if there was any chance of my having a relationship with another man, you would have been the one I would have wanted. I would have been compelled to at least try. Since I've never had those feelings for you, we can both be pretty confident that it's not going to happen. I am not gay; I do like women, although they don't seem to return the sentiment."

"I'm sorry I ever brought it up," I said.

"I'm not," replied Artie. "I'm glad we discussed it; had I realized it was on your mind, I would have cleared the air sooner."

I had almost forgotten all about it, but after Astrid and I moved to Rochester, I learned that Artie still carried it around with him. I had joined the same health club where

Artie belonged, and we played tennis indoors three days a week. The Saturday after I received the letter from Businetex was one of those days.

"Where's Astrid?" Artie demanded as I walked alone into the lobby of club.

Sometimes, when Artie and I played tennis, particularly on weekends, Astrid came along, either to watch us or to sit in the whirlpool.

"Sven had to go back to the dealer."

"It's practically new," protested Artie as we accepted towels from Linda, who worked the front desk, and headed for the locker room.

"It sounds like a coffee percolator when it idles," I replied.

"Is it a valve lifter?"

"No, it's a Saab," I grinned.

"Always the wise guy," said Artie, punching me lightly on the upper arm. "Do you think it's a major problem?"

"I think that car is a bomb."

"So you keep saying. Why did you buy it if you don't like it?"

"What's to like? It looks funny, the brakes feel terrible, I hate driving a stick shift, etcetera, etcetera."

"So why did you buy it?"

"Because Astrid loves that car, and I adore her."

"You are really gone," he laughed.

"I know," I agreed. "It's great."

"But you hate the car," he said.

"Yes, I do, but Astrid puts up with my griping because I bought it for her anyway."

"I'm surprised that you haven't decided that Sven is gay," mused Artie sarcastically, tying his sneaker.

"Oh, I know that he is," I said, picking up my racket and a can of tennis balls.

"How do you know that a car is gay?" demanded Artie impatiently.

"I saw him ogling a little red Porsche in Wegmans parking lot."

"I've seen you ogling many a Porsche," said Artie, leading the way onto our assigned court, and placing his ever-present bottle of Gatorade under the chair at the side of midcourt. "Maybe I should be wondering about you too."

"Maybe," I agreed. "I wonder about myself all the time."

"But not about being gay," said Artie, removing the cover from his racket.

"No, and I don't wonder that about you either. I wish you'd forget it; until you mentioned it, I had."

"All I remember is how much I want to cream you at tennis," said Artie, swinging his racket over his head to warm up before we started.

I played pretty well. Artie, as he did everything, still played tennis with all he had, and he won the best of three sets but it was close, 7-6, 4-6, 6-3. Later, when we were dressing after our showers, I remembered the letter.

"There's something I wanted to ask you," I said. "Have you received a letter from Businetex recently that they claim is sent to some highly compensated employees?"

"Are you talking about the famous negative option?"

"Yes."

"I got that one a couple of years ago; almost all the professionals get them," he laughed. "Sorry to disappoint you, but you're not that special."

"I'm not disappointed. What did you do about it?"

"Nothing."

"Astrid seemed to think it was something sinister."

"I don't agree, but if you feel that way, you're free to decline."

"I may do that."

"I'm sure the company will survive," he countered.

"I'm sure."

"If you want to hear an opinion different from mine, talk to Jim Deckle. He is the most paranoid man alive. He will give you every reason you want to hear and then some why you shouldn't participate."

Jim Deckle was my office mate. Meeting him for the first time, he seemed rather ordinary, average height, average weight, medium brown hair, and medium brown eyes situated in a non-descript face. He appeared absolutely benign but upon getting to know him, I quickly came to realize that looks don't always tell the full story. We were much like the odd couple; I think Charles Schulz had him in mind when he created the character Pigpen. I like neatness and order. I had to share an office with Jim, but I tried to have as little to do with him as possible, which wasn't easy because he was always at Businetex.

Soon after joining the company, I suggested to Artie that he lived in our office and was surprised to learn that he had a wife and two kids, although not many people had ever actually seen them. I was not the only one who found him strange, though. Deckle stories abounded around Businetex.

Jim thought that people everywhere were spying on him. We worked in a secure area, and everyone who knew the code was authorized to be there, but he still shredded every scrap of paper he used. Not believing that no one in his right mind would take the time to try to reconstruct his shredded garbage, he would wait until everyone else left the building and then burn the shreds in his wastebasket. He'd apparently gotten better at it because it hadn't happened recently, but our secretary told me that when he had first moved into that office, he had set off the fire alarms several times.

Beth had been the secretary for the group he worked in for almost five years and he was not her favorite person.

"He's a three dollar bill," she told me, rolling her eyes when she was sure that he was safely ensconced at a meeting, and well out of earshot.

"He seems a little odd," I agreed.

"You haven't a clue," she insisted. "Once, he went on a business trip and forgot to pack his suit. His wife showed up unannounced at my door at eleven-thirty at night with a brown paper Wegmans bag, insisting that I had to get it to the airline immediately, so that they could deliver it to Jim in time for his presentation at eight the next morning. The woman was probably terrified that if he didn't get the suit, he might actually come home."

"What did you do?" I wondered.

"After she had gone, I opened the bag and I swear, inside, rolled in a ball, was his navy suit, a white dress shirt, a striped tie and brown wing-tip shoes. I called the airline and found out that the next flight out was at six the following morning. I arranged to drop the suit off before I came to work, and I called Deckle at four in the morning, when I had to get up to do this, to tell him when and where to pick it up," she declared smugly.

I have Deckle stories of my own to tell. Last January, I stopped off at the office on the way home from a Super Bowl party to pick up a document that I needed for an early morning presentation. Beth had promised to leave it on her desk for me, and I had forgotten to look before I left on Friday. I needed several copies to pass out at the meeting, so I asked Astrid if she minded if we made a quick detour to the office on our way home.

It was very cold that night and the guard on duty recognized me, so he broke the rules and allowed Astrid to accompany me to my office. I picked up the document on Beth's desk and went to make copies, pointing out my office to Astrid and telling her that she could wait there. Astrid was about to walk in the open door when she heard a voice inside. There was Deckle, sitting at his desk, reading responses to his phone messages aloud, until he got just the right intonation and delivery. She watched him in silent amusement until he paused and then, in an effort at comedy, she applauded.

I came running when I heard the tirade that resulted. Deckle was having a fit.

"What is going on?" I demanded.

"This woman broke in here to spy on me," he sputtered, red-faced.

"That woman is my wife."

Astrid could hardly keep a straight face, let alone act contrite for being someplace that under the letter of the law, she shouldn't have been.

"The contents of my phone messages are confidential. I'm going to report her to the security guard!" he threatened

"Fine, you do that," I said calmly, "and first thing tomorrow morning, I will play all my saved messages from you over the public address system, to prove to everyone what a complete idiot you can be."

We had reached a stalemate and thus, he went back to his usual paranoia, and I went back to avoiding him wherever possible.

I was not happy to see him the Monday morning following my tennis game with Artie, but he was in an unusually friendly mood. He kept trying to start a conversation, and I couldn't get anything done.

"Jim, I've been meaning to ask you about something," I finally said, putting my pen down on the desk.

"What?" he asked suspiciously.

Had I replied "never mind," I think he would have ignored me for the rest of the day with relief, but I figured that I'd come this far, what the heck.

"Have you ever received a letter from Businetex that they claim they send to some highly compensated..."

He didn't even give me a chance finish. "Don't do it," he said.

"Why not?"

"It places you in danger," he replied with certainty. "I know that most people around here don't see it my way but I told them there was no way."

"Astrid agrees with you," I said, knowing that he was still wary of her after the Super Bowl Sunday incident.

"Your wife is an astute woman; listen to her."

"I just may," I agreed. "I was wondering if anyone else who works here agrees with you."

"Everyone here thinks I'm nuts about everything, but I don't care. I try never to deliberately put myself in a position where I feel vulnerable. Now that you brought up the subject, there have been some incidents over the past year that seem suspicious too. Would you like to hear about them?"

"Maybe some other time," I said, having had my fill of him for the day. "Right now, I'm late for a meeting."

"Any time you want to talk, let me know, Mitch," he said as I loaded papers into my briefcase. "I can make myself available any hour of the day or night."

"I'll keep that in mind," I said as I gratefully fled his company.

I was not thinking of Deckle or of anything else associated with Businetex on the fateful Friday that forever changed my life. I was thinking about how glad I was that the week was over, and that I had two glorious days to relax with Astrid. Our third anniversary had just passed and we were considering spending Saturday night in Niagara-on-the-Lake, if we could get a reservation. In late June, that might not be easy, but Astrid had promised to call them, and I was hoping that she had been successful.

She hadn't been able to get a room, but they had promised to call if there was a cancellation, so when the phone rang just as she was about to put the spaghetti we were having for dinner into the pot, I was filled with hope that we were in luck. Instead, it was Linda, the receptionist from the health club, calling for me.

"What can I do for you, Linda?" I asked pleasantly. Although we often made polite conversation and were on a first name basis, she had never called me at home before.

"I thought you would want to know," she said, sounding upset. "Artie Kornfeld collapsed on the racquetball court a little while ago. They're taking him to Rochester General."

"Did his knee go out again?" I asked.

"No," said Linda. "He was unconscious, and I heard someone say something about a heart attack."

My whole body felt like it had turned to stone. "I'll get right up there," I said quickly. "Thanks, Linda."

"Who was that?" asked Astrid.

"Linda from the health club. She thinks Artie had a heart attack. I have to get to General."

"I'm going with you," she announced, grabbing her purse from the counter, and checking the stove to make sure that she'd turned off all the burners.

I drove like a maniac, and Astrid kept warning me to slow down and be careful. I must have really been wild for her to have done that; she never criticized my driving. When we got to emergency, I was initially told that they would tell me nothing, unless I was a family member. Then, one of the doctors heard my name and said that I had been listed in Artie's wallet as the local person to contact in case of an emergency. All they could tell me was that they thought he had suffered a heart attack, and that he was being worked on in the emergency room. We were told to take a seat, and to wait for them to call us.

We were there for over an hour when Linda came in. She had gotten off her shift and couldn't find out anything over the phone. When she got no answer at my house, she decided to stop by on her way home. The three of us sat and waited for what seemed to be an eternity.

Finally, a young man in a white lab coat, I assumed an intern or resident, called my name. He asked us to follow him. I took that to be a good sign, assuming that we were going to be allowed to see Artie. He led us into a small room off the emergency department, not one of the usual treatment cubicles.

"I'm sorry," he said after he had closed the door behind him. "We did what we could but we were unable to revive him."

I just stood there dumbfounded, looking at him. I don't think it had really registered.

"Are you saying that he's dead?" asked Astrid. "Arthur Kornfeld is the name of the patient we are here to see."

"Yes," said the young man. "I'm sorry. Mr. Kornfeld died several minutes ago."

"I want to see him," I said, having finally found my voice.

"That will be okay," he said. "We need someone to make a positive identification."

I started to follow him, and Astrid was right beside me. "You can wait in the lobby," he said to her.

"I'm going with my husband," she announced decisively.

"Honey, why don't you wait with Linda?" I suggested.

"You don't want me there?"

"I do," I said, "but I think it's better this way."

"I love you," she said, kissing me lightly on the lips before allowing Linda to lead her to the lobby.

I followed the young man in the white lab coat behind the closed curtains of a silent, darkened cubicle. He flipped on the switch of the florescent light, but I didn't need it; Artie was lying on the gurney, still and pale, a sheet outlining the shape of his body.

I went over and took his hand. The man started to stop me and reconsidered. He was still warm, but I could tell by the feel of his skin and the way the hand was limp in mine that he was dead.

"This is Arthur Kornfeld," I said softly.

"I'm sorry," said the man. "We did all we could."

"Thank you," I replied.

"Will you be making the arrangements?" he asked.

"I have to contact his family," I replied woodenly. "Can I let you know?"

"We'll be taking him to the morgue. The funeral home will know how to handle it."

Astrid and Linda were both in tears when I returned to the lobby.

Astrid quickly dried her eyes and tried to hide it from me, but I knew. I put an arm around each of them. "It was Artie."

"Do you need help with the arrangements?" asked Linda. Artie and she belonged to the same church, and often sat together at Mass. She and I had something in common; we were both married to Lutherans.

"I have to tell his parents," I said. "They are the ones who have to decide what they want to do."

"Artie would have wanted a funeral Mass," said Linda. "Will his parents be able to arrange it?"

"His parents are Jewish," I said. "I really don't know."

Linda reached into her purse for a scrap of paper. She went over to the emergency desk and wrote something. "If you need any help, this is my home number," she said, handing me the paper.

Astrid and I got into the car. "Are you all right?" she asked.

"Yes," I replied.

"Would you like me to drive?"

"No; I'm fine."

We rode home in silence. I don't know what Astrid was thinking, but I was reliving the last time I had seen Artie, trying to remember if there had been some indication that I had missed that his life was about to end. It had only been the previous Wednesday, two days before, and as usual, he had beaten me at tennis. Even in retrospect, I thought that he looked and seemed fine. He had asked for Astrid and, as we were leaving, he had asked me to give her a hug and kiss for him.

"Come over and deliver it yourself," I had teased.

"I will," he had promised.

"When?" I had demanded.

"Maybe next week."

"Promises, promises," I chided. "You've missed dinner with us two weeks in a row. It's been so long, Astrid is not sure she remembers what you look like."

"Tell her I'm the better looking guy when you and I are in the same room," he had countered, and those were the last words that Artie ever said to me.

I unlocked the door and, automatically, punched the code into the alarm. "I have to tell Artie's family," I said.

"Do you want me to do it?" asked Astrid.

"No," I said. "I don't want to do it but it's my place, and as much as this news will hurt, I think it will be less painful coming from me.

Probably the only thing that went right that whole day was that Julius answered the phone. I don't think I would have been able to tell Alice. I know that a father is just as much a parent as a mother, but I couldn't have made myself be as hard with Alice as I could with Julius.

"This is Mitch Goldblatt," I said after Artie's father said hello.

"Mitch, what a nice surprise. Are you visiting your mother?"

"No, Mr. Kornfeld. I'm at home, and I have some very bad news that you have to hear."

I'm not a big believer in telepathy, but I think that Julius knew as soon as I said it what it was about.

"Oh?" was all he said.

"Artie collapsed at the health club this afternoon. They think he had a heart attack. I wasn't there when it happened, but I went to the hospital as soon as I heard. The doctors worked on him for a long time, but they couldn't do anything."

There was a long silence. I just stood there, holding the phone, not knowing what else I could do. There was a choking sob. I waited still longer.

"Thank you for calling," said Julius finally. I could feel the agony in his every word.

"Mr. Kornfeld, I am so sorry," I said. "This is a call I would have given anything not to have had to make."

"I know," said Artie's father. "I know that you loved him too."

"He was the brother I never had," I said, meaning absolutely every word.

Julius choked back another sob. "Mitch," he said after another long pause, "is there a number where I can call you?"

I gave him our number and, as an afterthought, the number of the hospital. I thought he might want to talk to the doctors who had treated Artie. "Call any time," I said. "I'll be here all night."

"Let me tell Alice and then, I'll want to speak with you."

I didn't envy him that job. I replaced the receiver and went to pick it up again.

"Let me tell Rifka," said Astrid behind me.

"I'll do it."

"Mitch," she said softly, "let me do this for you. It's hard enough; she'll be better if it's me. It will be better for both of you."

I knew she was right, but it felt cowardly, letting her do something that I dreaded so deeply. I started to protest and realized that I was cutting her off from me. "Okay," I said softly.

She was great. She commiserated with my mother just enough, and then, gently but firmly, got her to pull herself together, reminding Rifka that there were people who were going to need her help. By the time she handed the phone over to me, my mother was ready to offer me comfort, rather than the other way around.

"You are a saint," I said when I replaced the receiver.

"Remember that the next time you malign my car," she said, kissing me lightly on the forehead.

"Your car is still a bomb, and it is unworthy of you," I countered.

The phone rang. It was Julius Kornfeld. "Mitch," he said, sounding as relieved that it wasn't Astrid as I had been that Alice hadn't answered their phone.

"How's Mrs. Kornfeld?" I asked.

"As well as we can expect, under the circumstances," he said. "Both girls are on their way; that will help."

"What can I do?" I asked.

"If it's too much to ask, please say so," began Julius, "but Alice and I were wondering if you could handle the arrangements at that end. We've spoken to Kirschenbaum's, and they can do nothing until after sundown on Saturday. Can you contact someone there to have Artie sent home? I spoke to the hospital, and you are authorized to make any arrangements."

He sounded so composed when inside, I was screaming. "I'll see what I can do," I managed to say.

"The services will be on Monday at the chapel," Julius continued. "Will you be able to make it?"

"I'll be there," I assured him.

"That means a great deal to all of us."

"If you think of anything else that you need, give me a call," I concluded.

I sat down at the kitchen table and buried my head in my arms.

Astrid stroked my back lightly. "How are you doing?"

"I have a terrible headache," I said.

"You haven't had anything to eat since lunch. Let me make something."

"I'm not hungry," I protested.

"A sandwich and two aspirins."

"All right," I agreed, not moving.

She brought two turkey sandwiches and two glasses of orange juice to the table. "Sit up," she said, handing me two aspirins, which I obediently swallowed.

I picked up half a sandwich and bit into it with no enthusiasm. It had no taste at all.

"I know you don't feel like it but eat it anyway," said Astrid, working on her sandwich.

"They're going to give him a Jewish funeral," I said miserably. "The Kirschenbaum special."

She had attended my father's funeral, so she knew every tacky detail of that place as well as I did. Artie would have hated it.

"Can you talk to them?"

"Not about that. I have pretty much agreed with them over the years on the subject of his religion, but this feels all wrong to me."

"Would Artie have cared?"

I thought back to my childhood, to the funerals of the salamanders, swordtails and guppies, of Gabriel the angelfish. "Very much," I replied, "but I wouldn't know where to begin to arrange a Catholic funeral. Do you?"

Astrid shook her head. "What can we do?"

"I could talk to Linda, I suppose."

"I don't think she'd mind," encouraged my wife. "She seems very nice."

"She is," I agreed as I replaced the half-eaten sandwich on the plate and dialed the number written on the scrap of paper.

Linda was terrific. She knew a funeral director who she thought would cooperate, and she took care of everything. She called back, saying that a funeral Mass was scheduled for three the next afternoon, that the funeral director had contacted Kirschenbaum's and had arranged to transport the body to Brooklyn on Sunday. As I had instructed, Linda told the mortician that I would pay for any costs associated with the funeral Mass, and he didn't see why anyone in Brooklyn had to know about the local arrangements, if it would upset them unnecessarily. I wasn't sure that I was doing the right thing, but I knew in my gut that it was what Artie would have wanted. Linda said that she would call everyone she knew who would be interested in attending.

I did something that I would not have done under normal circumstances; I called Beth at home and asked her to help me notify the people who would want to attend the services. When she heard what had happened, she was more than willing to help. It was nearly ten at night, but we decided that when people heard why we were calling, they would forgive the hour. We split the list; Astrid took half of my list and called from her cellular phone. Somehow, we managed to get it all done in a time frame that would have seemed impossible.

Neither Astrid nor I slept much that night. I'm not sure whether I dozed off or if I was awake and daydreaming, but I spent the night reliving the years Artie and I had spent together. For some reason, movies we had seen together kept playing in my head.

Artie was a very disciplined person from the time he was a child. He was diligent about homework and projects that he considered important, and he watched extremely little television, although I never heard his parents try to restrict his viewing. I should have been so lucky. The only thing he ever did that seemed almost to excess was go to the movies. He liked any kind of movie, but his favorites were surprising, considering that he was usually disposed to intellectual pursuits.

His very favorite movie of all time was *Splendor in the Grass* with Warren Beatty and Natalie Wood. The first time he ever saw it, when we both were about twelve, we were together. I was sleeping over at his house and it was on *Saturday Night at the Movies*. The ironic thing is that we didn't even really want to see it, but Artie's parents were out for the evening.

"Why do we have to watch what you want?" Artie demanded of his sisters.

"Because we are the majority," replied Denise.

"There are two of us and two of you," countered Artie. "I'd say we've reached a stalemate."

"No, we haven't," countered Robyn. "Mitch doesn't live here; he doesn't get a vote."

"If you aren't interested, you can play racquetball or concoct one of your foul-smelling potions," added Denise.

We knew from experience that it was pointless to argue with the two of them, so we began to watch the movie, planning to leave when we got bored, but instead, we got involved. Two hours flew by. At the end of the movie, when Natalie Wood goes out to the farm and Warren Beatty is there with his wife, I looked over at Artie, and he had tears streaming down his face.

"I am in love with that woman," he informed me as we climbed into the twin beds in his room that night.

"What woman?" I wondered.

"Natalie Wood. Someday, I'm going to marry her."

"She's way too old for you," I protested.

"Now she is," he conceded, "but age doesn't matter so much when you're older. Besides, women live longer than men; they should marry someone younger."

I thought he would change his mind when he was older. To be perfectly honest, I didn't think *Splendor in the Grass* was all that great. I have seen that movie at least five times more since then, all but once with Artie, and I have come to consider it a so-so melodrama, but as far as I know, it was always Artie's favorite movie, and he always cried at the end, at least when I was with him.

That was another thing about Artie. He was very emotional. I don't mean that he was weepy or a crybaby, but he was completely comfortable expressing his emotions. I am the complete opposite. It's not that I don't feel things. I do, very deeply. I'm just very good at holding it in. Usually, I don't cry even when I'm alone. I'm not sure why; maybe I'm afraid that if I get used to letting it go, I'll lose my knack for maintaining control. Sometimes it's pretty hard, especially at the movies.

I didn't cry when my father died. It wasn't that I didn't love him; I did, very much. It was more that my father was always a quiet man, and I loved him quietly in return. He was quietly there in my life and he was quietly gone; his passing did not evoke that type of passion in me. After he died, and I sat stoically through the services and the Shiva that followed, Rifka had accused me of brooding, but that wasn't completely accurate. I missed the small things that he did most of all, and it was when I thought of those things that I felt the pangs of his loss. Fittingly, it was a quiet emptiness that remained with me. In light of that, the idea of a grown man crying over something that happened on a movie screen seemed silly to me. *Ghost* damn near killed me but I kept it in. Astrid went through four Kleenex.

There was this movie that Artie and I went to see when I was visiting him one weekend when we were both still single. It was called *The Unbearable Lightness of Being*, and it was about this young doctor and his wife during the fall of Prague, in 1968. The movie had just opened and Artie had been waiting eagerly to see it, so when my visit coincided with its Rochester release, I reluctantly agreed to go with him. It was playing at the Pittsford Loew's, which was a pretty good size theater, and the place was full.

Artie was very particular about where he sat at the movies. When we were kids, I was happy just to be going to a movie but as usual, he had a master plan.

"Why do we have to be here an hour before it starts?" I asked in exasperation the first time we went together, as we waited in the lobby for the previous show to let out.

"If we're not the first ones in, the choice seats will be gone," he explained, munching serenely on his popcorn.

Theaters were larger when we were kids. I'll bet the College, where we often went, held 300 or more. "There have to be enough good seats for some to still be left even ten minutes before," I protested.

"There are only two ideal locations in the theater," proclaimed Artie. "We're tall enough that they won't force us to sit in the children's section but our options are still limited. The best seats in the house are last row, center section, on the aisle. I prefer the left side but the right will do in a pinch."

"Now I know you've lost your mind," I said.

"No, not at all," he replied calmly. "I like the aisle because I can stretch out with my feet to the side. Leg room is very important."

By the time we were old enough to be allowed to go to the movies alone, we were about twelve, and he was quickly approaching his adult height of six three. I am less than an inch shorter, so I understood his point.

"There are lots of aisle seats," I pointed out. "Why does it have to be the last row?

"Because then, it's impossible for the talkers to sit behind you.

I couldn't argue with him there. I find it really annoying to be trying to listen to dialogue when someone behind me is describing her new curtains, or detailing his prostate surgery through the entire film. For some reason, Rochesterians seem particularly prone to this rude habit, but it happens everywhere. If people want to talk, I've never understood why they go to a movie; maybe some day one of these jerks will enlighten all of us. Of course, many of the same offenders tend to come in late, after the movie has begun, and disturb everyone in the process of finding a seat; I suppose in some respects, they have elevated rudeness to an art form.

"You'll like this," Artie informed me after I had agreed to go to see *The Unbearable Lightness of Being* with him. "We only have to get there half an hour before it starts. In Rochester, I find that's time enough to be in position to get our seats."

"Talkers aren't a problem here?" I asked hopefully.

"No, they're probably worse, but they come later," he replied.

"And I thought New York was bad," I said as we parked the car.

"It is bad," said Artie. "Rude people live everywhere."

"I guess that's true," I agreed as we bought our tickets.

Actually, *The Unbearable Lightness of Being* was a good movie, but it was depressing. By the end of the film, I could hardly stand it, and when it got to the part about their beloved dog, Karenina, and I realized what was going to happen, I had to get out of there. My chest felt like it was going to explode. Artie was paying rapt attention to the screen, but when I started to get up, he noticed.

"Where are you going?" he whispered.

"Men's room."

"The movie's almost over."

"I can't wait."

I went into the lobby and found the men's room. I didn't really have to go that badly; I needed to get out of that theater, to miss what was about to happen on the screen. I wasn't the only one who had that idea; there wasn't a free urinal in the place. I went into one of the stalls and bolted the door. Ordinarily, I don't bother to close the stall door just to urinate; I don't know why I did that night, but as soon as I was in there, the tears began to escape. Fully clothed, I sat down on the seat and wiped my eyes with toilet paper until I was able to stop crying. When I finally managed to pull myself together, I stood up and went to the bathroom. Afterwards, I went to the sink, washed my hands and looked at myself in the mirror. I couldn't see any telltale signs, and I went back into the theater.

The movie was just ending. Artie was crying so hard, he couldn't get up out of his seat. He just sat there while the rest of the people in the row climbed over him, or went out the other aisle. Finally, when we were practically alone in the theater, he put on his jacket, and wordlessly, we walked out to the car.

"Can you drive?" I asked as we buckled our seat belts.

"Sure," said Artie. "Why?"

"You seemed overcome."

"Do you want to know what happened after you left?" he offered.

"I pretty much got the idea."

"You could have stayed, you know," he said. "I wouldn't have thought any less of you had I seen you cry at that movie. It was an intensely emotional experience."

"I was afraid I was going to wet my pants," I protested.

"You were afraid that you couldn't hold it in all right," agreed Artie. "You know, Mitch, everyone has emotions. Crying at a movie is a great release; you really do feel better afterwards."

I hated him a little bit at that moment. I hated him for knowing me so well, and I hated myself just a little bit, for being too much of a coward to have stayed and watched the end of that movie. I still wish that I could cry at a sad movie and dismiss it as no big deal, but I can't. I wished I could have trusted him as much as he seemed to trust me, but it wasn't in my nature.

I remember so clearly the night that Natalie Wood died. Artie had come to realize that he was never going to marry her, but she was still, hands down, his favorite actress. I was single, living in my apartment in Queens. About three in the morning, my phone rang. I was really alarmed to hear Artie on the other end. He was openly crying.

"What's the matter?" I demanded, my heart filled with terror.

"She's dead," he sobbed.

I sat bolt upright in bed, thoughts of my mother, my sister, his mother, his sisters screaming through my mind.

"Who's dead?"

"Natalie Wood," he choked. "She was out on a boat with Christopher Walken and her husband, and she drowned."

I am not a cold person. I thought that Natalie Wood was a wonderful actress and a gorgeous woman, but I couldn't believe that Artie had called me at three in the morning to tell me this. "Are you kidding?" I asked incredulously.

"No. I wish I were. I woke up and couldn't sleep, so I put on the radio, and I heard it on the news. You were the only person I knew who would understand."

I didn't really understand, but I realized that he had called me for sympathy and comfort, so I gave it to him. "I'm sorry; when did this happen?" I asked, not knowing what else to say.

"Earlier this evening," he replied. "I can't believe it's over; I never even had a chance. If she had been married to me, I wouldn't have let it happen."

He was beginning to scare me. Artie, the person most firmly rooted in reality of anyone that I knew, sounded as if he was losing it.

"Artie, you didn't know the woman. The person you saw on the screen was playing a character."

"No, Mitch. I knew her. I never met her, but we were connected," he protested. "Somehow, some day, we were meant to meet, and now it will never happen."

"You'll meet the right person," I assured him.

"Maybe, but it won't be the same thing."

"No, I suppose it won't," I agreed.

It dawned on me that if there really was a heaven, maybe they had finally met. I'm not sure what I believe about what happens to us after we die, but during that night, thinking about Artie and Natalie Wood, I was hoping that they were finally together, and that Natalie Wood was as impressed with Artie as he had been with her.

At six in the morning, I decided to give up on pretending to sleep. I didn't mean to wake Astrid, but she's a light sleeper anyway, and when I began to fidget, she got up. She insisted on making a big breakfast, but I couldn't even stand to look at the food. I felt like a first class heel when I took my coffee and wandered around the house with it, leaving my plate untouched. I was so restless that I couldn't make myself stay still. I made some calls to the people I had been unable to reach the night before, and walked around aimlessly, in and out of the house.

Finally, it was time for us to change into our funeral clothes and leave. I punched the code into the burglar alarm and, automatically, headed for my car.

"Let's take Sven," proposed Astrid.

"Honey, I'm not in the mood today." My head was throbbing like someone was using a sledgehammer inside, and I still have to think about what I'm doing when I have to drive a stick shift.

"Ill drive," she offered, standing next to the driver's side door.

"If it means that much to you, fine," I agreed.

The church was in a suburban neighborhood, set back far from the road, and it was actually quite nice. I hadn't been in a Catholic church many times before, but it didn't look too much different from most synagogues, except for the statue of Jesus on the crucifix. Linda was waiting at the back end of the aisle.

"The family usually sits in the front pew," she said after we had exchanged pleasantries. "I thought the three of us could sit there, if that's okay."

"Sure," I nodded.

We took our places, Linda going in first, Astrid next to her and I was on the aisle. We had barely taken our seats when people began to arrive. There were a number of people I didn't know who nodded to Linda, fellow parishioners, I gathered. There was a respectably sized contingent of Businetex people as well. I noticed that Bob, my boss, came in with his wife. At our last Christmas party, one of my colleagues, after far too many Molson Goldens, had shared a long-standing office joke with those of us who hadn't heard it before: that Bob's wife looked like John Madden. He'd gotten a big laugh but it was true; she really did look like John Madden, and I found it very difficult to have any normal type of interaction with her, because that was all I could think about every time I saw her. I was glad that they decided to sit near the back of the church; I wasn't in the mood to make polite conversation with either of them.

Jerry Fallow, Artie's boss, took a seat in the pew directly behind us. He nodded to me and glared at Astrid, as if she was crashing some type of exclusive private party. I despised Jerry; most people who had any contact with him did. Artie referred to him as a sociopath, but he felt a little sorry for him too. Jerry was divorced, his kid lived in another city with his former wife, and he seemed friendless. Artie occasionally played racquetball with him; in fact, Jerry had been playing with him the day Artie died.

I hadn't allowed myself to look but now that the priest, two men and a woman were up on the altar arranging things for the services, I forced my eyes forward. The casket was at the front of the center aisle, only about six feet from where I was sitting. I couldn't let myself think of it as Artie.

I expected the Mass to be some kind of hocus-pocus affair but actually, it wasn't that far from what I had experience at Jewish funerals. The priest talked about Job, and how he was a good man who had his faith tested in so many ways. He compared Artie to Job, a good man who was unshakable in his faith. He said that we, the mourners, might have questions about why Artie had died when he was so young and had so much left to do, and that we might be tempted to question our own faith. He went on to say that sometimes, there are no answers in this life but our continued faith would assure us our place in the kingdom of heaven.   Apparently, he felt that there, the answers we sought would be forthcoming.   He also read from Paul's epistles, but I had more or less tuned out by that point.

Several times during the services, I glanced around the sanctuary. I had a really bad headache and was starting to feel pretty queasy.   Fortunately, the place was air conditioned and, if anything, it was too cold. I felt myself shivering slightly.

I didn't have to look to know that Jerry Fallow was still behind me. They sang a number of hymns, and he joined in on each of them, far too loudly and a bit off key. I stole a glance or two at him, and he was leaning back in the pew, a contented smile on his face. He appeared to be having the time of his life. Every once in a while, I caught him giving Astrid a dirty look.

The really bad part of the service was right at the end. The priest took this metal box on a long gold cord and began to walk around the coffin, swinging the box as he prayed.   The box contained incense, and smoke curled around us, spreading the acrid odor.   Somehow, this seemed like the hocus-pocus I had dreaded. It started to get to me, and I felt the room beginning to dissolve, but just when I thought I was actually going to pass out, they began pushing the coffin toward the door, and the woman who had assisted during the Mass indicated that we were to follow.

Linda, Astrid and I stood in the vestibule by the door, and the people who had attended passed by, offering their condolences.

Bob, my boss, and his wife, Bobbie, stopped briefly to talk to us. I thought he was going to give me a hard time about taking a few days off on such short notice but Bob was surprisingly understanding.

"Bob, thanks for coming," I said, shaking his offered hand. "I'm afraid I'm going to have to be gone for a few days."

"To Brooklyn, for the burial," he nodded. "I'm sure his family will appreciate you being there."

"Yes, his father asked me to come," I replied. "I know I have a stack of work on my desk…"

"No, don't worry about that," he reassured me. "I'll make sure that anything that can't wait is handled. We'll talk when you get back, but if there's anything I can do in the meantime, give me a call."

"Thanks, I will," I said as he nodded curtly to Jerry Fallow, his boss, who was waiting behind him.

"Nice funeral," said Jerry, extending his hand to me.

"Jerry, do you know my wife, Astrid?" I asked, my arm around her waist.

"No," he said, ignoring her completely and walking out the doors.

Finally, it was over, and all the mourners had gone, save for Astrid, Linda and myself.

"Linda, thanks for everything," I said.

"Was it okay?" she asked.

"Very nice," said Astrid, taking her hand warmly.

"I know Artie would have been pleased," I said.

"Will you be coming in to the club next week?" she asked.

"Probably on Thursday or Friday," I said. I didn't know if I would ever feel like playing tennis again, even if I did find another partner, but I used the Nautilus machines faithfully three times a week, and I didn't see myself giving that up.

"We'll talk then," she said.

Astrid and I walked to the car. She went right to the driver's side, and I didn't argue. We got in, fastened our seatbelts and then, I totally lost it.

Astrid had never seen me completely out of control before, but she knew exactly what I needed. She unbuckled my seat belt, took me in her arms, and just held me and let me cry. I couldn't have done anything else if my life depended on it. Finally, she sensed that I had vented most of what I'd been holding in. She handed me some Kleenex from a box between the seats.

"You did good," she said softly.

Then, she started the car and we drove home in silence. Wordlessly, we walked up to our bedroom to change our clothes.

"You're awfully pale," Astrid finally said.

"I have a brutal headache," I admitted.

"Do you want something?"

"I think I'd like to lie down for a few minutes."

"That sounds like a good idea."

I wasn't sure if she was going to join me or not, but a few minutes later, she brought the afghan from the guest room and covered me. Then, she lightly kissed my forehead, and I heard her bare feet padding down the carpeted steps.

Again, I don't know if I was asleep or awake, but I know that I relived every argument that Artie and I had ever had. Of course, in my present state of mind, they seemed to have all been my fault, and I was consumed with guilt that I would never have the chance to apologize. After a while, the throbbing in my head had dulled, and I realized that it was dinner time.

I didn't feel like eating, but I supposed that we had to have something, and it was my turn to cook. Usually, whoever got home first took care of dinner, but Astrid had been doing most of the cooking lately, so weekends were my domain.

Astrid already had dinner going. There was macaroni and cheese in the oven and glass dishes of applesauce on the table. I noticed a plate of Oreos on the counter near the coffeemaker. Comfort food.

My wife came over and gave me a gentle hug. "Hungry?"

"Not very," I confessed.

"You have to eat something. All you've had today is a cup of black coffee. You can't afford to get sick now."

"It smells good," I said. "I'll try it."

"Good," she said.

"Astrid, I'm sorry about before."

"For what?"

"For falling apart after the Mass.

Astrid put the pot holders she had in her hands down on the counter.

"Mitch, I'm your wife and I love you. You don't have to apologize for being a human being. I know what Artie meant to you. I thought it was going to be much worse than it was."

"Worse how?"

"I was afraid that you wouldn't be able to make it through the services. I was trying to figure out how I was going to get you out of that church without being the center of attention, if I had to.

"I was so proud of you today. You did a wonderful thing; you put aside your own beliefs to be the best friend Artie could have asked for. You conducted yourself with poise and dignity through that Mass, and you don't have to apologize to anyone for anything that has happened over the past two days."

"I don't know what I ever did to deserve you," I said. "I do know how lucky I am."

"We're both lucky," she said. "I know too well that not all marriages are as right as ours."

"Astrid, I'm afraid," I said, in what for me was a rare moment of candor.

"Of what?"

"Of what I'll do in Brooklyn, at the other services."

"You'll be fine," she reassured me.

"I'm not so sure."

"I'll be there with you; we'll handle it. Don't worry. Now, have some dinner," she said, putting a plate on the table at my place.

The food went down easier than I had expected, and it did make me feel better. After we had eaten, Astrid pulled out a tape and suggested that we watch a movie. It was *Sixteen Candles*. I knew what she was trying to do, and I was grateful. We had taped that movie because it was so silly that it always made us laugh. Even in our present frame of mind, it was good for a few giggles. I can't hear the name Long Duck Dong without at least cracking a smile. When the movie was over, Astrid suggested that we get to bed early, so that we would be fairly well rested for the drive to Brooklyn.

I was climbing into bed when Astrid offered me two capsules and a glass of water.

"What's this for?"

"It's Benadryl."

"My sinuses are okay."

"It will knock you out," she said. "You need to sleep."

I started to protest but decided that she was right. Although I hate to take pills of any kind, particularly ones that I don't need, I really wanted to sleep. I still had a dull headache, I was tired and I craved the escape. I gulped them down.

I didn't think the medication was going to work, but Astrid urged me to close my eyes and snuggle against her, and the next thing I was aware of was awakening at three in the morning in a cold sweat. I had been dreaming.

Actually, it was more of a nightmare. All the lizards and snakes of Artie's childhood were chasing me in a room that had no doors or windows.

Astrid whimpered as I jolted upright.

"It's okay, go back to sleep," I whispered as I climbed out of bed.

"Where are you going?" she asked in a tiny, sleepy voice.

"Bathroom."

"You okay?"

"Fine. I just have to pee."

She rolled over and burrowed deeper under the covers. When I returned from the bathroom, she was very still, and her breathing was slow and even.

I decided that I wouldn't risk waking her and quietly slipped downstairs. I can tell you with certainty that there is nothing on that's worth watching at three in the morning, even with cable television. I decided to look for a book.

Most of the books that I would have wanted to read were on the bookshelves in our bedroom. All of the volumes in our downstairs study were reference books and our college text books, which for some strange reason, both of us kept. I poked through the choices, and there wasn't much there that would hold my interest, until I came upon a volume of Romantic and Victorian poetry that Astrid had used for an English course. I remembered a favorite line of Artie's from when we were children. Whenever I suggested that he ask his father something, he always countered with "The child is father of the man." Once, I asked him where he heard that, and he told me that it was from a Wordsworth poem. Wordsworth was his favorite poet, and I decided that I would look for that line.

I started to read, and I have to admit that I liked it a lot better than I had expected. I found the line I was looking for in a poem called *My Heart Leaps Up When I Behold*, and I even found something that I hadn't expected. I found that the title *Splendor in the Grass* was also from Wordsworth. I wondered if Artie had known that before he saw the movie.

Around six, Astrid came downstairs. "How long have you been up?" she asked.

"Since a little after three."

"You didn't sleep at all?"

"I had five good hours."

"What have you been doing?"

"Reading poetry."

"That sounds thrilling."

"Actually, I kind of enjoyed it."

Astrid did not offer to take Sven to Brooklyn. I didn't really want to take any car that belonged to me there, but we drove the Subaru. Actually, I did most of the driving. Astrid kept offering to take the wheel for a while, but I found that by concentrating on the road or the radio, I could keep myself from thinking too much. Also, driving for eight hours tired me out, and I wanted to be able to sleep that night. I had convinced myself that it was the Benadryl that had given me the nightmare, and I was hoping that the combination of my childhood room and the long hours of driving would help me drop off on my own.

Rifka was delighted to see us. She was always glad to see us, but this was an unexpected visit, and she would have told anyone who would listen that it was an ill wind that blew no one any good. None of us said too much about the purpose of our visit, but Rifka had outdone herself in the kitchen: roast chicken, potato kugel, tsimmis and homemade challah. More comfort food.

"I made rugalach and strudel," she announced with a flourish as she cleared the plates.

"You shouldn't have gone to all this trouble," protested Astrid.

"It's no trouble to feed the people you love. Beside, you can use it. You look skinny."

"Ma!" I protested.

"Well, it's true," she sniffed. "You have your big muscles, but Astrid is thin as a rail, not that she isn't gorgeous."

"Thank you, Rifka," laughed Astrid.

Astrid is very thin. It isn't that she doesn't eat; she can and does usually eat almost as much as I do. She doesn't exercise either; she hates it. She is just one of those lucky people who have that type of constitution. I am of average build but well muscled. To stay that way, I work out regularly and watch my diet carefully. My sister Marilyn is slender, athough not as slim as Astrid, and she has been going to aerobics classes for as long as I can remember.

My mother, on the other hand, has fought a constant battle of the bulge. She tries to keep her weight down, but she loves food. Even when she joined Weight Watchers and enrolled in a senior exercise program, she still couldn't shed the extra pounds.

"Do you want tea with dessert?" asked Rifka.

"I think I'll skip dessert," I said.

"I made it myself," she protested, sounding hurt.

"That stuff isn't good for you."

"A little bit isn't going to hurt," she sniffed.

"I would like tea with mine," said Astrid.

I gave in and had two pieces of each. I should have passed, but I have to admit that nobody bakes better than Rifka does.

After dinner, I sat down on the living room couch and turned on the news. Astrid insisted that she would do the dishes, and she would not allow me to help.

"I've been shooed out of the kitchen," laughed Rifka, joining me on the couch.

"Is it a mess in there?" I asked.

"I washed most of the pots before you got here," said Rifka.

"I'll check on her in a few minutes," I said, beginning to channel surf during the commercial.

"Mitchell," said my mother, "what exactly happened to Artie?"

"He had a heart attack, Ma. They took him to the hospital, but they couldn't do anything."

"I don't understand," protested Rifka. "He was young, he was skinny, he was so careful with his health. Was he ever sick before?"

"Not that I know of."

"Then how could this be?"

"I don't know, Ma," I sighed. "I guess sometimes these things happen."

"Well, I have a lot of questions," sniffed Rifka.

I realized that I had a lot of questions too, but I hadn't thought to ask any. I had never questioned the doctors at the hospital or anyone else about how Artie had died, just like that with no warning. I guess I was so overwhelmed that my mind wasn't working, but what my mother was saying made me realize that there were many unanswered questions for me as well.

"Ma, I really don't want to talk about it right now."

"Hiding from the truth won't make it go away," said Rifka sagely.

"I know," I agreed, "but I'm not up to it now. I'm tired, I have a headache; maybe after the funeral."

"All right," said Rifka, but I knew that she was not going to drop it that easily. "You take it easy for a while, and I'll see if Astrid can use some help."

Later that night, lying in my childhood room with my wife beside me, I could not get warm. It was the end of June and the air conditioner was running, but I was chilled to the bone.

"Is it cold in here?" I asked Astrid.

"It seems about right to me. If you're cold, I can shut off the air conditioner."

"No," I said. "It must be me."

People can say all they want to about how much better the older houses were built; it's a myth. The walls in my parents' house were just as thin as in any other house when privacy was what you wanted. The noise of the air conditioner would cover any sound coming from my room and I was willing to sacrifice warmth for privacy. I didn't want my mother overhearing every word that we said.

"Come here and I'll see if I can warm you up," offered Astrid.

I willingly slid into her open arms.

"You're freezing!" she said.

"I know; I can't get warm."

"I'm worried about you, Mitch. Maybe we should try to call a doctor tomorrow."

"What for?"

"You've had a headache for three days, you're not sleeping, you're freezing when it isn't cold, you're not eating well; maybe he can give you something to help."

"I don't need a doctor," I protested. "I need for tomorrow to be over. If I can look back on it and say that I got through that funeral without making a jackass of myself, or worse yet, making it harder for the Kornfelds, I'll be fine."

"You will," soothed Astrid, gently stroking my back. "Tomorrow, it will be over and you will have done fine."

"I wish I had your confidence," I said, burrowing closer.

Gently, Astrid ran her fingers across my chest, fingering my nipple. I shuddered involuntarily.

"Cold?" she asked.

"No," I sighed. "You're making me want you."

"That I can do something about," she whispered, sliding on top of me.

Normally, I don't like to make love to my wife in my mother's house. There was nothing wrong with Rifka's hearing, and she always let me know that she knew. For whatever reason, it seemed that she disapproved. Tonight, I wanted to feel better so badly that I didn't care. I was glad that we'd left the air conditioner running.

I grabbed the hem of Astrid's nightgown and she helped me pull it over her head. I cupped her small breasts in my hands and felt the nipples contract at my touch. Her hand slid down across my belly, and gently, she guided me inside her. We began our journey, over those dark, velvet hills, drifting farther and farther away from our cares, from the sorrow, to a place where Artie had not died because he never had been. Where we were going, there was only room for the two of us and for those incredible sensations that somehow defied accurate recall once they had passed.

I slowed myself to try to prolong the journey, wishing that we could stay the way we were right now forever, but knowing that we would not be able to resist the sweet temptation of the reward that awaited us at our destination. The trick to making it last was to think of other things, nothing upsetting that would break the mood, but nothing that would make self-control more difficult. Long ago, I had discovered that trying to recall the presidents of the United States in the order in which they had served was very effective for me. By the time I got to Zachary Taylor, I felt Astrid's breath quickening, and I knew that if I didn't catch up with her, I would be left behind. I covered her mouth with mine and she responded, caressing my hair and pulling me even closer.

We were almost there, and I felt us soaring, higher and higher, until we were at the top of the hill. In one of those miracles of cosmic timing, we crashed over the crest together in pulsating spasms of pleasure. I pushed my face into Astrid's shoulder to keep myself from crying out and revealing to Rifka exactly what we were doing. A muffled gasp escaped me, and Astrid whimpered softly as we both sensed our shared climax coming to an end.

The journey back was never nearly so pleasant, a dark time-travel devoid of the delightful floating sensation of getting there. Afterwards, we lay side by side in my childhood bed, sweaty and exhausted. I was vaguely aware of Astrid trying to push closer to me, but I was more aware of feeling isolated, and somewhat betrayed that it had ended when I had willed it to last.

"What's the matter?" Astrid whispered, sensing that I was off elsewhere.

The sound of her voice brought me back her.

"Nothing," I whispered, kissing her silky hair.

"Mitch, I love you so much," she said softly, gently stroking my cheek.

Somehow, that helped because I knew that she was speaking the truth.

"I need you," I said, burrowing my face into her neck.

"I'm here," she said. "Now, close your eyes and go to sleep, and when you wake up, I'll still be here."

I slept pretty well that night; I always do when Astrid and I make love and it's good between us. When I awoke, around seven, I could tell by the smell of coffee in the air that Rifka was already in the kitchen. True to her word, my wife was right there beside me.

The funeral was to start at eleven that morning, but it promised to be a long day. The cemetery was on Long Island, and the Belt Parkway was under construction. "Expect delays" was the way they had put it on the radio in the car on our way to Kirschenbaum's.

I noticed immediately that the casket was different from the one at the Mass. It was in the empty chapel, and the lid was glaringly open. The family was receiving visitors in an adjacent reception area. My mother made a point of averting her eyes from the chapel as she made her way toward the Kornfelds.

Astrid and I, arm in arm, walked up to the casket. I was almost afraid to look. Artie was lying on the white satin dressed in a navy pin-striped suit. His flaming hair had been combed, but its usual disorder was still evident. In all the years I had known Artie, I had never seen him when he didn't look like he needed a haircut. He looked like he was asleep, but I expected him to look at me any second, with those piercing blue eyes and to say to me, "This is a farce!"

"I'll give you a minute," whispered Astrid as she gently let go of my arm.

"Well, Artie, you've really done it this time," I said softly when Astrid had gone. "I know that this isn't what you would have wanted, but we did it your way on Saturday, so hopefully that took."

I guess maybe I was hoping for some kind of a sign, but he remained still and quiet.

"I think that's going to have to be our little secret," I added to my captive audience. "I don't think your parents would be too appreciative. I'm going to miss you, buddy."

I didn't know what else to say to him. How do you let go of a part of yourself? "Give Natalie Wood a kiss for me," I added, as I turned to go.

Julius Kornfeld was watching me from the doorway. I don't know how much he heard; I still don't. "He looks so peaceful," said Artie's father.

"Like he's asleep," I added.

"How are you, Mitch?" he asked, taking my hand between both of his and shaking it warmly.

"I'm okay, Mr. Kornfeld. How's Artie's mother?"

"Mitch, I think we're close enough to be on a first name basis. We're Julius and Alice, okay?"

I nodded.

"We both are very grateful for all you've done."

"I wish I could have done more. I wish I could have done something to keep him...."

Julius put his hand on my arm, and I didn't finish. "I know," he said, his eyes meeting mine.

There was such hurt and grief in those eyes that I wanted to hug him but I didn't. The rabbi motioned that he was ready to start the services.

"I'll give you a moment alone with him," I said as I walked out of the chapel.

Alice Kornfeld was walking toward me. She took both my hands in hers; hers were colder than mine. Then, she fell into my arms. Neither one of us said a word to each other. From out of the crowd around us, Julius appeared and led her off. I exchanged solemn pleasantries with Denise and Robyn, but none of us were in the mood for extensive conversation.

Astrid and I were heading toward the chapel as the services were about to begin when I felt a touch on my arm. It was my sister, Marilyn.

"I didn't think you'd make it," I said, returning her embrace.

"I wanted to be here," she said, slightly breathless. "I thought you might need me."

"Is Bert here?"

Marilyn shook her head. "He had to work. I almost didn't get here; the Belt is ridiculous."

"You look good," I said, giving her the quick once over.

She was trim as ever, not quite as tall as Astrid but not short for a woman either. Her light brown hair had been sculpted very short on the sides and longer on top, the current style, but not the way I have seen her wear it in the past.

"Old age is catching up with your eyes," she laughed. "I have lots of gray hair, a few too many laugh lines and dark circles under my eyes. I'm a mess."

"You're beautiful," I said, and she actually blushed.

We filed into the chapel and took our seats two rows behind the family. From behind the now closed casket, the rabbi nodded to me.

I was very surprised when, about an hour after Astrid and I arrived at my mother's, Rifka had answered the door to find the rabbi who would perform the service on her stoop. He had never met Artie and wanted to know something about him, and the Kornfelds had suggested that he speak to me.

He was young, probably in his late twenties, and being a reformed rabbi, he did not have anything about him that readily identified him as a member of his profession. After we spoke for a while, I had the impression that he and Artie would have hit if off. He seemed articulate and intelligent. I didn't really know anything about him; it was just an impression I had.

I told him what I could about Artie. How do you explain so complex a man to a total stranger in fifteen minutes? I also suggested a passage that he might read during the service if he thought it appropriate. He, in turn, suggested that it would have far more meaning if I did the reading.

There isn't anything I wouldn't have done for Artie, but I just couldn't. I didn't trust myself, didn't think I could say those words and not have my voice betray what was in my heart. He may have thought me a coward but he said nothing.

The service was more or less the same as all the others I have attended. The customary prayers were said, and the rabbi said a few words about Artie, trying to tailor them to a person he had never met, which couldn't have been easy. Then, he looked down at a sheet of paper and read the passage I had suggested from Wordsworth's *Intimations of Immortality.*

Then sing, ye Birds, sing, sing a joyous song!
  And let the young Lambs bound
  As to the tabor's sound!
We in thought will join your throng,
  Ye that pipe and ye that play,
  Ye that through your hearts today
  Feel the gladness of the May!
What though the radiance which was once so bright
Be now for ever taken from my sight,
  Though nothing can bring back the hour
Of splendour in the grass, of glory in the flower;
  We will grieve not, rather find
  Strength in what remains behind;
  In the primal sympathy
  Which having been must ever be;

In the soothing thoughts that spring
Out of human suffering;
In the faith that looks through death,
In years that bring the philosophic mind.

I bit my lip so hard during the reading of that passage that I could taste the metallic unpleasantness of blood in my mouth, but I remained composed.

"What remains behind," said the rabbi, repeating the phrase he had just read. "The legacy of Arthur Kornfeld is large, extending into each of our hearts. He was a force of tremendous energy, and I do not believe that such energy dies. As we sit here today, thinking of our son, brother, friend who is not with us, I ask each of you to look inside your heart, and to think of what remains behind of Arthur Kornfeld."

I felt Astrid's eyes on me and I met her glance. Her expression told me that she understood what I was feeling without my saying a word. I had done nothing but think about Artie since Linda's call on Friday night. In my mind, all that remained behind was pain and emptiness. My wife squeezed my hand reassuringly. I returned the pressure.

"Arthur Kornfeld has left our physical presence, but he will always be with us," continued the rabbi. "His firm convictions in what he believed, his courage to explore new ideas, and his ability to be a friend, through good times and bad will remain with us. When the road is long and bumpy, we will feel his hand on our shoulder, and we will feel stronger, knowing that we are not alone, that his spirit remains among us. We will find strength in the energy that was Arthur Kornfeld. This is his legacy.

The twenty-third psalm seemed to follow naturally, and the service was over, the casket being wheeled out to the hearse, and the mourners filing out of the chapel.

"Why don't you let me drive,?" offered Astrid.

I silently shook my head as I helped my mother into the back seat of the car.

Marilyn wasn't going to the cemetery. I gave her a quick peck on the cheek.

"You take care, baby brother," she said, stroking my face gently.

"You too, boss lady," I countered.

When we were kids, I always complained when she tried to tell me what to do, and she always told me that she was older, so she was the boss.

We made pretty good progress until we passed Rockaway Parkway, and then things started to back up. The hearse crawled along with its line of cars following closely, headlights on to identify those of us who were part of the cortege. Things came to a total stop. To our right, there was another funeral procession of far greater size than Artie's. Behind the hearse, there were four vehicles, obviously made especially for carrying floral arrangements.

"Have you ever seen one of those before?" I asked my mother, pointing at one of the vehicles overflowing with arrangements of exotic flowers.

"Only once before," replied Rifka. "That's the way the goyim do things. I apologize, Astrid."

"I've never seen one before," replied my wife, studying the vehicle with interest. "It seems a little garish."

Perhaps the most remarkable feature of this other funeral was that the line behind the funeral cars, which stretched farther than I could see in my rear view mirror, consisted totally of limousines. They were of all colors, makes and models, and some of the license plates were from New Jersey. I have never seen that many limousines all in one place, but they did have one thing in common with the rest of us: they weren't moving any faster than we were.

Having nothing better to do, I looked inside the ones that didn't have tinted windows. There were several passengers in each, and most of them were dressed more appropriately for a wedding than a funeral. Although it was the end of June and quite warm out, most of the women wore fur stoles and lace dresses. The men were dressed in formal wear. Even more strange, almost every one of the passengers was sleeping. The evidence was compelling that they were not heading to the same place that we were. Things in my car were not nearly so serene.

"I know I have mints in here somewhere," my mother was saying as she rifled through her purse.

"I thought I put some in before we left home," said my wife, peering into her own purse. Astrid sometimes gets carsick on long rides, and sitting in traffic seemed to bring it on.

"My timing couldn't be worse, but I have to go to the bathroom," confided Rifka.

Anyone who is familiar with car travel in New York City knows what a monumental problem that can be. There was no way to get off at an exit; they too were bumper to bumper. My two passengers were miserable, the hearse was at a dead stop in front of the family's limousine with a long line of cars behind it, and three lanes of traffic were going nowhere. The procession next to us inched on along side of us with it's sleeping passengers. No doubt, the only one in our procession who wasn't having a fit at the delay was Artie; he had all the time in the world.

For some inexplicable reason it struck me as being funny. I tried to hold it back, but I couldn't and I started to laugh, just a giggle at first and then, full blown gales of laughter.

"What's so funny?" demanded Rifka.

"Nothing," I sputtered.

"Then why are you laughing?"

"I don't know," I choked, trying to stop but unable to control myself.

"Don't you think we'd like to be in on the joke?" demanded my mother, beginning to get angry.

Astrid understood. Laughter and tears are not all that far apart, and trapped in that car with my two unhappy passengers behind the stalled funeral procession, my hysteria was beginning to take over. Once again, there was nothing I could do. It was going to take three hours to make a ten mile trip no matter what I did, and I was overcome with the same sense of futility that I had experienced at being unable to do anything to help Artie.

"Here, wash your face," ordered Astrid, handing me one of those moist towelettes she kept in the zippered compartment of her purse.

When I continued to laugh and made no move to accept the towelette, she tore it open and began to wipe my face for me. The hysteria subsided, and I took over and washed my own face. It did make me feel better, and I was able to stop laughing. Rifka began to realize what was going on with me and, her anger gone, she leaned forward to massage my neck. Soon, the traffic began to crawl along, slowly but steadily and we finally got there.

I had to stop at the cemetery office so that Rifka could use the ladies room. She offered to wait until the funeral was over, but I decided that it was more important for her to be comfortable, and if we missed part of the burial, so be it. The only thing we really missed was the casket being lowered into the waiting hole, not my favorite part of the ceremony anyway.

Julius gestured for us to stand with the family, and I took my place at his side. Alice was huddled between her two daughters, and the three of them were weeping softly.

I really had to admire Julius. He stood there stoically, chanting along with the prayers as his only son was buried. He said the Yiskor, the prayer for the dead, and he didn't miss a word. He was completely composed, until the rabbi threw the first shovel of earth into the grave. When he heard the sound of those clods of dirt hitting his son's coffin, he crumpled in a sobbing heap against me.

I stood there and held him, not knowing what else to do. I felt like screaming but I didn't. Finally, he wiped the tears away with the backs of his hands, took the shovel that was stuck into the mound of earth that had been removed when the grave was dug, and threw a shovel full of earth onto the coffin. He just stood there frozen for a moment, then extended the shovel to me. I scooped up some of the earth and threw it in the open grave. When I turned away, Julius was gone.

There was a bench about thirty feet from the plot, and I went over to it and sat. The cemetery workers waited until all the mourners had gone before covering the grave. I have never been very religious, but we are not supposed to leave a grave until it is covered, and I waited and watched from the bench until I was satisfied that it the job had been completed.

When the workers were gone, I walked over and studied the bare rectangle in the grass. I realized that there was nothing more I could do there, nothing I could do for Artie, and I went back to the car.

Astrid and my mother were inside, waiting for me. I took my place behind the wheel, and Astrid wordlessly took my hand and squeezed it meaningfully. I returned the pressure. Amazingly, traffic was flowing freely, if at a higher volume. We made it home in half an hour.

"The Kornfelds will be expecting us," said Rifka, arranging rugalach and strudel on a plate and covering it with plastic wrap.

"We'll join you in a little while," suggested Astrid.

"No, we can go now," I said.

"I'm sure they'll understand if you need a few minutes," she said.

"If you're tired, you can join us later," I said.

Astrid shook her head, and the three of us walked across the street together.

The Kornfeld house was full of people, some of them familiar to me from childhood, and others complete strangers. There was an obscene amount of food and a flock of fussing women urging everyone to eat. I couldn't face the idea of food, but I did accept the Coke that Astrid poured for me. The headache that had been with me since Artie's death was back in high gear.

"Mitch, you look so pale, dear," said Alice Kornfeld, taking my hand between both of hers. She was shorter than I remembered her being in the soft bedroom slippers that mourners customarily wear. She looked about thirty years older than she had the last time I'd been in Brooklyn, about two months earlier.

"I'm all right, Mrs. Korn...Alice," I said. "I have a little headache."

"There's some aspirin upstairs in the medicine cabinet," she offered.

"If it doesn't go away on it's own, I may take you up on that."

"You know where it is if you need it," she said.

"Yes," I replied.

"I'm so grateful that you came," she said, her light blue eyes bloodshot with grief as they met mine. "It meant so much to me and Julius. I hope you will stay in touch with us, now that Artie is gone."

"For as long as you want me to. Artie was like a brother to me."

"I know, dear, and you are a son to us."

Astrid overheard this conversation and guessed what it was doing to me. "Alice," she interrupted, "I'll bet you haven't had anything to eat all day."

"I'm not very hungry," she protested.

"I know," said Astrid, "but you'll feel better if we get something in you. Come on."

Alice allowed herself to be led away, and I spoke briefly to Denise, Robyn and several of Artie's aunts and uncles, whom I remembered from all the time I had spent in that house over the years.

The house seemed so much smaller than I remembered. Rifka's house did too. Whenever we came home, I always marveled at how the place I remembered had been replaced with an identical replica in miniature. The food, the din of mingled conversation, the smoke and the walls closing in were suffocating me. I needed to get away from it, to be by myself. I decided to take Alice up on that aspirin and made my way upstairs.

The bedrooms were empty, their doors open. I peeked in Artie's room and it was just as I remembered it, same furniture, bedspreads, curtains, and his college pennant still on the wall over one of the beds. I couldn't stay there. Quickly, I went into the bathroom and locked the door, happy to be alone. That room was familiar too, but it was not as personal as Artie's room.

Someone had covered all the mirrors in the house, so there was a towel over the door of the medicine cabinet. Pulling the door back, I immediately saw the bottle of Bayer Aspirin on the middle shelf, and I poured two of the tablets into my hand, replaced the cap, then opened the bottle again and took a third tablet. I gulped the pills down with a handful of water and went to replace the bottle.

It was then that I saw it. The egg timer was in the corner of the medicine cabinet on the bottom shelf. I couldn't believe that it was still there. Apparently, no one in the Kornfeld house used an egg timer very often. Artie and I hadn't had our peeing contests with any regularity since grade school, although I can remember doing it when we were older, once or twice, as a joke. I picked the timer up and turned it over. It was so old that the sand had clumped, but after I tapped it several times on the palm of my hand, it began to flow. I watched until the last grain had gone through the hole. Then, I turned it over again.

There was a tentative knock on the bathroom door.

"I'll be out in a minute," I called.

I replaced the timer in its corner; the sand was still running through the hole. Gently, I closed the door of the medicine cabinet and opened the bathroom door.

"I'm sorry to disturb you," said Artie's aunt Bertha.

"I didn't mean to take so long," I apologized.

I walked down the stairs and mingled again, speaking to a few of the neighbors whom I hadn't seen for years.

After a while, my throat started to feel very dry and I decided to get a drink of water. Alice and Julius were alone in the kitchen.

"Excuse me," I said, when they looked up. "I just wanted a drink of water. I'll come back later; I didn't mean to intrude."

"Please come on in, dear," coaxed Alice, removing a glass from the cupboard, filling it with ice and the same bottled water I remembered from childhood, and offering it to me.

"We want to thank you for everything you've done," said Julius, putting his arm around me.

"If there's anything else I can do, I will," I offered.

"Mitch, dear, the rabbi told us that you suggested that he read that poem. I had forgotten how much Artie loved it. Wordsworth was his favorite poet, but I had already forgotten that the *Intimations* was his favorite work. Thank you for giving me back a little piece of my son," said Alice, beginning to cry.

"Alice, don't," pleaded Julius.

"Mitch understands," said Alice, wiping her eyes and kissing me lightly on the cheek. "We're losing more and more of Artie with every passing minute."

"I will never forget him, Alice," I reassured her. "I couldn't if I wanted to; he will always be a part of me."

"You're still so pale, dear," she observed. "Didn't the aspirins help?"

"Not too much," I admitted. "I thought I might go home and lie down for a while."

"Sure, you go on," said Julius. "I didn't realize you weren't feeling well."

"Just a headache," I reassured him. "I'll be fine."

"Rifka and Astrid don't have to leave yet, do they?" asked Alice.

"If you'd like them to stay, I'm sure they will," I said.

I had to get out of that house; I could hardly breathe. Astrid offered to come with me, but I asked her to stay, to make sure that Artie's parents were really okay. Alice was walking around, saying all the right things, but she didn't seem right.

I let myself into my mother's house and collapsed gratefully onto my bed. The air conditioner was running, and the cool air felt good after being in the stifling, crowded Kornfeld house for so many hours. I lay on the bed, staring at the ceiling, letting my mind drift wherever it would. The aspirins began to work and the pain almost disappeared.

I don't know how long I was there, but it must have been a while because the lights were off and it had gotten dark in the room. Suddenly, the door burst open.

"Mitchell, are you all right?" demanded Rifka.

I sat up quickly. "Ma, don't you believe in knocking?"

"In my own house, I should have to knock?"

Rifka had never been big on privacy.

"How did you know I was decent?" I challenged.

"I changed your diapers," declared my mother. "Maybe you've recently grown something I've never seen?"

I knew better than to argue with her. "Where's Astrid?" I asked instead.

"Poor Alice doesn't want to let her go. She agreed to stay for a while, so I promised to check on you. She was worried and so was I."

Rifka made her way for the lamp. "Why are you sitting in the dark?"

"My head feels better that way."

Rifka took a Kleenex from the box on the nightstand, sat down on the bed next to me and started wiping my face.

"Ma, what are you doing?"

"I dried your tears when you were a little boy; I can do it now."

"I'm not crying," I protested. I hadn't realized that I was, but my face was wet.

"Mitchell, there's nothing wrong with crying when you're sad. Did I ever tell you there was?"

"No, Ma."

"Well, then who did?"

"No one. I grew up; grown men don't cry."

My mother did not try to debate that one. "I want to talk to you about what happened to Artie," she said.

"All right," I sighed, "but not right now."

"Not last night, not now. When?"

"Tomorrow. We have all day tomorrow. We'll talk then."

"I'm going to hold you to it," she warned.

"We will; I promise."

"Is there anything I can do for you now? Would you like some tea, maybe?"

"No, I don't think so."

"Mitchell, I'll say just one more thing to you. Today is the day for you to mourn Artie. Tomorrow, it's time to get on with the rest of your life."

"Yes," I said.

"All right," said Rifka, standing up. "Sleep tight and don't let the bedbugs bite."

"Ma?" I said.

"Yes, my darling?"

I did the only thing I could at that moment. I buried my head in my mother's ample bosom and cried my heart out for Artie.

Chapter 3
Rifka

I actually slept very well the night after we buried Artie. I didn't even hear Astrid come in, and I was only half conscious of her undressing me, and coaxing me under the covers. I almost couldn't believe it when I opened my eyes the next morning to see that it was eight forty-five.

What was even more unbelievable was that my headache was gone. For the first time since Linda's phone call, I actually felt human.

"Welcome back," said Astrid.

"Have you been up for long?" I asked.

"Not too long," she said. "You looked so peaceful, I enjoyed watching you sleep."

"I didn't realize how tired I was."

"Rifka said you had been out for a while by the time I got back from the Kornfelds. You didn't even really wake up when I put you to bed."

"Thanks," I said.

"Did you let Rifka mother you a little bit last night?"

"More than a little bit."

"Good. I think she needed that. That was why I sent her to check on you."

I knew that she was thinking that some mothering was what I needed too, and she was right. She could tell by the way I was looking at her that I was feeling more like myself. I usually can't look at Astrid in my bed without wanting her, and she recognized the look of lust in my eyes. I stroked that golden hair, and she reached out to touch my face. Pulling her to me, I started to cover her with kisses and she responded, running her fingers gently through my hair. I rolled onto her, and she arched her back to help me get closer. We were moving together, me inside her, when the door to the bedroom flew open.

"Good morning, sleepyheads," greeted my mother.

I jumped about three feet straight up and rolled off my wife. "What is it, Ma?" I demanded, not bothering to mask my annoyance.

"Well, you must have gotten up on the wrong side of the bed," she remarked. "I'm leaving for my exercise class, and I'll be stopping at Waldbaum's on my way home. Is there anything special that the two of you want?"

"Not that I can think of," I said.

Astrid shook her head.

"All right then," chirped Rifka. "You two go back to whatever you were doing."

She closed the door behind herself.

"Hasn't your mother ever thought of knocking?" asked Astrid.

"Never," I said.

I looked at Astrid and she looked at me. Trust me, the mood was gone.

I have never understood how a woman, who thinks of herself as being as socially correct as my mother does, could have so little regard for the privacy of others. She has been this way for as long as I can remember.

Rifka's house was built sometime around World War I, and the doors all have those glass knobs that were used in most old houses. There were, at one time, locks on those doors, the kind that open with a big skeleton key, the same key for every lock in the house. However, those locks had been painted over so many times, I don't even know if they could be made to work if someone was motivated enough to take the time and effort to try to free the bolts. The only room in the house with a working lock was the bathroom.

Rifka and my father always slept with their door open. They must have had sex at some time during their marriage, but when Marilyn and I compared notes, neither of us had ever heard them. We were taught to keep our doors open too. The only time the door to the bedroom was ever closed was when Marilyn or I were sent to our rooms as punishment, "to think it over."

When we grew up and moved away, we started closing our doors when we slept at my mother's house, but that didn't keep her out. When Rifka had something on her mind, in she would come, and her answer was always the same.

"In my house, people live by my rules."

It wasn't so bad for Astrid and me; we didn't visit very often. Marilyn had been another story. My sister met her husband, Bert, when she was a freshman in college and

Bert was a sophomore. They dated for three years before deciding that they didn't want to wait any longer to get married. Marilyn and I never discussed this, but I'm pretty sure that sex was part of the reason. My mother told both of us when we were growing up that decent people saved themselves for marriage. You may have guessed that I didn't save myself. I consider myself a decent person but in my early twenties, I concluded that to do what my mother suggested would make me a candidate for sainthood, and that wasn't me either.

Marilyn, on the other hand, was very young when she met Bert. I know she wanted to wait for marriage to have sex, out of respect for Rifka, but I'm sure that Bert was losing patience, and Marilyn herself must have had normal urges. At the end of her junior year, they decided they wanted to get married, even though Bert was going to be starting graduate school and didn't have a job.

He had a teaching assistantship that paid his tuition, and his parents offered to give him a modest allowance, so that he could continue his education. They were not opposed to his marrying, and they liked Marilyn, but where the newlyweds would live was a problem. Bert's parents lived in a rather small apartment, and Bert shared a room with his younger brother.

My parents, on the other hand, had a house, and Marilyn had her own room. Both of our rooms were even furnished with double beds. When we were old enough to abandon the crib, Rifka bought us beds. I must have been about four-there was no baby after me to need the crib-and I remember accompanying my parents when they purchased my 'big boy bed,' as they chose to call it.

"I don't know, Rifka," mused my father as we stared at the mattress my mother had selected. "That bed looks awfully big for him. Maybe we should get the twin size."

"He's going to have this bed for a long time, Max. He'll grow into it," said my mother.

"The room is pretty small," persisted my father, "and the twin size looks big enough. I would fit in that."

"The twin size costs the same as a double bed," For Rifka, it was a no-brainer. "Why should we pay for room for one to sleep, when we could get room for two for the same money?"

"I understand that," agreed my father, "and I thought it made sense for Marilyn's room, but his room is much smaller."

"What's he going to do in his room that he needs so much space? He's going to sleep there; he needs a bed."

It was nearly impossible to win an argument with my mother. Three days later, the double size bed was installed in my room. It was a tight fit; if my mother turned sideways, she could fit between the wall and the bed when she changed the sheets.

Marilyn and Bert moved into her room after their wedding. Things might have actually worked out okay if Rifka had been a bit more sensitive to their needs. My father was just happy that his daughter was still under his roof. He liked Bert and had no problem accepting him as a son-in-law. My mother, on the other hand, was used to being privy to every detail of Marilyn's life, and after she was married, there were things my sister no longer cared to share with her mother.

Rifka seemed to have a sixth sense about when the newlyweds were in an amorous mood, and she would always wait until they were just getting started before bursting in on them on some pretext. After a while, they just about gave up on actually having sex in their bedroom.

I suspect that part of my mother's motivation for constantly invading the newlyweds' privacy was that she was afraid that Marilyn would get pregnant before they were ready for a family. No one was happier than Rifka when she finally did become a grandmother, and she was just as excited about Marilyn's second pregnancy as her first, but my sister did not have children until five years after her marriage. Both she and Bert had been working at pretty good jobs for a while when that happened.

Right after my mother left the house, Astrid went in to take her shower. Rifka had only one bathroom in the house, and before long, I became aware that my bladder was achingly full. I knocked on the bathroom door.

"It isn't locked," called Astrid.

"Do you mind if I come in?" I asked. "I have to pee."

She peeked out the corner of the shower curtain. "Help yourself."

I was standing in front of the toilet, remembering about playing lookout for Bert and Marilyn. I was seventeen when they got married, old enough to understand how frustrated they must have been. The bathroom was the only room with a lock, but Rifka used to get angry if they went in there together. They would usually wait until my parents were out of the house before sneaking in and locking the door. I would be posted somewhere near the stairs. If my parents came in, particularly Rifka, I would engage the intruder in conversation loudly enough to warn them. Then, Marilyn would hide in the tub with the shower curtain pulled closed, and Bert would come out innocently, as if he had been using the bathroom. When the coast was clear, I would go and get my sister.

I remember one time when Marilyn was hiding in the bathroom, and I wasn't able to spring her before Rifka went in. My sister was hiding in the tub, and my mother was doing all kinds of things that someone would do thinking she was alone in the bathroom. When my mother started pulling her face into contortions, apparently trying to simulate what she would look like after a face lift, my sister had started to giggle and almost gave herself away.

"Why are you smiling like that?" asked Astrid, toweling herself dry as I put the seat down and flushed.

"I was thinking about what Marilyn and Bert used to do in this bathroom," I said, washing my hands.

"What?" she asked.

"Would you like me to show you?" I offered.

Astrid laughed and locked the door. I had my wife right there on the bathroom rug in Rifka's bathroom.

At about twelve-thirty, Rifka came home with corned beef, pastrami and all the other goodies she could find at the Kosher deli.

"The artery clogging special," I observed.

"When was the last time you had it?" demanded Rifka.

"Last time we were here," I answered.

"Me too," she said. "Are you always so obsessive about what you eat?"

"No," laughed Astrid. "He's just giving you a hard time."

"That reminds me," said Rifka, "I wanted to ask yesterday, but you didn't want to talk. Was Artie still a vegetarian?"

"Yes," I said. "Ever since he was a kid."

"Was he still thin?"

"You saw him in the casket," I said.

Rifka shook her head adamantly. "No, I didn't. I never look."

"Why not?" asked Astrid.

"It's bad luck; I'd rather remember people the way they were," said my mother.

"Who told you it was bad luck?" I asked.

"I don't know. Did Artie eat a lot of dairy products?"

"Not too much that I knew about," I replied. "He drank skim milk most of the time, and to answer your question from before, he was still thin. Why?"

"We were talking about what happened to him at my exercise class on Saturday, and again today. The instructor said that it is very unusual for someone as young as Artie was, who's thin and has been a vegetarian for a long time, to have a heart attack and die like he did."

"Maybe your exercise class knows of someone he should sue," I replied.

"Be a wise guy," said Rifka, undaunted, "but I have a lot of questions about how this could have happened, and you would too if you were thinking clearly."

"These things happen, Ma. He was playing racquetball. He must have overexerted himself."

"He never exercised?"

"He did some type of physical activity every day."

"My instructor says that exercise is very safe, if you do it on a regular basis. She says that people who are inactive and try to do something strenuous are the ones who get in trouble."

"I don't know, Ma." I sighed, wanting this conversation to be over.

Rifka put the sandwiches on the table, but I had lost my appetite. I picked at my food disinterestedly.

"Rifka," said Astrid, "maybe there's heart disease in Artie's family."

"No," said Rifka. "Alice Kornfeld used to come to my exercise class before Artie died. I don't know if she'll come back after the Shiva's over, but she once said that neither she nor her husband have any history of heart disease in their families. They make you have a physical and answer all kinds of things before they let you join this program."

"I guess we'll never know why it happened," I said. "You said yesterday that today was the time to put it in the past."

"Did they do an autopsy?" asked Rifka, ignoring my attempts to end the discussion.

I pushed my plate away angrily. "I don't know, Ma! Would you like me to go across and ask the Kornfelds if they carved up their son's body before they allowed them to bury him?"

I got up from the table and stormed out of the house to the front stoop. My mother was like a dog with a bone when she got onto a subject.

Astrid came to sit beside me. "She means well, you know."

"The road to hell is paved with good intentions," I spouted.

"Why are you so angry?" asked my wife.

I hadn't thought that I was angry; I thought I'd had enough, and I didn't want to talk about it anymore.

"I suppose she makes me feel guilty."

"That's what mothers are for," smiled Astrid. "About what?"

"That I didn't ask more questions. That I readily accepted what seemed impossible. I took the word of some man in a white coat in an emergency room. I didn't even ask for his credentials; for all I know, he could have been the janitor."

"I don't know many janitors who rattle off as much medical jargon as he spouted. The safe money says that he's at least an intern."

"I should have asked more questions."

"You still can," said Astrid, the voice of reason. "Tomorrow, we're going back, and you can make some calls and see what you can find out. If you need to know, there probably are answers."

I have to admit that it annoyed me that Rifka had thought of the questions that I should have been asking, but when I began to think about it a little more calmly, I realized that I had even more doubts than she did. Artie was so damn compulsive about everything. When we ate together, he drove me crazy about nutritional value from the time we were kids. He was the only kid I ever knew who preferred fruit to candy, and the only junk food I ever saw him eat was popcorn, which is now supposed to be good for you. I went berserk in grocery stores with him, because nothing went into his cart until he had examined the entire label. I had once insisted that by the time he finished inspecting the container of skim milk we had stopped for, that the expiration date would have passed and it would have soured.

He was an exercise junkie. Aside from our tennis games, he played racquetball, bowled on an office league, and I know he swam daily at the health club. His arteries should have put the rest of ours to shame.

"I didn't mean to make you angry, Mitchell," Rifka was saying through the screen door.

"I'm not angry, Ma, but I don't know what you want from me. I don't have the answers that you want; I don't have the answers that I want either."

"It's just that I don't understand how this could happen," said Rifka. "If it could happen to Artie, it could happen to anyone."

My mother's eyes began to fill with tears, and I couldn't believe that I had been so dense. I stood and went in to her, taking her in my arms.

"Just because it happened to Artie at my age doesn't mean it will happen to me," I said.

"I know, I know, I'm just being silly," sniffled Rifka.

"You're not being silly," said Astrid, rubbing her back gently. "You're being a mother; it's allowed."

"I'm fine, Ma," I said, "and don't worry: I never play racquetball. I've never been all that crazy about the game."

"It's different when an old person dies," said my mother, pulling a tissue from the pocket of her slacks and wiping her eyes. "You still feel awful but it's different; I can't explain it."

"It's different when it's someone close to you," said Astrid.

"I suppose so," sighed Rifka. "When Max died, I thought I expected it, but it was still a surprise. Can you believe that? He'd had prostate cancer for five years, and I still didn't believe that he would die. Until the last year, he was never that sick."

"But they told us that it had spread when they found it," I said.

"Did you expect Daddy to die when he did?" Rifka demanded.

I averted my eyes. "I knew that it would happen, but if you're asking if I thought it would be that day, that month, no, I suppose not. It came as a shock, even though I'd known since they found it that it was likely to happen sometime."

"I knew that there was something wrong years before that," said Rifka.

"Why didn't you do something?" asked Astrid.

"I tried. He went to the doctors and they all made light of it. They did tests, they examined him, they took x-rays, and they insisted that there was nothing there. They said that all men have 'plumbing problems' when they get older. I insisted that it wasn't normal for a man to get up to go so many times every night, and to stand there straining for five minutes before anything would happen. I didn't have a decent night's sleep for ten years."

"What did they say?" questioned my wife.

"They said that I was a pain in the neck. I know that I can be stubborn."

I rolled my eyes.

My mother ignored me. "They told us that all the tests were normal, and that he shouldn't drink too much before he went to bed."

"What did they say when he had the back pain and they found out what was wrong?" I asked.

"They said he should have come to them sooner, before it had spread into his bones," sighed my mother.

The telephone rang. Astrid offered to answer it.

"It's Marilyn," she said, coming back into the living room. "She says that she'll still come for dinner, if you want her to, but Bert can't make it; he has a late meeting."

"Of course I still want her to," said Rifka, stomping off to the phone.

My sister Marilyn and my mother have a classic love-hate relationship; they feed off of each other. No one can exasperate Marilyn more than Rifka, but they can't seem to get through a day without having contact of some kind. Their phone bills are astronomical. Ever since I can remember, they have been practically joined at the hip.

I doubt that Bert really had a late meeting, unless he scheduled it after he heard he was expected at my mother's for dinner. Bert is always painfully civil to my mother, but I suspect that he can't stand the sight of her. He's a good guy but everyone has his limit, and I think Bert reached his long ago. I suspect that Bert could have forgiven Rifka for ruining his sex life during the first six months of his marriage. It's the cumulative actions over the rest of the years that have estranged them.

After six months at my parents' house, it was apparent to both Marilyn and Bert that the arrangement was not going to work. Bert decided to give up graduate school, take a job and find an apartment of their own. Marilyn would finish her degree, and he would go back to school after she graduated.

It turned out to be a good move for him, career-wise. He managed to find a good job in New Jersey. Marilyn had one semester left at Brooklyn College so they looked for an apartment in Brooklyn and Bert commuted. I guess when you're young, it doesn't seem so bad, but he had to take the subway to Manhattan, where he could get a bus to New Jersey, so he spent hours every day traveling to and from work. Marilyn could walk to school, so they didn't have the expense of a car, and they didn't buy much furniture. All that was in the apartment was a dresser, a bed and a table with four chairs. It wasn't for everyone but they were happy.

Rifka, however, would not leave them alone. She convinced Marilyn to give her a key, and she would go over and clean, bring them household items that she thought they could use and cook for them. I think that between the commute and working full time, Bert was too beat to notice. Marilyn asked Rifka not to come without calling when Bert was home and, for a while, she honored that request. Then, early one Saturday morning, Rifka let herself in with her key. I don't know if they were making love or just asleep, but Bert went ballistic. He screamed at my mother, bodily threw her out and gave Marilyn hell. Marilyn would never talk about what actually happened, but later that day, she showed up with a suitcase.

"My marriage is over," she had declared tearfully.

"That's fine," replied my mother. "If Bert doesn't want to be married to you, you always have a home here"

An hour later, Bert showed up. Rifka wouldn't let him in. Marilyn stayed in her room for hours and cried. Rifka stomped around like the cat who ate the canary.

Finally, my father interceded. Normally, he let Rifka have her way but this time, he was adamant. He went up to Marilyn's room to talk to her. Then, he called Bert and told him to come over.

"What do you think you're doing?" demanded my mother, when my father announced that Burt would be arriving momentarily.

"Stay out of it, Rifka," he said sternly. "This doesn't involve you."

An hour later, my sister went home with her husband, and the next time Rifka tried to use her key, the lock to the apartment had been changed.

A few weeks after Marilyn graduated from college, Bert found a different job, on Long Island, and he and my sister took an apartment close to where he was working. My sister took a job in a doctor's office, and a year later, they bought a home, the same house they live in now. Bert is now a regional manager for that same company. Marilyn too continued to work, taking only a short maternity leave when each of my nephews was born. She also took courses through the years and three years ago, she was certified as a physician's assistant. She still works at the office she started with straight out of college.

Marilyn breezed into the house, looking fresh and summery in her pastel colored short outfit. We don't look much like brother and sister. Marilyn has straight, light brown hair when she hasn't permed it, hazel eyes and a tiny nose. My father was dark, like I am, with a long, pointed nose. Rifka has dark eyes and the original from which my nose was copied. As for her natural hair color, she claims that even God can't remember that far back. As far as I can remember, it has always been one shade of red or another. Right now, it could best be described as auburn; I think it suits her. Both my nephews are the picture of Bert, with dark, curly hair and gray eyes, as if they had only one parent. Genetics are a funny thing.

"Where are the boys?" I asked, when it was apparent that Marilyn was alone.

"Camp," she said. "They left on Saturday."

"Already?" I asked. "It isn't even July yet."

"They always leave the last Saturday in June."

"I was looking forward to seeing them," I said petulantly. "I've been looking forward to having Ma tell some more embarrassing 'Uncle Mitch' stories."

I do love my nephews, but I had an ulterior motive for wanting them at any family dinner; Rifka is much less likely to stir things up when the boys are present. I guess she thinks she's setting a good example, and that they don't know what things are like when they're not around. David and Alan are pretty smart kids; I suspect Grandma would be shocked to learn what they really think about her.

"I had hoped that you would be glad to see me," said Marilyn, sounding wounded.

"Of course we are," said Astrid quickly. "Mitch is a little disappointed that we won't get to see the boys too."

"I know," winked Marilyn, giving Astrid a hug and then embracing me. "I just enjoy occasionally giving my baby brother a hard time."

"I didn't hear you come in!" said Rifka, running over to give her only daughter a big hug and kiss. "Bert couldn't get away early?"

"No, Ma," said Marilyn. "I told you that he couldn't make it."

"I thought he might change his mind," sniffed Rifka, "so I made enough, just in case."

"It smells good," said Marilyn. "What is it?"

After Marilyn had called earlier, Rifka had rushed out to the butcher around the corner, although she had already gotten lamb chops when she was at Waldbaums.

"It's veal cutlets, your favorite," announced my mother happily.

Marilyn frowned. "You know how Bert feels about eating veal."

"You told me he wasn't coming," protested Rifka.

"That's not the point," said my sister. "Bert doesn't approve of eating veal; he says the calves are mistreated."

"He eats lamb chops," sniffed Rifka. "Maybe he thinks they treat the lambs so nice? What a hypocrite!"

I have long since learned that it is futile to argue with my mother, but Marilyn lets her get away with nothing. Once they get going, she will challenge every word that comes out of Rifka's mouth. They argue and shout at each other, until one or both of them wind up in tears. Then, after everyone else's evening has been ruined, they kiss and make up and are back to lovey-dovey again. It always aggravates the hell out of me.

"Ma, don't start," I pleaded.

Marilyn is a pretty good sister, and I think she sensed that I'd had about all I could take in the past few days. "Ma, it's all right this time but please, don't do it again. It's disrespectful to my husband, and if you serve veal to me again, I won't eat it."

Rifka went off to the kitchen muttering to herself but she said nothing more.

We managed to catch up on what had been going on in each others' lives, as we set the table and helped Rifka bring the food into the dining room. My mother really had outdone herself and we all enjoyed the meal.

"Mitch," said Marilyn, pouring cups of tea as Rifka passed a plate of cake, "I didn't get a chance to ask you the other day; what actually happened to Artie?"

"He collapsed playing racquetball," I replied. "They said it was a heart attack."

"That makes no sense," said my sister.

"That's all I know," I shrugged.

"He was a thin, active vegetarian with no family history of heart disease," said Marilyn. "That's very unusual."

"You sound like Ma."

"This time, she makes a lot of sense."

"Thank you!" said Rifka.

"It all happened very suddenly," said Astrid. "We didn't have time to ask a lot of questions."

"What were the results of the autopsy?" asked Marilyn. "It was too soon for the results of the toxicology studies to be back before you left, but they must have reached a preliminary conclusion."

I pushed my untouched dessert away. "I don't know," I said, "and I'm getting really tired of this obsession. I said I would check into it when I got back and I will. Can we please drop it for now?"

"Just let us know what you find out," said Marilyn.

"Fine."

Rifka reached into her apron pocket and removed a slip of paper. "I wrote down some questions."

I turned around and stared at her, making no move to accept the offered square. "Do you never give up?" I demanded.

Rifka's eyes started to fill with tears again. "You know he was like one of mine," she said softly.

"We know," said Astrid, accepting the proffered slip. "Mitch will find out what he can and we'll let you know."

Marilyn went over to comfort my mother and shot me a dirty look. I knew that I was the heavy in this situation. I took my wallet out and accepted the slip from Astrid. "I'm putting your list in my wallet so I'll have it with me, Ma. Okay?"

Rifka dried her eyes and nodded.

"I'm sorry, Ma," I said. "I didn't mean to upset you. I want some answers too, but I don't have them yet."

"Okay," sniffled Rifka.

"How about if Mitch and I do the dishes, so you and Marilyn have some time to visit?" offered Astrid.

"Mitchell do the dishes?" laughed Rifka.

"He does them at home," said Astrid. "He isn't a bad cook either."

"See, Ma? You live long enough, you see everything," laughed Marilyn.

***

We got an early start the next morning. So early, in fact, that we hit part of the rush hour, and it took us forever to get out of New York City. We made up some time because the midweek traffic was pretty light along Route 17, and we stopped only once, for gas, in the Catskills.

About an hour later, I was cruising along, lost in my own thoughts, only vaguely aware of the Neil Diamond tape in the cassette player of the car.

"Promise not to be angry," said Astrid.

"About what?"

"I know we just stopped, but I have to go to the bathroom."

"No problem," I said. "We're almost in Hancock, and I remember that there's a McDonalds there."

"I'm really sorry; I should have skipped the coffee at Rifka's, and I should have gone when we stopped," apologized my wife.

"Astrid, it's no big deal. To be honest, I can stand to go too." My bowels had been pushing uncomfortably for the last few miles, and I was thinking that I might not be able to make it to Cortland, where I had intended to stop for lunch.

My wife is not a good car traveler. Aside from her tendency to get carsick, she becomes fidgety from sitting too long, and she hates public rest stops. I'm pretty easygoing about all those things, but she feels guilty about asking me to stop.

I pulled into a spot in the parking lot and shut off the ignition. "Do you want something to eat here too?"

"We can wait, unless you're hungry."

"Whatever you want," I said as we went through separate doors.

I was surprised that Astrid was nowhere to be found when I came out of the men's room. It had taken me a while, and I expected her to be waiting. I checked to see if she'd gone back to the car, but she wasn't there. Sliding into one of the booths, I sat back to wait for my wife, but when five minutes more had passed, I was beginning to get worried.

A woman came out of the ladies room, and I almost asked her if she had seen Astrid, and if she could go back in and check on her for me, but I decided against it. Astrid probably would have been mortified, and the woman had a little girl about three and an infant with her. I remember wondering if both children were hers. She was a blonde woman with china blue eyes, but the little girl she led by the hand had dark curls and the greenest eyes I've ever seen. The baby resembled her, with downy wisps of blonde hair and blue eyes; I was not sure if it was a boy or girl.

Just when I was about ready to go into the ladies room myself, Astrid emerged. I could tell immediately that something was wrong. Her eyes looked strange and the usual lithe bounce was missing from her step.

"Are you ready?" she asked.

"Yes," I said.

Before I could get out another word, she was ten feet ahead of me, out the door of the restaurant, heading for the car. I called her name and she stopped but didn't face me.

"What happened?" I demanded, terrified that something awful had occurred of which I was unaware.

"Nothing," she replied, opening her door and sliding into the passenger seat.

"What's wrong?" I asked gently as I got behind the wheel.

"Nothing. Really, I'm fine."

I could see that she'd been crying, and she knew that I knew. I just sat there motionless, watching her for several moments.

"I don't know what's the matter," she finally said. "I suppose the stress is beginning to catch up with me."

"Come here," I said, holding my arms open to her.

She moved close to me and buried her face in my neck. "I'm being silly," she said.

"That's fine," I said, rubbing her back gently.

She began to cry softly, and we sat there while I cradled her in my arms. Finally, she wiped her eyes and moved away. "I'm okay now," she said. "I'm sure it's just the stress of the past few days."

"You're probably overtired," I said. "Why don't you try to take a nap for a while."

"You know I can't sleep in the car," she protested. "I think I'd feel better if you let me drive."

"You really want to?"

She nodded. "I do, if you don't mind."

"Sure," I said, hopping out of the car and walking to the passenger side.

She slid over the console and was behind the wheel before I got the passenger door open. "There is something that we need to talk about," she said as I slid into the passenger seat.

"What is it?"

She shook her head. "It's not new; it will keep."

"Tell me now."

"This isn't the right time or place. I'd rather wait."

"Whenever you're ready."

"Fasten your seat belt and prepare to fly!" she said with a little laugh, but it was forced, and I knew that something still weighed on her.

I closed my eyes and leaned back, but sleep would not come. Normally, I can sleep anywhere, but my mind was so full of racing thoughts that they didn't even make sense. The one recurring central theme was that there was more to Artie's death than we knew.

We got home around five o'clock. I should have been worn out after eight hours in the car, but I was restless and unsettled.

"You wouldn't happen to remember the name of the doctor we spoke with in the emergency room the night that

Artie died?" I asked Astrid casually as I set our suitcase on our bed.

"Yes," she said, not even breaking the rhythm as she vigorously brushed her hair. "It was Feldman, same as my boss."

"What would I do without you?" I asked, kissing the nape of her neck.

"Hopefully, we'll never know," she said.

"I thought I might give him a call," I said casually.

"Why?"

"To get the answers to some of Rifka's questions."

"Do you have any questions?"

"Many."

"Aren't you tired? It will keep."

"I feel like I need to do this right away."

I called the hospital emergency room and asked for Dr. Feldman. I was told that he was with a patient, but that they could ask him to call me when he was free. I had a better idea.

"I'm going to take a ride up to General," I told Astrid. "I think I may have better results with this guy if we speak face to face."

"Would you like me to come with you?"

I really did want her to but she looked exhausted. "Why don't you take a long bath and veg out in front of the tube? I can handle this one on my own."

"If you're sure you don't mind," she said.

"Soak an extra five minutes for me," I said, kissing her lightly on the forehead on my way out.

The emergency waiting area was almost empty when I arrived. I went to the reception desk and asked for Dr. Feldman.

The woman dialed a number and asked for Dr. Feldman. Then, she told them that I was there and I wanted to speak with him.

"Please have a seat," she instructed. "Someone will be with you as soon as they can."

I took a seat and impatiently watched the minutes elapse on the clock on the opposite wall.

After nearly an hour, a young woman came out of the emergency department. "Mr. Goldblatt, I am Dr. Weber. What can I do for you?"

"There must be some mistake," I said. "I asked to speak with Dr. Feldman."

"Dr. Feldman is busy," she said. "I am a doctor; I can answer your questions."

"All right," I said, trying to mask my annoyance, "but first, can you tell me just who Dr. Feldman is?"

"He's the chief resident," said Dr. Weber.

"Were you in the emergency room last Friday night?" I asked.

"I was on duty part of the night," she acknowledged.

"My friend, Arthur Kornfeld, was treated for a possible heart attack. He didn't make it."

"I'm sorry," said Dr. Weber. "What can I do for you?"

"Did you treat Mr. Kornfeld?"

"We get a lot of patients here. I honestly don't remember."

"Do that many of them die?" I asked sarcastically.

"Unfortunately, some of them do," she replied evenly.

"Do young, thin, fit vegetarians usually die of heart attacks?"

"Not as a rule," she replied, "but it isn't unheard of."

"I'd like to know if an autopsy was performed and what the results were," I said.

"I couldn't give you that information," she said defensively. "Medical records are confidential."

"I had authorization to act for the family."

"Did you sign a consent for an autopsy?" asked Dr. Weber.

"No. Does that mean that it wasn't done?"

"Not necessarily. If the circumstances of your friend's death were in any way uncertain, the medical examiner has the authority to order a post mortem, with or without consent."

"I would like to know if an autopsy was done and what the results were," I reiterated.

"I don't have the authority to give you that information. Perhaps you should call in the morning and make an appointment with the director of emergency medicine."

I was starting to get really annoyed; I knew when I was being stonewalled. "I won't have time to do that," I said calmly, "because first thing tomorrow, I intend to have my lawyer file a malpractice suit against this hospital and Dr. Feldman. Then we'll see what I can and cannot find out."

"I understand your frustration," said Dr. Weber. "Why don't you wait here and I'll see if I can get some further information for you."

"I'll be here for ten minutes longer," I said and when her eyes met mine, I knew that she knew that I meant business.

About two minutes later, Dr. Feldman himself came out of the emergency department. "Mr. Goldblatt," he said curtly, "I'm very busy. What can I do for you?"

"I'm a busy man too, and I've already been kept waiting almost an hour, until you were good and ready to send your lackey out to stonewall me," I replied tersely. "If you'd rather answer my questions under a subpoena, we can try it that way."

"A subpoena for what?" he asked stonily.

"I suspect that a charge of malpractice would get your attention, not to mention the hospital's."

"You'd be wasting your time," he said. "We did everything by the book when we treated your friend. Your suit would get nowhere."

"It would get my questions answered," I replied. "It would probably annoy you personally and the hospital administration as well, and it might get you and the hospital some very nasty publicity."

"And what is the point?"

"The point is that I want straight answers to some questions and I'm not getting them."

"What are the questions?"

I hadn't really formulated a specific list but I remembered Rifka's sheet of paper, and I removed it from my wallet for effect. "First of all, was an autopsy done?"

"Yes," said Dr. Feldman.

"Did you have a signed consent form?"

"We didn't need one," replied the doctor, shaking his head. "The medical examiner has the authority to order an autopsy in the case of an unattended death, and your friend's father gave his verbal consent over the phone."

"All right," I said, "what were the results?"

"I'm not authorized to tell you anything about that. All I will say is that it was inconclusive."

"Can you tell me what the cause of death was on the death certificate?"

"That's a matter of public record. Cardiac arrest."

"But what was the cause?" I persisted.

"I can't tell you that."

"Can't or won't?"

"Mr. Goldblatt, you have my sympathy. I understand that Mr. Kornfeld was your close friend; his father told me that as far as the family was concerned, you were his brother, or I wouldn't be talking to you at all. The fact is that Arthur Kornfeld was essentially dead before he got here. He was given CPR and we did everything we could to revive him, but nothing worked. That doesn't make any of us feel very good, but sometimes, that's just the way things happen. If you feel you have to sue us, that's your right."

"I don't want money," I said. "I want answers; I want to know what happened."

He had turned to go back into the emergency department but he faced me again. "I don't have the answers you want."

His eyes met mine and I saw something there that I didn't quite understand. "It's been a long night," he said wearily. "I get off at eight and I plan to stop at the Wendy's on Portland near the hospital for some coffee, and then I'm going home to sleep for the better part of the next thirty-six hours."

He turned and walked back into the emergency department.

I was angry and frustrated as I walked back to my car. I didn't know any more than I had before, and I had even less hope that I would be able get any answers. I was fuming at the arrogance of Dr. Feldman. The guy was so cocky and sure of himself. I knew more about his plans for the evening than I did about what I came to find out.

I started the ignition and froze. Quickly, my mind scanned back over the conversation. Why had Feldman told me where he was going after work, unless he expected me to meet him there? But if that was what he had in mind, why hadn't he just said so? I decided that there was no harm in stopping for a cup of coffee before I went home.

I pulled into the parking lot of Wendy's and glanced at the clock in the car. It was seven twenty-five. I decided to check in with Astrid.

"Did I get you out of the tub?" I asked contritely when she picked up the phone on the fourth ring.

"No, perfect timing," she said and I could hear that the bounce was back in her step, even over the phone. "I'm in bed with a bag of M&Ms waiting for Jeopardy to start. What's up?"

"Not much," I conceded. "I spoke with Feldman; he wasn't very helpful."

"Well, come on home, then," she said. "I'll save you some M&Ms."

"Sounds good but I have a stop to make first. Feldman made some cryptic comment about a cup of coffee at Wendy's, so I decided I'd have one too and see what materialized."

"Don't be too long," she said as we ended our conversation.

I was ready for my third refill when Feldman came in. We were the only customers in the restaurant and, when he saw me, he proceeded right to my table.

"Coffee, Dr. Feldman?" I offered.

"Thanks," he said after studying me quickly. "By the way, I'm Jay."

"Mitch," I said, offering my hand, which he shook. "Can I buy you some dinner?"

"No, thanks anyway. It takes me a while to wind down before I'm ready for food. Just coffee will be great."

I returned with two cups. He declined the cream and sugar I'd brought and took a long sip of the hot, black liquid.

"Is there something else that you wanted to tell me?" I asked.

"This is against my better judgment," he began, "and I've never done anything like it before."

"Like what?"

"Like what I'm about to do," he said, taking another gulp of coffee. "By the way, if you mention this conversation to anyone, I'll deny it ever happened."

"Okay," I said, "what is it?"

"I'm not positive about what it means, but something struck me as odd. I told you that an autopsy was done on your friend. I read the report and he was in excellent shape, probably healthier than you or me. There's no good explanation for his death there. It had to be some type of arrhythmia but the question is, what caused it?"

"I'm listening," I replied.

"There were toxicology studies done too, and the final results aren't back yet, but there was blood work done when he was in the ER. There was nothing in the sample that shouldn't have been there; no poisons, illegal drugs or anything like that, but there was something strange."

"What was that?"

"His Digoxin level was high."

"What does that mean?"

"Digoxin is a drug used to stimulate the heart. It was used on Mr. Kornfeld when we were trying to get his heart to restart and sustain a rhythm. His blood pressure was extraordinarily low when the Critical Care unit got to him, and we were unable to bring it up after he got to the hospital."

"Do you think he was given an overdose?" I asked.

The doctor shook his head. "I know the dosage was right; I checked it myself before it was administered, and I reviewed the chart later on. The problem is, I'm pretty sure the blood that was tested was drawn before the drug was administered."

"What are you trying to say, Jay?" I asked, putting my coffee down and studying him intently.

"I'm saying that if the blood tested was taken before he was treated, there was something in his blood that shouldn't have been there, unless he was being treated for a heart condition, which to the best of our knowledge, he wasn't."

"Something that could have caused the heart attack?"

Feldman nodded.

"Are you sure?"

"Am I sure that it could have caused the heart attack? Yes. Am I sure when the blood that was tested was drawn? No. There was so much going on that night, so much confusion. Friday is a terrible night in emergency; we were mobbed, and there were a lot of people scurrying around, doing all sorts of things at the same time. We all knew that Mr. Kornfeld's condition was extremely critical, and we did everything we could to save him. No one was paying much attention to sequences and details."

"I understand," I said nodding.

"Is there any reason that you would suspect that someone would have wanted to harm your friend?" he asked.

"No," I said adamantly. "Artie was a little different, but most people he knew liked him. I can't think of anyone who was his enemy."

"Good," said Jay Feldman. "Then the blood tested was probably drawn after he was treated, and that's the explanation. That makes me feel better."

"Thank you, Jay," I said.

"For what?" he asked. "I didn't really have the answers you were looking for."

"No," I said, "but at least for a moment, it seemed as if you saw Artie as a person, rather than another statistic."

"Mitch, when one of my patients dies, I take it very personally. I can't let it get to me for long, but take my word for it; it matters."

"I'm glad to hear that."

"You know, I could be in a lot of trouble for telling you what I did. When I mentioned it to my superiors, they were adamant that unless I was sure of when the blood was drawn, I was not to mention it to anyone."

"If it comes down to needing the information, how could I get it without involving you?" I asked.

"An attorney could subpoena the autopsy results and possibly the hospital medical records."

"I won't tell anyone but my wife where I got this information, "I promised.

"Fair enough," said Feldman, "but if you do, remember: this conversation never happened."

***

Astrid had dozed off with the television on. I shut it off and began to undress. Then, I stopped what I was doing and went down to the kitchen. It was a little after nine-thirty, still early enough to call my sister.

"Something wrong?" asked Marilyn.

"No," I said. "I was wondering if you could answer a medical question for me."

"If you're sick, go to the doctor," she said.

"It's not about me. I want to know about some kind of heart drug that sounds like digit. I don't remember the right name."

"Digitalis?"

"It's like that," I encouraged.

"Digoxin?" she asked.

"That's the one.

"It's used to treat heart conditions, usually heart failure," said Marilyn. "It's a fairly common prescription."

"What would it do to a healthy person?"

"It depends on how much. It could cause an irregular heartbeat."

"Could it kill a healthy adult?"

"Under certain circumstances, if the dosage was high enough. Why do you want to know?"

"I can't give you all the details of how I found out, but there is a possibility that Artie had a high level of that drug in his system."

"That wouldn't be all that odd," said Marilyn. "When the heart is not pumping vigorously enough, they often give a high dose initially to stabilize the patient, and then follow up with a prescription for a smaller dose."

"What if it was in his system before he was treated?"

"That would be very odd if he wasn't under a doctor's care for a heart problem. Is that what happened?"

"That's the problem; nobody knows."

Astrid came downstairs just as I was hanging up the phone. "Who were you talking to?" she asked sleepily.

"Marilyn."

"Everything okay?"

"With her, it is."

"Did you find out anything from Feldman?"

"I promised him I would tell no one but you where I heard this."

Astrid slid into one of the dinette chairs. "And he agreed that you could tell me?"

"He was wearing a wedding band; he didn't even try to dissuade me." I repeated what I had learned.

"How could the drug have gotten into Artie's system before he got to the hospital?" she asked.

"That's what I intend to find out," I said, removing Rifka's slip of paper from my wallet and writing Digoxin on it, before I forgot the name of the drug again.

My mother had posed some legitimate questions. She had no idea that she had opened a major can of worms. When Marilyn and Bert were first married, Rifka once told Bert that she was always right, and that Marilyn took after her, so he should always listen to his wife. I hate to admit it publicly, but I will acknowledge in confidence that my mother has a pretty good track record, but there is nothing I hate more than when Rifka is right. Somehow, it always forebodes big trouble.

Chapter 4
Bob

Everyone who never worked for my boss, Bob McCann, thought he was a great guy. That's because the rest of us, who were unfortunate enough to work under his supervision, spent a great deal of time trying to make him look good.

If you think that this was altruism on our parts or some deep seated loyalty to Businetex, you have either spent your life in a closet or are totally unfamiliar with the business world. Rifka had a favorite expression when I was growing up. She was forever telling my sister and me that cream rises to the top. In the corporate world, there's a more apropos, if crude, saying: shit floats. No matter what disagreements there might be over procedure or policy in Bob's group, those of us who worked for him were united in our desire for him to float up in the ranks of Businetex, and out of our lives.

It's not that Bob was such a bad supervisor; as people in that type of position go, he was top of the line. His training was as an engineer, and he was adequate if not exceptional in that field. He was superior at what he did now; unfortunately, he did not do anything that was the least bit useful. Bob was the consummate brown-nose; what he did best was to deal with all the political bullshit without making enemies. The way he usually handled this was by agreeing with everyone he spoke to, hoping that the various parties never got together long enough to discover that he had sided with all of them.

To put the levels of competence within our organization in perspective, the better engineers and technicians knew how just about every feature of the new ink jet printer we were about to release worked. Bob knew how to turn it on and off. Most of the other supervisors at Bob's level and Jerry Fallow, Bob's boss, knew there was an on/off switch, but had no idea where to find it. The vice presidents above Jerry had no idea whether or not it had an on/off switch and if they ever did need that information, someone's head was going to roll. Our illustrious CEO wouldn't have recognized an ink jet printer if he tripped over one.

Bob liked to think that everyone who worked for him liked him, and thought of him as one of the guys, so periodically, he would corner us and talk to us as if he thought we were buddies. This always made me very uncomfortable; I would have much preferred that he just leave me alone. My opinion of him would have been the same. I didn't know anyone else in our group who would actually admit to liking Bob. Deckle may have been the ultimate paranoid, but he was not far off the mark when he said that every time Bob patted him on the back, he had the distinct impression that he was looking for a nice, soft spot into which to slide the knife. It scared me, but that was one instance where Deckle and I actually agreed.

The morning after Astrid and I returned from New York, Bob was waiting for me when I came into the office.

"Mitch," he called, "do you have a minute?"

I figured that some kind of trouble had arisen while I was gone, and he was going to dump a pile of work on me, but he just wanted all the details of Artie's funeral. I gave him the abridged version and that seemed to satisfy him.

"Boy, that was a real shock," said Bob. "Artie always seemed so healthy."

"He was healthy, Bob," I said, sensing an opportunity, "and frankly, I don't understand how it could have happened. You've had access to the division personnel files; did he have any medical problem the rest of us didn't know about?"

"I haven't seen his file recently," said Bob, "but I don't think so; I never remember the guy being sick, even with a cold. In the years he worked for Businetex, he never missed a day of work that I can remember."

"Did Jerry every mention anything about him being sick?" I persisted.

"No, I don't think so. Why don't you talk to him?"

I was hoping to avoid that at all costs, but I knew better than to burn bridges, particularly in the business world.

"I hate to bother him; I know how busy he is."

Bob nodded. "But I'm sure he wouldn't mind. You know, he was playing racquetball with Artie when he collapsed."

"I'd heard."

My eyes wandered to the bookcase behind Bob's desk and settled on the picture he kept there of himself with his family. I always found it fascinating because it was the only place I had ever seen Bob with a beard, although everyone who had been with the company longer than I had thought it odd to see him without one. Until just before his fortieth birthday two years earlier, Bob had always sported a full beard. He had grown it in college and the smart money said that he would never shave it off, but when he took up scuba diving and had trouble getting a good seal on his mask, he had no problem sacrificing facial hair for his new passion.

Actually, he was not a bad looking man, slim and tall with wavy, blond hair and dark eyes. He had retained his carefully trimmed mustache, which was much darker than the hair on his head, and I heard more than one person describe his appearance as distinguished.

Bob had a favorite story that he told to anyone who commented about his missing beard, or who never knew that he had one. When he shaved it off, his youngest child, Brittany, was just two. He emerged from the bathroom clean-shaven, and Brittany began to scream in terror. For over a week, she would not even stay in the same room with Bob; she was terrified of the stranger. She had never seen her father without a beard. Bob thought the story made him sound like a regular, good guy. I thought it made him sound like an asshole.

The rest of the picture was actually kind of interesting too. It was obviously taken at Disney World and Bob was in the center, hugging Mickey Mouse. His sons, Brandon and Brett, were standing off to the side, looking bored, and Bobbie, looking nauseous, was holding the infant Brittany, who was obviously crying.

"...will be ready on time, but now we may have to push back the date because of the manual," Bob was saying.

I had tuned him out, but I thought I understood the gist of what he was saying.

"How bad a problem do we have?" I asked, hoping that he would fill in the part of the conversation I had missed.

"It was coming along pretty well, but Artie had such an active hand in the compiling that I don't think anyone else is ready to step in where he left off. We can't very well release our new ink jet printer with no user's manual or give a voucher for one at a later date; it looks like we're going to have to miss our deadline, and that makes the company look bad on Wall Street. The investors are not interested in the mechanics of the operation; all they want to know is the share price and the amount of the dividend."

I realized that Bob's concern was not about what had happened to Artie, but that he might look bad if the release of our product was delayed; it didn't mean much to him that a man was dead.

"There has to be another technical writer who can pick up where Artie left off," I said. "One of the guys who worked for him, maybe?"

"Actually, Jerry didn't have a writer in mind. He was thinking along the lines of someone in more of a managerial role. The people who worked for Artie are all capable writers. What is really needed is someone who will dot the i's and cross the t's. Do you know of anyone who you think would fit?"

I was surprised that Bob would ask. I recalled a conversation we had a few months back.

"I wanted you to know, Mitch, that we're been very pleased with your work," Bob had said.

"I appreciate you telling me that," I had replied. "It's always nice to hear that you're appreciated."

"You are," Bob had agreed, "but now, if you want to get ahead in this organization, you're going to have to learn to play the game."

"Just what game is that?" I had wondered.

"Being part of the team," Bob had replied. "The consensus is that you aren't a real team player."

That surprised me. I felt that I had made a positive contribution to the organization, and I said as much. "I was under the impression that creativity and innovation are desirable in a working environment."

"Creativity and innovation just confuse the issues. The powers that be are looking for people who do their jobs without ruffling any feathers."

"I'm disappointed to hear that," I had said. "I came to Businetex because I thought I would have the chance to put my talents to use."

"That's unfortunate," he had replied. "We thought that you were a good fit, but you're probably too intelligent for your job."

I'll admit I was shocked. "Is this your personal feeling or the opinion of those above you?" I had inquired, trying to keep my voice even.

"All I'm willing to say is that it's a feeling in the organization," was his answer.

I suppose I should have given some serious thought to moving on at that point, but you have to look at it from my point of view. I had given up a job I liked, in Connecticut, I had moved here, my wife had taken a job that was certainly less than the one she had in New York, and we made a commitment to stay in this area, at least for a while, even if it took sacrifices on both our parts. If Astrid wanted to be near her mother, at least for now I would do the job I was hired to perform, and I would try not to ruffle too many feathers unnecessarily, but I wouldn't promise to like it.

That previous conversation was in my mind as I tried to discern his motives for asking my input on the matter of someone to supervise the completion of the manual.

"I can't think of anyone offhand," I said to Bob, "but I'll give it some thought. If you would like me to look over what's been done so far, I'm willing to see if I could finish putting it together, but I might need help with some of the things that are on my desk, if I'm going to take on the manual now."

"That's no problem," said Bob. "I'm sure Jim Deckle will be happy to do what he can to help you out."

I wasn't thrilled that I would be working so closely with Deckle, but I had to admit that he was a capable engineer and could easily handle anything I would have to abandon.

"Fine," I said. "I'll go over to Artie's office this morning and see if I can get a feel for where he was headed."

"You know, Mitch, there's something in this for you too," said Bob meaningfully.

"I want the J-6 to go out on time just as much as anyone else does," I replied.

"I know that," said Bob, "but that wasn't what I meant. If you can pull this off, you're a shoo-in to take over Artie's job."

"Me?" I asked incredulously. "I'm an engineer; I don't know anything about writing. I spell worse than a third grader."

"You'd be managing twelve people," said Bob. "There are a lot of people who'd give anything to be in your position."

"I don't think I'd feel comfortable working at a job where I'm not secure about what I'm doing; I don't think I'd be interested."

Bob shrugged. "That suits me," he said. "You know, I'd hate to lose you, but you don't have to make a decision now. Take a look at the manual; see what you can do and think about it."

From Bob's office, I went across the building to the area where Artie had worked. Outside Artie's former office, Maggie was sitting at her desk, filing her nails. She looked up quickly when I came up to the desk and dropped the nail file.

"Hangnail," she said, smiling. "It keeps snagging all the papers."

She sounded a bit defensive, as if I would think she was goofing off. That never would have crossed my mind. Maggie had a reputation at Businetex for being one of their most capable secretaries; Artie had often expressed his appreciation of her clerical abilities.

"I didn't mean to interrupt you," I said pleasantly. "I promised Bob that I would take a look at what Artie was doing to compile the manual."

"Bob called and told me to give you what you needed," agreed Maggie. "I was putting away a few things around the office; Artie's personal items are in the two boxes on the desk. I guess it's okay if you take them; he probably would have wanted you to have his things."

"Thank you," I said. "I thought I might try looking over what he had on the computer."

"Sure, help yourself," said Maggie.

I walked into the office and looked around. The office and the top of the desk had been stripped bare, save for two cardboard boxes. The darkened computer was undisturbed on the work station against the wall. I went over and flipped on the power switch. The screen began to glow.

"Mitch?" said Maggie softly from the doorway.

I turned around expectantly. "Yes, Maggie?"

"I'm sorry about Artie," she said softly, her eyes glassy and filling with tears. "We weren't exactly close, but I really liked working for him. I'm going to miss him."

"I know what you mean," I said.

Maggie was something of a legend around the office. At the very least, she had to be well into her thirties, because she had two college age children, but she could easily have passed for ten years less. She worked out regularly, and her body was evidence that the program she followed was working. She looked like the former popular cheerleader type, but the strange thing was, at Businetex, she had no friends. Most days, you could see her sitting alone in the cafeteria, eating her customary salad, and you never saw her giggling with the other women near the coffee machine, or stopping to gossip by the copier. She was known behind her back as "the ice queen" and yet, she was not unfriendly in the few dealings I had with her.

I heard a rumor about Maggie on the first day I started work. The scuttlebutt was that she and Bob were doing the horizontal tango on a regular basis. I have never given much credence to office gossip, but I hadn't worked there a week when Bob himself confirmed the rumor.

I cannot imagine ever wanting to cheat on Astrid, but if I did, I am sure I would not go around advertising what I was doing. Bob seemed almost proud of himself.

"I know you're new here, Mitch," he said after approving a change to the J-6 that I had proposed, "but I was wondering if you've noticed Artie's secretary, Maggie?"

"He introduced us," I agreed casually.

"What did you think of her?"

"Artie says she's the best secretary he's ever had."

"I was asking for your impression. Do you think she's nice-looking?"

"It's hard to ignore that she's a very attractive woman," I conceded.

"You should see her without her clothes," he winked at me.

It wasn't long before I learned that Bob and Maggie met every Wednesday, during their lunch hour, in her van in the parking lot outside our building. They thought they were being discreet by arriving there separately - she had given him a key - but everyone in the building knew about it. They would make love in the van, and then he would take her out to lunch. Bob did not tell me how long this had been going on, but Deckle, in one of his friendlier moments, had confided that he had known about it for at least ten years.

Maggie didn't wear a wedding ring. She had a picture of her children on her desk, and rumor had it that she was still married, but no one knew anything about her husband. Bob did wear a wedding ring, and everyone knew that he thought of himself as a family man. A family man who was getting a little on the side, I guess.

I had no trouble figuring out Artie's password; Natalie72038, his own private tribute to the only woman he had ever loved. I started looking through his files, and before long, I found what I was looking for. After all these years, I knew pretty well how his mind worked, and Artie was nothing, if not organized. The planned layout for the manual was all there; it fit easily on two floppy discs. I felt confident that I could get it put together with very little trouble. I took the two discs, slipped them into my shirt pocket, and lifted one of the two boxes.

"I think I have what I need," I told Maggie on my way out. "I'll come back later for the other box."

I'll bring it over," she offered.

"It's a little heavy," I warned.

"I don't mind," she said, walking into the office and returning with the other carton.

We walked across the building together, but we didn't speak. I didn't know what to say to her. I suspected that she was a very lonely woman, but I did not approve of what she and Bob were doing, and it made me feel uncomfortable to be around her.

It wasn't that hard to understand why Bob was attracted to her; she was very stylish and the subject of much gossip among the other women in the office. She dressed a bit better than anyone else in the building, much too well for a secretary. Her jewelry was simple but obviously expensive, and the rumor mill buzz was that Bob had given her the bracelets, necklace and rings that she always wore.

If that was the truth, I couldn't have blamed him all that much. About six months earlier, Bob had called me into his office. With a flourish, he had opened the lid of a large box that I recognized to be from one of the most expensive jewelers in the city. Inside, was an absolutely gorgeous gold and diamond choker. Astrid would have given her eye teeth for that piece. It was elegant, simple and obviously very costly.

"It's beautiful," I said.

"My wife has been a little bit down about having a birthday," he explained with a grin. "It's the big 4-0."

"That should cheer her up," I observed.

"Do you think she'll like it?"

"If she doesn't, I know my wife would be happy to take it off her hands; I'm sure she'll love it," I assured him.

Several days later when Bob and I met at the coffee machine, I happened to ask him how Bobbie had enjoyed her necklace.

"Oh, she returned it," he said, pouring a packet of Sweet 'n Low into his coffee.

"She didn't like it?" I asked incredulously.

"It was too short to fit around her neck, and she said it was so fancy, she could only wear it on the rare occasions when we were dressed formally, so I told her to exchange it and get whatever she wanted."

"So what did she get?" I couldn't resist asking.

"A new Kirby vacuum cleaner," he replied.

I had looked at him, assuming that it was a joke, but as far as I could tell, he was completely serious.

Deckle had a meeting every Thursday morning, so he was not in our office when we got there. I unlocked the door and allowed Maggie to walk in first. She put the carton she had carried down on the desk.

I put down the box I was carrying and turned to her. "Thanks, Maggie."

"If there's anything else I can do to help, let me know," she said. "I was Artie's secretary for three years; I have some idea of what he was doing."

"I appreciate it. Maggie," I said, almost as an afterthought, "would you happen to know if Artie was having some type of a serious medical problem?"

"Not that I know of. I don't remember him ever being sick."

"Well, thanks," I said.

Maggie started to leave and then stopped. "Come to think of it, I took a message for him a while back. It was from a doctor's office, asking if he could come in at a different time."

"Do you happen to remember the name of the doctor?"

"No, I don't think so," she said, shaking her head.

About fifteen minutes later, I was sitting at my desk, poking through the boxes I had removed from Artie's office, when the phone rang. It was Maggie.

"Mitch," she began, "this is almost too silly to mention, but I think I remember the name of the doctor that called Artie."

"What is it?"

"I'm not positive but I think it was Dr. Mintz. This is going to sound really stupid, but on my way back to the office, I decided to get some gum from the vending machine in the lobby and there was a type of candy called

'Krystal Mintz.' It jolted my memory. I think that was the doctor's name and that was how he spelled it."

I thanked Maggie and pulled out the phone directory. There were three doctors named Mintz. The first was a gynecologist so I pretty much discounted that possibility. The second was located in Scottsville, no specialty. That was possible but a little far away. The third was an internist in the city. I dialed that office's number. I told them that the doctor had been recommended by a friend of mine, and I wanted to make sure it was the right Dr. Mintz. They would not tell me whether Artie was a patient.

As usual, Astrid was my savior. She remembered that one of the women in her office was a patient of Dr. Mintz, and she called and made an appointment, giving her friend as the referral. She was allergic to the toner from her office's copier, so before she left for her appointment, she deliberately spread some on her hands to give her a rash and stated that she was there to have it checked. Denying that she had been exposed to any known allergen, she mentioned to the doctor that she was under a lot of stress. When he asked why, she replied that she had just lost a close friend, a patient of his.

My wife definitely deserved an Oscar for her performance. The doctor confessed that he was as shocked as we were to hear that Artie had died. The last time he had seen him was three months ago, when Artie had eaten a salad in a restaurant where there was later an outbreak of hepatitis A, and he had stopped in for a Gamma Globulin shot.

Astrid mentioned in parting that her husband had played tennis with Artie just two days before his death and felt terribly guilty. Had he known that Artie had a heart problem, they never would have played. The doctor reassured her that there was no reason to feel guilty; had Artie asked him about playing tennis, he would have given his enthusiastic okay. To his knowledge, there was nothing wrong with Artie's heart.

I was astounded that Astrid managed to get an appointment with the doctor, and to find out so much of what we wanted to know within hours of my learning that he existed. I wondered aloud how good he could be if he had immediate openings. Astrid said that they told her that she had picked an opportune time to call; they had taken a cancellation immediately before and were allowing her to fill that time. She was even more impressed that to treat the rash, the doctor had given her a sample of the same over-the-counter hydrocortisone cream she had used on it for years. He told her that he thought that it was a mild contact allergy, but that if it wasn't gone in two days, she should call him. Her impression was that he was a pretty good doctor, and if he thought Artie was healthy, he probably was.

"So what now?" asked Astrid.

"I don't know," I admitted.

"Maybe it's time to accept that sometimes things happen for which there are no good explanations," suggested Astrid.

What she was saying made a lot of sense. I had gone through Artie's belongings and found nothing too interesting. Nothing, that is, except for a slip of paper with the name Drucilla, and a phone number. I promised that if, after I checked that out, there was nothing new, I would try to put it aside and move on.

Bob was beside himself with joy when I was able to tell him that I saw no reason why the manual could not be completed within a week. Artie had essentially finished everything that needed to be done; he would have been ready to send it to the printers the Monday after he died. That day had come and gone, but if we put a rush on it, the printing could still be finished in time to make our deadline just over two weeks away, if only on a wing and a prayer. Bob was leaving on his vacation the day after the printer was scheduled to be introduced, and I think it would have upset him more than anything else to miss being in the picture that was released to the media.

I returned to my office after my meeting with Bob and Deckle was there waiting for me.

"Mitch," he said, "can I get you some coffee?"

I looked over at him, surprised. This was not the type of thing Deckle made a habit of doing.

"No, thanks, Jim. I think I'm coffeed out for today."

I sat down at the desk and saw the note I had written to remind myself to call the number I had come across among Artie's things. Deckle was just sitting at his desk, doing nothing. I preferred privacy to make that call, so I decided to do some of the work I had neglected in deference to the manual until I was alone. I started going through my files and was surprised to find that the work had been completed. I looked up at Deckle.

"Did you do all this?" I asked.

"Yup," he beamed. "I stayed until four this morning, but I finished it."

"Why?" I asked.

"Nothing more important than making our deadline," he said happily. "I wanted you to be free to work on the manual."

"That was very considerate of you, Jim, but what about your work?"

"I went home for a couple of hours of sleep and a shower, and I've been doing that this morning."

"You're going to burn out putting yourself under that kind of pressure," I said. "I didn't need this so soon; you could have taken the rest of the week, and I could have finished what you didn't accomplish."

"I do my best work under pressure."

"Well, I appreciate your help," I said, searching through my briefcase for Artie's floppy discs.

"Mitch, there is something you can do for me," said Jim.

"What's that?" I asked, trying to sound neutral but feeling apprehensive.

"I heard that Bob told you that you were up for Artie's job, and that you said you weren't interested."

"Where did you hear that?" I asked. "That was a private conversation."

"The walls around here have ears," he said meaningfully. "I've been warning people about that for years, but nobody takes me seriously."

"Who did tell you?" I persisted.

"Let's just say it was a reliable source."

"And?"

"If you decide you want the job, that's fine, but if you don't, will you put in a good word for me?"

"Jim, you're no more qualified for that job than I am," I protested. "You're an engineer; you don't know anything about writing and, no offense, but you spell worse than I do."

"I'm a fast learner," protested Deckle, "and all the people who would be working for me could cover what I didn't know. My word processor has a spellchecker, and Maggie is the kind of secretary who knows how to make her boss look good."

"I doubt that you'd even enjoy the work."

"I'd be supervising twelve people; that's definitely a big step up the ladder to the top; I know I'd enjoy that."

"Have you ever been a supervisor before, Jim?"

"No," he confessed.

"It's not always all it's cracked up to be."

"I'd like to find that out for myself; will you put in a good word for me? I also heard that if you don't take the job, you will have the chance to give your input on who should get it," he added sheepishly.

It was so ludicrous to me that I wanted to laugh, but he was absolutely serious. Actually, I supposed he might not be any worse at that type of job than many of the other people in similar positions. "Sure, Jim," I finally said. "If you want the job and they'll listen to me, I'll suggest that they offer it to you."

"Thanks, Mitch," he said, coming over and extending his hand.

I shook it not to seem rude but I felt silly. "Have you heard any other interesting rumors?" I asked, more to tease him than seriously hoping for information.

"I heard that you will be acting for Bob while he's gone," he said. "I'm looking forward to working for you."

I was less than thrilled by that idea. I knew that Bob would be gone for two weeks, but I hadn't counted on being put in charge in his absence. I had hoped that without him to hassle me, I would have two relatively relaxing weeks to recover from what had been going on lately.

Deckle finally left the office to use the copier, and I picked up the slip of paper that I'd found in Artie's belongings and dialed the number. It was a store on Monroe Avenue near twelve corners that sold houseplants.

"Is Drucilla there?" I asked.

"This is Dru. How may I help you?"

"I'm a friend of Artie Kornfeld," I said. "My name is Mitchell Goldblatt."

"Mitch! Of course!" she said excitedly. "Artie talked about you all the time. How is he?"

I wasn't prepared for that. "Well, Drucilla, I have some bad news. Artie died last week."

"Oh, my God!" she gasped. "You're not going to tell me that he had AIDS or something?"

"No, no, nothing like that. He had a heart attack."

"I told him that all that strange stuff he ate wasn't any good for him," she said knowingly.

"Drucilla, I was..."

"Dru, please," she interrupted. "I hate the name Drucilla."

"Dru, could we meet someplace?"

"Well, I don't know," she said suspiciously. "We don't know each other, and I'm not looking to meet anyone right now."

I could not believe that she seemed to think I was trying to make a move on her. "I don't think you understand," I said quickly. "I wanted to talk to you about Artie. My wife and I would be happy to have you come to our house, or you and I could meet someplace public."

"I have an hour for lunch at one," she said, a lot more receptive when she realized that I wasn't some lunatic on the prowl.

"I could get away then," I said. "Where do you want to meet?"

"There's an Arby's on Monroe Avenue near 590; do you know it?"

"Yes," I said. "One o'clock?"

"About ten after."

"I'll see you then."

I realized after I hung up the phone that I hadn't asked her what she looked like, but I needn't have worried. Even though the place was fairly busy, I spotted her immediately. She was standing right next to the door, looking like a hippie who had misplaced her generation. Her dull blonde hair was long and stringy, parted in the center and hanging down straight. A good shampooing wouldn't have hurt it at all. She wore one of those crinkled-looking skirts that went nearly to her ankles, in muddled brown colors, over a black leotard top, Birkenstock sandals and two large earrings, one a cross and the other a hoop with a peace symbol inside. Around her neck, a large Maltese cross hung from a leather thong.

"Hello, Mitch," she said as I walked in the door. "You look just like your pictures."

"Dru, it's nice to meet you," I said, offering my hand.

She shook it quickly.

"What would you like?" I asked, gesturing to the counter.

"I'll buy my own," she said.

"Please, let me. I was the one who asked you to come."

She shrugged and told the girl behind the counter what she wanted, and I did the same. We sat down opposite each other at one of the tables.

"Why did you want to meet?" she asked.

"I told you that Artie died last week," I said. "It was very sudden; he wasn't sick. I was going through some of his things, and I found your name and number on a slip of paper. I didn't remember his mentioning you. I was wondering how he knew you, and if maybe you knew something about him that I didn't, that would help explain how he could have just collapsed and died of a heart attack, with no warning."

"I was completely shocked when you told me he was dead," she said. "We hadn't been in touch recently. I probably haven't seen him for three months."

"How well did you know him?"

"Pretty well, I suppose. We saw each other regularly for a little more than a year, but it's been over for a while. We were still friends, though. I occasionally called him just to talk, and we went out as friends a few times, but I've been dating someone pretty seriously lately, so I kind of lost contact."

"How and when did you meet, if you don't mind my asking?"

Dru laughed, and I could see how she could have been considered attractive, if you liked her type. She did have nice teeth; they looked well cared-for too.

"You'll like this. We met at a Natalie Wood retrospective at the Dryden, about three and a half years ago."

I smiled. "That certainly fits."

"He told me about all the times you saw *Splendor in the Grass* together."

"That was his favorite," I said wistfully.

"I prefer *Marjorie Morningstar*," sniffed Dru. "Anyway, we met during an intermission, started talking and we became friends. One thing led to another, and after a while, we started dating."

"What happened?" I asked.

"What do you mean?"

"Why did it end?"

Dru gave a little laugh. "Artie was a very smart guy, but if you knew him as well as I think you did, I don't have to tell you that. He realized that all we had in common was Natalie Wood and sex; that's not much to base a relationship on."

My look must have given away my surprise.

"What?" she asked.

"I'm surprised that he never mentioned you," I said.

"Artie wasn't the type to kiss and tell," she replied.

"No, I suppose not," I agreed. "I don't think I would be compromising your honor to ask if you were ever aware of a serious medical problem that he might have had."

"Just the opposite; he was always so full of energy. He was tireless in bed," she added, averting her eyes.

I was sitting there, wishing I had known about her when he was alive. It was even possible that they had been sleeping together when I accused him of being gay.

"Do you happen to know if he was taking any kind of medication while you were dating?" I asked.

"Never!" she said insistently. "He ate a lot of weird stuff, like tofu and hummus but he didn't trust medicine at all. For a while, I was taking all kinds of vitamins. He told me that all the vitamins a person needs are available in a healthy diet. He was even skeptical about herbs. I was into that for a while. That's part of why we were so wrong for each other. I try out every fad that comes down the 'pike

172 What Remains Behind

and then give it up quickly. Artie had to research everything completely before he would even try it. He was the least spontaneous human being I have ever met."

"At times, he did seem spontaneous," I observed, "but even then, he always had a plan."

"That was the big problem between us. We weren't on the same wavelength. He had an agenda for everything, and I prefer to experience life as it comes. That, and the fact that I am an avowed carnivore, with no wish to be enlightened to the benefits of vegetarianism didn't make our future together appear too rosy," Dru added, gesturing to the empty wrapper from her Giant Roast Beef sandwich.

"I guess you've told me what I wanted to know," I said, picking up the garbage from our lunch as we stood to leave.

"Well, it was nice to meet you," said Dru. "Thank you for telling me about Artie. I'm sorry to hear it but I'm glad that I know."

"Thank you for meeting me," I said.

I couldn't help but think that Drucilla was one strange woman. She said that she and Artie were just friends before he died, but I would have expected more of a reaction than I'd gotten from someone who had been his lover for more than a year.

It was almost quitting time and I was working on the final draft of the manual later that afternoon, when my phone rang.

"Mitch?" said an unfamiliar female voice.

"Yes?"

"It's Dru; I assumed that you worked at Businetex since Artie did, so I got your number from the operator. I hope you don't mind."

"Not at all. What can I do for you?"

"I couldn't get Artie out of my mind all afternoon. Did I tell you that I was sorry?"

"Yes, I think you did," I said. I didn't remember her having said so, but it seemed the polite response.

"I know you may think it's strange that I didn't act sad or more upset," she said.

"People react to things like that in different ways."

"It's just that I don't think that this is permanent," she said.

"I don't understand."

"I believe that Artie is in a better place, in a higher kingdom and someday, I too will be there, and we will meet again. It's not really good-bye for us; it's only so-long."

"I hope you're right," I said, unable to think of any other appropriate response.

"I don't expect you to agree with me or even to understand," said Dru. "I just wanted you to know."

Before I could say anything else, she had hung up. I couldn't help but think that she and Artie had been more alike than she thought, and I probably would have told her so, had I been given the chance.

***

The J-6 ink jet printer was very well received by the business community when it made it's debut on the expected date. The local papers had extensive coverage of its features, and positive reactions to its ease of operation and reasonable price. The stories were accompanied by a large photo of the machine, with Bob and Jerry flanking George Stanton, the president of Businetex. The caption said that this was the new product that Businetex Corporation was counting on to reverse some of the cash flow problems the company had been experiencing in recent months.

Astrid studied the photo and laughed.

"What's so funny?" I asked.

"Take a look at Jerry," she said. "He looks like the mad scientist."

I hadn't paid that much attention to the photo, but she was right; Jerry Fallow was not what many people would have considered a nice looking man, but he looked downright bizarre in that photo. He was not exactly short, but at five foot ten he was shorter than he wanted to be, and thus had a habit of standing on his tiptoes when he was next to taller people. This gave him a strange stance, like some type of large wading bird. His steely gray hair was reminiscent of a bird too, a belted kingfisher. It appeared to have started out as a brush cut that somehow went wrong. He was hardly handsome but his mustache, rather than providing a focal point for an otherwise ordinary face, was a lopsided eyesore that grew in with large bare areas. Add to this that his eyes, such a pale shade of blue that they seemed to lack color, had a sort of wild, deranged look about them and you get the idea: he was one weird-looking dude.

The J-6 made its debut on a Friday, and when I got to work the following Monday morning, it was obvious that if anything, the sense of elation in our office had grown over the weekend. Not much work was getting done, which was fine with me since Bob was gone, on vacation for the next two weeks. I didn't have to worry about him breathing down my neck while I got a feel for what I had to do while I was in charge during his absence.

I had barely settled into my office when Jerry showed up.

"Mitch," he called from my doorway.

"Hello, Jerry," I said warily.

"Did you happen to see the article in Friday's paper?"

"How could I miss it?" I asked. "We had a pretty good sized spread."

"Did you like the picture?"

"Very nice," I lied.

"I'm sure you've got everything covered here," he said, "but if you need anything, just give a holler. Maggie is working for me now, and I told her to give you anything you need.

I silently wondered how that arrangement was going to work. Jerry went through secretaries faster than anyone I've ever known. Maggie was his seventh since joining Businetex only two years earlier.

"I appreciate that," I said.

Jerry made no move to leave my office.

"Did you need something, Jerry?"

"I was wondering if you were up for a game of racquetball sometime?"

"Racquetball isn't my game."

"Tennis then," proposed Jerry. "I'm not very good but I like to play."

"I haven't played since Artie died," I protested. "I'm probably rusty already."

"Then we'll be evenly matched. Is tomorrow okay?"

I did not want to play tennis or anything else with Jerry Fallow, but I didn't see any graceful way out. "It will have to be late," I said.

"I'm free all night," he agreed eagerly. "Is eight okay?"

"Sure," I nodded.

"I'll reserve the court," he said happily as he bounced out of my office.

All day Tuesday, I was so busy trying to get everyone in our group to focus on our new product that I almost forgot about my tennis date with Jerry. We were developing a new printer that would be part of what had the working name Gulliver. Businetex was trying to develop an entire portable office that could be contained in something the size of a salesman's sample case. This was to include a computer, cellular fax that could double as a scanner and, a very small but full-function ink jet printer. It was hoped that the whole unit could be priced under a thousand dollars. If successful, the demand would be incredible. What company would not want its people to have the facilities of a full office while on travel? We were talking about something that could be carry-on luggage on a plane. The main problem we had encountered in the early stages of development of the printer was not sacrificing features for the small size.

Had it not been for Deckle, I'm sure I would have stood Jerry up.

"I hear you're schmoozing with the boss tonight," he said as he came into our shared office.

"Huh?" I said, looking up at him, wondering how he was familiar with that term.

"I heard about your tennis game later."

"Oh, that," I replied, going back to the presentation I was revising without letting on that it had completely slipped my mind.

"This would be a good time to feel him out on what we were talking about before," suggested Deckle.

"What was that?" I asked apathetically.

"About you recommending me for Artie's job," he reminded.

"I hardly think this will be the time or place," I protested. "We're playing tennis; this isn't a business meeting."

"Don't kid yourself. Everything these people do is about business. You're not going to back out on me?"

"If the opportunity presents itself, I'll put in a good word for you; if not, I'll mention it when I think the time is right."

"Thanks, buddy," said Deckle happily. I was uncomfortable about Deckle thinking of me as his buddy, but I let it pass.

Jerry was eagerly awaiting my arrival at the health club.

"Am I late?" I asked apologetically.

No, I'm a little early," he said.

Linda was thrilled that I was going to play tennis again. "Mitch!" she said happily, "I didn't see your name on the court reservations."

"Jerry reserved the time," I said, accepting the clean towels that she offered.

"Do you want me to sign you up for some more sessions this week?" she asked happily.

"How about it, Mitch?" asked Jerry eagerly.

I felt trapped. I didn't really want to do anything I didn't have to with Jerry, but I didn't know how to decline without hurting his feelings. "Why don't we see how it goes first?" I proposed. "When you see how rusty I am, you may not want to play with me again and then, you'll be stuck."

"Oh, I doubt that," said Jerry, clapping me on the back.

We changed into our tennis clothes and walked toward the court. Jerry was in front of me and I was amazed that he was really in very good physical shape. He had to have been in his mid-fifties, but he was solid and well-muscled.

We walked onto the court, and Jerry began to look around for a place to put a bottle of Gatorade.

"Under the chair at midcourt is usually a good place," I offered.

"Thanks," said Jerry. "Artie got me started on this stuff, and it's really helped. I used to have problems with leg cramps, and now I rarely get them. You ought to try it; it keeps your electrolytes in balance while you're playing."

"I've never had any problem with cramping," I said, "but I'll keep it in mind if I do."

Artie had always tried to get me to drink Gatorade while we played. Personally, I can't stand the taste of the stuff, but he seemed to like it. He claimed that it helped his game, but every time I tried it, by the middle of our court time, I'd have to pee so bad that I couldn't even play.

It turned out that Jerry and I were pretty evenly matched. We each won one set and he took the tiebreaker on the third. I had to admit that I didn't mind him on the tennis court nearly as much as I did at work.

"How about it, Mitch?" he asked when we were dressing after the game. "Would you like to play again?"

"Sure," I said, "but until Bob gets back, I'm going to be too swamped to make any definite plans."

"I'll call you after next week to set up a time," he promised.

"I'm looking forward to it," I said, managing to conceal my sarcasm.

It was Astrid who came up with a solution to my problem. Have I told you that the woman is a genius?

"Why don't you get Deckle to play racquetball with Jerry?" she proposed. "Maybe then he won't have so much time for tennis with you."

"I don't even know if Deckle plays," I protested.

"If he doesn't, I'm sure he'd be willing to learn, if he thought it would earn him a few brownie points."

I got into work at six-thirty the next morning. I had so much to do that I was hoping to get a head start while the office was quiet. Deckle was already at his desk.

"Don't you have a home?" I asked in exasperation as I opened my briefcase on my desk.

"Good morning, Mitch," replied Jim cheerily, oblivious to my dark mood. "You're in bright and early."

"I have a lot of work," I said tersely.

"How did your tennis game go?"

"It was strictly social, but I'm going to give you a pointer, Jim, and you are going to owe me big time for this."

"What's that?" he asked expectantly.

"Jerry is desperate for a racquetball partner. If you would like to spend more time with him, there's a definite opening there."

"Racquetball, huh?"

"Do you play?"

"Well, no, I never have," confessed Deckle, "but how hard can it be? I'm sure I can fake it."

Fortunately, my brain was in relatively high gear for that hour of the morning.

"Jim, that's absurd. If you really want to play, why don't you ask Jerry if he would teach you, instead of pretending you know how."

"Do you think he would?"

"He might even be flattered," I suggested.

I was intently typing away on the computer hours later when Deckle came bounding into the office.

"I did it!" he beamed.

"Did what?"

"I asked Jerry to teach me to play racquetball, and he agreed," he announced happily. "We're playing tonight and, depending on how it goes, we may play every night this week!"

"Good," I said. "Some exercise won't hurt you at all."

"Mitch, thanks. I owe you; I won't forget."

"Happy to help," I said, going back to what I was doing.

"Mitch?"

"Yes, Jim?"

"Do I need any special gear or a uniform?"

"A racquetball racket would help."

He was making a list. "A sporting goods store would have it?"

"Yes."

"What should I wear?"

"Shorts, a tee shirt and some type of court shoe should do it," I replied. "Running shoes will do in a pinch. And eye protectors; getting hit in the eye is no fun at all."

"Very good," he said, writing all of it down. "I'll run over to the mall and get all that stuff on my lunch hour."

He was even in a pretty good mood late that afternoon when his phone rang and it was Astrid. Normally, Deckle freaks out if he has to speak to Astrid; he still holds a grudge over her overhearing him rehearsing his phone messages. I was on a long distance conference call and she couldn't get through on my line, so she dialed his number.

"Mitch, your wife is on my phone," he interrupted.

"Ask her if I can call her back."

He started to protest, and then thought better of it. He gave her the message and turned to me. "On her cellular phone," he said.

I finished my call and dialed Astrid. "What's doing, honey?"

"I'm at the dealer with Sven."

"What happened?"

"I got on the expressway and he began to buck like a bronco. I decided to get it checked out instead of risking getting stuck."

"Why don't we trade that bomb in on something reliable?" I proposed.

"It isn't Sven's fault!" she protested defensively. "They think it's a plugged injector, probably from dirt in the gas. It could happen to any car."

"Do you need me to pick you up?"

"No, I'm hoping they can do it while I wait. I just wanted to let you know that I'm going to be home late."

"That's not a problem," I said. "I have a lot to do here. Why don't I wait, in case you need a ride?"

"Great," she said. "If you need to get me, I'll leave my phone on."

I had kind of lost track of the time, but the phone ringing insistently on Beth's desk was driving me crazy. Finally, I decided that whoever it was would not just go away if I ignored it, and I decided to pick it up. The female voice at the other end was unfamiliar.

"Who is this?" she asked.

"This it Mitchell Goldblatt. May I help you?"

"Oh, Mitch," she said absently. "This is Bobbie McCann. Is there anyone else around?"

"I think everyone's gone for the night. Can I help?"

"I don't know," she said. She sounded really strange.

"I thought you were going on vacation," I said.

"We are; I'm calling from Cancun. I guess I wanted to talk to Jerry; I don't know."

"Is there a problem?"

"Yes," she said, her voice breaking. "There was an accident today."

"What kind of an accident? Are you or the children hurt?"

"No, we're fine," she said.

"Well, that's good," I encouraged. "Is Bob there?"

"No," she said softly. "There was a diving accident; Bob is dead."

"Bobbie, is anyone there with you?" I asked.

"My mother. We brought her along to help with the kids."

"That's good," I said encouragingly. "Can you put her on the phone?"

I heard a shuffling noise on the line, and then a voice, "Yes, hello?"

"Hello," I said. "This is Mitch Goldblatt. I worked for Bob. Bobbie tells me there was an accident. Do you know what happened?"

"Yes," said the woman, "a little bit. By the way, I'm Irma West, Bobbie's mother."

"Hello, Mrs. West. Can you tell me what happened?"

"Bob went out on a diving charter to Cozumel this morning," she said. "Roberta had a bus trip to Tulum, and I was here with the children. A few hours ago, the police came to the room and said that Bob was underwater and became separated from the rest of the group. By the time they found him, he'd run out of air in his tanks and they took him to a hospital. Apparently, it was too late."

"I'm very sorry," I said. "How can I help?"

"I don't know," replied Mrs. West, starting to become upset. "If my son were here, he'd know."

"Would you like me to call him?"

"You wouldn't mind?"

"No," I said, scribbling his name and the name of his firm on Beth's note pad as Bobbie's mother gave them to me. "Is there anyone else you would like me to contact?"

"Roberta was wondering if you would call Father Drummond, our parish priest."

"I'll take care of it right away," I promised.

I took down her phone number at the hotel and gave her my home and office numbers. I still couldn't believe what was happening, but I went into high gear after I hung up from talking with Mrs. West. I managed to get Bill West, Bobbie's brother, at his office in San Francisco. He had his secretary book a flight while we were still on the line. It turned out that he was a lawyer, and he knew much more than I did about what needed to be done in Mexico. He thanked me profusely.

I called the hotel in Mexico and got Bobbie on the line. She was far more composed than when we first spoke, and sounded relieved that her brother was on the way.

"Would you like me to fly down there?" I offered. "I'm not sure what I could do, other than offer moral support, but if you need my help, you have it."

"Thank you, Mitch," she said. "You've done more than I had even hoped. I don't know why I called the office; I didn't know what to do or who to call."

"You did the right thing," I reassured her.

"Did you speak with Father Drummond?"

"He wasn't in and I didn't want to leave that kind of message; I'll try again later."

"I appreciate it," said Bobbie. "He's been Bob's family priest all his life; he even baptized him. He's going to take this very hard."

"Do you need me to fly down there?" I offered again.

"I don't think so," said Bobbie. "When Bill gets here he'll know what to do."

"If you change your mind or need anything else, give me a call."

"Thanks, Mitch."

After I hung up with Bobbie, I dialed Astrid on the cellular phone.

"I was just trying to get you," she said. "Sven is good as new and I'm on my way home. How about if we grab a bite out?"

"Would you be very disappointed if I picked up a pizza on my way home?"

"Hard day?"

"Worse than you can imagine," I replied, not wanting to break that kind of news over the phone while she was driving.

"I'll call the pizza in and you pick it up," proposed Astrid. What would you like on it?"

"Surprise me."

"Anchovies and pineapple," giggled Astrid.

"Sounds good."

No one could have accused me of being close to Bob, but I never wished that any harm would come to him, and the news of his death affected me more than I would have guessed. Forty-two was pretty young to die, and Bob was what people categorize as young and vital. Certainly, you hear about diving accidents, but scuba was his passion and his certification was one thing that he made a point to keep current. Considering all the other things I knew he had done, it seemed pretty safe. He had gone skydiving on several occasions. Bungee jumping was another activity he enjoyed. For his birthday last year, Bobbie had arranged for him to fly with one of the Thunderbirds during an air show. He had gone on a safari in Kenya when all foreign tourists had been warned that it was considered unsafe; he hadn't even contracted the severe form of dysentery that went through the rest of the group. A few weeks before his death, he had been trying to arrange a trip to Nepal, and was even trying to find out if he could join an expedition to climb Mount Everest. Anything that was dangerous and challenging was of interest to Bob.

I did not feel the tearing sense of loss that I had when Artie died; it was more a sense of shock that this could happen to Bob. I suppose that a part of me believed that there had been some mistake, and that Bobbie would be calling back to say that because of the language barrier, there had been a misunderstanding.

I managed to get hold of Father Drummond right after I spoke with Astrid. He sounded like an older man, and he did not take the news well. He asked many questions for which I had no answers, but he did finally promise to handle all the funeral arrangements. I didn't know if this was what Bobbie had in mind, but I thanked him and told him that I was sure the family would be grateful.

"Hello, pizza man," said Astrid cheerily as I walked into the house.

"I see the bomb got you home in one piece," I said, setting the pizza box on the counter.

"I told you it wasn't his fault," she said protectively.

I put my arms around her and nuzzled her neck just a little bit too long.

"What's wrong?" she asked immediately.

"I had a phone call from Bobbie McCann before I left."

"I thought they were going on vacation."

"She was calling from Mexico. There was a diving accident."

Astrid already looked shaken. "What happened?"

"I didn't get all the details but it's bad. Bob is dead."

The color drained from my wife's face. "He's dead?"

"Yes," I said softly.

"How can that be?" she said, looking confused. "First Artie and now this? How can this be happening?"

"I don't know," I sighed.

"I didn't even really like Bob," admitted Astrid.

"Neither did I," I confessed.

Astrid fell into my arms and cried for a man that neither of us liked.

***

I awoke in the middle of the night with a start, having the feeling that something was wrong. Astrid was not beside me in bed.

"Honey?" I called.

"In here," she answered from the bathroom.

I got out of bed and squinted at the clock; it was ten minutes past four. I peeked into the bathroom through the open door, and saw Astrid, sitting on the floor with her back propped against the wall, a washcloth draped over her forehead.

"What's wrong?" I demanded.

"I'm sick," she said. "I guess I ate something that didn't agree with me."

I lifted the washcloth and felt her forehead. She didn't seem to be running a fever. "Should I try to get hold of a doctor?"

"No," she said, getting to her feet and putting the washcloth on the sink. "I think I gave back whatever it was that did it; I'm feeling better."

When the alarm went off, I tried to convince her to take the day off, but she wouldn't hear of it. I would have loved to have taken the day off, but I suspected that the office would be in chaos, so I didn't even seriously consider the possibility.

Deckle was waiting for me when I got to work. "I heard the news," he said, trying to sound properly somber but not quite succeeding. "I wonder who Jerry will pick to fill Bob's job?"

I was in no mood for Deckle today. I couldn't fall back asleep after I had awakened with Astrid, and I was tired and out of sorts.

"For goodness sake, Jim. Bob isn't even cold yet and you're already picking at the remains. What does that make you?"

Deckle looked surprised. "I didn't think you and Bob were all that friendly."

"We weren't, but I certainly never wished him dead. He was young, he had a family and I feel horrible about what has happened."

"I feel bad too," said Deckle, "but Businetex is going to go on without him, and as I see it, you and I are the major contenders for his job."

"If you want it that badly, I hope you get it," I said.

"Do you really mean that?"

"Yes."

"If Jerry offers it to you, will you suggest that he give it to me?"

"Sure," I said. What I did not add was that if he was given the job, I would take Artie's old job or whatever was available that would prevent me from working for him.

Beth knocked on the office door. Her eyes were red-rimmed, as if she had been crying. "The funeral is set for Saturday," she said.

"That was smart," said Deckle. "He should get a good turn-out, since people won't have to take time off from work."

Beth choked on a sob, and I went over to put my hand on her shoulder. She leaned against me and buried her face against my chest.

"Why don't you take a hike, Mr. Sensitivity?" I asked Deckle curtly.

"What did I say?" he asked defensively, but he did leave the office.

Gently, I led Beth to my chair and eased her down. Then, I pulled some Kleenex out of the box on the shelf behind my desk and handed them to her.

"I'm sorry," she sniffled. "I don't know what's gotten into me. Bob was okay as a boss but we weren't close."

"I know," I soothed. "It was a shock. Coming on top of what happened to Artie, it's bound to affect all of us more."

"I'm sorry I got so emotional," she said.

All morning long, people were coming in and out of the office, making it impossible to get any work done. Just before noon, Maggie knocked on my door.

"Come in," I called.

"Hello, Mitch," she said softly.

"How are you doing, Maggie?"

"I've had better days," she said, the corners of her mouth twisting into the beginnings of an ironic smile.

"I'm sorry."

"I know what you probably think of me," she said.

"I try not to judge people."

"It wasn't the way it looked," she said. "I really did love him."

I didn't know what to say to her but she didn't wait for a reply.

"Jerry wanted to see you in his office when you have a minute."

"Tell him that I'll be right over," I said.

"Thanks, Mitch," she said, starting to leave.

"Maggie?"

"Yes, Mitch?"

"Is there anything I can do to help you?"

"No," she said, shaking her head, "but thanks for being the kind of person who would ask."

Jerry was sitting at his desk, tapping his pencil absently when I knocked on the frame of his open door.

"Mitch, come on in," he invited. "Have a seat."

I always felt uncomfortable in Jerry's office, like I was entering the lair of some dreaded beast. Artie had once joked that rumor had it that Jerry was the model for Hannibal Lecter. I don't think that was accurate; Jerry was much scarier.

"What can I do for you, Jerry?" I asked as I edged nervously into the offered chair.

"It's more a matter of what I can do for you. Bob told me that you didn't want Artie's job."

"I was flattered," I protested, "but I felt that someone who was qualified in that field would be more effective."

"Yes," said Jerry. "Well, now Bob's job is open. Do you have any suggestions for his successor?"

"Jim Deckle is interested."

"I know that. Do you think he's qualified?"

"From a technical standpoint, I think he's probably more qualified than Bob was."

Jerry tapped his pencil and studied me. "Would you be willing to work for him?"

"Not if I had any other alternative," I replied candidly.

"Exactly!" said Jerry. "And you are not alone. Apparently, he has been lobbying for Artie's job, which I will tell you right upfront, I have no intention of offering him. He's managed to start the rumor that the job is as good as his, and I have already been approached by four of our best technical writers, requesting a transfer on the basis of that rumor alone.

"What I called you here to ask is if you will accept Bob's job if I offer it to you."

I wasn't sure that I really wanted the dubious honor of more work and more aggravation, but heaven knew who Jerry would bring in to take over our group if I declined. "Yes," I said softly. "If you offer me the job, I will accept."

Jerry extended his hand. "Congratulations on your promotion. I'll be making the announcement this afternoon. You can move into Bob's old office any time after Beth is able to get it cleaned out."

I hardly felt like congratulations were in order. I don't know what I wanted or expected. Maybe I had hoped to see Jerry mourn Bob just a little bit; I don't know.

"Congratulations," said Beth when I passed her desk on the way back to my office.

"For what?"

"Maggie just called to tell me that you're my new boss."

"Yes, I suppose I am," I sighed.

"I hope that's okay," she said anxiously.

"Beth, I'm sorry. It's more than okay. There is no one I'd rather work with. I'm not myself today."

"None of us are. I'm happy it's you, Mitch."

"Thanks," I said, returning to my desk.

"You got it, didn't you?" asked Deckle before I was even in the door.

"I suggested that Jerry give it to you," I reported.

"You did?" asked Deckle, surprised.

"I promised you that I would."

"What did he say about me?" demanded Jim.

"He said that he wasn't prepared to offer you the job, even if I turned it down."

"I wonder why?" asked Deckle.

"I don't know, Jim," I said. I couldn't bring myself to tell him the truth. "Why don't you ask him?"

It was lunchtime but I had no appetite. I picked up the phone and dialed Astrid's number. Her secretary said that she'd see if she was available.

"Hi!" said my wife cheerily as she came on the line.

"How are you feeling?" I asked.

"Oh, much better. It must have been the salad I had for lunch yesterday; I ate at my desk. Who knows how long it was out of the refrigerator before I got it!"

"As long as you're okay."

"What's up with you?"

"Not too much. Jerry offered me Bob's job and I accepted. The vultures are already picking over the carrion."

"It does seem heartless," agreed Astrid, "but I suppose that a company the size of Businetex can't stop over the loss of one employee. You should try to be a little happy; I'm very proud of you. I must say that Jerry showed unusually good judgment in this instance. This is the first good decision he's made since he's been with the company."

"I don't get a raise," I said. "I was already at the same salary level as Bob.

"I think we'll manage," said my wife.

***

Saturday was a gray, gloomy day. I remember thinking that I was getting far too much experience at attending Catholic funerals, as I pulled into the parking lot of the suburban church barely a mile from Bob's home.

Astrid and I slipped into a pew a few rows from the back of the church and sat down. A few minutes later, Jerry came in.

"Hello, Mitch," he said, offering his hand. "Hello, Ingrid," he said, nodding to Astrid.

I started to correct him, but Astrid tugged on my sleeve and returned his greeting. I was afraid that he was going to want to sit with us, but he waved to someone near the front of the church and kept walking.

The services were about to start when I caught sight of her walking down the aisle. She looked even taller than usual in her slim black dress, black brimmed hat, black stockings and high-heeled black pumps.

Astrid felt me stiffen. "Who is that?" she whispered.

"Maggie," I whispered. I had confided in Astrid about Bob's liaison when I first learned of it.

"What's she doing?" asked Astrid.

Maggie was strutting determinedly toward the front of the aisle. Bobbie was standing silently beside Bob's coffin, her two sons at her side, and Maggie was headed straight for them.

I jumped up and followed her quickly down the aisle. "Maggie," I said softly, putting my hand on her arm.

She stopped and faced me. "Oh, Mitch," she said, looking as if she wasn't totally aware of her surroundings.

"Why don't you come and sit with us?" I offered.

"I should be up there," she said hollowly, gesturing at the coffin.

"Maggie," I said softly, "don't make it harder than it has to be."

She allowed me to lead her back to the row we had chosen. Astrid slid over to make room for us, and I introduced the two women. Halfway through the services, Maggie began to sob. I shrugged at Astrid helplessly.

"Do something," she whispered.

I took Maggie's hand and tried to calm her down, but she buried her head against my shoulder and sobbed harder. I helplessly patted her back and looked over at Astrid. She shrugged.

Finally, Maggie reached into her black clutch bag, pulled out a handkerchief, wiped her eyes and blew her nose. "I have to get out of here," she whispered to us.

"Are you okay?" asked Astrid softly.

"Yes. I just need to go. Thank you both."

Quickly, she stood and bolted from the church.

I hadn't been paying much attention to the services. I was aware of Jerry Fallow, leaning back against the pew several rows in front of us, singing along with all the hymns, a bit off key, his voice louder than everyone else's. It seemed that nothing could get Jerry going like a good funeral.

The priest read something from Corinthians by the apostle Paul, not one of my idols, and to tell the truth, I was so preoccupied with keeping Maggie from causing a scene that I couldn't have given a good account of what went on. When they started waving that box with the incense, I knew that the services were over.

Bobbie was greeting people at the back of the church, looking somber but completely composed. I did my best not to think of John Madden in a black dress, but the resemblance was always startling. She introduced us to her mother, brother and Bob's mother, who was a patrician-looking female version of her son. All of the mourners were stone-faced and impassive; I couldn't help but think that at least a few tears would have seemed more appropriate.

"Thank you for handling that woman," Bobbie said to us both. Our eyes met and I realized that there was no point in denying what we all knew to be the truth.

"If there's anything else we can do for you, please let us know," said Astrid.

"A few people are coming back to the house after the burial," she said. "Could you join us?"

"We wouldn't want to intrude," I protested. We had spent some time with the McCann family at company activities, but we weren't what I would have characterized as close friends.

"I would consider it a favor if you have the time to stop by," she replied.

I had hoped to skip the burial, but it seemed that we were expected to attend.

"We'll be there," said Astrid, squeezing Bobbie's hand.

We were walking back to the car from the graveyard behind the church, where they had buried Bob next to his father, when Astrid slipped quickly into the bushes and vomited.

"Honey, what's the matter?" I asked, rushing to her side.

"The smell of that stuff they burn did me in."

"If you're sick, I'm sure Bobbie will understand if we go straight home."

"I'm fine now," she assured me.

Astrid and I had never been to the McCann home. It was a large, stately old house on a tree-lined street that backed up to a private golf course. The neighborhood screamed old money. It was not a place I would have chosen to live. I was feeling really out of place as I rang the doorbell.

Bobbie's brother answered the door. "Please come in," he invited. He was even larger and taller than Bobbie, but instead of being endowed with the abundant head of tousled dark blonde hair that his sister sported, Bill West was bald with just a trace of dark hair cropped short along the sides of his shiny pate. He was not an exceptionally good-looking man, but there was a twinkle in his dark eyes that suggested that in a social situation, he would be personable enough.

"Mitch, Astrid, thank you so much for coming," said Bobbie.

"Bobbie," I said, taking both her hands, "we haven't had a chance to tell you just how sorry we are about Bob."

"Thank you."

We were introduced to a few friends and neighbors. Irma West and Mrs. McCann were also there. It was a sadly small crowd for someone like Bob, who had considered himself a man of stature.

"I still cannot understand how this could have happened," sniffed Bob's mother, Stella, when we were all seated in the McCann's impeccably decorated but stuffy living room.

Bobbie gave her an exasperated look. I remembered Bob mentioning how it was a good thing that his mother had decided to move to Florida after his father died, because she and Bobbie despised each other. "What is it that you want to know, Mother McCann?"

"How could the accident have happened and why weren't you there to help him?"

"Now, what could she have done?" demanded Bill defensively.

"I've told you what happened," said Bobbie tersely. "We planned this vacation because there were things of interest to all of us in the area. Mom was to take the kids to the beach, I had plans to explore several Mayan ruins, and Bob was to spend the week scuba diving."

"You could have gone diving too, instead of driving miles on a bus into the jungle," accused Stella.

Astrid looked like she was thinking about choking the woman, but she sat stiffly beside me and said nothing.

"I am not certified to dive," replied Bobbie defensively, "and Bob could have taken one day to visit the ruins with me, but he didn't. You seem to be trying to place the blame on me, but if you have to find fault, your perfect son did this to all of us!"

"Roberta!" snapped Irma West.

"Look, Mother," said Bobbie, obviously struggling to hold her temper, "this needs to be said. Stella has been making all sorts of comments and insinuations; I think we should clear the air."

"We'd probably better be going," I said.

The friends and neighbors took the cue and all muttered their agreement, heading for the door.

"Mitch, I would appreciate it if you and Astrid would stay," said Bobbie, making no move to stop anyone else from beating a hasty retreat.

"We don't want to intrude," protested Astrid.

"You're not," said Bobbie, clasping Astrid's hand. "You have been good friends to me, and I will feel better having you both here."

My wife sat down next to Bobbie on the sofa, and I eased uncomfortably into a wing chair.

"Where are the kids?" asked Irma West.

"They're in their rooms," said Bill. "The boys are playing video games and Brittany was asleep when we got home; she's upstairs in her bed."

"Now," said Bobbie, focusing on Stella McCann, "you seem intent on blaming me for what happened to Bob, but let me tell you, I could have predicted it, and there is nothing I could have done to stop it. Your son was a real hot dog; he always had to show everyone up."

"You're jealous because he excelled at everything he touched," sniffed Stella.

"He was an inconsiderate show-off," said Bobbie.

"Now, come on you two," said Bill. "You're both under stress; try to calm down before you both say things you'll regret."

"And some wife you are," said Stella, ignoring Bill completely. "Your husband isn't even cold yet and you're spitting on his grave! This is a far cry from the Norman Rockwell family in the pictures you and Bob used to send."

Bobbie gave a cold, angry laugh. "We were the perfect Norman Rockwell family, if you didn't look too closely. The problem is that Bob was only here when the pictures were taken. Otherwise, he was at work, doing some daredevil stunt, or cavorting around heaven knows where, while I was holding things together. It was all an illusion, just like this house, which Bob had done by a decorator without consulting me. He didn't know or care that I loathed the way it looked; he was pleased at the way it came out, because it fit the Norman Rockwell image of which you are so enamored."

Astrid fidgeted uncomfortably and I didn't know where to look.

"Bob worked very hard; he deserved a comfortable, stylish home that pleased him," defended Stella. "He also needed to relax. If he enjoyed the water, certainly you wouldn't have begrudged him the opportunity to pursue that hobby?"

"No," said Bobbie, "but let's talk about what happened. Bob was supposed to be diving with a partner, but when they came upon an old shipwreck, he went off on his own, without giving the other diver a second thought. When they found him, his air tanks were empty. A diver is responsible for checking his equipment; maybe he panicked when he became lost and used his oxygen faster than normal, but more likely, he just didn't bother to make sure that his tanks were filled properly before he left. I don't dive and I wouldn't have known how to check his tanks. What would you have had me do?"

"You didn't have to be sixty miles off in a jungle somewhere," said Stella, rising up in her chair to reveal her full height. She had to be close to six feet tall.

"I have always been interested in archaeology; it was my major in college." said Bobbie. "I have willingly put aside my career plans to raise our family, but that doesn't mean that my interest isn't still there. The ruins at Tulum are one of the best preserved Mayan sites; it was too good an opportunity to miss. Besides, I have put up with twenty years of your son's selfishness. I've sat in hotel rooms with small children in every God-forsaken place you can imagine, while Bob went off seeking thrills. This time, I told him that either we took a vacation that all of us would enjoy, or we would vacation separately. Cancun was Bob's choice, but it was acceptable to me and the children too."

"I don't know what poor Robert ever did to deserve your venom, Roberta," said Stella haughtily.

"Maybe I should have introduced you to his mistress," said Bobbie, her anger taking over.

"How dare you!" gasped his mother.

"How dare I? She was at the funeral; ask Mitch and Astrid."

"I don't believe you!" said Stella. "I told Robert that you were a hateful witch the first time I met you. He could have done so much better!"

"Now, just one minute!" said Bill angrily.

Bobbie seemed almost in a trance. "You don't believe that Bob had a mistress? Why not? You know what they say: like father, like son!"

The blood drained from Stella's face; she was so white that I was afraid she would faint. "Could someone call a cab for me?" she whispered.

"I'll drive you to your hotel," said Bill, sounding defeated.

"Just take me to the airport!" fumed Stella.

"I'm so mortified!" said Irma when they had gone. "How could you, Roberta?"

"I only spoke the truth; I wish I'd said that and more a long time ago. I loved Bob, but he was no saint, and I won't have that woman blaming me for all his shortcomings. She's never liked me and I've never liked her, and hopefully, I'm done with her now."

"I'm ashamed of you," said Irma. "You didn't have to throw Bob's father in her face. He's been dead a long time, and if she wants to forget that he died in another woman's bed, that should be her right. She's still your mother-in-law and you should treat her with respect."

"You're entitled to your opinion," said Bobbie, "but if you feel that way, please go home. I don't want you under my roof tonight."

Mrs. West picked up her purse. "When you're ready to apologize, I'll be waiting," she said, closing the front door softly behind her.

Bobbie looked at me and Astrid. "I'm not sorry for any of what I said to them, but I do want to apologize to the two of you. I meant for us to get to know each other better. I had no idea that things would get so far out of hand; I'm sorry if you were embarrassed."

"Don't worry about it," I said, for want of some meaningful reply. "A lot of things are said in the heat of emotion."

"Nothing that was said wasn't true," said Bobbie, "but you were embarrassed."

"Mortified," agreed Astrid.

She looked at Bobbie and Bobbie looked at her, and the two of them began to laugh hysterically. To this day, I have no idea what was so funny. I guess you had to be female to get it.

"I can't even imagine what my brother's going to say when he gets back," said Bobbie, wiping her eyes, when their laughter had subsided.

"He seems like the supportive type," observed Astrid. "I think all of you needed a 'time-out.' Why don't you go up to your bedroom and lie down for a while? We can wait for your brother and tell him that you were exhausted."

"I haven't been able to sleep much since the accident, and I am tired," admitted Bobbie, "but I'm too keyed up to sleep now."

"Why don't you lie down and rest?" suggested my wife.

"Would you come up with me?" she asked Astrid.

Astrid looked at me questioningly.

"I'll hold the fort," I volunteered.

I poured myself a cup of coffee from the urn on the dining room table, and grabbed the *Democrat and Chronicle* that I spied on the kitchen counter. I was about halfway through the real estate section when I heard footsteps on the stairs. I looked up and saw Brandon, at sixteen the older of the two boys. I had seen the boys at the funeral, but one of the adults had ushered them quickly out of the church after the services were over, so we hadn't spoken. I hadn't seen Bob's small daughter; I'd assumed they left her with a sitter.

"Hi," he said shyly.

"I'm Mitch Goldblatt; I worked with your dad."

"I remember," he said. "Your wife found the chocolate ice cream for us at family day."

"Right," I said.

"Where's my mom?"

"She went to lie down for a few minutes. Can I help?"

"Brett has something in his eye and I can't get it out."

"I'll have a look," I offered.

The boy led me back to one of the bedrooms. Brett, four years his brother's junior, was sitting on the bed, his hand over his left eye.

"Mr. Goldblatt thinks he can get it out," said Brandon.

"Mitch," I said. "Mind if I have a look?"

Brett shrugged.

I turned on the desk lamp and gently pulled the lids away from the eye. It was teary and red.

"Do you see anything in there?" asked Brett.

"Well, let's see," I replied. "There's a sneaker, a rake..."

Brett smiled slightly.

"Wait a minute," I continued. "There's the culprit: an eyelash, right next to the teapot."

The corners of Brandon's mouth turned up slightly.

"Can you bring me a really wet Q-tip?" I asked.

The older boy went out of the room and returned a few minutes later with a box of Q-tips and a paper cup full of water.

I dipped one of the Q-tips in the cup and pulled back the lid. "Got it!" I announced, handing Brett the Q-tip with the offending lash on its end.

"Thanks, Mitch," said Brandon.

"It didn't even hurt," said Brett.

"Good," I nodded. "Is there anything else I can do for you two?"

"I don't think so," replied Brandon.

"I'm sorry about your father," I said.

Brandon shrugged. "He wasn't such a great dad."

"I hate it when you say that!" blurted Brett angrily.

"No one's perfect," I said, "but I'm sure he did the best he could."

"He was the only dad we had," said Brett, lying down across one of the beds and burying his face in the pillow.

His brother stood impassively watching. I went over and patted the younger boy on the shoulder.

"You know, Brandon," I said, "you shouldn't take anything you may have overheard earlier too seriously. Sometimes, when people are under a lot of stress, they say things they don't mean."

"It wasn't just what we overheard," said Brandon coldly. "I've known what my father was really like for a long time. Brett knows a little bit too, even if he doesn't want to admit it."

"Maybe I don't see things the way you do," said Brett, sitting up again. "Could you stay here with us for a while?" he asked me.

"Sure," I agreed, sitting on the edge of the bed next to him. "I wasn't doing anything important."

"Is Mom okay?" asked Brandon.

I studied the boy for a moment. He was tall and lean, built like Bob had been, but with darker hair and lighter eyes. His younger brother, who resembled him but had lighter hair and darker eyes, obviously worshipped the ground he trod.

"She's exhausted," I said, "but she's a good lady; I think she'll be fine after a little rest."

"Brandon keeps saying he wasn't worth getting upset about, but I loved him even if he did some things wrong," said Brett, pacing nervously across the room. "Is it so bad if I only want to remember the good things now?"

"No," I said, shaking my head. "My dad wasn't perfect either, but I still loved him, and I felt awful when he died."

Brett turned his back and started to shake with sobs. When I walked over and put my arm around him, he turned to lean against me.

"It's okay," I soothed, rubbing his back. "I don't know everything your dad did or didn't do, but I know it's okay for his sons to love him."

Brandon stood there awkwardly staring at us, looking lost and sad. No one had to tell me that the one who held it in sometimes suffered most of all. I held out my free arm to him and he leaned against me and his brother.

"You don't have to worry about your mom," I told them, "because she has two pretty great sons to help her over the rough spots."

"I wish we had a dad like you, Mitch," said Brandon.

"I wouldn't mind a couple of sons like you guys either."

The bedroom door creaked on its hinges and the three of us faced the noise. A head of blonde curls peeked through the opening.

"Britt, this is Mitch," said Brandon, picking up the little girl, who rubbed her eyes sleepily.

"Hi!" she said, burrowing her head shyly into her older brother's neck.

"What's that you have?" I asked, noticing the fairly large book in her hands.

"That's her favorite book," said Brett, wiping his eyes on the backs of his hands. "It was Mom's when she was little. She makes everyone read it to her about a million times."

"May I see?" I asked.

The little girl looked up at me with two eyes that were like bing cherries. She looked exactly as I remembered Shirley Temple in those old movies, when she was pushing five. "Yes," she said nodding.

I smiled when I saw the title. It was *One Morning in Maine*, Marilyn's absolute favorite book when she was a child. I would never admit it but I liked it too. At age three, hearing about someone meeting a bear while picking blueberries is high adventure, especially when you've spent your whole life in Brooklyn and consider a squirrel to be a wild animal.

"That was my sister's favorite book when she was little," I said.

"How old is she now?" asked Brett.

"Old enough to have sons the same age as you guys."

"Will you read it to me?" asked Brittany.

"I'd be happy to," I replied.

I sat down on one of the beds and Brett sat next to me, while Brandon cuddled his little sister on the other bed. I opened the book and sat reading *One Morning in Maine* to Bob's kids, momentarily filling the void of the father they had lost or maybe never had.

Chapter 5
Inga

I can best describe my mother-in-law by paraphrasing Winston Churchill's impression of Russia. Inga is a riddle wrapped in a mystery inside an enigma. Astrid repeated this to her mother and Inga was pleased, although she said it made her sound much more romantic and mysterious than was actually the case.

What I do know about Inga is that if she is in my life for another fifty years, I don't think I will have any better idea of what makes her tick.

I remember a conversation Astrid and I had about Inga, shortly after I first met the woman who was to become my mother-in-law. Astrid and I were not yet married, and I suppose we were still finding our way with each other.

"I sense that you didn't like my mother," she observed as we were driving home from the hotel near our apartment, where she had introduced me to Inga and Gus Lindstrom over dinner.

"That's not true," I protested. "She's very elegant; you can tell just being in her presence that she's refined."

"She wasn't lying when she said that had she cooked, the meal would have been even better," said Astrid. "She's a woman of many talents."

"You don't have to tell me that," I agreed. "She created you."

"You didn't seem to warm to her," persisted Astrid.

"I think first meetings are always awkward," I observed.

"Did you find her aloof?"

"No, not aloof," I said. "I think we were both wary with each other. Possibly, it was the accent."

"You think my mother has an accent?" wondered Astrid incredulously. "She's been in this country for over forty years."

"It isn't always noticeable but there's something about her that seems European. I don't know. She didn't say very much."

"My mother makes it a point to stay out of other people's business," said Astrid. "She has very strong opinions, but she never expresses them casually."

In the time I've known Inga, I've come to know that this is true. The world would be a better place if more people were like Astrid's mother.

"I didn't expect her to discuss her political views," I protested, "but I had hoped to get to know her. She's a good listener, but she said very little about herself."

"I think she told you almost as much as I know about her. She came to America as a young bride, when she and Daddy decided that the economic opportunities were superior here. Much of his family had already emigrated, and when an uncle offered to help him get a job and start a life in America, he eagerly pursued the opportunity. Mom was the only child of older parents who died before I was born."

"I wasn't looking for a dossier," I protested. "Your father seemed a lot more friendly, and I'd always heard that men are brutal with their daughters' boyfriends."

"My father wants me to be happy; I like you so he likes you."

For as long as Astrid could remember, Gus, her father, worked as a foreman at Delco products, always on the second shift. As a result, Astrid spent little of her childhood with him. He was always asleep when she left for school, and he came home after she had retired for the night. On Saturdays, he spent the day with his male buddies. It was only on Sundays that the family spent the day together, attending church and having dinner afterwards around the polished mahogany table in the dining room.

"He seems to regret that he wasn't around more when you were a child. Wasn't that a problem for you and your mother?"

"You will learn that my mother doesn't try to change what others around her choose to do. She accepts their decisions with cool grace. You will learn this firsthand. When Daddy was assigned to the second shift, she developed her own interests. She worked part-time, did some volunteer work, and spent time with me. All of us had a very full life. It might have seemed that she made the best of what others around her were doing, but honestly, looking back on it, I think she had more control than we realized."

I didn't really get to know either of Astrid's parents well at that first meeting, but I did forge a bond with them as our relationship progressed. I remember Gus Lindstrom as a boisterous, good-natured man who loved his beer and, when he could get it, his Aquavit. He had a certain earthy charm, and it was obvious that he adored his women, but he was different from the people I usually associated with. I've been told by others that he was typical of a middle-aged blue collar laborer; I don't know. I do know that we got along fine as father-in-law and son-in-law, although I never knew him well enough to say he was my friend. I do know that Rifka, with no justification, despised him, labeling him crude, an opinion that I did not share.

I've always thought of my mother-in-law as having a regal presence. For some reason, Astrid took exception to this when I expressed my opinion to her.

"You make her sound like some proper dowager," she said, wrinkling her nose in distaste.

"That's not what I meant," I protested, "but the proper part isn't wrong. I have never seen her wear slacks, even on the most bitterly cold day of the Rochester winter."

"Neither have I," confessed Astrid, "but she is sixty-four years old. She was raised in another country at another time. I suppose wearing a skirt or dress seems right to her."

"Or maybe she realizes that it would be a shame for her to hide those legs," I teased.

"You think Mom has nice legs?"

"Very nice," I replied.

"What do you like about them?"

"I don't know; they look like yours."

"Slender and well-shaped," said Astrid.

"And she's modest too," I replied.

"We're talking about my mother."

"And how you got your good looks from her," I added.

"You think my mother is pretty?" asked Astrid coyly.

"I do," I agreed but it was more than that. She has a way about her that exudes elegance. The creamy, fair skin of her face is unblemished, and every golden blonde hair is tucked neatly into a French knot, even at the earliest hour of the morning. "I think your mother is pretty, but what I like most about her is the way she is with you."

Astrid learned her impeccable manners at an early age from her equally well-mannered mother, but my wife is quick to point out that her mother's coolly composed demeanor belies the affection that she lavished on her only daughter.

"I wish you could have been there," said Astrid, the first time she told me about the hours of her childhood spent playing dolls with her mother. "When we played together, I got to dictate all the rules of the game. It was as if I was the mother, and she the obedient daughter. When I expressed an interest in learning to swim, she took swimming lessons with me at the YMCA, although she was terrified of water. You call her regal and yet, at times she can be almost child-like."

"I believe it," I replied. "The first time I saw her with Ole, I couldn't believe it was your mother, romping on the floor, laughing like that over the antics of a kitten. I never imagined that your mother liked animals. If I had know how much the gift of a kitten would delight her, I would have gotten her one myself."

"Even I didn't know that about her," admitted Astrid. "My mother is still capable of surprising me."

I could see how that was true. The only thing about Inga that is completely predictable is that anytime I think I have her figured out, she will do something to surprise me. As well mannered as she is, I have seen her cut people down swiftly and efficiently. Heck, she's even done it to me. If you ask her a question that she doesn't wish to answer, she will look almost through you with those steely blue eyes and coldly declare "That is not something you need to know" with emphasis on the word 'you.' I can tell you firsthand, it is lethally effective.

Astrid has a lot of her mother in her, but I can tell you for certain, if she could duplicate the look in those eyes, I never would have married her. My wife's eyes flash when she is angry, but the coldness and cunning of Inga's look is not there. I admire many things about Inga, but I could never live with a woman who had eyes like that.

With all the chaos in our lives the past summer, we really hadn't had the chance to spend much time with Inga. Rather than complaining about the lack of attention, she tried to be understanding.

"I know there have been many demands on your time recently," she sympathized as we sat around her dining room table, having dinner.

"We're so busy that we're going to have to put off taking a vacation this summer," said Astrid.

"Oh?" said Inga casually as she cleared the table.

"At least for now," I explained as I carried the platter and bread basket into the kitchen. "Later on, when things are more under control, we'll try to get away, even if it's only for a weekend."

"Do you think that is wise?" she asked.

From her tone, both of us knew that she disapproved, although she made no other comment and did not try to change our minds.

"Wise or not, it's what we need to do," said Astrid.

Inga served dessert and let the matter drop.

***

The day we returned from Brooklyn from Artie's funeral, there had been a notice in the waiting mail informing me that I was being summoned to serve on a grand jury. As if regular jury duty wouldn't have been enough of a hassle, this was a full four weeks of service, five days per week.

Businetex and the other large companies in the area have a policy of paying their employees through their entire term of service on a jury, so there is a high likelihood of being selected. It was not that I minded serving on a jury; I believe that it is everyone's civic duty and I am a firm supporter of our justice system. It was just that the timing was so rotten. I had a bit more than three weeks notice that the rest of my life would have to be put on hold for four weeks. At the time, Bob didn't think it would be much of a problem for me to be away, as long as the J-6 came out on time. Now, things had changed drastically. Bob had just died, I had taken over his job only the previous week, our new printer was not coming along as quickly as we had hoped, and Astrid and I desperately needed the vacation we had decided to postpone.

My wife kept telling me that we needed to talk about something, but every time we started, we would be interrupted. I was putting in fourteen hour days and was, quite frankly, exhausted. I fell asleep during more than one conversation, and I'm horrified to admit, once I even dozed off while we were making love.

I told Jerry about my impending grand jury service immediately after he promoted me to Bob's former job.

"This is a lousy time for you to be away, and four weeks is a long time, Mitch," he said, as if I had control over the situation.

"I might be able to postpone it if I call them," I offered, "but according to the notice, if I do that, I have to give them a firm date for service within the next six months."

"That's no good," he said, shaking his head. "How are we supposed to know when it would be a good time for you to be away? Things change day to day around here. Let me make some calls and I'll take care of it."

"You can do that?" I wondered.

"Consider it handled," he assured me.

When I checked back with him, true to form, he had done nothing.

"Why didn't you tell me about this sooner?" he demanded.

"I did tell you, right after I took over this job," I reminded him. "You promised to make a call to take care of it."

"There was a lot of confusion around here back then," he shrugged. "I can't say I remember that conversation."

I wound up reporting as instructed, and of course, I was chosen for a jury. I wish I could have the same kind of luck in having my name pulled out of the box when there's a door prize or a raffle at stake.

Because Astrid had an assigned parking spot downtown that she rented by the month, we decided that we would ride into the city together, and if we couldn't get out at the same time in the evening, we would meet at Inga's house, which was only a block from the city bus line.

Most days, I was later than Astrid, so she and her mother had the opportunity to visit, which seemed to please both of them. On a few occasions, I arrived at Inga's first and we engaged in our usual small talk.

On my first solo visit, Inga observed that Astrid looked tired.

"We've both been working hard," I replied. "We both have demanding jobs."

"You should make more of an effort to rest on the weekends," she countered.

I sensed that she had something on her mind and I said as much.

"It is just an impression I had," she said.

"And what was that?" I pressed.

"I think your weekend plans may have been too much for Astrid."

It seemed to me that she was blaming me for something, and I didn't understand why. "Specifically, which weekend plans?"

"Activities that tire Astrid,"

Bobbie McCann had called Astrid the week after Bob's funeral. It surprised me but they seemed to have hit it off and had spoken regularly ever since. According to Astrid, Bobbie thought that I had done something unusual for her children, and she mentioned that the boys had both expressed an interest in spending some time with me. Astrid had suggested that we take them out on a Saturday afternoon and we had.

"Taking the McCann kids out was her idea, if that's what you meant."

"I know that," agreed Inga, "but apparently, you had no objections. I think it was too much for her, even if she will not say so, and I would like you to keep that in mind when you plan activities in the future."

"Things went very well," I protested.

We had taken the kids to a matinee of *Free Willy* at the movies, and they seemed to enjoy themselves. What's more, it was a pretty good movie; Astrid and I enjoyed it much more than we had expected we would. Brittany, who insisted on being included, had gotten a bit restless, and Astrid had to take her potty four times. I was a little worried that something might be wrong, but Astrid was sure that Brittany just enjoyed the change of scenery. Afterwards, we had eaten at the Spaghetti Warehouse, and the kids behaved fine. In fact, we'd all had a good time.

It had gone so well that I was beginning to think that it was time for Astrid and me to consider starting a family of our own. I had mentioned the idea to her that night, as we were lying in bed.

"I've been giving that some thought too," she admitted. "We need to talk."

We should have talked it over right then, but somehow, I fell asleep.

"Mitchell, you and Astrid need to spend more time together. You must make time to talk and really listen to each other," said Inga.

This was as close to meddling as Inga ever came. "Did Astrid say something to you?" I asked.

"She said that you two have not even had time for a conversation in weeks."

"She's right," I confessed, "but I'll be through with this jury thing in a few weeks, and things will settle down."

"As long as you are aware of the situation," said Inga, ending the conversation.

Usually, we did not have all that much to say to each other, so I wound up drinking tea and eating enough of Inga's fabulous cookies to completely ruin my appetite for dinner. When I was early enough, I would walk over to the health club, which was only three blocks away, for a quick work-out before returning to Inga's to meet Astrid.

In the evenings, I usually made a quick run in to the office, just to keep up with what was going on. Jerry had allowed Deckle to be acting supervisor in my absence, and the rest of the people who worked for me were on the verge of mutiny.

"You have no idea what is going on here," said Beth, on her way home for the day as I was coming in.

"Enlighten me," I said.

"Jim is scheduling all sorts of meetings with no purpose other than to exert his authority."

"I've been canceling most of them," I said.

"As quickly as you cancel them, he reschedules. He also sends at least a dozen memos a day, including his daily reminder that all correspondence should be shredded before disposal."

"Ignore them," I advised.

"It isn't that easy," she protested. "I work for him now."

"It's only temporary," I soothed. She had already threatened to quit twice, but I was hoping I could convince her to stick it out. "I'm looking forward to working with you again."

"I have no control over what is done to him," she warned me. "People are reaching their limits."

His office had already been stuffed with shredder confetti and another night, everything had been glued down with super glue.

"You don't think anyone would hurt him, do you?"

"I think many of us would like to, but no, I don't know of anyone who is psycho enough to do that, other than Deckle himself."

"He's a little off but he's harmless," I assured her as I closed her car door for her.

The nice thing about serving on a grand jury was that Astrid's office was only a block away from the Hall of Justice, and most days, we were able to eat lunch together. I never knew exactly when we would break or how much time I would have until it happened, so I would call her when I was free and she would decide where we were to meet, depending on the time and her schedule. This was almost the only time we had together when we were awake, so we really looked forward to our lunches.

One afternoon during my second week of service, I had a longer than normal lunch break, but it was too short for me to take the car and run in to work. Astrid didn't have much time but she did agree to meet me for a quick bite.

"You go down to Fruit and Salad Company and get on line," she instructed. "I'll join you in about twenty minutes."

"What if I get to the front before you get there?" I asked.

"Get me half a turkey on white and a small salad," she said.

I was just paying for the food when she arrived, so she gestured that she would reserve a table in the crowded restaurant. I joined her and we were so engrossed in conversation that I didn't notice the tall, slender dark-haired stranger approaching our table.

"Astrid! I thought it was you," said the man excitedly. "I'd heard you were back; you look fabulous!"

"Hello, Jeffrey," said my wife softly.

No one had to explain to me who he was; I knew it had to be Jeffrey Laslo, Astrid's former husband. I certainly could understand how Astrid had been attracted to him; even I noticed that he was a particularly good-looking man. It was obvious by the way that they stared in our direction that many of the women in the restaurant had made the same observation. To Jeffrey's credit, he seemed oblivious to the attention his looks commanded.

I stood up and offered my hand. "I'm Mitch Goldblatt," I said cordially.

Jeffrey took my hand and shook it warmly. "It's a pleasure to finally meet you," he said, meeting my gaze with eyes the color of pale green crystals. "To tell you the truth, I've been curious about the man who convinced Astrid to take his name."

Actually, he gave me far too much credit. When Astrid and I decided to marry, I had assumed that she would keep her name, since she was known that way professionally. It was she who announced her intention to become Astrid Goldblatt. As she put it, "With my looks and that name, I'll certainly turn a few heads!"

"May I join you?" asked Jeffrey, gesturing at the empty chair at our table.

Astrid looked uncomfortable but my curiosity was in high gear. "Please do," I invited, moving my napkin and iced tea to make room for his tray.

"Are you two working downtown?" asked Jeffrey as he arranged his food on the table.

"I'm back with Wilson-Locke," said Astrid. "Mitch works at Businetex but he's on jury duty."

"I hope not in Judge Connell's court this afternoon," said Jeffrey nervously.

"Grand jury," I clarified.

"Oh, that's a relief," said Jeffrey. "Having lunch with one of the jurors on my case would be excellent grounds for a mistrial."

"I thought you weren't trying cases anymore," said Astrid.

"I'm doing a favor for a colleague. He asked me to be part of the defense team. Specifically, he wants me to sit in on part of the testimony, and make suggestions about the cross examination. Some aspects of the case involve my area of expertise."

"You specialize in a particular area?" I asked.

"Matrimonial law, usually," he agreed. "I hope you two never need my services."

Astrid glanced nervously at her watch. "I'm going to have to get going. Are you coming, Mitch?"

"If you don't have to be back yet, why don't you stay and keep me company?" invited Jeffrey. He had hardly made a dent in his large Chef's salad.

"I have another hour," I said.

Astrid looked nervous. "I'll see you later, at Mom's," she said, slinging her purse over her shoulder.

I stood and kissed her on the lips. "Knock 'em dead," I said.

She gave the two of us one last wary glance and walked out of the restaurant.

"You both look very happy together," commented Jeffrey.

"We are happy," I agreed.

"Good," he replied. "I only wish the best for Astrid. I don't know if she's mentioned that I got married a few months before you two did."

"Yes, she did."

"Monica and I have been happy too. I didn't know how Astrid would feel about this, so I didn't say anything, but we're expecting our first child in September."

"Congratulations," I said.

"Thanks. I didn't think I'd ever want to risk having another child after Astrid and I lost our baby, but time has put things in perspective, and now I'm looking forward to fatherhood."

Although I'm sure that everyone else in the restaurant had gone on talking and doing what they had been, for me it was as if the world had stopped. Inside my head, there was absolute silence except for those echoing words "Astrid and I lost our baby."

Jeffrey was still talking, but I didn't hear what he said. Finally, he stopped and said my name several times.

"Yes," I replied.

"Are you all right?" he asked. "Is something the matter?"

"No, Jeffrey," I said, trying to sound composed when inside, I felt as if my whole world had fallen apart. "I just remembered a call that I promised to make, and I may already be too late. You'll have to excuse me."

"Of course," he said. "I'm really glad we had the chance to meet."

"Me too," I said, shaking the extended hand, "and good luck with the baby."

"Thanks," he said to my back as I bolted from the place.

I didn't know where I was going as I loped down the street, but when I got to the Genesee river, I stopped and stood by the railing, staring down at the water. My wife had neglected to mention one small detail of her relationship with her ex-husband. This was the first I'd heard that they had a child together.

The rest of that afternoon was a blur to me. I don't remember going back to the jury room, but obviously, I did. I couldn't concentrate on any of the cases we heard, and I'm ashamed to admit, I voted them based on what the majority felt. I know that wasn't fair when my actions were determining the fate of another human being, but it was all I could do. Luckily, the last two cases were scratched from our schedule for the afternoon, and we were dismissed early.

I got to Inga's house a few minutes after she had arrived home. She still worked part-time at McCurdy's downtown store four days a week, the same job she'd had since Astrid started attending school full-time.

Ole, her kitten that had grown into a large orange tabby, was delighted to see me. Normally, that cat followed Inga everywhere, like a shadow, but for some reason, he had taken a liking to me, and anytime I was around, he would find some way to make physical contact, purring like the engine of a race car.

"Inga," I said as soon as I was in the house, "we need to talk." I leaned down and picked up Ole for affect. That cat despised being picked up, but for some reason, he tolerated it from me. Astrid and Inga would get scratched to ribbons if they tried it, but when I lifted him, he'd tense up at first and then settle down until I let him go. I think this has always been a sore point for Inga, although she would never admit it.

"About what?" she asked, trying to sound cool, but I knew she was nervous.

"About the baby that Astrid had with Jeffrey."

The relief that flooded over Inga's face was apparent. "Oh, she told you. Thank goodness!"

"She didn't tell me," I said quietly. "I heard about it from Jeffrey."

Inga looked as if someone had just told her about the death of a good friend. "That is something you will have to discuss with Astrid."

"Astrid has had four years to discuss it with me; I think if she intended to, she would have gotten around to it by now."

"She meant to tell you," said Inga wearily.

"She didn't," I said coldly, "and now, I want you to tell me."

"It is not my place," said Inga. "That was a very painful time for all of us. It is not easy for Astrid to speak of it at all, even with me."

"Don't you think it would make it easier for her if I knew what happened and she didn't have to recount all the details?" I demanded, trying to sound like the voice of reason. "I think I have a right to know."

"I agree that you have a right to know about the baby, but why do the details matter? Jeffrey and she had a child, a son. He lived for only two days. It was the most painful period of Astrid's life. What good will it do to bring it all back again?

"She's my wife; I need to know."

"You married her contingent on your approval of her former life?" demanded my mother-in-law.

"No, of course not," I replied as I gently set the cat down.

"Then what is different now?"

"I thought we were so close, we were almost one," I said softly. "Now, I find out that I don't even know this woman."

"You do know her," said Inga. "You know how she is now."

"And you don't think that a husband has a right to know everything about his wife's past?"

"No," said Inga, "I do not."

"I wonder if Gus shared your feelings," I mused.

"I know that he did," she declared self-righteously. "There were some things in my past that I preferred to forget; that was acceptable to him."

"Because he never found out?" I asked.

"No," said Inga. "I told him that there was something in my past before we were married. He chose not to know the details."

"But I wasn't given the right to choose. You can hardly equate some small thing that you chose not to share with something as serious as a previous marriage that resulted in a child."

"It was equally important," protested Inga.

"You were never married before you met Gus," I protested.

Inga said nothing, but the way she quickly looked away answered adamantly that I was wrong.

"Gus was your second husband?" I asked. "Astrid never mentioned that you were married more than once.

Inga turned to me with a look in her eyes that could only be described as desperation. "Astrid does not know; you must not say anything to her; she will only be confused by it."

I silently stared at her for several moments, not able to find the right words. "Astrid doesn't know?" I replied, barely above a whisper.

Inga shook her head. "Gus and I decided before she was born that there was no reason to tell her. I do not know what possessed me to tell you."

"I don't know how you could have lied to Astrid for her entire life."

"I did not lie," protested Inga. "I made an omission. It was something that had no bearing on her life, and you must promise me that you will not tell her what you have learned."

"Did you have other children?"

"No," said Inga. "Astrid is the only child I have ever had."

"So now you hope to put a secret between Astrid and me," I accused. "Is it your hope that if I'm keeping something from my wife, I will let the matter of the baby drop?"

"No," said Inga. "I never intended for you to find out about my past. You caught me completely off-guard."

"I find that hard to believe, Inga. You are the most controlled human being I have ever known."

"You do not know me as well as you think," she replied, the slightest hint of a smile turning up the corners of her mouth.

"I still have to know about the baby," I said.

"But you will not tell Astrid about me!" she ordered. "You must promise!"

"I will give you some time to tell her yourself, but no, I will not promise to keep something like that from my wife. I think what she did was wrong, but I won't behave the same way. If you don't tell her, eventually I will."

"All right," said Inga, "but you will allow me some time?"

"Yes," I said, "but I won't wait forever. I don't believe in keeping secrets from my wife and before today, I thought she felt the same way."

"She does feel the same way," said Inga. "I know how much your marriage means to her."

"Then why didn't she trust me enough to tell me about the baby?"

"The two of you were so happy. After she and Jeffrey divorced, she told me that she would never again allow herself to be tied to one person. She vowed that she would not remarry. When she met you, I was wary but when I saw the two of you together, I became convinced that your marrying was right for my daughter. After the baby died, she thought that she would never again have happiness in her life. When the two of you were together, and life was more wonderful for her than she ever dreamed that it could be, she did not want to bring back that awful time. It was a mistake, yes, but I can understand her motives."

"Tell me about the baby," I insisted.

"There is not much to tell."

"Tell me what there is."

"Jeffrey and Astrid were wrong for each other from the day they met," said my mother-in-law, sitting stiffly in one of the chairs in her living room.

I sat down on the couch and the cat jumped up beside me. He settled happily in my lap and began to purr loudly. "Why do you say that?"

"You have seen Jeffrey; he is very nice looking. Astrid liked him, but I never saw anything in her that would indicate to me that she was in love. At the time, many of her friends were marrying. She had finished college and begun to work, but personally, she was at loose ends. Jeffrey had recently passed the bar, he had a job and was looking for a wife. They were two nice people who were wrong for each other, but they decided to get married.

"Gus did not like Jeffrey; he said Jeffrey acted like he thought he was too good for us, but he was equally adamant that marrying him was Astrid's decision to make, and we should not interfere. Perhaps I was wrong not to confront Astrid, but I chose to abide by Gus's wishes and we gave them a big, formal wedding."

"They were married for almost five years," I said. "Surely, it wasn't all bad."

"At first, they seemed happy enough," agreed Inga, "but steadily, there were increasing signs of trouble. Jeffrey was very hurt that Astrid insisted on retaining her maiden name, and he wanted her to stay at home, while she insisted on working. I am not saying this as a criticism of him; some men are just that way, but Jeffrey is a dominant individual. He wanted to be the boss in his home and in his marriage, and you and I well know that our Astrid has a mind of her own."

"One of the things I've always loved most about her," I said.

"One of the reasons I thought you were right for her," agreed Inga. "Jeffrey was most anxious to start a family, but Astrid did not feel ready for motherhood. This was a major bone of contention between them. After three years of marriage, Astrid decided that they did not want the same things, and she asked Jeffrey for a divorce. He was crushed; he said that if it was his fault, he would change. They decided to try a marriage counselor. I suppose that some of those people are qualified, but this person was no help at all. She said that marriage was a series of compromises, and suggested that having a baby might cement the relationship. Jeffrey pushed and Astrid felt that maybe she was not being fair, so reluctantly, she agreed.

"It took almost a year before she got pregnant, and they were fairly happy during that time. Jeffrey could be very charming when he was getting his way. Astrid had an uneventful pregnancy, but the delivery was another story. She very nearly died, and the baby had some serious medical problems. They could not save him."

"My God," I said with a sigh.

"Astrid was devastated," said Inga. "Jeffrey took it very hard as well. Some couples would have pulled together, but their relationship was not built on a solid foundation. In their case, it opened a gulf between them that they could not close again. Jeffrey was so consumed with his own sense of loss that he was powerless to help Astrid. They were like two wounded animals who would let no one near them. Astrid did not want to return home with Jeffrey, and he was so defeated that he agreed to a quick, amicable divorce. Gus and I brought Astrid home with us until she had recovered physically, and when she expressed an interest in working in New York, we urged her to go. We thought that maybe the healing that had not happened would take place more quickly if she was in new surroundings."

I put the cat onto the sofa and stood. I paced around the living room silently, trying to take in all I had just heard. It was a lot to handle. "What was the baby's name?" I finally asked.

My mother-in-law looked through me with those cold eyes. "That is not something you need to know," she replied.

I walked silently toward the door.

"Where are you going?" demanded Inga.

"That is not something you need to know," I said as coldly as I could manage. The effect was not lost on her.

"You must wait for Astrid," she said. "The two of you need to talk."

I said nothing and opened the front door.

"The baby's name was Peter," said my mother-in-law defeatedly.

I closed the door and resumed my place on the sofa. Wordlessly, Inga and I sat in that room and waited for Astrid.

I can't honestly tell you if it was a long or short time later that my wife finally arrived. She let herself in with her own key and found us posed in our places.

"What's up?" she asked expectantly, kissing my cheek in greeting. I did not move.

"I have a bridge game tonight," said Inga. "I am going to leave now, so you two will have some privacy."

Both of us listened to her moving around in the kitchen. We heard the back door shut, the sound of a car starting and we were alone.

Astrid bent to pet the cat and he jumped back into my lap. "What went on here with you two?" she asked.

"Inga was telling me about your baby," I said softly.

The color drained from Astrid's face. "She had no right!"

"Don't blame your mother," I said coldly. "I already knew about it; I forced her to fill in the blanks."

"I was going to tell you," said my wife.

"When?" I asked. "You've known me for four years."

"I've tried to tell you several times," said Astrid. "It never seemed like the right time, or we were interrupted."

"If you had wanted me to know, you would have found the time and the way," I said. "I've spent the last three years of my life married to a stranger."

"How long have you known?" asked Astrid. "Why didn't you come to me?"

"Jeffrey mentioned it at lunch today, after you left," I said. "Don't give me that look; he didn't do it to start trouble. He honestly thought I knew."

"I'm sorry," said Astrid.

"That's too little too late," I said, rising from the sofa.

"Let's talk about it," said Astrid.

"I don't feel like talking now. I have to get out of here; I'm suffocating."

"Let's go home," suggested Astrid.

I shook my head. "I need to be alone." Then, I walked out the front door and down the street without looking back.

I didn't know where I was going, but when I passed the health club, I turned around and went in. I was hurt and angry and felt that I would be more rational after a workout, but I didn't have my gym bag. Luckily, the pro shop was open, so I was able to pick up a pair of trunks and a shirt. I happened to be wearing my running shoes. The club was not too busy at that hour and I planned to see if the trainers would squeeze me in for a session on the machines, but if not, I would take a swim or just sit in the whirlpool. When I came out of the shop, I bumped into Jerry Fallow.

"Mitch, nice to see you," he said. "We really miss you around the office."

"Two more weeks," I said, rolling my eyes.

"How about a little tennis?" he asked.

"I didn't reserve a court," I said, "and I don't have my racket with me."

"I did," he winked "and I'm sure you could borrow a racket; the club keeps some around for their tennis classes."

I wasn't really in the mood for Jerry, but the tennis part didn't sound like a bad way to work off my frustrations. "Aren't you playing with anyone?"

"Jim Deckle is supposed to meet me in fifteen minutes, but I'm sure he'll understand," said Jerry. "Just between us, I hate to play tennis with him."

"He isn't any good?" I asked.

"He's finally catching on to racquetball," said Jerry, "but he thinks he knows how to play tennis because he's watched it on television. He's not exactly Ivan Lendl."

I smiled. "He does try hard."

"That doesn't make up for the fact that he's an asshole," said Jerry. "Did you know he plays tennis with a racquetball racket? Says he's used to that one and doesn't see the point in switching."

I knew that Deckle would be furious, but in the mood I was in, I didn't care. "If you're sure it won't be a problem with Jim, I'd like to play," I said.

"Great," replied Jerry.

We got off easy; Linda found a racket for me to use in my exact grip size, and she promised she would handle Deckle for us, so we headed off to the locker room together.

"Mitch," said Jerry, swigging Gatorade from the bottle as we took a short break between sets, "do you think Bob's death was a little suspicious?"

I was surprised by the question. "It sounds like it was an accident. Why? Have you heard something different?"

"No, not really," said Jerry, wiping the back of his neck with a towel. "Deckle seems to think there's something sinister there, although I'm not sure why."

"It's too bad there wasn't anyone Bob knew on the dive with him. Then, we might get a better idea of what happened," I said.

Jerry looked at me strangely. "He knew his diving partner for years; the guy is a vice president at Businetex."

My surprise was evident. "Bobbie never mentioned that."

"I'm not sure she knew about it," said Jerry. "There was an account of the accident in *The New York Times* that quoted Bob's partner on the dive, and the name was familiar. I stopped by his office, and it was the same person."

"It does seem odd that Bob's wife didn't know," I mused.

"Not that odd," said Jerry, walking to his side of the court. "The guy's name is Walter Nelson. Walt and Bob worked together about ten years ago, when Bob was working on faxes, but they hadn't seen each other in years. Walt said they were both surprised to see each other when they boarded the boat that morning; neither one knew the other was in Cancun, let alone booked on the same diving charter."

I whizzed an ace past Jerry. "Had they known each other well?"

"Your serve is brutal tonight," said Jerry. "They shared an office for a few months, but Walt was promoted and left the department. He's been riding a rocket; rumor has it that he's George's right hand man."

"George Stanton, the CEO of Businetex?" I asked.

"One and the same," said Jerry as we switched sides between games.

"Did you talk to Walt about what happened?" I asked. I was creaming him.

"You must have been practicing since the last time we played," said Jerry, as I put another game under my belt. "I spoke to him; he said that they were exploring a sunken ship, and Bob just vanished. Walt looked for him for a while, but when he realized it was taking a long time, he went for help. Walt only learned to dive recently, and it sounds like he didn't know what to do on his own. The people in charge of the charter immediately followed Walt back to where he had last seen Bob. They found him inside the wreck, and he was out of air. His equipment was intact, it was functioning; the air tanks were just empty."

"Doesn't sound like anything sinister there."

"I didn't think so, but you know how Deckle is. He even checks the men's room for bugs and cameras before he'll use it."

"He's a little strange," I agreed, as we walked toward the locker room.

"Would you like to play again sometime?" asked Jerry.

"After I'm done with this jury thing."

"I'm looking forward to that too," agreed Jerry.

We decided to leave separately, in case Deckle was waiting around. We both knew he would be easier to live with if he didn't know the real reason Jerry had canceled their tennis date.

I took my time showering and changing. When I came out of the locker room about twenty minutes later, I was surprised to find Astrid sitting in the lobby, waiting for me.

"Linda told me you were here," she said. "Please come home with me and let me apologize."

"All right," I said, not wanting to take it up in the lobby of the health club.

We walked out to the car together. "Do you want to drive?" she asked, offering me the keys to Sven. It was her idea of a peace offering, but I wasn't ready to let her off the hook.

"Not particularly," I replied.

She shrugged and got behind the wheel. We drove in silence until we were almost home. "I wish you'd talk to me," she said.

"What do you want me to say?"

"I don't care; anything."

"Sven is a bomb," I replied.

She smiled slightly. "I even prefer that to your silence."

"The time for talk was four years ago, after we started dating; three years ago, before we got married."

"You're right," she agreed, pulling into our garage. "I have no defense; I screwed up, and I'm asking you to forgive me."

"Why didn't you tell me?" I asked as I put my key into the door of the house. "I feel betrayed, like everyone else knew something that I should have known, and they were laughing behind my back."

"Not everyone knew, and certainly, no one was laughing," said Astrid. "Will you let me tell you about it now?"

"Yes, I'm willing to listen."

"Good," said Astrid, nodding.

She kicked off her shoes and led the way into the living room. She sat on the loveseat with her long legs curled beneath her, and I sat on the couch.

"Okay," I said. "Tell me about your marriage to Jeffrey."

"I never should have married him," she began. "I knew that even as I was walking down the aisle."

"Why not?" I asked.

"Because I didn't love him. I liked him, I thought he was handsome, but I never loved him. I wasn't sure exactly what love felt like, having never experienced it at that time, but I was sure that it wasn't what I felt for Jeffrey. I thought I might learn to love him, but over the course of our marriage, I came to dislike him."

"He's a very good-looking man; were other women a problem?"

Astrid smiled slightly. "No. One thing I have to give Jeffrey credit for is that he was always a one-woman man. When I was with him, he always behaved as if I was the only woman in the room. That's part of his charm."

"Then what did go wrong between you?"

"He always had to be in control. He believed that he was entitled to make all decisions that concerned the two of us, without consulting me. I felt like I was losing myself and turning into an extension of him."

"So why didn't you end it?" I asked.

"I tried. I told Jeffrey that it wasn't working out and that I wanted a divorce. He knew this marriage counselor from his matrimonial work, and he insisted that we hadn't given the marriage a fair chance, because we hadn't tried counseling. He has always pushed counseling to all his clients, so at least his motives seemed honest.

"The marriage counselor told him that he had to allow me more independence, which he agreed to try, and she told me that I was being unfair by refusing to start a family. She insisted that sometimes, in a troubled relationship, the parents' love for a child is what cements the bond."

"And you bought that crock?" I asked incredulously.

"I thought that maybe I'd been unfair to Jeffrey. He'd wanted children for some time, and I wasn't ready. I thought that maybe if we had a child and I loved that baby, I would learn to love it's father. Obviously, that was pretty stupid."

"So you got pregnant?" I asked.

"I agreed to try, but it didn't happen right away," continued Astrid. "Jeffrey was trying so hard to make things work that I actually thought there was hope for us. He consulted me before making decisions, he agreed that it was all right for me to keep on working, even after we had a family, and he seemed to have gotten over his anger that I didn't take his name. He was so happy when I finally got pregnant; he promised that he was going to be the world's best husband and father."

"How long did that last?" I asked.

"All through my pregnancy. He went to natural childbirth classes and read all sorts of books about parenting; if I even mentioned that I was in the mood for something, he would move heaven and earth to get it."

"It must have been a happy time for you," I said.

"It should have been," agreed Astrid, "but from the very early stages of my pregnancy, I had a sense that something was wrong."

"Were you sick?"

"No, I felt great. I never had morning sickness, and everything went along exactly as my doctor expected. He wouldn't even do an ultrasound, because there was a strong heartbeat, and I was young and healthy. He didn't believe in routinely performing extensive prenatal tests when there was no reason to suspect a problem.

"When I entered the later stages of my pregnancy, I was sure something was wrong. The baby almost never moved. I have heard all these stories about how a woman can feel life inside her; the only sensation I felt when it seemed that the baby might have moved was pressure in one spot, like a gas pain. My doctor reassured me that every pregnancy was different, and that some babies were more active than others. He said that what probably was happening was that my baby had adopted waking and sleep cycles that were the opposite of mine, and I was sleeping through the periods of activity.

"And no one took your concerns seriously?" I asked.

"In all fairness to Jeffrey, I must say that he did. The doctor dismissed my fears as the nerves of a first-time mother, but Jeffrey went to see him and expressed concerns too. He insisted that if I felt strongly that something was wrong, he thought it should at least be checked out. The doctor claimed that there was nothing to be checked and advised him to give me a lot of reassurance, which he really tried to do."

"When did you find out that your fears were justified?"

"Not until I delivered," said Astrid. "I woke up in the middle of the night and the bed was soaked, and I don't mean a little damp; Jeffrey and I were drenched. I woke him and he called the doctor. I was having no pains, and the doctor didn't believe that my water could have broken, because I was almost a month early, and I hadn't been at all dilated two days earlier. He said I must have wet the bed."

"I suppose that was possible," I said.

"I didn't think so," said Astrid, "because what woke me was that my bladder was achingly full, and I had control. Anyway, Jeffrey reassured me that everything was fine, insisted on changing the bed himself, and told me that the doctor said he would see me the following afternoon, unless something changed before then.

"When I got to his office, he still wasn't sure that my water had broken, and I still wasn't dilated, but the size of my stomach was visibly smaller, so he told me to go into the hospital for some tests."

"What happened?"

"I don't remember everything that happened, but after they examined me, they decided to induce labor. I'm still not sure if they knew there was a problem with the baby then. After they gave me some medication, I started having contractions but I still was not dilated very much. I was in labor for eighteen hours, and they were preparing me for a Cesarean when the baby finally came.

"He sort of cried when he was born, but it wasn't a normal sound, and they whisked him quickly away without letting me see him. I kept asking what was wrong, and they would only tell me that the doctors had to check him over, and then, they would know more."

"What was wrong?" I asked softly.

Astrid's face crumpled, and she went into the kitchen, returning several minutes later with a box of Kleenex. She wiped her eyes, blew her nose, and I should have told her that it was enough, but I was so hurt that she had not told me, until I found out on my own, that I couldn't bring myself to do what would have been the compassionate and mature thing.

"Jeffrey saw him when he was born and said he was very blue. He only weighed a little over four pounds and was obviously premature; his lungs were not fully developed."

"They can usually treat that," I said.

"Yes," said Astrid, "but he was also born without functioning kidneys, and his heart had a defect that would have needed correction, had he lived."

I went to her and took her in my arms, and she buried her head in my shoulder for a few minutes before going on.

"I don't know everything that happened after he was born," continued my wife. "Because my water broke so long before the birth, the amniotic sac was open and an infection developed. Almost immediately after the delivery, I spiked a fever and was deathly ill for three days.

I was in and out of consciousness, and when I finally came out of it, my baby had died.

"Peter," I said.

Astrid looked surprised that I knew his name. "Jeffrey wanted to name him Jeffrey Junior, but I wouldn't have it. I insisted that my child would have an identity of his own. We compromised and named him after Jeffrey's father and mine. Peter Gustav.

"They didn't want me to go to the funeral; I had been so sick that they advised against my leaving the hospital, but I insisted on being there. That was the only chance I ever had to see my child. Right before Peter died, they had allowed Jeffrey to hold him. My mother says that when I was delirious with the fever, I kept asking for my baby, saying I wanted to hold him. I don't remember any of that and they never brought him to me. Mom says that I was too weak or she would have insisted on it.

"At the funeral home, I asked if I might hold him for just a minute, but the undertaker said that he couldn't let me, that it was against the law. I later found out that wasn't true; Jeffrey had ordered him not to allow it. I believe that he truly thought that was best for me, but he took away the only chance I might have had to touch my child, and I could never forgive him. I still can't."

"I'm sorry," I said.

Astrid wiped her eyes again. "I'm not saying that what I did was right, but now maybe you can understand why I didn't tell you; it isn't easy for me to even think about what happened."

"You should have told me long ago," I said.

"Would it have made a difference in the way you feel about me?" she asked.

"No, of course not."

"You're right, of course," she said. "I should have told you when we briefly discussed having children, before we were married."

"You said that you wanted to someday, but that you didn't think you'd be ready for a while; was that a lie?"

"No," said my wife. "I knew the first time we met that I wanted to have your children, and I'm more sure than ever about that now, but I'd be lying if I said I wasn't afraid."

"Did they ever tell you why your baby was born the way he was?" I asked.

"They didn't know. They seemed surprised that I didn't miscarry. My doctor also admitted that at least some of the problems would have shown up, had I been given more extensive prenatal tests, but all the doctors I've spoken to since agree that under the circumstances, they would have followed the same course. They told us that there was no reason to believe that we couldn't have a healthy child if we tried again."

"Why did your marriage end, Astrid?"

"I still believe that Jeffrey is basically a decent man, but we were never right for each other. After Peter died, we were both in such pain that neither of us could make room for the other. Although he denied it, I always felt that he blamed me."

"For what?"

Astrid shrugged. "For creating a child that wasn't perfect; I think that even though he never said so, he thought that I was somehow at fault."

"But you weren't. If anything, you tried to do something to prevent it, and they dismissed your concerns."

"That's true," she agreed, "but I'll tell you something that I've never told another living soul. I do blame myself."

"Why?"

"Because I didn't want my baby the way I should have," she said. "We had a child for the wrong reason, to try to save a marriage that had no business being saved, and although I loved Peter with all my soul while I was carrying him, and every day since, I didn't want him the way I should have. I didn't really want a baby, and maybe losing him the way we did was my punishment."

I put my arms around her. "That's crazy," I said, kissing the top of her head. "It was no one's fault, especially not yours."

She looked up at me, her eyes brimming with tears. "Will you forgive me for not telling you?"

"I already have," I said. "I won't say that I'm not hurt; it still smarts that you didn't trust me enough to confide in me, but I can only imagine the hell that you went through, and I'd never want to be responsible for your suffering more over it."

"I didn't tell you when I should have," said Astrid, "and the longer I waited, the harder it became."

"There's something I know that I don't think you do," I said.

"What is it?" she asked.

"I'm not sure I should tell you; you'll probably be upset, but I think there have been enough secrets."

"I want to know."

"Jeffrey's wife is pregnant," I said.

"Good," she said nodding.

"That's not the reaction I expected."

"If he can put it behind him, maybe I can too. I've been thinking lately that you and I should start a family. As soon as I decide that I'm ready, I get so scared that I can't bring myself to actually go through with it. Maybe we shouldn't analyze it too much and just do it."

"I wouldn't want to push you into anything," I said.

"I know. That's one of the many things I love about you. Do you still love me?"

"I don't know what you could do to make me stop loving you," I said, "but I know that it would have to be a lot more than this." She fell into my arms and I began to feel hopeful that everything would be all right.

Later, lying in bed, Astrid kept trying to get closer and closer to me. "I love you so much," she whispered in my ear.

"I love you too," I replied, kissing her forehead.

"Make love to me," she whispered. "I want us to make a baby."

"Are you sure?"

She nodded.

I took her in my arms and kissed her. Her breathing quickened and she stroked my chest, which always got me going but this time, it wasn't working. When she reached down to guide me into her, it became apparent that it wasn't happening for me.

"I'm sorry," I said, jumping from the bed, pulling on my pajama bottoms and bolting down the stairs. I suppose it wasn't the first case in history of someone being betrayed by a penis, but it was the first time that mine had let me down.

Astrid was right on my heels. "Mitch," she said softly, putting her hand on my shoulder, "it isn't your fault; it's mine."

"You aren't the one who couldn't perform," I said.

"I tried to push it before you were ready," she said. "I did the same thing to you that Jeffrey did to me. I'm ashamed of myself."

"I do love you," I said.

"And you do forgive me?"

"Yes," I said. "I'll do whatever it takes to make it better for you. I want you to finally heal; it's gone on longer than it should have."

"I've known since I met you that you're the most wonderful man alive, but it's nice to have it proven once in a while," she said.

"Why don't you go back to bed? It's late."

"You coming?" she asked.

"I don't think I can sleep yet."

"If you're not sleepy, there's something else I want to tell you."

"More secrets?"

"No," said Astrid. "It was just something that happened that I didn't share, and now I would like to."

"All right," I said.

And then, she related what had happened at the McDonalds in Hancock and why it upset her so.

Astrid was drying her hands in the ladies room when a woman came in with two children, a little girl about three or so and an infant.

"Hurry, Mommy!" the little girl urged.

"The child was dressed in a romper that buttoned at the shoulders and the woman was struggling to unfasten it with one hand while she held her squirming baby with the other. The little girl was holding herself and bouncing," related Astrid.

"Hold still, Dani!" the woman ordered. "I'm trying to help you."

"Mommy, my pee-pee is coming out!" wailed the child.

Astrid felt sorry for them. "Would you like me to hold the baby while you help your daughter?" she offered.

"You wouldn't mind?" asked the woman skeptically.

"Not at all," said Astrid, taking the baby.

The infant looked at her uncertainly at first, but when she smiled and said hello, he gave her a big smile and settled down.

"He had blond hair so fine he looked almost bald, and big blue eyes; he was very cute. I amused him by playing peek-a-boo in the mirror."

"You finish going while I get your brother," the woman was telling her daughter.

"I need you, Mommy," sobbed the little girl. "My pants are wet!"

"I can hold him until you finish," Astrid offered.

"I couldn't ask you to do that," protested the woman. "It may take me a while; I have to go too."

"It's okay," Astrid reassured her. "I was finished."

"Mommy!" called the little girl.

"Thank you," said the woman, going back into the stall. "It's okay, Dani; it's just a little damp. We can dry you off with paper and it will be fine."

Astrid was wearing a pair of hoop earrings that had little teddy bear charms dangling from them, and their shininess attracted the baby. He reached for them and touched her face. Astrid laughed and the baby laughed. He touched her nose and she touched his. They were happily amusing each other.

The woman came out of the stall, led her daughter to the sink where they washed their hands, and took the baby back from Astrid. "I hope he wasn't any trouble," she said.

"He was an angel," said Astrid. "How old is he?"

"Six months," replied the woman, taking her daughter's hand. "Thank you so much for your help."

As they were leaving, really as an afterthought, Astrid asked, "What's his name?"

"Peter," called out the woman as she exited the ladies room.

"I just fell apart," recounted Astrid. "I don't even know why I reacted the way I did. I probably shouldn't have offered to take her child, and she never should have given him over to a stranger, but that's what happened."

"And you couldn't help but think that you should have had a little boy named Peter, and for the second time, someone had taken one from you," I finished for her.

"Yes," she said softly.

I put my arms around her and held her against me. "It won't happen again; you will not have another child taken from you."

"You can't promise that."

"I have no basis for saying so," I said, "but I know that it won't happen; I feel it in my gut, and I am sure."

"I will find a way to make this up to you," she promised. "You have to forgive me."

"I told you, I already have," I replied.

"But I can feel that you're still resentful," she insisted. "I know it's a stretch but haven't you ever put off doing something that was really important, just because you never found the right time?"

"I'm sure I have," I agreed. "I just can't think of anything at the moment."

"I'm glad to hear that," said Astrid, "because I was worried that you never took care of that letter."

"What letter?" I asked, wrinkling my brow, trying to remember.

"Oh, Mitch!" said Astrid in exasperation. "The letter from Businetex, the one you promised to reply to weeks ago.

"Look, it's not the end of the world," I said. "I put it in my briefcase; I'm sure it's still there."

"It had a deadline," Astrid reminded me. "Do you remember when that was?"

"Not off the top of my head," I admitted.

I went into the study and rummaged through my briefcase. The envelope had been pushed to the bottom and was crumpled but still intact. "It's here," I replied, trying to smooth out the wrinkles with the side of my hand.

"When do you have to let them know?" asked Astrid, her brows knit in a frown.

She looked over my shoulder as I searched for the date. "Day after tomorrow," I said. "See, no harm done."

"No, not if you attend to it immediately, and we make sure that it arrives in their offices before the close of business on the day after tomorrow. Will you let me take care of it?"

"I still don't think this is any big deal, but if it means that much to you, sure, go ahead," I agreed.

"I'll type the letter on the computer and you can sign it. I'll mail it tomorrow."

"I can put it in the mail at the Hall of Justice," I offered.

"No, I'll take care of it," she said.

"You don't trust me to mail it," I accused.

"No, if you say you'll do it, I believe you," replied Astrid. "I'll just feel better if I send it special delivery with a return receipt. That way, we'll know that they've received it and we can put it out of our minds."

I didn't understand why this letter was so important to her, but obviously, it was. Had she not insisted that I decline, I have to admit that I probably would have just ignored it. "Whatever you want to do is fine with me," I agreed as I scribbled my name at the bottom of the reply she had printed.

"I'll take care of it," promised Astrid.

***

The next afternoon, when I called and asked Astrid about meeting me for lunch, she declined.

"My stomach has been off all day," she protested. "I'm just going to sip a Coke at my desk."

"Was it too off for you to mail that letter?" I asked, figuring that if she had put that off, I would know that she was really sick, and I would insist that she see the doctor immediately.

"I took care of it first thing this morning," she assured me.

I wasn't sure if she was still upset about the previous night, angry at me about having forgotten the letter, or if her stomach was really just off, but I told her that I would see her later.

"Mom wanted us to have dinner with her tonight; I told her that my stomach wasn't up to it, and she volunteered to make chicken soup. What do you think?" she asked.

"Do you want to?"

"Saves us from having to cook."

"Sure, why not?" I replied.

It was obvious from the empty teacups on the coffee table that Astrid had arrived at her mother's quite a while before I did. When Astrid opened the door for me, the cat went right between my legs and almost tripped me. I picked him up and walked into the living room. Today, instead of tensing, he perched contentedly in my arms and was purring so loudly, he sounded like a power saw.

"That cat is an excellent judge of character," said Inga as I kissed my wife in greeting. Apparently, she was pleased by Astrid's account of my behavior since she had last seen me.

"He almost maimed me today," I protested but I too was pleased; that's as close as Inga comes to giving a compliment.

"Hard day?" asked Astrid.

"You cannot imagine some of the things people do to each other," I replied, rolling my eyes. Grand Jury procedures are secret, and that was as explicit as I could get. "Are you feeling better?"

"I'm fine now," replied Astrid. "When you called, I was green, but I was so hungry when I got here that Mom made me a snack. I must have picked up a bug; it goes away but it keeps coming back."

"Maybe you should see the doctor," suggested Inga.

"If I don't get rid of it soon, I will," promised Astrid.

Inga went into the kitchen to check on dinner, and Astrid and I were alone. "I wanted to ask you about something I heard at the health club last night," I said.

"What?"

"I played some tennis with Jerry Fallow. He mentioned that Bob's diving partner, when he had the accident, was a vice president at Businetex who he'd known for many years. Did Bobbie ever mention anything about that to you?"

"No," said Astrid. "I doubt that she knows. How did Jerry find out?"

"Bob's diving partner was mentioned in an account of the accident in *The New York Times*. Jerry recognized the name and checked it out. It was the same Walter Nelson."

"That name sounds so familiar. Wasn't that the name of the vice president who gave Artie that award last year?"

"I don't remember," I admitted. "It may have been Walter Nelson."

"Is he a man in his early fifties, short, heavy and bald?" asked Inga, who was coming back into the room.

"He looks like Humpty Dumpty," I said, recalling how one of my co-workers had described him to me that way before the only time we met, briefly shaking hands at a reception. "Why?"

"I met a man by that name a few weeks ago, at a wake," she said. "He was quite charming."

"Did he work for Businetex?" asked Astrid.

"I did not ask," said Inga, "but he could have. The couple that died both did."

"Who were they?" I asked.

"They did volunteer work at the hospital with me. Andrew and Marianne Cody; did you know them?"

"The names aren't familiar. What happened to them?"

"It was very sad," said Inga. "They had a cottage on Coneseus lake that they were converting to a year round home. While they were renovating it, some solvent they were using on the floor caught fire, and the whole place went up in flames; they were trapped inside."

"What did they do at Businetex?" asked Astrid.

"They both had been there a long time," said Inga. "He was a patent attorney, and I am not sure what she did; I know she was a supervisor to a number of people, because they were all at the wake."

"That's odd," said Astrid. "We know of four people who recently died, and all of them knew the same man. What does that suggest to you?"

"That he goes to a lot of funerals?" I asked facetiously.

"It could be a coincidence," said Astrid, "but it certainly is food for thought. I wonder if there is a connection."

"That," said Inga, "is not something you need to know."

Chapter 6
Jerry

J erry Fallow had a nickname around Businetex. People didn't use it to his face but everyone knew who the "rubber stapler" was. As it was explained to me, a rubber stapler looks enough like the real thing to fool people but it does absolutely nothing. If you try to get it to do what's it's supposed to, you're the one who looks foolish. The name was given to him before I joined Businetex, but I had to admit, it was incredibly appropriate.

I doubt that anyone actually would have had the nerve to use Jerry's nickname to his face, but had that happened, it might not have made any difference. Jerry was one of those people who were often described with the phrase "the lights are on but nobody's home." Actually, in Jerry's case, often, it was more like a night light. He did not come across as a bright guy.

Jerry had only been with Businetex for about six months when I started working there, and it didn't take me long to size up his abilities.

"What's the story with Jerry Fallow?" I asked Artie one evening as we walked toward our court for one of our tennis games.

"He was a gift from a former disgruntled vice president," explained Artie. "He got wind that his removal and replacement were in the air. Before they had time to give him his walking papers, he decided to hire someone, Jerry, to coordinate all the departments of his division. In the process, he managed to alienate several of the better managers, who were well-qualified and eligible for the position. His determination to advertise and fill the job from outside the company, through a headhunter, led to three of them accepting outside jobs and leaving Businetex."

"What's Jerry's background?" I asked as we tightened the laces on our tennis shoes.

"Jerry had a thirty year undistinguished career with another company before accepting the offer at Businetex. He was a supervisor for an engineering group at large mid-Atlantic corporation. In one of those rare strokes of luck that some people have a knack for encountering, he learned of the Businetex job just as his company was offering a rather lucrative early retirement offer. He was able to qualify for a full pension and benefits, while accepting a six figure salary in his new position,"

"We should be so lucky!" I said.

"Amen," nodded Artie. "The irony of the situation was that any one of the managers who already worked for Businetex would have happily accepted Jerry's job for twenty-five thousand dollars less, and probably would have been much better at what he was doing. The scuttlebutt in his division is that his former company has probably declared an annual holiday in honor of our former vice president, for ridding them of an incompetent nuisance."

"If he's so bad, why haven't they dumped him?" I wondered.

"Actually, the higher-ups at Businetex have a reasonably high opinion of Jerry. They don't have to deal with him day to day. Also, because he rarely does anything, it isn't often that he presents them with problems, which is exactly the way they like things."

"I find it hard to believe that someone as high up as he is can always skirt trouble," I protested between games.

"Every once is a while, he gets grazed by a bullet," said Artie, whizzing his racket through the air above his head, "but not often, and when he does, he can usually find someone to bail him out."

I found that out for myself when it looked as if the manual was going to be late, delaying the release of the J-6. The top floor got pretty excited and put pressure on Jerry. He, in turn, put the responsibility on Bob who, in turn, laid it on me. I took care of it, the word was passed on, Bob, Jerry and the higher-ups looked good, and the business Gods smiled on them once again. In most corporate tales, the people at the top only look as good as the people working under them actually are. Jerry was again blessed; most of the people working in the departments of his division were very good.

I have to say that when I returned to work after my Grand Jury service was over, I was certainly met with a warm welcome. Beth pounced on me with a big hug and kiss. The engineers and technicians who worked for me chipped in and bought a large welcome back cake from

Wegmans. They brought me coffee at my desk, and all of them wanted to know what they could do to help me get readjusted. I have never felt so appreciated.

Deckle was unexpectedly cordial as well. I thought that he would resent my return, but he seemed genuinely glad to see me.

"If you need my help, let me know," he announced cheerily.

Later that afternoon, I found out why everyone was so glad to see me. While I was gone, we had missed two deadlines on the new Mini-6 ink jet printer that was to be part of Gulliver, and the top brass were leaning on Jerry, who in turn had been pressuring Deckle, who in turn had issued even more memos, and had scheduled a number of extra meetings.

"Why didn't you let me know that you were in a bind?" I asked Deckle.

"I knew there wasn't anything you could do," he said defensively. "The problem is that the people who were supposed to be working for me weren't doing their jobs. I had everything under control but they didn't."

"Did you tell them specifically what each one needed to accomplish, and the time limit for achieving that goal?" I asked.

"Well, not exactly," said Jim. "They're professionals; they're supposed to take some initiative. They knew what the deadline was; they didn't want to make it so that I would look bad."

I had only been at work for two hours and already, I was exhausted. "That's not managing, Jim," I said. "The people who are working for you are not there to make you look good or bad; you have to direct them to accomplish what you need done. If they run into obstacles, you have to be the one who can find the way around them. There are some very talented people working in this division, but without some sense of direction, all you have is confusion."

"They don't like me because I'm tougher on them than you are," protested Jim defensively. "They want to make sure that they don't have to work for me permanently. Now that you're back, they'll try extra hard to make you look good, so that I look like a jerk."

"That's so ridiculous, I won't even dignify it with an answer," I replied. "I have work to do."

By noon, I had discovered that three engineers, two of them software experts, were working on the same problem, a clogging of the printer's ink flow, a mechanical problem. Nobody was tackling the most serious fault, the fact that this printer was just plain slow, something most likely to be solved by software changes. I reassigned jobs and convinced Jerry that progress was being made.

I wasn't hungry at lunch time after all the cake in the morning, so I decided to work right through, but I did take a break to call Astrid. She hadn't been feeling great that morning, and although she didn't complain, I knew it had been an effort for her to get ready and out of the house.

"Don't worry about me," she reassured. "I think I'm just tired. If I can arrange to take a couple of days off just to rest, I'm sure I'll be fine."

I was so swamped that we hadn't been able to get away, even for a weekend, all summer, but we did make a point of trying to spend most of our free time relaxing together. The previous weekend, we had done nothing more strenuous than meeting Bobbie and the kids at Golden Phoenix for some Chinese food on Saturday evening.

"I don't think I can get away anytime soon, if that's what you had in mind," I said dubiously. "Things took a slide while I was gone."

"How bad is it?"

"Everyone was very glad to see me," I laughed.

I had just hung up the phone when Jerry stuck his head in the open door of the office. "Got a minute?" he asked.

"Sure," I replied.

He came in, pushed a chair next to my desk and settled himself in it. "Things have been overlooked while you were away," he said neutrally. "They're turning the heat up on me."

"I've got a line on it," I replied. "I've been looking over some of the work that was done; actually, quite a bit has been accomplished. It's more a matter that no one took the trouble to coordinate things."

"I knew I could count on you," said Jerry.

I had long since learned not to take any of his flattery seriously. "From what I've been told, morale has been pretty low around here."

"If Gulliver doesn't show some real progress, there have been hints that it could be scrapped. "The rumor mill has been using the word 'layoffs.'"

"Is there anything to that?"

"All I know is what I've heard through the rumor mill," he replied.

That was bull. At his level, I would have made a serious wager that he was privy to the thinking at the top, particularly where the idea of scrapping Gulliver was concerned. If he didn't want to tell me, at least he could have been honest.

"If people get nervous, they'll be more concerned about lining up other jobs than doing one that may hold no future," I said. "Boosting morale is important."

"In that area, I have some good news."

"Oh?"

"It's not definite yet, but Walt Nelson is working on arranging a little reward for the professionals who worked on J-6. I can't give you all the details, but I will tell you to keep Labor Day weekend free."

"What kind of reward?" I asked.

"It sounds like some kind of a trip," said Jerry. "The company wants to show it's appreciation to the people who got the J-6 out on time. It sounds like they may include all the groups in Business Machines that have made their deadlines in the last six months. I don't have any details."

I decided that I wouldn't get my hopes up until I heard something more definite. "Was there anything else you needed?"

"How about getting together for some tennis?" he asked. "You should have more time now that your jury thing is done."

"I certainly hope so," I said.

"Is Wednesday all right for you? Around seven?"

"Actually, Wednesday is good. Do you want me to reserve the court?"

"I'll take care of it. Deckle and I have a racquetball date tonight."

I had just gotten back to work when Deckle came in. "Was that Jerry?" he asked.

"Umm," I said, not bothering to look up.

"Did he say anything about me?"

I couldn't resist. "Yes, as a matter of fact, he did."

"I hope you told him that none of it was my fault!"

I looked up and smiled. Then, my face changed when I saw him. He was wearing a black suit, black tie and white shirt. He looked like an undertaker. "What's with the outfit?" I asked.

"I have to go to a funeral. What did you say to Jerry?"

"Nothing."

"What did he say about me?" persisted Deckle.

"He said that the two of you are playing racquetball tonight."

"Oh, that," sighed Deckle. "You scared me."

"Sorry, I couldn't resist. By the way, who died?"

"I don't think you know him. Guy by the name of Al Finnegan. He was a supervisor in Industrial Chemicals. We worked together on copier fluids for a few years."

Deckle was around my age, definitely no more than a couple of years older, but he had started at Businetex straight out of college, and it always seemed that he had been with the company forever.

I don't know what made me pursue it but nevertheless, I did. "What happened to him?"

"He was fixing his car and it slipped off the jack. He was home alone, and by the time his wife got back from the grocery store, he was beyond 911."

"There seems to be an epidemic of that going around," I mused.

"Cars slipping off jacks?"

"No. Businetex employees dying," I replied, thinking of what Inga had said a few weeks earlier.

"I'm glad that you said that," said Deckle excitedly. "We both know what everyone around here thinks about me, but I've noticed it too. Maybe we ought to send out a memo warning people to try to be more careful. I know that I'll certainly take it to heart."

Oh, great, I thought. Here I was, adding fuel to his paranoia.

"I don't think you have to worry, Jim. Unless you have permanent designs on my job, you're probably safe. Everyone I've heard of who's died has been a supervisor."

"Really?" said Deckle. "I wonder if that means something?"

I had said it tongue-in-cheek, but thinking about it, I wondered too. "It means that I should look both ways before crossing the street," I joked.

"I'll see you later, Mitch," he said.

"So you're on your way to *Finnegan's Wake*'" I teased, unable to resist.

"I'm not sure they're having a wake but yes, I'm on my way to his funeral," replied Deckle, completely devoid of a sense of humor.

I mentioned the conversation to Astrid that evening.

"I didn't want to mention it until I had something more concrete," she said, "but I've been asking around a little bit, and I've come across something odd. There have been a disproportionate number of deaths among Businetex employees in the past six months."

"Now you're starting to sound like Deckle," I responded. "Any company with twenty thousand employees is going to have a large number of deaths in an area this size. They are a major employer."

"That's true," she agreed, "but I've made a kind of informal list. Look at this."

She went to her briefcase and pulled out several sheets of paper. On them, she had sections for name, age, date of death, cause and prior known illnesses. There were seventeen entries on her list. Four had existing conditions that could have proven fatal, and three were over sixty-five, but the rest were between the ages of thirty-two and fifty-nine, in apparent good health. That left ten unexplained deaths out of a population of twenty thousand. Hardly an epidemic.

"But those are just the ones that we know about. Add Finnegan to the list and you have eleven. Statistically, it may not be significant but it doesn't feel right."

"Where did you come up with those names?" I asked.

"Mostly from people I work with, although one came from a client who mentioned that he was on his way to a funeral."

"How many of the people who died were supervisors?" I asked.

"I don't know; I never thought to ask."

"Listen to us," I said with a nervous laugh. "I think I've been spending too much time around Deckle, and you've been watching too much *Murder, She Wrote*."

"Would it bother you if I checked it out a little more?" she asked.

"As long as it doesn't become an obsession."

Astrid had arranged to take the next two days off, to give herself some time to rest, and to see if she could shake her persistent bug. Although she insisted that she was fine, I knew that she still wasn't herself. It was the middle of August, and even in Rochester, there were still dog days. The heat and humidity seemed to make her feel worse. It had gotten so bad one day that she had called the doctor and was trying some antacid he had suggested. It didn't seem to help very much.

"What are you doing up so early?" I asked when I stepped out of the shower the next morning and found her brushing her teeth.

"It's easy to get up when I don't have to go to work," she laughed.

"What are you going to do with yourself all day?"

"Just take it easy. I may meet Bobbie for lunch later."

"You just saw her," I pointed out.

"The kids were there; we hardly had a chance to talk. Do you have a problem with that?"

"Yes, I'm jealous," I said.

"That I'm having lunch with her?"

"That she's having lunch with you and I can't," I replied, kissing her as I went out the door.

Astrid was anxiously awaiting my return that evening. "The list has grown to forty-six," she announced when I was barely in the door.

"What list?" I asked. My day had not been easy.

"The list of people who have died who worked for Businetex. I didn't count retirees; do you think I should have?"

"That's what you wasted your day off doing?" I asked incredulously.

"I happened to mention it to Bobbie while we were having lunch. I guess we got a little caught up in it. She knew of two people, other than Bob and then, she had this great idea. We started calling funeral homes."

"You've got to be kidding!"

"I thought it was a stroke of genius. Some of them wouldn't talk to us at all, but others were very helpful."

"I'm surprised they didn't send some men with nets to get the two of you," I said, pouring myself a glass of iced tea.

"We told them that we were reporters doing a story," said Astrid. "You'd be surprised how cooperative people can be when you seem concerned that you're spelling their names right."

"You need to go back to work, and Bobbie definitely has too much free time on her hands," I said.

"There seems to be a pattern here," said Astrid, ignoring my comments. "Bobbie sees it too, and she wants to know if it has anything to do with Bob's death. I think she has a right to know; don't you?"

"I guess so," I sighed, "but be careful."

"Of what?"

"I'm not sure; it's just a feeling I have."

***

By mid-morning the next day, one of the software engineers in my group had a breakthrough on our printer, and with a simple adjustment, had increased its speed by fifty percent. That was still too slow, but what he found showed us how to attack the problem, and two people were already at work on the modification. I was so optimistic that I was checking through my calendar to figure out a good time for me to take a vacation when Jerry came by my office.

"I wanted to remind you about our tennis date tonight," he said.

"At seven."

"Right. Oh, by the way, I do have some good news. It's all set; all professionals who worked on the J-6 are going to be invited to St. Thomas, Virgin Islands, this Labor Day weekend."

I gave a low whistle. "They're really going all out this time."

"They wouldn't include the technicians or secretaries, but I did convince them to give some gift certificates for the company store to everyone not invited on the trip."

"That hardly seems fair," I protested.

"Well, the weekend is being called a 'strategy session' for future projects. There will be meetings scheduled, so it is a working trip, but don't worry; there'll still be plenty of time to enjoy the surroundings," said Jerry. "They're picking up the tab for activities; some of them are pretty amazing. The company writes the whole thing off as a business expense, and we get a free vacation in paradise. Everybody wins."

"Are you trying to tell me that spouses are not included?"

"No, I don't think so," said Jerry. "As I understand it, it's Businetex employees only."

"If Astrid is not included, I'll tell you right now that I won't be there."

"I don't think the big boys will appreciate your refusing their hospitality."

274 What Remains Behind

"Labor Day weekend is my time," I said curtly. "If they want me there, they can reschedule during working hours. I'm not spending the holiday weekend without my wife."

"I'll never understand you people who put your family before your career," said Jerry. "I'd probably be slinging hash somewhere right now had I done that."

"Don't you have anyone you care about, Jerry?" I couldn't resist asking.

"I have a son," he said. "I suppose I care about him, even thought his mother ruined him."

"Do you see much of him?"

"I don't see him at all. That bitch I married saw to that."

"I'm sorry," I said.

"Thanks. I'll see you at seven."

I was afraid that Jerry would be angry at me after our earlier conversation, but he seemed happy to see me when I came into the health club. He went on to the locker room as I stopped to chat with Linda for a few minutes.

"You look particularly fetching, ma'am," I teased. Instead of her usual jeans and tee shirt, she was wearing a navy and white sailor style dress. Linda was not a bad looking woman; dressed as she was, she looked almost glamorous.

"Thanks, Mitch. Actually, I just came from a funeral."

"Not my favorite way to spend an afternoon."

"Mine either," she agreed. "You know, I didn't think about it, but it was kind of strange. This was the second one this week, and both were pretty similar to what happened to Artie."

"They were young and healthy and had heart attacks?" I asked.

"Yes. Both of them were long time members here. Steve, the man whose funeral I went to today, had heart surgery ten years ago, but he hadn't had any symptoms since then. He worked out three times a week, faithfully, and was never sick. Last Saturday, he took his dog for a walk along the canal path. The dog came home without him. He had collapsed and died during the walk."

"How old a man was he?"

"Fifty-two," said Linda, "but to look at him, you would have guessed forty, tops."

"Linda, did he work for Businetex?"

"I couldn't swear to it, but I think he did."

"What did he do?"

"He was a chemist," she replied. "He did some kind of research. Why?"

"Oh, just curious," I said.

"I know for a fact that the other guy who died worked for Businetex," she related.

"Oh, really?"

"The management here wants us to keep it quiet, but he was just like Artie. He collapsed on the racquetball court. He was only twenty-eight."

"What did he do?"

"I know he was a lawyer who worked for Businetex, but I don't know exactly what he did."

Jerry came back into the lobby, dressed for the court. "Coming, Mitch?"

"We'll talk later," I promised Linda as I went to join Jerry.

"I'm sorry if I was short with you this afternoon," said Jerry as I began to change my clothes.

"Your personal life is none of my business," I replied.

"My ex-wife isn't my favorite subject."

"We don't have to talk about her," I said. "We don't know each other very well, and I was just wondering if you had family around here."

"No, I don't have family here or anywhere else."

"That must get pretty lonely."

"I don't know," said Jerry, picking up his Gatorade and racket, leading the way to the court. "Family has always been more of a problem than a comfort to me."

"That's too bad," I said.

He seemed to want to talk. "My old man was a drunk. When he got loaded, he was mean. I can't remember too may times when he was sober. My mother couldn't take it after a while; she left when my brother and I were kids. The old man raised us. He was a lousy father, but he was the only one we had. Soon after he died, my brother also died."

"I'm sorry," I said.

"Thanks. I was pretty lonely after they were gone. I met my wife and we got married. Things were okay until the kid came along. Then, there were all sorts of problems."

"I've heard that children can put a strain on a marriage."

"I was a good father!" said Jerry adamantly, slamming an ace past me.

"I'm sure you were," I agreed.

"When I was nine, I saw my father give my mother the worst beating I can remember; I think that was what finally pushed her into leaving. I resolved then that I would never take a drink in my life, and I never have; even through four years of college, when everyone else got stinking drunk all the time, I never even tasted alcohol. To this day, I have never tasted it; not one drop! I never wanted to be the kind of father that my old man was."

"That's pretty impressive," I said, not knowing what else to say.

"No one can say that I wasn't a good father. I even potty trained the kid when my wife didn't know where to start. Three years old and still in diapers; it was a disgrace."

I said nothing; I felt like I was peeping through a gap in the curtains of someone's window; someone I didn't know.

"I told the kid I'd give him five bucks if he peed in the toilet; no more of that silly potty chair," continued Jerry proudly.

"I'm surprised that worked with a three year old. He must have been very smart to understand what money was worth at that age."

"Oh, I taught him the value of a buck," said Jerry. "When he was about two, I started him on an allowance, and if he wanted something, he had to pay for it himself."

"That's pretty young to understand about using money."

"Yeah, maybe." He took a long swig of his Gatorade and sat down on the chair at midcourt. "It didn't take the kid long to cash in though; maybe an hour or so. Then, I asked him how he'd like to go double or nothing."

"Double or nothing?" I repeated, mystified.

"Yes," said Jerry. "I told him if he crapped in the toilet, I'd give him a ten, but if he did it in his pants, he'd lose the five. A few hours later, he cashed in again. Then, I offered him double or nothing one last time."

"For what?" I asked, after just missing with a long lob.

"For standing up to pee like a man. My wife had him sitting down like a little girl."

"And he did it?"

"Right then and there," agreed Jerry. "He made me stay and watch while he went over and did it. Then, I gave him his twenty bucks, and I told him that now that we knew he could use the toilet, if he ever wet or messed his pants again, I was going to beat the living daylights out of him."

"And he was trained after that?" I asked.

"Oh, he screwed up once or twice, but I followed through with a beating each time, and it wasn't long before he stopped. You have to let a kid know that you mean what you say."

The whole thing seemed a little sick to me; I didn't know Jerry's former wife, but I had a gut feeling that she was justified for keeping him away from their son.

"How old is your son now?" I asked conversationally.

"Seventeen," replied Jerry, taking another long gulp of the Gatorade. "Boy, this stuff tastes really strange; it burns going down. They must have changed the formula since the last time I bought it."

"Don't drink it," I advised.

"I'd better get used to it," he sighed. "I buy it by the case at Sam's Club; this must be from the new batch."

"What is your son doing now?" I asked. He seemed to be resting more than normal tonight, but I didn't want to rush him if he was tired.

"His mother ruined him," said Jerry. "She was always too soft with him and now, we've got the results. He's in a special school; they say he's a manic-depressive, but I think that's something my ex's pansy shrink made up to drain cash from me. Of course, I'm footing the bill for this nonsense."

"I'm sorry, Jerry. It's a shame that you've had so many bad things happen in your life."

"Thanks, Mitch. I did the best I could."

"I believe you," I said as he served.

We were at the end of our court time. Jerry picked up the balls and the bottle of Gatorade. Normally, he finished it off by the time we were done, but tonight, the bottle was still probably a quarter full. "This stuff is really terrible," he said, looking at the bottle before tossing it into a trash barrel in the corridor. "If the rest of them taste like that, I may see if I can get a refund."

"Maybe you can switch it for another flavor," I suggested.

"Yeah," he agreed. "Mitch, I'm sorry that I rattled on like that."

"No problem, Jerry. I didn't mind listening."

"I hope that means that we can play again sometime."

I was feeling really sorry for him. Don't get me wrong, I still didn't like Jerry. At best, he was strange, and at worst, he showed signs of being mentally unbalanced, but he had been through a lot, and I got the idea that he was pretty lonely.

"If you'd like to set up a regular weekly game, I'm sure I could fit it in," I offered.

Jerry grinned widely, something he didn't usually do; he looked weird, like the Cheshire cat from *Alice in Wonderland.* "I'd like that," he said. He staggered a bit, and I thought that was odd; usually, he was very well coordinated.

"Wednesday is a good night for me," I said. "Astrid is taking an evening course, so I'm usually in no hurry to get home."

"Wednesdays are fine," agreed Jerry happily. "They'll be even better if I don't have to play with that idiot Deckle." He sounded funny, like his speech was starting to slur.

"Are you all right?" I asked him.

He nodded. "For some reason, I'm a little tired tonight; I guess I'm not as young as I used to be."

"None of us are," I agreed.

We walked out of the locker room together, and I stopped to talk to Linda for a moment. "I'll see you tomorrow," I said to Jerry.

"Oh, by the way, I do have a little surprise for you," he said with a giggle.

A giggle from him was more than bizarre.

"Oh?"

"I got permission for you to bring your little wifey on the trip with you," he beamed. "I spoke to Walt and told him that if it hadn't been for you, the umanal would have been late, and the J-6 would still be gathering dust."

He had no idea that he misspoke, and I didn't point it out, but Linda and I both looked at him strangely.

"Are you sure you're all right, Jerry?" I asked.

"Just tired," he muttered, stifling a yawn.

"Do you want a lift home?" I offered.

Jerry rubbed his face. "No, no, I'm fine," he said, seeming to come out of it. "You'll get official notice tomorrow by email, along with everyone else, but you're the only person who can bring his little wifey, and I wanted you to know why."

"Thanks," I said uncertainly as he walked out the door.

"He was strange tonight," said Linda.

"Very," I agreed. "He was unusually talkative on the court. I think he was embarrassed that he told me so many personal things."

"He almost acted drunk," mused Linda.

"On, no," I said adamantly, "Jerry doesn't drink; he's never touched alcohol in his life."

***

I was soundly asleep late that night, and I was dreaming about the phone ringing. Then, I heard Astrid's voice and realized that it was not a dream. I jumped upright, my heart pounding in frantic cadence.

"No, that's all right," Astrid was saying. "He's awake; just a minute."

"Who is it?" I asked, my voice still thick from sleep.

"It's Jim Deckle; he says it's an emergency."

I took the phone. "Jim?" I murmured sleepily. "What time is it?"

"About two-thirty, I think. I'm sorry to call at this hour, but I thought you would want to hear what happened."

"What's the matter?"

"Jerry Fallow had a car accident earlier tonight."

"I played tennis with him a few hours ago."

"He must have been on his way home. He got onto the expressway going the wrong way, and he had an accident."

"And they were supposed to notify you in case of an emergency?" I asked, confused.

"No. The police found my business card in his wallet; I wrote my home number on it for him after we started playing racquetball, in case he wanted to reach me. He never called."

"What hospital is he at?" I asked. "I'll meet you there; he doesn't have any family to speak of."

"He's not at a hospital," said Deckle. "He's dead, Mitch. He's at the morgue. They think he was driving drunk."

I was fully awake now. "That's impossible! He told me just tonight that he's never had a drink in his life."

"I don't know, Mitch. The police seemed pretty sure. They want me to come down in the morning, to identify him."

"Will you do it?"

"I told them I would."

"I'll see you at the office, then," I said. "And Jim?"

"Yeah, Mitch?"

"Thanks for calling."

"No problem."

I replaced the receiver in the cradle of the phone. Astrid was sitting up in bed, watching me. I didn't say a word to her. I got out of bed, went into the bathroom and threw up. Then, I sat down on the floor and leaned against the wall, closing my eyes, waiting for my head to clear.

I didn't hear Astrid come in, but she was there, wiping my face with a cool washcloth. The cobwebs began to disperse.

"What happened?" she asked.

"Jerry Fallow got on the expressway going the wrong way and managed to get himself killed. The police seem convinced that he was drunk, but I know that couldn't be;

he told me just tonight that he's never had a drink in his life."

"It isn't all that unusual for a person with a drinking problem to lie," said Astrid, sitting beside me on the bathroom floor.

"His father was an abusive alcoholic," I recounted. "I believed him when he told me that he didn't drink."

"Another Businetex fatality," said Astrid grimly.

"Linda told me about two more."

"This is getting scary," said Astrid. "I don't buy the coincidence explanation anymore."

"It's a little too weird," I agreed. "You know, Jerry was behaving strangely when he left the club."

"How?"

"He giggled."

"Jerry Fallow?" asked Astrid. "That guy looked as if his face would crack if he even smiled."

"He was unsteady on his feet too," I added.

"What about his speech?"

"It sounded funny, almost slurred."

"Are you sure he didn't have anything to drink?"

"Nothing but..."

"But what?"

"The Gatorade!" I said. "He complained that it tasted strange."

"Why did he drink it?" asked Astrid, always the voice of reason.

"He bought it by the case; he said that they must have recently changed the formula. I have always thought that it tasted awful, so I didn't think much of it when he complained."

"Where's the bottle now?"

"In the trash in the hallway of the club, near the tennis courts."

"How early do you think Linda gets up?" asked Astrid.

"It's going to be pretty early this morning," I replied.

I waited until six before I tried Linda. A man answered, probably her husband. He sounded awake, but Linda was half asleep when she came on the line. It took me three tries at explaining before she understood who it was.

"Mitch, what time is it?"

"A little after six and I'm really sorry to wake you, but this is urgent,"

"It's okay," she said, and I could hear her moving around.

"Jerry Fallow had a fatal accident last night," I said.

"Oh, my God!" she gasped, sounding fully awake now.

"After our tennis game, he threw a bottle of Gatorade in one of the trash barrels in the corridor near the tennis courts. If at all possible, I'd like to get that bottle back."

"What's today? Wednesday?"

"Thursday."

"They pick up the garbage this morning. If the barrels were emptied last night, it's in the dumpster."

"So it's too late?"

"Maybe not. Let me call over there and see who's on this morning. A couple of the guys on the janitorial staff owe me favors."

I sat anxiously by the phone, sipping coffee and waiting. At ten to seven, the phone rang.

"Success!" said Linda. "Jose was there; he owes me big time. The bottle is in his locker."

"You're a peach," I said.

"I'm happy to help. Is there anything else I can do?"

"Linda, you don't happen to know what became of Artie's gym bag the night he died, do you?"

"No," she said. "I thought you had it."

"No. I even asked his father after he cleaned out Artie's apartment; he never saw it either."

"How odd," said Linda. "I'll ask Jose if he knows anything, but I doubt it; the guys here are bonded and they're very honest. I know they wouldn't have taken it."

"I'm sure they wouldn't have," I agreed. "I was wondering if it could have been put in a closet or someone's office for safekeeping."

"I'll ask, but I don't think so."

The police had contacted Jerry's former wife, but she refused to make any of the arrangements. She told them they could send him to the dump, for all she cared. Deckle and I discussed it, and we decided that whatever Jerry had been, he deserved a decent burial. We decided that we would split the cost. He didn't really want to go alone, so I went with Jim to the coroner's office. There was no mistake; the body was Jerry's. Afterwards, we spoke briefly with the police. They were not too interested in what I had to say about his never having had a drink; the preliminary results of their tests showed that Jerry's blood alcohol was over .2, more than double the number considered to be intoxicated in New York. We had stopped to pick up the Gatorade at the health club, and we turned it over to them, but they felt it only strengthened their case; they were ready to proclaim Jerry's death a DWI fatality. They told us that luckily, the vehicle he ran into was a tractor-trailer, and the driver had escaped with cuts and scratches. They were not very sympathetic about Jerry, and I can't say I blamed them; I've always considered drunk drivers to be a particularly despicable life form.

We arranged for the services for Jerry to be held at a funeral home. He was not a member of any church, so Deckle asked his minister to officiate. Turnout was particularly light for someone in Jerry's position; apparently, the people at Businetex either looked upon drunken drivers about as kindly as the police did, or they would rather play golf on a sunny August Saturday morning. I kept thinking that Jerry wouldn't have enjoyed his own funeral at all, and he probably would have had a fit that Astrid attended with me.

Apparently, his wife had reconsidered her initial decision concerning his remains. The funeral director notified us that a lawyer had arranged for Jerry's body to be returned to Baltimore after the services, to be buried next to his father and brother.

We were getting into the car after the funeral when a woman called out to me.

"Mr. Goldblatt?"

"Yes?" I replied.

"I'm Laura Martin," she said.

I looked at her blankly. I would have guessed that she was in her mid-forties, slender and fairly attractive, with straight, dark hair that fell over the shoulders of a plain, black dress. Her light brown eyes were flecked with green that glinted in the sunlight.

"I'm sorry," I said. "Do we know each other?"

"I'm Laura Martin Fallow," she replied. "I dropped the last name when Jerry and I divorced."

"It's nice to meet you," I said, extending my hand. "This is my wife, Astrid."

Laura Martin shook my hand lightly and nodded to Astrid. "Would it be possible for us to talk for a few minutes?"

"Why don't I catch a ride with Bobbie?" offered Astrid. "There was something I wanted to talk to her about anyway."

"I didn't mean that you had to leave, Mrs. Goldblatt," protested Laura.

"No, it's fine," reassured my wife. "I really did want to spend some time with Bobbie. Mitch can pick me up at her place whenever you're through."

We watched silently as Astrid walked briskly over to Bobbie's van and climbed into the passenger side.

"What can I do for you, Ms. Martin?" I asked.

"Call me Laura, please. Do you have time for a cup of coffee?"

"I'm Mitch; do you have a car?"

"Yes," she said, "a rental. I don't know my way around here very well but I did see a Wendy's when I got off the expressway."

"I know where it is; I'll meet you there."

I tried to make it as easy as possible for her to follow me, and I waited for her to get out of the car so that we could walk in together. She insisted on paying for the coffee and I let her.

"Now, what was it that you wanted to talk about?" I asked.

"I was told by the police that you and a Mr. Deckle took care of the funeral arrangements. I wanted to thank you."

"No problem," I said.

"I wanted you to know that I spoke with Jerry's lawyer, and there was a will; there is money for funeral expenses, so I instructed him to make sure that both of you are reimbursed."

"Thank you," I said, still not sure what to make of her.

"I assume that the police told you what I told them when they first called," she said.

I nodded.

"You must think that I'm one cold-blooded bitch."

"I try not to judge people."

"That's admirable," she said with a wry smile, "but sometimes impossible when you don't know the whole story. I will tell you that my first reaction to the news of the accident was that it was another ploy by Jerry, to avoid paying for Brian's schooling. He tried to get out of it more than once. Did he ever tell you anything about me?"

"He mentioned you once, very briefly."

"Jerry never had any friends that I knew of when we were married, or before, so I was surprised to hear that there were people here who cared about him."

"Jerry had his quirks," I said, "but he was still a human being. I'm sure that you thought there were some good things about him; the two of you were married for quite a while."

"I loved him once," she said softly. "I think that's what he despised most about me."

"I don't understand," I protested.

"He considered my affection for people a sign of weakness," she sighed, taking a sip of coffee. "I tried to get him to realize that he had to change some things about himself for us to stay together and be happy. Jerry and I were happy when we were first married, but after Brian came, the trouble began. Jerry's father was controlled by alcohol, and Jerry was determined never to become the kind of monster that raised him. I admired that determination, but he could not see that, in his own way, he was just as abusive."

"He hurt your son?" I asked.

"Physically, he was rough with him but not brutal. Emotionally was a different story; he was incapable of showing that child a single bit of warmth or tenderness."

"But he spoke of his son with affection," I protested.

"In his own way, I'm sure that Jerry loved Brian, but not for who he was. From the time our son was small, it became evident that he was not like other children. He scored so high he was off the charts on all the standardized tests, but he did poorly in school. He would go through periods where he was wild, out of control, and at other times, he was so quiet that you couldn't get a word out of him.

"When he was eight, he slit both of his wrists. The pediatrician recommended a psychiatric evaluation. Jerry wouldn't hear of it. Instead, he made him stay in his room for two months, except for school and meals. Six months later, Brian swallowed almost a full bottle of one hundred aspirins. After he was out of the woods, I insisted on psychiatric treatment, and Jerry refused to pay for it. I got a job and paid for it myself."

"But if Brian improved with treatment, surely Jerry came around."

"Brian has his ups and downs. Manic-depressive illness can be treated, but it is not cured. On medication, he can be controlled, but Brian is not reliable about taking it. Like many people with his condition, he likes the highs of the manic phases and is powerless to help himself when the depression takes over. He will have to have some type of supervision for the rest of his life."

"It can't be easy, having a child with such a serious problem," I sympathized.

"You have to understand that Brian is a charming, intelligent young man, and I love him with all my heart," said Laura, "but I understand that he is the way he is, and there is nothing I can do to change that. Jerry couldn't accept it; he could never admit that his child was less than perfect. I begged him to talk to someone, to get some help, for all of our sakes. He wouldn't even consider it. He said that the boy's problems were caused by my coddling him, and that if we made him into a man, all the nonsense would stop. The older Brian got, the more severely Jerry punished him, until I had no choice but to get a divorce and a restraining order, to prevent Jerry from doing his son any further harm."

"Do you know what caused your son's problem?" I asked.

"They say it's hereditary," replied Laura.

"Jerry had his quirks, but his behavior hardly fit the pattern you describe."

"I assumed you knew about his brother."

"He told me he had a brother who died after they lost their father. He didn't give me the details and I didn't ask."

"I never met Larry," said Laura, "but from everything I've heard, he was a classic manic-depressive. He was always in trouble in school, couldn't hold a job for very long, and went through periods where he didn't say a word to anyone for months on end. From what I've been told by people who knew him, he was far more likable than Jerry, but his behavior usually wound up driving away anyone who got close to him. He was never diagnosed or treated, but having lived through it with my son, I'm certain that he suffered from the same illness."

"What happened to him?" I asked.

"Jerry came home from work one day and discovered him in the basement. He had hanged himself."

"Wow," I said.

"Jerry didn't like to talk about it, but I know that it was very painful for him."

"Laura, did the police tell you what happened to Jerry?"

"They said he was in a car accident."

"They said he was drunk and got on the expressway going the wrong direction."

"That's impossible!"

"There's no doubt that he was driving the wrong way," I said, "and they did a blood alcohol test; he was intoxicated."

"I don't care what they said. I knew Jerry probably as well as anyone else in this world knew him, and I would bet my life that he would never take a drink, let alone get drunk."

"Would he sneak it?" I asked. "He was drinking some Gatorade that we suspect was laced."

"If that's so, he didn't do it, and he didn't know what he was drinking. Jerry wouldn't voluntarily drink alcohol; I'm positive of that."

"That was my feeling too," I agreed.

Laura looked at her watch. "I have a plane to catch."

"Laura, Jerry mentioned that his mother left when he was a child," I said. "Is she still alive, and would you know how to locate her?"

"I don't know, Mitch," she said, shaking her head. "No one has heard from her since Jerry was nine. I know I shouldn't judge her; heaven knows, I had to leave my marriage too, but there was no excuse for her abandoning her sons the way she did. I think that was unforgivable."

"I agree with you," I said.

I saw her out to her car.

"Thank you for listening to me," she said. "I don't know why it mattered, but I didn't want you to think of me as some kind of a monster."

"I don't," I assured her. "Laura, are you and Brian going to be all right financially?"

"I didn't come to you for money," she protested.

"I didn't think you had, but this was pretty sudden; I'm not trying to pry; I'm genuinely concerned."

"Don't be," she said. "I have a job and I haven't accepted anything for myself since the divorce. As I told you, Jerry left a will. He was pretty secure, financially; most of his estate goes to Brian. Although he arranged it so that I have no access at all, and Brian has little control over the money, unless he is able to live without psychiatric treatment, it should be sufficient to meet his needs as things now stand. Thank you for asking."

"Take care," I said.

"Mitch, thank you for being his friend."

"I don't know that we were really friends," I protested.

"Believe me, you're as close to a friend as he ever got," she said, sliding behind the wheel.

I closed her car door, still not sure what to make of what I'd heard. I watched her drive off and got into my own car. On a whim, I dug through my wallet for the card one of the officers had given me when Jim and I went to the morgue, and punched the numbers into my cellular phone. As luck would have it, officer Coffey was there.

"Yes, Mr. Goldblatt," he said when he came on the line. "What can I do for you?"

"I was wondering if you tested that bottle of Gatorade that I brought in."

"I was going to give you a call about that on Monday," he said. "We did find something odd. It would have to have been laced with ethyl alcohol."

"What is that?"

"Pure alcohol. It's not readily available to the public; do you happen to know where he got it?"

"I have no idea," I said. "Mr. Fallow didn't drink."

"Well, based on how he laced his Gatorade, I'd say he was drinking pretty heavily the other night. It tested at over one hundred proof, stronger than most whiskey."

"He drank three quarters of the bottle," I said.

"It's amazing he was still conscious," said the officer. "It's a shame, too. Had he passed out somewhere, he probably would still be alive, although the next morning, he might have wished he were dead."

"Officer Coffey, I don't think Jerry spiked that Gatorade himself," I said.

"Do you know who did?"

"No."

"Did Mr. Fallow have any enemies?"

"He didn't have too many friends, but I can't think of anyone who disliked him enough to want him dead."

"Then I would say that maybe you didn't know Mr. Fallow as well as you thought you did," he replied.

Maybe no one did, I thought. His life had certainly been every bit as strange as his death was.

Chapter 7
Bobbie

O n my way to meet Astrid, I was aware that my head was throbbing as if there was a jackhammer inside. Funerals seem to have that effect on me. Astrid and Bobbie were waiting for me in the living room when I arrived at the McCann house. I carried the large carton that I'd taken from the trunk of my car inside. In the box were the personal effects that had been in Bob's office.

"Where do you want it?" I asked Bobbie, after I had given Astrid a quick peck on the cheek in greeting.

"Just put it on the floor," she said. "I'll go through it in here."

"I meant to bring it over before but things kept coming up," I explained.

"That's all right," replied Bobbie. "I wouldn't have had time to look at it before now anyway."

"Where are the kids?" I asked.

"Brandon is up in his room, sulking. He's been strange all week; I hope he's not getting sick."

"Sixteen is a tough age," said Astrid. "I think my mother was ready to trade me for two eight year olds!"

"I'm sure my mother didn't realize that was an option, or you'd be sitting here with two younger women," agreed Bobbie.

"Where are Brett and Brittany?" I asked.

"Over looking at a neighbor's new puppies. They think if they spend enough time there, I'll give in and allow them to have one."

"Any chance of that?"

"Would you be interested in an English Sheepdog?" asked Bobbie.

"Absolutely!" I said enthusiastically.

"Not!" added Astrid, equally adamant. "Two people who are away at work all day have no business having a dog."

"The 'nays' have it," laughed Bobbie, pouring me some coffee from a carafe on the coffee table.

I sank down on the couch and took a long gulp, massaging my throbbing left temple.

"Something wrong?" asked Astrid.

"Just a little headache."

"Do you want something for it?" offered Bobbie.

"I think it will go away on its own if I can get my mind on something else."

"Maybe I can provide a distraction," proposed Bobbie, gesturing at the carton on the floor. "Shall we?"

"Maybe you'd like some privacy when you do that," I suggested.

"I'd like you two to stay for dinner," she said.

"I told her it was too much trouble," interjected Astrid.

"We'll get take-out," said Bobbie. "I could use the company."

"Our treat," I offered.

"Deal," said Bobbie. "Oh, look at this."

"That was the picture he kept on the shelf behind his desk," I said.

"I've always hated that picture," said Bobbie.

"Why?" asked Astrid.

"Take a good look at us, at our expressions."

"I found it kind of fascinating," I confessed.

"Would you like to know what was really going on?" asked Bobbie. "The boys both wanted to go to Kennedy Space Center. Bob and I spent a week at Disney World every year, and they had been there so many times, it had lost its charm, but Bob insisted that we had to go there. He said that we didn't want to miss all the fun. We did what Bob wanted, but the boys sulked for the entire trip."

"Kennedy Space Center sounds interesting," I said. "Couldn't you have done both?"

"We could have," agreed Bobbie, "but you didn't really know Bob; he was like a little kid. For him, leaving Disney World early would have been a major sacrifice."

"Did you like Disney World?" asked Astrid.

"I could take it or leave it, preferably leave it, but I kept telling myself that at least we were vacationing together, as a family. That year, I had the flu, and all I wanted to do was stay in the hotel room and sleep, but

Bob wouldn't hear of it. He insisted that I go everywhere he did. I couldn't have gone on any of the rides, even if I had felt well, because someone had to take care of Brittany, but that made no difference to him; he had to have his way or he was impossible to be around."

"That was pretty insensitive," said Astrid.

"It was vintage Bob," sniffed Bobbie. "He always assumed that if he was enjoying himself, everyone else was, and I generally humored him, but on that vacation, he crossed the line. Brittany had such bad diarrhea when that photo was taken that we wound up spending all night and most of the next day in the hospital emergency room with her, while they gave her intravenous fluids. Bob kept insisting that I was overprotective when I told him that diarrhea in an infant was nothing to fool around with; I wanted to take her to a doctor as soon as it started, but he wouldn't hear of it. Only after she became listless and lethargic did he become as frightened as I had been all day long. For everyone else, that vacation was the epitome of misery, but he remembered it as a fun time and immortalized it in a picture."

"The photo loses its charm in the translation," I said.

"For your sake, I wish you weren't so bitter," Astrid said to Bobbie.

"I'm getting over it. I did make peace with Maggie."

"You two saw each other?" I asked, wide-eyed.

"Purely by accident. My mother and I finally buried the hatchet, and last Saturday, she took the kids to the zoo. After a while, the walls started to close in on me, so I went for a ride. I didn't even know where I was going until I found myself at the cemetery. You can imagine my surprise to run into Maggie, placing flowers on Bob's grave."

"She's mourning him too," I said softly.

"I understand that," agreed Bobbie, "but before I had a chance to say a word, she lit into me. She told me that I made his life a living hell, and he deserved better."

"That wasn't true," said Astrid, patting her hand.

"I realized that she was upset," continued Bobbie, "but she was so wound up, there was no stopping her. She even told me that for years, everyone has referred to me as 'John Madden in drag.'"

I couldn't make myself look at her.

"I didn't know who John Madden was then," continued Bobbie, "but I understood that she meant it as a put-down. I let her go on until she was done; I surprised myself; I remained extremely calm. When she paused for air, I told her that I understood that she was mourning him too."

"What happened?" asked Astrid.

"She said she was sorry and fell into my arms sobbing. After she calmed down, we sat there on the grass and talked. Her circumstances are not too different from mine; actually, we have a lot in common."

"Like what?" asked Astrid. From her tone, I gathered that she would not have been so forgiving.

"We were both married to men who were incapable of giving us the romance we craved. Despite my appearance, I'm a woman, I feel feminine, and I like to be treated that way. It was ironic that what Maggie most loved about Bob was that he brought romance back to her life. He sent her flowers at her desk with no card; he bought her little pieces of jewelry, for no occasion, that were demure enough that she could wear them all the time; he took her to lunch. It meant the world to her. If he'd done those same things for me, our marriage would have been so different."

"If her marriage is so unhappy, why doesn't she divorce her husband and find someone else?" I asked.

"You could ask the same about me," said Bobbie. "Her husband is kind to her, and he's a wonderful provider. He helped rear their children, and in most ways, they're a happy family, but he's addicted to sports. He watches them on television, he bowls, he golfs, he has season tickets to everything. She is bored by it. When she tried to tell him what she needed, that she would like it if he sent her flowers sometime, according to her, without even looking away from the television, he said that if she wanted flowers, she should call a florist and order whatever she liked."

"It's not the same," protested Astrid.

"I know," said Bobbie, "but she said that one of the reasons she stays with him is because if she did order the flowers, when he got the bill, he would pay it without flinching, whatever it was, and he would never say a word in complaint. He wouldn't have noticed the flowers unless they were dressed in uniforms and squaring off against each other, but if they were what she wanted, it would have been fine with him."

"That still doesn't make up for having an affair with someone else's husband," said Astrid.

"Should we be talking about this when Brandon is in the house?" I asked uncomfortably.

"Oh, Brandon knows all about Maggie," said Bobbie. "He's known since he was thirteen."

"How?" I asked.

Astrid glared at me.

Bobbie took each of our hands. "It's all right," she said to Astrid. "I want you both to know about all of this. I think we are close enough.

"Brandon was looking for a pen, and Bob's briefcase was open on his desk. He looked inside and saw a box from Mann's Jewelers. He shouldn't have opened it without permission, but he did, and the bracelet inside was engraved with Maggie's name and Bob's.

"Brandon went to Bob and confronted him. Bob told him that this is how things are in the real world, and he'd better get used to it. He told Brandon that he didn't have anything to worry about, that we would never divorce; we were a family forever."

"That was a pretty cruel thing to do to a kid that age," I said.

"That was the only time Bob and I ever fought about Maggie," said Bobbie. "Brandon didn't come to me, but he couldn't handle it by himself either. That night, he locked himself in the bathroom and wouldn't come out.

He wouldn't betray Bob but he felt disloyal to me. It was a hellish position for a child. I finally convinced him to let me in and, from his ramblings, I guessed what he had learned. I had to lie to my child; I told him that I knew, and that it didn't matter to me even though it always had, very much. After I managed to calm him down, I told Bob that if he ever brought his mistress into our home again, I would leave him, and he would never see his children. I knew that he wouldn't stop seeing her, but I would not allow him to wave her in my face ever again. He was very careful after that."

"That doesn't make up for the harm it did to Brandon," said Astrid.

"No," said Bobbie, "and that's part of the problem now. He wants me to mourn Bob as my lost lover, because he thinks that will validate his feelings for his father, but I can't do that because my lover is still alive."

I suppose the look on my face revealed my feelings rather clearly. Astrid was unable to meet my gaze, so I realized that she already knew.

"Don't look so shocked, Mitch," laughed Bobbie. "Bob and I truly deserved each other. I really believe it was a marriage made in heaven, or wherever matches that are meant to be are created."

My head had begun to pound even harder. "I didn't expect that," I admitted.

Bobbie nodded. "There is something else, as long as I'm making a clean breast of it all, but first I want to see where Brandon is."

"How long have you known?" I asked Astrid when Bobbie left the room.

"She told me last week, when I took those days off and we had lunch. She asked me to allow her to tell you herself."

"He's fallen asleep," said Bobbie when she returned. "Let me finish before the other two get back."

Astrid and I both nodded.

"I met Lou in the library. He's in real estate, so he has pretty flexible hours. He was browsing the best sellers between appointments, and we started talking. When we ran into each other a second time, we made arrangements to meet on a regular basis. We would browse through the books and then go for coffee. After a few months of friendship, we began going to a hotel together. He too is married, with a family, and he was very clear right upfront that he would never want to jeopardize that. He loves his wife, and he believes that she loves him. I don't know why it happened; I guess both of us were looking for something that was lacking in our lives, a little excitement or romance. Call it what you will."

"Did Bob know?" I asked.

"I'm not sure," admitted Bobbie. "If he did, he never said anything about it to me. I don't think that Lou's family knows; in his line of work, it's not unusual for him to have meetings at all sorts of strange hours. Apparently, he's very successful at his career, and it wouldn't even be unusual for a woman to call him at his home to arrange a meeting, although I never did. My children do not know, and I plan to keep it that way."

I certainly had no problem with that. In fact, that was about the only thing I'd heard in the past hour with which I didn't have a problem.

"Didn't the dishonesty bother you?" Astrid asked hesitantly.

"At first it did," admitted Bobbie. "Then, about five years ago, I found out the extent to which Bob would go to deceive me, and all bets were off."

"What happened?" I asked.

"After Brett was born, we decided that we only wanted two children, and we wouldn't have any more, but a few years later, Bob decided that he wanted to try for a little girl. We discussed it again, and I still didn't want another baby. The boys were old enough to be in school full time, and I was hoping to take some graduate courses, and maybe do something related to archaeology. Bob agreed that I was entitled to pursue my career, but I later learned that he had decided to get his own way without consulting me.

"When I went to take my birth control pill one morning, the tablets in the new prescription did not look the same as the old ones. I called the pharmacy, and they said they had given me the same thing I always had, so I brought it in to be checked by the pharmacist. They were artificial sweetener tablets!"

"But you had no proof that it was Bob who changed them," I said.

"Other than finding a bottle of artificial sweetener in his desk drawer, no, but I took no chances. I went right to the doctor and had myself fitted for a diaphragm, which I wore faithfully every time Bob and I were together. Then, I told Lou what had happened and explained that I would like to have his child. He was reluctant at first, but he finally agreed. I knew that we had no long-term future, but I wanted a part of him that I could keep. So the child that Bob tricked me into having became my gift to myself. Brittany has always been particularly precious to me."

"Did Bob know?" I asked.

"No," said Bobbie, "and Brittany and the boys will never find out either; that wouldn't be fair to them."

"I wish you hadn't told us," I said, rubbing my forehead. My headache was getting worse by the minute.

"I'm sorry," said Bobbie. "I hope it won't change the way you feel about her or me."

"No," I said, "it won't; it's just something I would rather not have known."

"I never did finish telling you what happened at the cemetery," said Bobbie. "I wound up comforting Maggie, as strange as that sounds. She couldn't tell her husband what was eating away at her; as far as she knows, he had no idea about Bob. It sounds like she doesn't have many friends either."

"She isn't popular at work," I agreed.

"Before she left, she told me that she could never understand why Bob stayed with me, despite what he told her about wanting to keep his family together, but she said she now knows why he loved me so much. I protested that I didn't think that Bob had loved me for a long time, but she insisted that she knew that he did. She said that I am the kindest person she's ever met. I thought she was trying to butter me up, but she sounded sincere."

"Whether she meant it or not, it's true!" insisted Astrid.

"Thank you," said Bobbie, her eyes starting to fill with tears. "It means so much more to me coming from you."

"You're very important to us; you're a wonderful woman, Bobbie," I said.

She swallowed hard and forced herself to go on. "After Maggie left the cemetery, I sat down by Bob's grave and had a long talk with him. I told him how angry I was about some of the things he'd done, and how sorry I was for some of the things I'd done. I don't know why but sometimes we were what only could be described as mean to each other. For some reason, we just seemed to feed off each other that way. I told him that whatever had been wrong between us, I never wanted him dead."

"Of course you didn't!" said Astrid. "The accident wasn't your fault."

"No, but you know how we blame ourselves for all sorts of things over which we have no control."

Both of us nodded in agreement.

"When I finished my conversation with my dead husband, I stood to go and it hit me. I began to think about how we were when we first met, and I just stood there all alone and cried, the only time I've shed tears for him since it happened."

"Despite everything, you still loved him," I said.

"Yes," said Bobbie, "but until that moment, I didn't realize it."

Just then, Brett and Brittany came bursting into the house.

"Mommy," pleaded Brittany, "can't we please have a puppy?"

"I don't think so, sweetheart," said Bobbie. "Maybe sometime but not right now, and I think we'd get something smaller."

"They're so cute!" said Brett.

"Everything is cute when it's a baby," replied Bobbie.

"Where's Brandon?" asked Brett.

"He fell asleep; please don't wake him. I don't think he's feeling well."

"Will you read to us, Mitch?" asked Brittany.

"Sure," I agreed.

"What are you going to read?" asked Brett.

"Whatever you pick," I replied.

"What was your favorite book when you were little?" asked Brittany.

"Oh, that's easy," I laughed. "*Where the Wild Things Are*. I wasn't real little when I first read it, but I always suspected it had been written just for me."

"We have that!" said Brett.

"Oooh, too scary," said Brittany.

"I never thought it was scary," I said. "I gave all the monsters names of my teachers and relatives, so it was like a bunch of people I knew."

"Neat!" said Brett. "Will you show us?"

"Sure."

Brett ran up the stairs with Brittany right on his heels.

"Are things okay between us, Mitch?" asked Bobbie, when they were gone.

"Fine."

"Really?"

I walked over to her and kissed her lightly on the forehead. "Do you know who John Madden is now?"

Bobbie laughed. "Yes. I asked Brandon, and he found him doing commentary on a sports show. Supposedly, he was a pretty good coach."

"For the Oakland Raiders," I said.

"I can see the resemblance," winked Bobbie.

"You know, he isn't bad-looking," I observed.

"And people don't mess with either of us," added Bobbie, and the three of us were able to laugh about it.

"Mom!" called Brett from the top of the stairs, "Brandon locked himself in the bathroom, and he won't come out!"

"Use the one in my room."

"He called me a bad name!" added Brett.

"Just drop it," said Bobbie. "Maybe I should go up and check on him," she added to us.

"Would you like me to do it?" I offered.

"Brandon would probably prefer that; he hasn't had much to say to me lately. Would you mind?"

"Not as long as you know that I'm going say what I think, not what you want him to hear," I warned.

"That's fine; I'm not sure myself what I want him to hear. If you say what's in your heart, I have no problem with that."

Our eyes met and I knew I wouldn't betray her, but I'd give her son what he needed if I could. She knew it too.

I got to the top of the stairs and Brett was waiting for me. "Are you going to read to us?"

"Yes," I said, "but I'd like to talk to Brandon first. Can you give us a few minutes alone?"

"I guess so," agreed Brett.

"Let me show you something first," I said, hoping to find a way to occupy him and Brittany while they waited. I took the book that he was holding and opened to a page with illustrations. "My friend Artie showed me that if you put tracing paper over the pictures and trace the outlines, you can make them look even more like the people you name them for. You can change the noses and eyes, add warts, hats and mustaches; anything you like. Do you have any tracing paper?"

"I think so, in my desk drawer," said Brett.

I got him and Brittany started on copying the illustrations and went to the bathroom door. It was still shut. I tapped lightly.

"I told you to get out of my face!" yelled Brandon.

"It's Mitch, Brandon. Do you mind if I come in for a minute?"

He said nothing but I heard the lock turn.

"May I come in?" I asked through the closed door.

"It's open."

I turned the knob and walked in. Brandon reached behind me and turned the lock again.

"How are you doing?" I asked.

The boy shrugged. "I'm doing all right."

"We were a little worried about you," I said. "Is there anything I can do to help?"

"No, I don't think so," said the boy. "I don't feel like I can be around anyone else without saying something mean."

"Hit me with your best shot," I offered. "I think I can take it. Are you thinking that I have a big nose? You should see the original it was copied from."

The corners of his mouth turned up just the slightest little bit. "I didn't mean it that way," he said softly, "and your nose isn't so big. I just feel like I have to hurt people who come near me, so they'll go away leave me alone. Do you know what I mean?"

"Yes."

"I want people to feel as bad as I do; do you ever feel that way?"

"Most of the time lately," I said, and I was only half kidding.

Brandon gave an empty little laugh. "I thought I was losing my mind."

"I doubt that; you sound pretty normal to me."

"Has Astrid ever done anything bad?" he asked.

"Of course she has," I replied. "There is no one who has never made a mistake."

"That wasn't what I meant. Has she ever done something that made you really mad?"

"Just recently," I admitted.

"What did she do?"

I considered how much it was appropriate for me to tell him. "She didn't tell me about something that I thought I had the right to know. I found out about it by accident, from someone else."

"And it hurt your feelings?"

"It was more complicated than that. I felt that her not telling me was a betrayal of my trust."

Brandon nodded. "What did you do?"

"I confronted her about it. She apologized and, after a while, I forgave her."

"Because you're a good guy," said the boy.

"You give me far too much credit. First, I went off by myself to sulk, and then I let her sweat for a while. I finally realized that I was suffering as much as she was, if not more. I still don't like what she did, but I love her and I had to separate the two. For myself, I couldn't not forgive her. Do you understand what I mean?"

The boy nodded sagely. "Mitch, you didn't like my dad too much, did you?"

My first instinct was to lie, but he was looking at me in a way that only children can when they suspect that you won't level with them. "Most of the time, I thought he was a pain in the rear," I said, "but I miss him and I wish he was back."

Brandon wordlessly nodded his head and turned to look out the window. I saw his shoulders begin to shake, and I realized that he was sobbing convulsively. I put my arm around him, and he slumped against me.

"This is good, Brandon," I said quietly. "This is just what you need."

After a while, the sobs tapered off. I reached over to grab a few tissues from the box on the toilet tank and offered them to him.

He wiped his eyes and blew his nose. "Promise me that you won't tell anyone about this," he urged.

"It's between us, but you have no reason to be ashamed. It's perfectly all right for you to grieve for your father; no one could find fault with you for that."

"I can't stop thinking about him," said the boy. "I don't mean to but it just happens."

"You have to try to remember the good things; I know there had to be good things."

The boy nodded.

"As for the bad things, you have to consider them to be mistakes, and you have to forgive him because he was a human being, and we all make mistakes; he wasn't perfect, but he was still your father, and you can't help it that you loved him. You were supposed to love him; you were a good son."

"But you won't tell anyone that I cried?"

"No," I said, "but you're far too much like me for your own good."

"What do you mean?"

"I'm not too good at dealing with my feelings either; that's something I have to work on."

"I have a headache," he said.

"So do I," I agreed.

"Do you want some Tylenol?" he offered, opening the medicine cabinet.

Something caught my eye on the bottom shelf. Automatically, my hand reached for it. "I haven't seen one of these very often," I said, fingering it gently.

"It's an egg timer," he said. "Mom uses it to time the thermometer when we're sick."

"Good idea," I said, returning it to where I had found it.

"You look like it means something else to you," said Brandon.

"It reminds me of a friend of mine."

"Your best friend?"

I nodded. "He used to be."

"Did you two have a fight?"

"No. He died."

"I'm sorry," said the boy.

"Me too," I agreed.

We each swallowed two of the Tylenol tablets, crumpled up the little paper cups that we'd taken from the dispenser, and tried a hook shot for the wastebasket. Both shots went in at the same time.

"Mitch, are you and Astrid going to have children?" asked Brandon.

"I hope we will, someday."

The boy nodded. "Will you still be our friend, even then?"

"I'll have to be extra nice to you then," I grinned. "Do you know how valuable good baby-sitters are?"

"If you have kids, I'll sit for free," vowed Brandon.

"Don't make promises that you won't want to keep, my pal," I said, putting my arm around his shoulders, "but I will remind you that you promised to sit when you tell me that you can't because you have a hot date."

The boy smiled slightly.

"I promised Brett and Brittany that I'd read to them," I said.

"I'll come too, in a minute," he said.

"Splash a little cold water on your face before you do," I said, winking at him as I closed the door behind me.

The two younger children had traced the outlines of several of the monsters in Maurice Sendak's wonderful illustrations. Brett showed quite a talent for art; one of his drawings looked exactly like Bob's mother.

"That looks like Grandma McCann," said Brandon, sinking onto the bed next to his brother.

"That's who it's supposed to be," said Brett. "Maybe I'll send it to her."

I couldn't help but smile at that thought, but I said nothing.

"Brett, I didn't mean what I said before; I'm sorry," said Brandon.

"I know," agreed the younger boy. "Forget it."

"Brandon, can we get these books?" asked Brittany, handing him a card that she'd pulled from a children's magazine that was on the nightstand.

"You have to ask Mom," he said.

The little girl ran off with the card and Brett handed me another drawing.

"That's the one I always called Rifka," I said. "She has long red hair and she looks bossy."

"Who's Rifka?" asked Brandon.

"My mother."

"You call her by her first name?" asked Brett, sounding really impressed.

"Not to her face he doesn't," laughed Astrid, who had just appeared in the doorway.

"Was she the boss in your house?" he asked.

"There and anywhere else she went," I said.

"Mitch!" laughed Astrid. "You shouldn't tell him that."

"We like bossy women," said Brandon. "Women like Mom."

"Bobbie and I are getting hungry," said Astrid to me. "How would you like to make a pilgrimage to see the Colonel? The one on Panorama Trail is probably closest."

"Can we go too?" asked Brett.

"Sure, if you want to," I replied.

When the four of us got downstairs, Brittany was whining unhappily as Bobbie explained why she couldn't order the books offered on the postcard.

"It isn't just those books, sweetie. Every month, they send you other books, and you have to send back cards to tell them that you don't want them. It's too much trouble. Sometimes, the cards come late, and the books you don't want are delivered; it will be better if we go to Borders and buy what you want.

Astrid and I looked at each other, wide-eyed. "A negative option!" we said in chorus.

"Yes," said Bobbie, "but I think she's too small to understand the terminology."

"Guys," I said, turning to the kids, "can you wait for me out by the car for a few minutes?"

"Why?" asked Brandon.

"We have to talk to your mother about something," said Astrid.

Brandon looked at us suspiciously.

"It will only take a few minutes," I promised.

"All right," he agreed, leading his brother and sister out of the house.

"What's going on?" demanded Bobbie.

"We may have figured out the common link between the people who have died," I said.

"I'm all ears," replied Bobbie.

"Did Bob ever get a letter from Businetex about life insurance?" asked Astrid.

"He had insurance from them since he started working there. They deducted the amount from his paycheck each month, and I filed a claim after he died."

"This was different," I explained. "This was about the company taking out insurance on his life, paying for it, and making Businetex the sole beneficiary."

"I don't remember anything like that. No, I'm sure Bob never mentioned it. What would be the purpose of that?"

"As the letter explained it, they did it to compensate the company for your value as an employee, in the event of your death," I replied. "I was told that more often, it was used as an inexpensive method of borrowing money."

"It doesn't sound familiar to me," said Bobbie. "If Bob did get that letter, he never mentioned it."

"Well, it was a thought," shrugged Astrid.

The kids were waiting for me out by the car. "Ready to visit the Colonel?" I asked.

All three nodded enthusiastically. We got into the car and took off. After a while, I noticed that they were extremely quiet.

"Want some music?" I offered.

"If that's okay," said Brandon.

"Sure," I replied. "Do you want to look for a radio station or do you want a tape?"

The tape player turned out to be a real treat for them; Bobbie didn't have one in her van, and Bob's tape player was off-limits. I let them go through the tapes and play what they wanted. I suppose the tapes that Astrid and I had probably weren't what they would have chosen, but they seemed to enjoy Neil Diamond as much as we did.

I ordered the food, and while I was waiting for my order, I saw the boys huddled together near the doorway.

"Tell him," I heard Brandon say.

"What do you think he'll do?" asked Brett nervously.

"This isn't one of the 'torture safaris,'" replied Brandon.

I picked up the bags and went to join them. Brandon took one of the bags from me and I held the door so that they could go out.

"Mitch?" said Brett uncertainly.

"Yes?"

"Please don't be angry at me."

"Why would I be?"

"I have to pee real bad."

The Colonel only had a storefront with no rest rooms. "That's not a problem," I said, looking around. "There's a McDonalds right over there; they'll have a bathroom."

"I'm really sorry," said Brett.

I could see that his bottom lip was quivering, as if he was fighting tears. "Don't worry about it," I reassured him. "To be honest, I can stand to go too."

I could have waited until we got back to the house, but he was so upset that I wanted to make him feel better, and I didn't really want to send him into the restaurant men's room alone.

"Can I go on the slide?" asked Brittany as I pulled into a vacant parking space. There was a small McDonalds theme play area adjoining restaurant.

"If Brandon doesn't mind watching you," I agreed.

"You're afraid of the slide, Britt," said Brandon.

"No I'm not!" she protested.

"You always used to be."

"I was when I was little but now, I'm a big girl."

"I'll watch her," Brandon assured me.

I led Brett toward the back of the restaurant and into the men's room. Both urinals were in use but the stall door was open.

"You go ahead," I said.

The boy went in and turned to me. "There's room for both of us."

I hesitated for a moment before joining him. He had already started, and standing next to him, I had such a strong feeling that Artie was there with me, that I actually imagined that he touched my shoulder. I finished long before Brett did; the poor kid must have really had to go. Inside my head, I heard the unmistakable laugh and that familiar voice saying 'Gotcha again!'. A lump formed in my throat, and I struggled to swallow it down.

"Mitch, I'm really sorry," said Brett as we were washing our hands. "I know I should have gone before we left, but I forgot."

"Brett, it's no big deal," I said, trying to reassure him. "Have I done something to make you afraid of me?"

"No," said the boy softly.

"Brett, you can ask me anything, any time. I like to think that we're friends. Sometimes, I may say no, or I may not know the answer, but I won't be angry at you for asking. Okay?"

The boy nodded but he still looked guilty, like he'd done something awful.

"Let's go find your brother and sister," I suggested.

Brittany was sliding down the slide, giggling delightedly as Brandon stood close by, making sure she didn't fall as she climbed up the ladder.

"Are you guys ready?" I asked.

"Oh, can I go one more time?" pleaded the little girl.

She looked so happy, I couldn't refuse. "Twice," I said with a wink.

She ran happily up the ladder and slid down. The second time, I caught her at the bottom and scooped her up into my arms.

"Okay?" I asked.

"Okay!" said Brittany, hugging my neck. "It was fun, Mitch."

I looked at her two brothers, standing soberly next to me like two old men. "Anyone else like to try?" I asked.

"We're too big," said Brett quietly.

"I'll push you through if you get stuck," I laughed.

"The food will get cold if we don't get it home soon," said Brandon. "Mom and Astrid might get mad."

"If it gets cold we'll reheat it," I said. "You guys have to lighten up."

We got into the car, and I realized what it was that disturbed me about these children. Their reactions were very strange. The whole time we were in the car, they sat silently or quietly listened to the tape player. My sister and I used to have our best battles on the move. Marilyn and I would squabble so much that we often had to be separated, one in the back seat and one in the front. These kids never argued among themselves. I've known many adults who behave worse.

They didn't know how to laugh or play either. The most I'd seen from the boys so far was a smile, and even that seemed reluctantly coaxed. The thing that distressed me most was the fear; I didn't understand why, but what I had seen in Brett earlier bordered on terror. I thought about every moment I had spent with them, and could not come up with a single thing that should have evoked that kind of reaction in the boy.

Astrid and Bobbie had the dining room table set when we came in with the food.

"Mommy!" blurted Brittany excitedly, "we stopped at McDonalds so Mitch and Brett could go potty, and I went all the way down on the slide!"

"You did? You used to be afraid."

"She loved it this time," said Brandon.

"I'm big now," said Brittany. "I was scared when I was little."

"Oh," said Bobbie, smiling affectionately at her daughter. "I'm very proud that you were so brave!"

"Can I sit next to Mitch?" asked Brett.

"Maybe Astrid would like to," said Bobbie.

"I want to sit next to Astrid!" insisted Brittany.

"Okay," said Bobbie. "We'll let Mitch sit at the head of the table. Astrid can sit next to him and Brittany can sit on her other side. Brett, you sit next to Mitch and Brandon will sit next to you. I'll sit opposite Mitch. Is everyone happy?"

All of us nodded silently. She had taken charge with authority and yet, there was not the feeling of being bossed that Rifka conveyed. I remembered what Brandon said about bossy women, and I was thinking that Rifka could have learned a thing or two from Bobbie.

I noticed during the meal that Astrid was picking disinterestedly at her food and wasn't really eating at all. I was starting to become really concerned about her. She insisted that she was feeling better, but she still didn't seem to be herself.

"My assistants and I will clean up," I insisted, after we had finished eating.

Brett and Brandon nodded their assent.

"I'll put the leftovers away," Astrid volunteered.

While I cleared the table and scraped the plates, Brett rinsed and Brandon loaded the dishwasher. Bobbie took Brittany upstairs for her bath. By the time Bobbie returned, you never would have known that a meal had been eaten.

I had promised Brittany that I would read her a story before she went to bed. For some reason, the boys enjoyed hearing me read, even from Brittany's books.

"I've never heard of this one," I said as she handed me *Madeline*; it was about a group of little girls in a French boarding school, with a headmistress called Miss Clavel. When I opened the front, it was obvious that this was another of Bobbie's hand-me-downs. Printed in a childish scrawl inside the front cover was the name Roberta Claire West.

I'll admit that there's a bit of ham in me, and instead of just reading it straight, I decided that I wanted these children to have some fun. I think I needed the reassurance of seeing some childlike reactions from them. I took a red straw hat with little white flowers off one of Brittany's dolls and sat it on my head when I was reading about Madeline or the little girls; I read those parts in a little, tiny voice. In a falsetto voice, with a pair of wire-rimmed glasses perched on the bridge of my nose, I read the parts about Miss Clavel. I had appropriated the glasses from a teddy bear that sat on a shelf above the bed, and they were much too small for me. I pranced around the room, doing my best impression of a little girl or a proper headmistress.

Brittany squealed delightedly at my antics, but the boys barely smiled. Finally, I stopped, looked right at them and said, "I'm trying hard to be funny; you'll hurt my feelings if you don't laugh."

They actually seemed to relax and enjoy themselves after that. I tried to teach Brett my Miss Clavel walk, and even Brandon got into it, showing us what we looked like from the back. Brittany, despite her best efforts to stay

326 What Remains Behind

awake, dozed off when we were about halfway through the book.

"Let's try not to wake her," I said softly, pointing to their sister.

Brandon turned on the night light and shut off the lamp. "We can go in my room," he offered.

I followed them down the hall and sat on one of the twin beds.

"You were a pretty funny Miss Clavel," said Brett.

"I sounded like I did at my Bar Mitzvah," I laughed.

The boys looked at me puzzled.

"Do you know what a Bar Mitzvah is?" I asked.

They both nodded. "I went to one once," said Brett, "and Brandon's been to six or eight."

"Some Bat Mitzvahs too," said Brandon.

"Have you ever been to one when the Bar Mitzvah boy's voice keeps breaking?" I asked.

"I never noticed," said Brandon.

"Don't look so serious," I said. "This is a funny story."

To my amazement, I found myself telling one of the embarrassing "Uncle Mitch" stories that Rifka loved to tell my nephews.

"My voice is deep now," I said, "but when I was a kid, it was pretty high. I studied really hard for my Bar Mitzvah, because I was afraid of looking foolish in front of all those people. The one thing I didn't count on was that I was nervous, and my voice was starting to change.

Through the whole thing, my voice kept breaking and I sounded just like Miss Clavel.

Brandon and Brett both nodded sympathetically.

"My father was so proud that morning when he helped me get dressed in my new suit, and I was sure he was really disappointed in me. When the services were over, he burst into tears. Of course, I wanted to die."

"But it wasn't your fault!" protested Brett.

"It turned out that he wasn't crying because he was disappointed. He said that I had been so perfect that he couldn't help himself; he had never been more proud of me. Here I had gone through my whole Bar Mitzvah sounding like Miss Clavel, and he was delighted.

"That must have been so embarrassing," said Brett.

"It was," I agreed, "but it was funny because nobody else noticed. After about the fourth or fifth time my father hugged and kissed me and told me how proud he was, I kept wondering if I could have pulled off doing something really funny and gotten away with it; I was kind of sorry that I didn't try."

"Did your father always hug and kiss you?" asked Brett.

"On special occasions. We always kissed each other good-bye or good-night. Why?"

"My dad never kissed me," said Brett.

"Are you sure?" I asked.

"Not that I can remember," insisted the boy.

"Me either," said Brandon. "He used to kiss Brittany, but she's a girl, and she's just a baby; maybe he did when we were babies, but I don't remember it."

"I guess every family is different," I said. "Mine are definitely kissers."

"It sounds kinds of nice," said Brett.

The boys made me promise to come back up to say good-night before I left.

Astrid and Bobbie were deeply involved in conversation when I joined them in the living room.

"We were trying to figure out how much money would be involved if this was being done for the insurance," said Astrid, holding the list she had created of names of people who had recently died.

"Even if some of them were insured, it doesn't seem like the money would be enough," said Bobbie. "How much cash do you think would be needed to turn things around?"

"The figure that's been mentioned in the press is two hundred million," I said.

Bobbie gave a low whistle. "That's a lot of money. How much do you think they could have insured each person for?"

"I have no idea. A million would probably be tops; I can't imagine an insurance company giving them more than two million each unless they could prove the person had an extraordinary talent."

"Astrid and I have been asking around for a few weeks," said Bobbie. "We now have a list of around seventy-five people who have died in the past year, but not all of them were professionals, and even some that were may not have been what would be considered highly paid. By the law of averages, some people who were made the offer had to have turned it down; you and Jim Deckle did. If we consider only people who fit the profile, we would have thirty at most."

"And that's the flaw in our theory," said Astrid. "It would take too long for them to get as much as they need inconspicuously."

"Maybe the deaths are just a strange coincidence," I said. "There is something I'd rather discuss right now, though."

"What's that?" asked Bobbie.

"Your children," I said. "There are some things that I find pretty disturbing, and I was wondering if you were aware of them."

"Mitch," said Astrid softly, her tone a warning.

"No, please go on," urged Bobbie.

"They don't know how to be kids," I said. "They don't play, they don't laugh; it doesn't seem normal."

"Mitch, how could you?" asked Astrid, looking stricken.

"It's okay, sweetheart," said Bobbie, sliding onto the couch next to Astrid and taking her hand. "I know what Mitch is saying; he isn't wrong. I've been worried too lately, especially about Brandon; he just isn't himself."

"I think Brandon is working it out," I said.

"Did something happen?" asked Bobbie.

I weighed what a mother had a right to know against my promise to her son. "He's starting to deal with his feelings a little more."

"Good," nodded Bobbie, and I was grateful that she didn't demand the details.

"I'm more worried about Brett," I said. "He actually seemed afraid of me earlier. I've gone over and over it in my mind, and I can't figure out what I could have done for him to react that way."

"Exactly what happened?" asked Bobbie.

"After we picked up the chicken, he had to go to the bathroom. He was absolutely terrified when he had to tell me. The boys were talking to each other, and I heard them mention 'torture safaris.' Does that mean anything to you?"

Bobbie nodded. "That was what they used to call our family car trips behind Bob's back. I understand why Brett was so upset. He was afraid of what was going to happen when he asked you to stop."

"I'm lost," I confessed.

"Bob used to come up with these places that we could go on family vacations," she said. "He would get tour books and maps, plan a route and make up a schedule. For him, it was a major production."

"It sounds like the way he ran our office."

"He would decide how far we had to go each day, and he would set a time for us to get there. Nothing made him angrier than having to deviate from his schedule. When the kids were small, that was very hard. They would get restless and fussy and need to stop. When they got older, Bob would tell them what the day's schedule was and how long we were going to travel. If he decided that we would go three hours without a stop, that is what he did, no matter what anyone else wanted. If they kids had to go to the bathroom, he told them they had to wait."

"To be fair," said Astrid, "kids sometimes ask to go because they are bored; I remember I used to do that in the car."

"I'm sure that was it some of the time, but sometimes, they really had to go, and Bob would not stop. He berated them for not 'taking care of business' before we left."

"He used that line at work too," I interrupted.

"If he did give in and stop, he would always point out something that everyone thought would be fun and say that we couldn't do it, because we had used that time for a rest stop. I used to carry a bottle and sometimes plastic bags and toilet paper for emergencies, but when the boys got older, it was humiliating for them.

"These trips went on every summer until Brittany was born, even though everyone but Bob hated them. That last year, I was seven months pregnant, and he decided that we would go to New Hampshire to see Franconia's Notch. It's a beautiful area, but there wasn't too much for the boys to do there, and I had my doubts, but Bob insisted that it would be fun.

"All three of my pregnancies were very different; with Brittany, I felt wonderful most of the time, except it seemed that she was always pushing against one organ or the other. Toward the middle of my pregnancy, I was carrying very high and I had shortness of breath. Later on, she dropped low, and I had almost constant pressure on my bladder. On that trip, Bob wouldn't even stop for me. I can tell you that I couldn't always hold my bladder for two hours after I had the urge, and it is not easy for a woman seven months pregnant to pee in a bottle in a moving car."

I looked away, embarrassed.

"Couldn't you explain how you felt?" asked Astrid. "If he understood how uncomfortable you were, surely he would have been more accommodating."

"Oh, I did better than explain," laughed Bobbie. "I showed him how it felt!"

"How?" I couldn't resist asking.

"We stopped overnight near a small town, and I went into a drug store to pick up some Tums for Bob. I was looking along the shelf when I spotted a laxative that promised 'dependable relief in fifteen minutes to an hour.'"

"You didn't!" gasped Astrid.

"I was so angry that I did," said Bobbie. "In the morning, before we left our motel room, I mixed it in a glass of orange juice and he didn't even know it was there. Then, I offered to drive. I told the boys very clearly that we would not be stopping until we got where we were going.

"It took about forty-five minutes before Bob felt the effects. 'I need to stop,' he told me. I told him that we'd be there in another hour and fifteen minutes. There really wasn't anyplace along the route we were traveling, or I might have given in; he looked so miserable that I was almost sorry for what I had done. After about fifteen minutes more, he asked if I had any plastic bags; I told him there weren't any. He sat there, writhing and twisting. I didn't stop until I knew he had messed himself."

"He must have gotten the point," I said.

"Oh, he got the point," said Bobbie acidly. "He made sure not to let me drive again. After we got home, I told him that if he wanted to take another car trip, he could go without me and the children. That was the last one we took, but even when we were going somewhere in the area, he was the same way. He would not stop unless he needed to."

"He was pretty attached to his schedules at work too," I said.

"How could you two have stayed together so long, being so mean to each other?" asked Astrid, more of herself than to Bobbie. "I could never have done anything like that to Mitch, and I couldn't see him doing it to me either."

I shook my head adamantly.

"That was just our way, Astrid. We seemed to thrive on challenging each other to the limit. I realize that it wasn't very mature, but that was how we dealt with each other. We met and married when we were pretty young; maybe neither of us ever grew up."

"But now that Bob is gone, don't you think it's time for a change?" I asked. "Couldn't you see your way clear to show your boys that they can be a bit more comfortable with themselves? As annoying as it can be, I'd feel better refereeing a battle between those two than watching Brett quake with fear because he had to go to the bathroom. That unnerved me."

"Mitch, that's not fair!" said Astrid protectively. "Bobbie is doing the best she can. A lot has changed in her life."

"I'm not trying to be critical of anyone, least of all Bobbie," I protested. "I think anyone would agree that she's a terrific mother. I'm just worried. They're kids; they should be driving us nuts doing kid things, but they don't. There should be some happiness in their lives; they've had their share of pain at an earlier age than most people do."

"I appreciate your defending me, Astrid, but Mitch is right, and I'm grateful that he cares so much. Brett wasn't afraid of you, Mitch. He was afraid that if he disappointed you, he would lose your affection."

"That will never happen."

"I know," agreed Bobbie, "but I'm not quite sure how we can convince Brett of that. I suppose I have failed him badly."

"You're much too hard on yourself," protested Astrid. "You need some time to get your own bearings."

"The kids are more important than what I need at this point. I have something to add to what I told you earlier.

Let me just make sure there are no little ears lurking around."

Bobbie went toward the stairs.

"Are you all right?" I asked Astrid when we were alone. "I noticed that you didn't eat very much."

"I'm fine. I was disappointed that Bobbie didn't know about the letter. I was sure we'd figured it out; I couldn't get it out of my mind while we were eating, and it killed my appetite. From the beginning, that deal made me uncomfortable."

"I know, but I would be more upset it there was a connection," I said, rubbing the back of my neck.

"You okay?" she asked.

"My neck is a little tight."

She came behind me and began to gently massage my upper back and neck. The woman has magic hands.

Bobbie came back into the room. "Brandon is in the shower and Brett and Brittany are asleep. Now would be a good time for me to finish."

Astrid and I nodded.

"Last weekend, after I went to the cemetery, I realized that my life does have to change. My children need stability; I know that my sons crave male attention. I also realized that now that Bob is gone, I would never have a normal relationship with anyone else, as long as I continued to see Lou. I told him on Wednesday that I won't see him again."

"That must have been very hard for you," I said.

"I've had to keep myself from calling him more than once, but so far, I haven't given in. I've also given some serious thought to moving to the west coast, to be nearer my brother."

"Take some time before you make such radical changes," said Astrid gently.

"It's just a thought right now. I don't know that it makes much sense; my boys hardly know Bill. They are much closer to you, Mitch."

"I care about them, Bobbie."

"I know that, but I'm afraid that I'm being unfair. It seems like I'm imposing on the two of you. You have enough in your own lives without taking on the four of us too."

"We don't mind," said Astrid.

I nodded in agreement.

"Oh, when you asked about getting a letter from Businetex before, I forgot to tell you, I did get one," said Bobbie.

"About what?" I asked.

"It seems they have decided to invite me to the Virgin Islands, in Bob's place, for Labor Day weekend."

"We've been invited to that too," said Astrid. "Are you going?"

"I didn't think you would be included," said Bobbie to Astrid. "Now, I wish I could do it."

"A change of scenery might do you good," I suggested.

"It probably would," agreed Bobbie, "but I don't want to be away from the children while Brandon is having such a rough time. Usually, I can leave them with Mother, but it's Brandon the younger two look to for reassurance. I don't think it would be fair to put that burden on him right now."

"You may be right," I said. "I don't want to seem rude, Bobbie, but it's been a long day. Would you mind if we called it a night?"

"Of course not," she said. "I've been inconsiderate; it never occurred to me that you might be tired."

"I'm not really tired," I said. "More like wrung out. I did promise the boys I'd look in on them before we left."

I felt very old as I walked wearily up the stairs. Brittany's room was right at the top. I peeked in the open door. She was lying on her side with her thumb in her mouth. She had been covered with the sheet but she had managed to kick it off. I covered her again and kissed her lightly on the top of her tousled curls. She did not stir and I tiptoed back out.

I looked in on Brandon next. He was stretched out on his back, fully clothed, on one of the beds. There was an afghan on the chair, and I unfolded it and covered him. It was too short, but I guessed it was better than nothing. I looked at him sleeping. The expression on his face was one of worry; he looked like a lost child. On impulse, I kissed him on the forehead. His face relaxed and I went into Brett's room.

Brett was asleep, half on and half off the bed. As gently as I could, I got him back on the mattress and put the covers over him. He frowned slightly but did not awaken. I brushed the hair off his forehead and kissed him softly. I was closing the door behind me when I heard him call out.

"Mitch?"

"Go back to sleep," I whispered. "I didn't mean to wake you."

"That's okay," he said sleepily, sitting up.

I went back into the room and sat on the edge of his bed. "Astrid and I were getting ready to leave; I was checking on you, like I promised."

"Mitch, today was the best day of my whole life!"

"I'm glad you had a good time today, Brett, but this was only the beginning of many good times to follow. There will a lot of better days ahead."

"I love you, Mitch!" he said, throwing his arms around me so violently that I almost slid onto the floor. Then, embarrassed, he added, "I don't mean like you love a girl."

"I know what you meant," I said, putting my arms around him and gently patting his back. "I love you and Brandon and Brittany too. You are all very important to me."

I wasn't watching where I was going as I walked out of Brett's room, rubbing the back of my neck. I didn't see Brandon standing in the hallway; he startled me.

"Do you still have a headache?" he asked.

"No, it's better. It's just been a long, hard day."

"I was awake when you came in before," he said. "I felt dishonest not letting you know."

"You looked like you needed something," I said. "My father always used to look in on us and kiss us good-night before he went to bed, and it made me feel safe; I thought it might make you feel that way too."

"He did it even when you were my age?" asked Brandon.

"Even after I was married," I said. "The first time, he scared poor Astrid half to death, but she said that once she knew what he was doing, it made her feel safe too. My family was just like that; kind of a *Where the Wild Things Are* bunch."

"Very different from what I'm used to," said Brandon.

"I'm sorry; I shouldn't have done it; I didn't mean to embarrass you."

"You didn't," he said, his gaze meeting mine. "It was nice. It made me feel like I was special."

"You are special."

"Do you miss your father?" asked Brandon.

"All the time."

"How long has he been dead?"

"More than two years."

"And it doesn't go away?" asked the boy.

"It's changed since it first happened. It's easier to think about him now; sometimes, it's comforting."

"Did you cry when your father died?" asked Brandon.

"No," I said. "My father was sick for a long time; I had a lot of time to get used to the idea that I was going to lose him. Near the end, he was in terrible pain, and the people who loved him had to watch him suffer. I didn't want him to go, but I was kind of relieved that it was over for him."

Brandon nodded.

"It wasn't that I didn't feel anything, Brandon. I told you earlier that we are too much alike; I wouldn't let myself cry."

He came over and hugged me, and I hugged him back.

Wearily, I walked down the stairs. Astrid was waiting for me by the door.

"Thank you for dinner and for everything else you've done," said Bobbie.

"Don't mention it," I said.

As an afterthought, I walked over and kissed her on the cheek. She looked surprised.

"What was that for?" she asked.

"That is because you are one terrific lady who certainly knows how to raise great kids," I said.

She looked embarrassed but I knew she was pleased.

Chapter 8
Astrid

I should have realized that something was not right with Astrid and I should have insisted that she see the doctor long before she did, but I was so distracted by all the chaos at Businetex that I must admit, I let my personal life slide a bit.

By the time the week before Labor Day arrived, we couldn't ignore it any longer. "Honey," I said, as I held a cold washcloth to her forehead after she had vomited her breakfast, "we have to face it; you're sick. You can't hold anything down for more than a few hours, and you're exhausted all the time. Hopefully, it's nothing worse than a stubborn bug, but whatever it turns out to be, we need to find out so you can be treated."

"You're right," she agreed weakly.

I think she was really frightened that Monday morning when she called the doctor for an appointment; I know I was.

"I made that call," she said in greeting when I answered my phone later that morning.

I was relieved that she had followed through on her promise.

"My regular doctor is away until Wednesday. They said they could get me in immediately, but I'm more

342 What Remains Behind

comfortable seeing someone I know. Since I've waited this long, I doubt that a few more days will matter," she told me.

I'm not sure that I agree with that logic," I protested.

"I think I did the right thing. Right after I knew I had the appointment scheduled, I started to feel better. I'm going in to work this afternoon."

"Don't you think you should give yourself more time? You were so sick this morning, I felt like a jerk leaving you," I confessed.

"I'm fine now," she assured me. "I'll see you later."

On Tuesday, Astrid called me at work, sounding relieved.

"I think I know what's the matter with me," she said.

"Did something happen?" I asked.

"Nothing to worry about," she said lightly. "I think I know why I've been feeling so awful. I suspect that I have a urinary tract infection."

"What makes you say that?"

"All morning long, I've had the feeling I have to go, even when I don't. I had an infection once, back in college, and that was one of the symptoms. It can make you feel really awful. I've been drinking water by the gallon. Keeping your urine diluted is supposed to help, and cranberry juice is supposed kill the bacteria; I'm going to get some on my lunch hour."

"I hope that's all it is," I said.

"We'll know for sure tomorrow morning," she replied.

I didn't bother to tell her about my morning. I figured that it would keep until I got home and, if she was really sick, it could even wait until she was better.

I had been surprised when earlier that morning, a little after nine, Beth buzzed me."

"Walter Nelson is here to see you," she announced in her most businesslike tone.

I went right out, wondering what a vice president of the company could want of me.

"Mitch," he said, offering his hand.

I shook the hand uncertainly. We had only met once, and I'm sure he didn't remember shaking my hand out of all of those he shook that day.

"Mr. Nelson, what can I do for you?" I asked.

"Oh, please, call me Walt. I wanted to thank you for the good job you've been doing for us," he said. "Jerry kept me posted."

"I appreciate your saying so," I replied.

"As you know," he said, "I'm just 'the little cheese' but I'm here on behalf of 'the big cheese.'"

Hearing him say that struck me funny, but I managed to control myself. I merely nodded and waited to hear what was on his mind.

"We were wondering if you think you'd be able to hold the fort down until we find someone to replace Jerry."

"You want me to do his job?"

"We'd like you to take over what he was doing until we can find someone permanent," replied Nelson. "We think you are familiar enough with the division to keep things going during the search. Of course, you can use his office, and his secretary will do what she can to help you."

"It's flattering that you have so much confidence in me," I said, "but what about my job?"

"We will trust you to pick someone who's able to fill in for you while you're gone. After you've trained Jerry's replacement, you can step right back to where you are now."

"You aren't considering me for Jerry's job?"

"On a permanent basis?"

"Yes," I replied. "I realize it's a jump for me, but I think I'm capable; you must too or you wouldn't be asking me to fill in."

Nelson gave a booming laugh. He really did look like Humpty Dumpty. At five foot six, he had to look up at me when we talked, and with his bald head on his neckless round body, he had the physique of a huge egg. "It's nice to meet someone so young and ambitious, but you are hardly qualified to take over the job permanently. We're looking for someone with many years of experience as a manager. We probably will hire from outside the company; that worked out very well the last time."

I decided right then and there that the man was an idiot. He thought I was good enough to fill in until they found someone, and good enough to train Jerry's replacement; what more did they want?

"I think that I am qualified," I said, "but of course, that's your call."

"Well, I suppose you may surprise us. To be honest, George wasn't too keen on letting you fill Bob's job, but Jerry insisted that we give you a chance, so I agreed that you could have your shot. I have a lot of influence for a 'little cheese,'" he laughed.

His laugh was a combination of the bray of a donkey and the scream of a hyena; it was really irritating.

"You said earlier that you were pleased with my work," I said. "Was that the truth?"

"Oh, so far, you're doing fine," he said, slapping me on the back. "If you keep it up, I see no reason why you shouldn't keep your present job, after the trial period is over."

"I didn't realize there was a trial period," I said tersely.

"Three months," said Nelson. "We told Jerry that you would be evaluated after that time, and a decision would be made. Didn't he mention it?"

"This is the first I've heard about it."

"Well, it's nothing to worry about," said Nelson. "I'm sure you'll come through with flying colors."

At that moment, I came to a decision. I knew that I was working for the wrong company, and I knew that I couldn't stay there, no matter what they decided about my future.

"So, how about it, Mitch?" Walt was asking. "Can we count on you to take over the wheel for the short term?"

I knew that the job market was not the best it had ever been, and I'd been part of the corporate world for far too long to ever burn a bridge when it wasn't absolutely necessary. "Of course, I'll do what I can," I offered.

Walter Nelson pumped my hand enthusiastically. "It's nice to know we can count on you," he boomed.

I waited until I was sure he was gone before I began to flip through my Rolodex. I always kept a list of headhunters who called me with job opportunities. I placed calls to three of them who had contacted me recently, and told them that I was about to begin an active job search.

"Are you willing to relocate?" asked the third one I contacted, someone I had dealt with back when I was living in Connecticut.

I hadn't really given it much thought, but I knew that I had to give him some leeway. "I know that my wife won't be happy about leaving the area," I told him, "but I'll do what I must. If she's really against it, I'll try to stay within an hour or so by air, and I'll commute home on weekends." I knew that if I wanted to make a move that would be beneficial career-wise, it was unlikely that I could continue to work in Rochester.

Later that afternoon, I spoke to Tony Sullivan, one of the engineers who worked for me.

"I was wondering if you would be willing to fill in for me for a while," I asked.

"Are you finally taking a vacation?" he wondered.

"I wish I could," I smiled. "I've been recruited to take over for Jerry, until the company finds a permanent replacement."

"I'm sure you're on the short list," he said.

"No, I'm not under consideration," I told him. "There's no chance that this will be a permanent move for you either; I want you to understand that."

"They should work for you for a while; they would know that you're the logical replacement for Jerry. You're the best boss I've ever had."

"Thanks, Tony. It means a lot to me coming from you. Are you interested in the job?"

"Very much so. Thank you for having enough confidence in me to ask," he replied exuberantly.

I knew that Deckle would be disappointed and probably angry at me, but after his performance while I served on grand jury, I couldn't put the people who worked for me through that again. Not if I intended to come back to my job, when I was unceremoniously replaced by Jerry's successor.

"Do you have a minute?" I asked from his doorway.

"Sure, Mitch, come on in," he said happily. "Give your old chair a try!"

"I only have a minute," I replied, stepping into the office but remaining on my feet. "I wanted you to hear this directly from me. I've asked Tony Sullivan to fill in for me while I take over Jerry's job during the search for his replacement."

Deckle's face fell. "How could you do this to me? You know I'm ready to move up."

"I considered you," I lied, "but since there was no chance that it would be a permanent promotion, I thought I would spare you the hassle of moving into a new situation, only to have to return to your old job after a short time."

I don't think he totally believed me, but at least he was fairly cordial when I left his office.

Before leaving for the day, I went over to Jerry's old office. Maggie was sitting at her desk, staring off into space.

"A penny for your thoughts," I said.

"You're here," she said softly.

"Yes," I replied. "I've been asked to fill in for Jerry until they find a replacement."

"I knew that, but I didn't think you'd be willing to work with me," she said dully.

"Why?"

"Word around the office is that life gets dangerous when I'm around," she said as she dissolved into tears.

I went over and gently took her arm. "Come on in here," I said, gesturing to Jerry's office. She allowed me to lead her inside, and I closed the door. I didn't think that anyone who happened to walk by needed to watch her falling apart.

She leaned against the wall and began to sob. I let her cry for a few minutes. Then, I pulled some tissues from my pocket and offered them to her.

She wiped her eyes and blew her nose. "I'm sorry."

"No need to apologize. I think everyone's unnerved by so many deaths in such a short time."

"People are calling me 'Poison Maggie,'" she said.

"That's dumb. You had nothing to do with any of it."

"Two of the people worked with me, and the third, well..."

"I'm not superstitious," I said.

Maggie opened a door and walked into a bathroom adjacent to the office.

"I didn't know Jerry had his own bathroom," I said.

"He didn't want anyone to know," replied Maggie. "He was very proud of it, but he was terrified that someone else would want to use it. He was a very strange man."

"Yes," I agreed.

She left the door open, and I heard the water running. "Come on in and look around, if you want," she invited.

I walked tentatively through the door. She was carefully blotting her eyes with a paper towel.

"Wow," I said, "he had a shower and everything."

"I suppose it's yours now," observed Maggie.

"Only temporarily; Nelson made that very clear."

"'I'm just the little cheese but I'm here for the big cheese,'" boomed Maggie, doing an excellent imitation.

I smiled. "I didn't think it was the first time he'd used that line."

"He says it every time he meets someone new. Doesn't he have any idea that he sounds like a moron?"

"Apparently not," I said, looking around the bathroom. "What's in here?" I asked, gesturing to a closed door.

"Oh, it's just a closet."

I looked at her and then opened the door. There was a case of Gatorade on the floor, and on a hook on the back wall, there was a very familiar looking gym bag.

"Isn't that Artie's gym bag?" I asked.

Maggie shrugged. "It could be. Artie always kept it in there. He and Jerry shared the cases of Gatorade too. He was the only other person I know of who Jerry let in this bathroom."

"But Artie collapsed at the health club. How did the bag get back here?"

"Jerry must have brought it back with him. I didn't know it was there; take it if you want."

I lifted it from the hook and opened the zipper. Tentatively, I peeked inside. There was a towel, an extra pair of sweat socks, a can of tennis balls, racquetball eye protectors and a bottle of Gatorade about half full. I picked up the bottle carefully.

"Do you mind if I take this?" I asked.

"There's a whole case down there," she said. "Why don't you take a fresh one?"

"This is the one I want."

"Suit yourself," shrugged Maggie.

"Maggie, did Jerry have a personal file here in the office?" I asked.

"I think I remember seeing one. Do you want to look at it?"

"If you wouldn't mind."

She opened one of the file drawers and searched for several moments; then, she handed me a folder about an inch thick.

I thumbed through receipts, a bill from a dentist, two insurance policies and a packet of letters. About halfway through the pile, I found what I was looking for.

"Bingo!" I said, more to myself than to anyone else.

"What is it?" asked Maggie.

"I found what I was looking for," I said.

"I'm glad," she replied.

"Maggie," I said, suddenly having a thought, "did Bob keep a personal file in his office?"

"Why do you ask?" she wondered suspiciously.

I thought about how much to tell her. "I find what's been going on around here to be pretty alarming. I think I've come up with a link between several people who have recently died; I'm trying to find out if Bob's death was really an accident."

"There's no file in his office that I know of. I know you didn't approve of what Bob and I did," she added.

"I didn't approve," I agreed, "but I think you're a good person, Maggie."

"I could lose my job for what I'm about to tell you."

"It won't leave this office. You have my word."

"That's good enough for me. Bob did keep a personal file; after he died, I went into his office and took it."

"Where is it now?" I asked.

"Underneath the liner of my top desk drawer. I promise you that's the only thing I took. I know that Mrs. McCann knew about us, but there were receipts and things. I didn't know how much she knew. If someone found it, the only use it could have had was to hurt her or me."

"Maggie, I don't want to hurt either of you. I like you, and Bobbie McCann is a close friend. I just want to see if something is in there."

She looked hesitant.

"I'll tell you what," I proposed. "You look through it and see if you can find a letter from Businetex. What I'm interested in specifically is a letter about the company taking out insurance on his life, making Businetex the beneficiary."

I sat down at Jerry's desk and waited. A few minutes later, Maggie returned and placed an envelope in front of me.

"I think this is what you want," she said.

I removed the letter from the envelope and read it. The final gap had been closed.

"Thank you, Maggie," I said. "And if you don't mind a suggestion, I think you ought to run the rest of that file through the shredder. As you said, a lot of harm could be done if it were to find its way into the wrong hands."

Maggie studied me for a moment. I had no idea what she was thinking. "I suppose you're right," she sighed. "I'll take care of it immediately."

I was on my way out of the office when I heard her say my name.

"Mitch?" she called softly.

I turned to face her. "Yes, Maggie?"

"Your wife is a very lucky woman."

"That's nice of you to say," I replied. "We're both lucky."

"Yes," said Maggie, "I guess so."

***

Astrid was really excited when I put the two letters on the kitchen table in front of her. "This is it!" she said excitedly. "This has to be the link!"

"So it would seem," I agreed, "but don't get too excited. It still doesn't add up. Remember when we discussed this at Bobbie's? Nothing's changed; they couldn't get the sum of money they need fast enough."

"But there is a pattern!" she said excitedly.

"I'm more concerned about you right now than I am about this," I said. "How are you feeling?"

"I don't know if it's just in my mind, but I seem to feel better since I started drinking the cranberry juice. I still have some pressure but I don't feel as wrung out."

"Good," I said, "but that's not enough to keep you from seeing the doctor tomorrow."

"Nine o'clock. Hopefully, he'll give me a prescription and that will be the end of it."

"Hopefully. I did find something else today," I added.

"What?"

"The bottle of Gatorade that Artie was drinking the night he died, or at least I think that's what it is."

"What are you going to do with it?"

"I'd like to find out if there is Digoxin in it but I'm not sure how I'd do that."

"Marilyn might know," suggested Astrid.

I kissed her enthusiastically. "You're a genius!"

I punched the button on the auto dialer next to Marilyn's name.

"Yes, hello?" said my sister expectantly.

"Marilyn, hi, it's me."

"How are you, baby brother?"

"Fine. Astrid's fine too," I added, before she had the chance to ask.

"You sound like a man on a mission," she observed.

"So to speak."

"What do you want me to convince Ma to do now?"

"This has nothing to do with Ma. I want to ask you a medical question."

"I'll try to tell you what you want to know," she said, "but if you're sick, you should go to a doctor."

"Marilyn, I'm not sick. You're starting to sound like Ma. I want to know how I can find out if some liquid contains a certain drug. How would I do that?"

"There are labs that do analysis," she said.

"They could tell me if it contains Digoxin?"

"I could tell you if it contains Digoxin. It's not that difficult. Our office has a machine that tests for that drug. Any lab could do it."

"Can you do it?" I asked.

"I don't know," she said. "I could probably tell you if it was present; I don't think I could tell you the exact concentration."

"If I got a sample to you, you could tell me if the drug was present?"

"Mitch, what's going on?"

"I've come into possession of a bottle of Gatorade that I think Artie was drinking before he died. I want to know whether it has Digoxin in it."

"Take it to the police," said Marilyn. "It might be evidence."

"Marilyn, it's been missing for two months. I'm not even sure how it got where it was, who had it, or even if it is the right bottle. I learned enough on Grand Jury to know that nobody will consider it to be evidence of anything. I just want to know for myself if there is Digoxin in it. Depending on the answer, I'll decide what I'm going to do."

"This is against my better judgment," said Marilyn, "but if you Fed Ex it to me, I'll take it in to the office and see what I can do."

As soon as I got off the phone, Astrid and I poured some of the Gatorade into two small bottles, sealed the tops with tape, placed them in a box, and cushioned them with paper and Styrofoam peanuts. I didn't want to wait until morning to send it, so we drove it over to the airport. Now, all we could do was wait to hear from Marilyn.

***

Astrid sounded upset when she called me at my office the next morning. "I don't have an infection," she said. "My urine specimen didn't show anything."

"I suppose that's good news," I said, "but what is making you feel so bad?"

"I don't know. He says that whatever it is, he doesn't think it's serious. I may have had the beginning of an infection and the cranberry juice cleared it up, or it may be a bug that's hanging on. They're running blood tests. He wants me to come back in first thing Friday morning. He says he wants to see the test results before he does anything. He did tell me not to worry," she added dubiously.

"I suppose two more days isn't that long," I said, trying to console her.

"No, but that pretty much rules out my going to St. Thomas."

"I'll see if I can get out of it too," I offered.

"No," said Astrid, "I think you should go. Now that you've taken over Jerry's job, your presence would be missed."

"I told you how I felt about that and about this company," I said, wondering for a moment if it was possible that someone was somehow listening in on our conversation, and feeling like an idiot for thinking the way Deckle did.

"You've also told me how you feel about burning bridges," said Astrid. "You go; I'll be fine."

"I won't enjoy myself," I said miserably.

"You'd better not," she laughed.

A little while after I spoke with Astrid, I impulsively picked up the phone and dialed Bobbie McCann's number.

"I thought I should tell you about something I learned yesterday," I began.

"You found the letter. I just finished speaking with Astrid," she added sheepishly.

"I thought you had the right to know," I said.

"I won't ask where you found it."

I didn't offer to tell. "Did Astrid tell you that she won't be going to St. Thomas after all?" I asked.

"She told me that she'd been to the doctor and has to go back on Friday, but she didn't mention that she wasn't going on the trip."

"She wants me to go and realistically, I probably will have to, but I was wondering if I could ask a favor of you? Would you mind very much keeping an eye on her while I'm gone?"

"You're doing me the favor," said Bobbie. "My mother is staying with us while her apartment is being painted. I will look upon any excuse to escape as a gift from God."

"How long is she staying?" I asked.

"About two weeks, or until we kill each other, whichever comes first. The smart money is on homicide."

"At least the kids should enjoy having Grandma around," I said optimistically.

"Well, Brittany seems to like it. Grandma has taught my daughter to climb into bed with her every night; I'm really grateful for that," said Bobbie sarcastically. "Brandon and Brett are sharing a room so that Mom can have Brett's room, and they are at each other's throats. Brandon has been seeing a lot of a girl he knows from school, and Brett is feeling left out and, I think, a bit envious. I have never heard so much squabbling about such nonsense in my life."

"I'm glad to hear it," I laughed. "It sounds a lot like normal sibling rivalry."

"And you wished this on me?"

"You know they would still give up their lives for each other," I said.

"I do know that, but I liked it better when they got along," said Bobbie. "Astrid and I may just run off together and send you home to my mother!"

***

The plane to St. Thomas was scheduled to leave at noon on Friday. A bus was leaving for the airport from the Businetex parking lot at ten-thirty, so Astrid dropped me off at work on her way to her doctor's appointment.

We kissed each other good-bye longingly. "You call me the minute you're done with the doctor," I instructed.

"If you don't hear from me before take-off, you call me. I have the phone right here," she said, patting her purse.

I decided that I was going to try to get some work done before I left. Maggie seemed put out that I kept giving her things to do; Jerry had arranged for her to go along on the trip before he died, even though all the other secretaries had been excluded, and she was watching the clock. At nine forty-five, I finally gave up and told her that she could go. No sooner did she leave than the phone started ringing.

"Hello?" I said on the fourth ring.

"It's me," said Astrid happily. "I'm done with the doctor and he was right; it's nothing bad. He gave me a prescription to have filled, and I should be fine. How would you like some company in St. Thomas?"

"I'd love it!" I said enthusiastically.

"I called Bobbie and convinced her to be impulsive for once in her life. She's coming too. I hope that's all right."

"That's great," I said. "Is it okay for her to be away now?"

"The boys urged her to go; the kids will be fine with Mrs. West, and Bobbie is losing her mind with her mother there."

"Great," I said. "I'll talk to Beth."

"Bobbie called Walter Nelson's office. His secretary said that tickets will be waiting for us at the counter, and she promised she would make the room arrangements."

"What exactly did the doctor say? Why have you been sick?"

"I'll tell you later, when I see you."

After I hung up, I started to think about the trip, and I realized that it might be awkward for Bobbie and Maggie to keep on running into each other all weekend. I decided to stop at Beth's desk on my way to the bus.

"What are you doing here?" she demanded when she saw me. "Mr. Nelson said that you had already gone two hours ago, when he dropped off the bags."

"The bags?" I asked, mystified.

"Yes," said Beth. "He brought the two suitcases he said you forgot and asked me to have them messengered to the airport. He didn't want them on the bus; he said they were too important, and he didn't want you to get on that plane without them. I sent them over more than an hour ago; they must be there by now."

"I have no idea what you're talking about," I protested.

"I don't know; you'll have to speak to Mr. Nelson. I just did what I was told. Also, your sister Marilyn called and she wanted you to call her back. She said she was at work and she has the answer to your question."

I took the message slip and dialed Marilyn's number on Beth's phone. "Sis," I said when she finally came on the line, "what have you got?"

"I got your package yesterday, and I ran the test as soon as I got to work this morning," she said. "What you suspected is true; it does contain Digoxin. I can't give you any exact figure but I'd guess there's a pretty high concentration."

"Thanks," I said.

"What are you going to do now?" she asked.

"I'm not sure."

"Be careful, baby brother," she admonished.

"More than ever, boss lady," I replied.

"Bad news?" asked Beth.

"I'm not sure what it means yet," I said.

"Well, don't ask me; I only take the messages," she said curtly.

"Since you're in such a good mood, I'd like to ask you for a favor," I said.

"What?"

"I was wondering if you could call the hotel and make sure that they haven't put Mrs. McCann in a room anywhere near Maggie."

"Maybe Maggie deserves to squirm."

"Maybe," I agreed, "but Mrs. McCann deserves better."

"You're right; I'll make the call. I'm just a little upset that I was left out. A hundred dollars at the company store is a far cry from a weekend on a Caribbean island."

"I'm sorry about that too," I said, genuinely meaning it. "I didn't agree with the decision, but I was not consulted. Secretaries were not included, but if you subscribe to Deckle's Law, you may be the lucky one."

"How's that?"

"Deckle says that whenever the company does something nice for you, watch your back. He claims they always have an ulterior motive. Who knows? This could be a going away party. When we get in on Tuesday morning, there may be pink slips waiting for all of us."

"He couldn't take too much stock in his own law," sniffed Beth. "He's going."

"He decided that if he was going to be screwed, it would happen anyway, so he might as well take advantage of the trip. He also figured that they couldn't fire every professional whose group has met a deadline in the past six months.   That's too far-fetched even for Deckle's imagination."

"Do you think that secretaries are immune from getting the ax?"

"No, I suppose secretaries don't get special treatment either," I sighed.

"Unless they're sleeping with the right people," sniffed Beth.

"Even if it's true, that was beneath you."

"I'm sorry," she said, lowering her eyes.

"I'll tell you what," I proposed.   "I'll bring you a souvenir."

"For real?" she asked.

"What would you like?"

"I've heard that watches are cheap there," she hinted.

"Okay. I'll bring you a watch; a nice one."

"You really don't have to. I'm being a brat; I'll make the call."

"Thanks," I said.

"Mitch?" called Deckle.

"Yes, Jim?"

"Are you going to meet the bus?"

"In a minute."

"Let me get my bag and we'll walk together," he said.

I wondered how friendly he would be when he learned that Astrid was meeting me on the plane.

"Mitch!" called Beth as Deckle and I were about to leave the office.

I turned around expectantly, and she quickly caught up with us.

"Something strange is going on," she said.

"What's that?"

"Mrs. McCann just called and asked if I could arrange a spa appointment for her. I called Frenchman's Reef and asked to talk to someone in charge of the Businetex trip. I know in the past, they have sent a team of people down days before to arrange all the bookings, but they claim no one from the company has arrived yet, although check-in for guests starts at three today. That is where you're staying, isn't it?

"Yes," I replied.

"Don't you find that odd?" wondered Beth. "They confirmed the room reservations, but they couldn't schedule Mrs. McCann for the spa. They said that's handled by the Businetex reps."

"Okay, thanks Beth," I mused absently, still wondering about those suitcases that I couldn't recall ever having heard about.

"You must have asked the wrong thing," said Deckle. He raced back to Beth's desk and dialed the phone number in his travel packet and asked to confirm his helicopter tour of the island. A few minutes later, he replace the phone and gave us a perplexed stare. "They told me the same thing."

"Surprise, surprise," said Beth sarcastically.

"This makes no sense," said Deckle. "The last time I went on one of these trips, they met us at the airport in limousines, picked up our luggage, and gave us tickets for all our excursions. What's going on?"

"I don't know," I said, "but something doesn't seem right. First those suitcases that I know nothing about, and now, no Businetex reps on hand for our arrival. On both of the other trips I've taken, there was a hospitality team in place when we got there."

Deckle went back to the phone and made another call. "Well, the plane is leaving on time," he said.

Beth went back to her desk and looked in her directory. She dialed a number and waited. "Hello, Emily," she said. "This is Beth down in printers. I was wondering if you could tell me who took care of arranging the hospitality staff for the St. Thomas trip." There was a pause as Beth listened intently. "Oh, really? I see. Well, thanks."

"What?" I asked, studying the strange expression on her face.

"She said that she booked the hotel rooms but Walter Nelson took care of all the other arrangements himself. This is a man who won't even pour himself a cup of coffee. She knows nothing about any of it, and you can't ask him, because he flew down to St. Thomas last night, so that he could be there to greet everyone when they arrived."

"But you said he was here this morning," I said.

"Him or his identical twin," Beth insisted.

"There couldn't be two of them; nature couldn't be that cruel," I said. "I wish there was some way that we could find out what he's up to without tipping our hand.

"There may be," proposed Deckle.

Both Beth and I had forgotten that he was there, but now we both gave him our undivided attention.

"How?" I asked.

"Let's go to Jerry's office," he said. "Less chance of anyone walking in on us there."

We followed him in silence and I closed the door behind us. "What did you have in mind?" I asked.

Deckle walked around the room, closing the bathroom door, looking under the furniture, and even unscrewing the mouthpiece on the phone. I couldn't believe it; he was checking for bugs!

"It's risky but we could see what's in his e-mail," said Deckle when his search proved fruitless. "That's one area that's really vulnerable to surveillance. I never use it for anything important myself."

"How would we do that?" I asked.

"We need his employee number," said Deckle.

"That's easy," said Beth. "Those are listed in the directory that all the secretaries have. She dashed out and came back a few minutes later with a booklet.

"The next part is harder," said Deckle. "We need his password."

"How are we going to get that?" I asked.

"It's usually obvious," said Deckle. "Most people used their pet's name or their birthday. Something easy for them to remember."

He was right; my password was Astrid followed by our wedding anniversary; Artie had always used Natalie followed by her birthday.

I picked up a copy of the company magazine that was sitting on the shelf behind the desk. The front had a brief profile of each of the officers.

"March 25, 1939," I said.

Deckle sat down at the computer and began typing. "That's not it," he said. "It isn't his name either. Is he married?"

"Divorced," I said, reading through the article, "and he lives alone; I doubt that he has a pet. He would probably mention it, to make him sound more like one of the guys."

"Try fifteen sixty-four," called Beth, putting down the phone directory. "That's his address."

"No," said Deckle, "that's not it. You wouldn't happen to know if he has a nickname?"

"'The little cheese,'" Beth and I chorused.

"Eureka," said Deckle a moment later. "Let me print it out."

I went over to the printer and anxiously ripped the sheet off.

Good job so far. Did you handle loose ends? George.

"George Stanton!" gasped Deckle.

"This is coming straight from the top," I replied.

"Anyone want to guess what Stanton's password would be?" asked Beth.

"I don't think we should do that," protested Deckle. "He's the president of the company, for God's sake!"

"If you won't do it, move over," I ordered.

Deckle didn't even ask. He typed in 'big cheese' and waited.

The computer died.

"What did you do?" I demanded.

"I put in what I hoped was his password," he replied.

"Try my computer!" urged Beth.

Deckle ran toward her desk.

"It wasn't the computer," he said. "The server is down! What are we going to do?"

I thought about Astrid, planning to meet me. "We'll go to the airport," I decided. "Maybe we can find out more about what's going on there. Someone from Businetex is always there to see a charter off."

Beth looked at her watch. "It's already too late," she said. "There's no way you'll make the bus."

"Astrid dropped me off this morning," I said. "I don't have my car."

"I'll drive," offered Deckle.

I hated to be in the car with him. Deckle was a lousy driver, and his car was as slovenly as everything else about him, but I was desperate. I couldn't put my finger on it, but something about the events surrounding this trip was making me extremely uncomfortable. I hoped that I would figure it out before my wife and I boarded that plane.

"Keep trying the computer. If the server comes back up, try to finish what we started.," I said to Beth, jotting down my cell phone number on her pad. "Call me if you learn anything new."

"Come on, Mitch," said Deckle impatiently. "We're going to miss the plane!"

We still had time to make it to the airport, so I wasn't concerned about that as we set out. I tried to ignore Jim's driving as I moved the fragments of information that floated in my head, trying to put them into a scenario that made sense. We were on 390, about three exits from the airport, when traffic came to a stop.

"What's going on?" I muttered.

"Must be an accident," replied Deckle.

We later found out that it was exactly that. A tanker truck had collided with a car and slid off the road. It was filled with gasoline, and some of it had leaked. No one was going anywhere until the spill was cleaned up.

My cell phone rang after we had been stuck in traffic for a while. "Mitch," said Beth excitedly, "The system came back up a few minutes ago. You'd better listen to what I found in Stanton's mailbox."

"Something that explains things?" I wondered.

"I'm not exactly sure what it means. Listen. 'Bon voyage party set for three o'clock. Approximate location: Bermuda Triangle. Souvenirs sent in care of Goldblatt. Loose ends aboard. They should get a real bang out of it! Walt.'"

The color must have drained from my face, because Deckle was calling my name, asking me what was wrong.

"I know what it means," I said. "I know what's in those suitcases, and I've got to stop that plane. It means that…"

I heard several beeps.

"What's that?" asked Beth.

"I forgot to charge the battery on my phone and it's low. I'll plug it into the cigarette lighter and call you back," I said.

I didn't hear what she said in reply because my phone went completely dead.

I knew that Deckle would have the same phone as I did. Businetex had an arrangement with one of the local wireless companies, and the plan offered to employees was by far the cheapest service available in the area. "Jim, where's your phone cord?" I asked.

"I don't have a phone," replied Deckle.

"You don't have a cell phone?" I asked incredulously.

"Waste of money," he said. "Who would I call?"

"At the moment, you might want to call the police, to warn them that there's a bomb on that plane."

"And people think I'm paranoid," he said, shaking his head.

I repeated Walter Nelson's message to Stanton for him. "What would you think that meant?" I demanded.

I have never seen anyone's face go that white. I thought he was going to pass out, which would have been a problem, being that he was behind the wheel, save for the fact that we hadn't moved in at least half an hour.

"Well, I'm not getting on that plane now!" he declared indignantly, when he finally found his voice.

"You really are a moron," I said. "Of course you aren't getting on that plane, but one hundred-fifty of our coworkers and my wife have no idea that they are walking into a trap. We have to warn them."

"Well, call Beth back," he said curtly. "We aren't moving; get your cord out of your suitcase and plug your phone into my cigarette lighter."

"I didn't bring the cord," I said sheepishly.

"Who's the genius now?" he retorted sarcastically.

"I suppose I deserved that," I conceded, "but we have to get out of here."

"There's nothing I can do," he protested, assessing our situation.

Unfortunately, he was right. We were in the center lane and about midway between two exits and traffic was packed solid on all sides. Our options were limited.

"I'll walk," I decided, starting to open the car door. "I'll find a phone at the next exit."

"Mitch, it's too far. There's no phone right at the exit and I doubt that you know the area. By the time you find one, it will be too late to stop the plane. Besides, you may need my help."

I stopped and thought for a moment; he was right. I sank dejectedly back into the passenger seat.

After about an hour of not moving at all, we started to inch forward. Apparently, they had closed the opposite side of the road between two exits. Four police cars, lights flashing, were parked in the median and troopers were directing traffic on our side to drive across to the cleared roadway.

"It's about time!" said Deckle. "If we don't get there soon, I'm in big trouble. I have to piss like a racehorse!"

"Thank you for sharing that," I said sarcastically. To be honest, I was getting pretty nervous, and my own bladder was reminding me it was there. I had been making an effort not to think about it. When I get nervous, my bladder always does the two-step; when Astrid is nervous, she gets diarrhea.

Finally, we neared the exit and a sheriff's deputy was directing everyone onto the ramp. Naturally, it was going slowly because three lanes of traffic had to merge to a single lane. I thought of trying to stop to talk to him, but he was impatiently waving us on, and I sensed that he would not be receptive to my plea for help. We tore into the airport entrance, parked the car and raced for the terminal.

"Where are you going?" I demanded as Deckle started for the men's room.

"If I don't take a whiz right now, I won't be any use to anyone," he said.

"All right," I agreed, glancing at my watch. "I'll meet you at the gate. That plane is supposed to be leaving right now. We'd better hope they're late!"

I got to the gate and my blood started to circulate again. I could see the plane out the window!

"Is that the Businetex charter?" I asked.

"Yes, sir, but I'm sorry; you're too late."

"It's still here!" I protested.

"It's pulling away from the gate right now," said the agent. "You can go to the ticket counter and see about catching a commercial flight."

"My wife may be on that plane!" I said. "You can't let it go."

"There's nothing I can do," said the woman.

"What if I told you there's a bomb on that plane?" I asked.

"Just a minute, sir," said the woman.

I could tell by her expression, as she reached for the phone, that she thought I was some kind of a nut, and she was calling for help, rather than stopping the plane. I saw a pay phone and ran for it. As quickly as I could, I dialed Astrid's cellular number, hoping that her phone was in her purse, that she still had it on and that she'd answer it. Relief flooded through me when I heard a ring, rather than the "out of service" recording.

"Hello?" said my wife.

"Thank God!" I said. "Astrid, you have to get off that plane. You can't take off!"

"Mitch! You missed the flight. Where are you?"

"I'm in the terminal. You and Bobbie have to get off that plane!"

"We can't!" she said. "It's not such a big deal. Catch a later flight and meet us there."

The woman at the phone next to me was looking at me strangely, obviously listening to my conversation. I didn't want to attract any more attention to myself than necessary.

"Astrid, listen to me carefully. I think Sven is on that plane with you! You have to get off!"

"Have you lost it?" she asked.

"I said that I think Sven is on the plane with you," I repeated deliberately.

"I'm sorry," I heard an unfamiliar female voice say in the background, "cellular phones are not permitted on the aircraft. You'll have to shut it off immediately."

"I have to go," said Astrid. "We'll see you there."

"No!" I screamed as arms grabbed me from behind.

"Is this the man?" asked a uniformed airport guard.

The agent I'd spoken with at the gate nodded. "That's him."

"You'll have to come with me, sir," he said, keeping a firm hold on my arm.

"Where are we going?" I asked.

"To the airport security office."

"You have to stop that plane!" I demanded. "I have reason to believe there's a bomb aboard!"

"Please come with us and we'll sort all of this out," replied the man, obviously trying to humor me to get me out of the terminal without alarming any of the passengers.

"You don't understand," I protested. "My wife is on that plane."

"That must be the woman who called; they're in this together," said the man to the agent."

I saw Deckle coming along the concourse and he saw me. I saw him hesitate, but he didn't acknowledge that we were acquainted. "All right," I said, "but first I have to call my mother-in-law, Inga Lindstrom. She's in the book under Gustav; you can check it out. She has a right to know what's going on; her daughter's on that plane."

"You'll get to make your call later," said another man who took my other arm. "Right now, you have to come with us."

Deckle nodded at me imperceptibly, and I stopped struggling and followed my captors.

I wasn't on the plane, so I can't give a first hand account, but Bobbie and Astrid later filled me in on enough of the details for me to represent the events with what I feel is some accuracy.

"That was Mitch," said Astrid, after the stewardess, certain that the phone was no longer in use, left them.

"Why did he miss the plane?" asked Bobbie.

"He didn't say," she replied, "but that was the strangest conversation we've ever had. He was really insistent that we had to get off this flight. He kept repeating that he thought that Sven was on the plane."

"Your car?"

"Yes. Isn't that weird?"

"Could he have been trying to tell you something else?" asked Bobbie. "Maybe it was like code, because he couldn't talk. Brandon pulled that on me two days ago, when he arranged to sneak out late at night to meet a girl."

"Brandon has a girl friend?"

"She called him last Sunday and asked if he could help her practice her softball pitching. Apparently, she's hoping to make the team when school starts. Brandon has had a crush on her for months, and they've started spending a lot of time together. Two nights ago, they made plans to meet in the park at midnight, only he said something about a dozen bottles in the recycle bin at curbside. I was only listening out of one ear, and it made no sense until I looked in on the boys and he wasn't there. After a few minutes, it came to me that you park at curbside and a dozen is twelve."

"What did you do?" asked Astrid.

Bobbie laughed. "I put on my sweats over my nightgown and I sneaked up on them. They were both pretty embarrassed. He's grounded until school starts."

Astrid laughed. "It sounds familiar."

"All too familiar," agreed Bobbie. "Believe it or not, Bob and I used to do things like that all the time in high school. I hate to see Brandon getting involved so young; look how Bob and I turned out."

"I forgot that you knew each other then," said Astrid. "Mitch and I missed so many things by not meeting sooner. There are so many little things that we don't know about..."

"What is it?" asked Bobbie when Astrid stopped talking in mid-sentence.

"I think I know what Mitch was trying to say," whispered Astrid. "He's always telling me that Sven is a bomb."

"I don't understand," protested Bobbie.

"He kept saying that we had to get off the plane," said Astrid. "He repeated that he thought that Sven was on the plane with us twice."

Bobbie's face drained of color. "My God!" she gasped. "What are we going to do?"

"I don't know," admitted Astrid. "but I'm not taking any chances about anything now. I wanted to tell Mitch first, but I think now's a good time to tell you. I found out this morning that I'm pregnant."

"Astrid, that's wonderful!" said Bobbie happily.

"Bobbie, we have to think of a way to get them to land this plane. We have to get off!"

Bobbie looked out the window. They were rapidly climbing to cruising altitude. "How are we going to do that?"

"I'm not sure," said Astrid, "but we're going to come up with something."

"Honey, you're very pale; try not to worry," soothed Bobbie.

"I need the bathroom."

Bobbie watched her bolt for the lavatory.

"Feeling better?" she asked when Astrid returned to her seat.

"I've been throwing up all morning, and now I have diarrhea," said Astrid. "It's probably just nerves."

"Astrid, I hate to ask you to do this, but if you fake a miscarriage, they might land the plane and take you to a hospital."

"I don't like that idea much," said my wife.

"Can you think of anything else?"

Astrid shook her head and ran for the lavatory again.

"Can I do anything for you?" asked Bobbie when Astrid returned.

"I'm really feeling awful," said Astrid. "I'm sure I can convince them I'm sick; let's go for it."

Bobbie nodded. "I'm not superstitious; you'll be fine."

Astrid nodded slowly. "Bobbie, I have to go again."

She stood and her knees buckled.

Bobbie grabbed her to keep her from falling. "I'm going with you," she announced.

Bobbie more or less carried Astrid back to the lavatory and helped her inside. "Astrid, I'm not going to leave you," she said, helping her to sit on the toilet. I can't close the door but no one can see past me."

"This isn't going to be pleasant," said Astrid. "I'll be okay if you wait outside."

"Astrid, I have three kids; I've done this many times before. It doesn't bother me if it doesn't bother you."

Astrid was ashy pale and beads of sweat were forming on her forehead. "I'll feel better if you're here with me; I'm really sorry."

"Don't be," said Bobbie, wetting a paper towel and wiping Astrid's face. "I want to stay."

One of the flight attendants tapped Bobbie on the back. "Is something wrong?" she asked.

"My friend is sick," said Bobbie. "She's pregnant and I'm afraid she may be having a miscarriage," she added in a whisper.

The flight attendant peeked alongside Bobbie just in time to see Astrid retch violently into an airsick bag.

"She doesn't look well," agreed the stewardess. "You don't think this could be morning sickness?"

"She's never had pains like she is now," lied Bobbie.

"Let me talk to the cockpit," said the woman.

"Astrid, do you think you can go back to your seat?" asked Bobbie when the woman was gone.

"I'll try," she agreed. "Bobbie, I think something really is wrong."

"Are you bleeding?" asked Bobbie worriedly.

"No, "but when I move, I have a stabbing pain in my side."

"Just take deep breaths and try to relax," said Bobbie as she brought Astrid back to her seat.

"Do you mind if I put my head down for a few minutes?"

"No," said Bobbie, lifting the arm rest between them, "That's a good idea; stretch out on top of me."

Astrid put her feet up and her head in Bobbie's lap and Bobbie rang for the stewardess.

"Yes?" inquired the same flight attendant who had admonished Astrid about the phone earlier, but not the same one who had checked on them in the lavatory.

"We need some help," said Bobbie. "Astrid is pregnant and something is very wrong."

No sooner had she said it than Astrid tried to sit up and cried out.

"Are you in pain?" asked the stewardess.

"Yes," said Astrid softly, "I'm pregnant, and I think that something is happening to my baby. Please, I need a doctor."

The woman looked at her. "You are very pale," she agreed. "Could it be morning sickness?"

"It's not the same as what I've had," said Astrid. "I feel a lot worse; I've never had pain before."

"We spoke to another flight attendant, and she was supposed to talk to the cockpit. Could you find out what's happening?" asked Bobbie.

"Yes," said the stewardess, walking briskly down the aisle.

"You were very convincing," said Bobbie when she had gone.

"Bobbie, I wasn't acting," whispered Astrid. "The diarrhea seems to have stopped, but there's a stab in my side every time I move. I feel awful; I think something is seriously wrong." Astrid's skin was almost gray and sweat was pouring down her face.

"You're going to be fine," Bobbie said with a lot more confidence than she felt. "It's probably just unusually bad morning sickness." She didn't believe that for a minute, but there was no sense in frightening Astrid any more than she already was. Besides, Bobbie was frightened enough for both of them.

"Bobbie," said Astrid softly, starting to cry, "I lost a child once; I don't want to lose this baby."

Bobbie caressed her forehead. "You're not going to lose the baby," she said, wiping the tears from Astrid's cheeks. "I'm going to get you off this plane, to a hospital. You have to trust me. Okay?"

Astrid nodded. She tried to sit up again and cried out.

"What's the matter?" asked Bobbie.

"I have pressure," whispered Astrid. "I think I have to pee. Can you help me get back to the bathroom?"

Bobbie tried to help her to her feet, but when Astrid stood, she cried out and her knees buckled. Carefully, Bobbie eased her back into her seat.

"Astrid, honey, try to lie still and stay calm. If you really have to go, just do it. It will be okay; I'll make sure you're okay."

Astrid closed her eyes and nodded slightly.

Bobbie sensed someone in the aisle next to her. When she looked up, Maggie was standing over them. "Is something wrong?" she asked.

Bobbie looked like she was going to tell her where to go, but then, her face softened and she reconsidered. "Astrid isn't feeling well," she said instead.

"I just found out that I'm pregnant, and I think something is wrong with the baby," said Astrid, tears starting to roll down her face again.

"What can I do to help?" asked Maggie, taking Astrid's hand and patting it reassuringly.

"Could you stay here with her while I go give that Barbie doll stewardess some grief?" asked Bobbie.

Maggie slid into Bobbie's seat and lowered Astrid's head gently into her lap. "Don't you worry," she soothed, stroking my wife's sweat drenched hair reassuringly.

"Bobbie and I are going to see to it that nothing happens to you or your baby. You can count on that."

Bobbie nodded and walked down the aisle. I have mentioned before that Bobbie bore a striking resemblance to John Madden. That included size; she was tall and broad, not fat but solidly built. She walked up to the two stewardesses, and in the confined space of the galley, her six foot one inch two hundred forty pound frame was impressive.

"My friend is really sick," she said. "She may be having a miscarriage, and she needs medical attention. Will you please do something?"

"She isn't any better?" asked the one who had been near the lavatory.

"If anything, she's worse."

"She didn't look too well," agreed the second one.

"I'll speak to the captain," said the first flight attendant.

"Please do it quickly," ordered Bobbie.

When she returned to her seat, she saw that Maggie had managed to get some of the other travelers to find a pillow and blanket for Astrid. Beads of sweat were pouring down my wife's face and her color was gray, but Maggie was cradling her protectively, and she seemed calmer. Bobbie slipped into Maggie's seat.

A few minutes later, the captain of the aircraft came to check on Astrid. The passenger Bobbie sat down next to had paramedic training, and when Bobbie told him about Astrid, he went over to see if he could help.

"Her pulse is weak and thready," he told the captain. "I suspect that her blood pressure may be low; she could be bleeding. I can't say what's wrong with certainty, but she needs immediate medical attention."

While all of this was happening, I was being unceremoniously carted off to the Public Safety Building. I tried to convince the sheriff's deputy who drove me there in handcuffs that he had to do something to stop the plane, but I could tell by the way he acted that he thought I was a mental case, and that I would get no serious help from him.

After serving on a Grand Jury, the participants are usually treated to a tour of the jail. I can tell you that everyone who takes that tour is sure that the jail is one place he or she never wants to go again, but here I was a few weeks later, being taken back, this time not as a visitor. They put me in a holding cell with the others who had been arrested but had not yet been processed.

I was pretty scared by this point. I knew that Astrid and Bobbie, not to mention one hundred fifty of my co-workers were on that plane. I was sure that there was a bomb aboard, scheduled to go off at three o'clock. I didn't even have the email messages to show them; Deckle had the print-out from Stanton in his pocket, and Beth had the one from Nelson. I knew that I had no credibility with these people; my story sounded far-fetched even to me, and I knew that it was true. I was powerless to do anything as long as I was in custody, and I was going nowhere until they decided whether to charge me with a crime or spirit me off to a psychiatric hospital for evaluation.

"You're lucky," said the officer who showed me to the holding cell. "It's a slow day."

If that was a slow day, I didn't want to see a busy one. There were three tough-looking black men in their early twenties, who looked like they might have been gang members, huddled together on a bench. They silently glared at me and the officer from under their identical backward baseball caps. On the floor, a young blond boy was asleep in a puddle that may very well have been of his own doing. I couldn't swear even now that he wasn't dead, but no one seemed at all concerned.

There was a toilet without a seat against the far wall, a roll of paper on the floor next to it. When the officer brought me in, an elderly man wearing three coats, a stocking cap and several pairs of pants rushed to sit down on it. He did not look all that unusual for a street person save for the fact that this was Labor Day weekend, and the temperature was in the mid seventies.

As I came into the cell, a very thin middle aged man with a stubble of beard, dressed in a soiled tan raincoat, rushed toward me. When he was about four feet away, he opened the raincoat. All he was wearing was the raincoat and a pair of worn out running shoes.

"Eddie, cut that out," ordered the officer.

"I'm buck naked!" he shouted at me.

"So I see," I said softly.

"Now!" ordered the officer. "You stay away from him or you'll be sorry."

Eddie closed his coat and backed away.

"He's harmless," said a soft female voice from across the cell. I looked up and saw the deep brown eyes of a very beautiful woman meeting my gaze.

She looked Hispanic, probably in her early twenties, impeccably groomed and dressed. I couldn't believe that they would actually put her in with this group of misfits.

"I'm going to be the next Mrs. Farrell," she informed me, making kissing noises at the officer who had been my escort.

That statement was greeted by catcalls from the three toughs.

"Are you going to give me grief today, Chico?" demanded officer Farrell.

It was then that I realized that the beautiful woman was, in fact, a man.

Officer Farrell shut the cell door behind me. I don't know why, but for some reason, the others in the cell just ignored me. I considered that to be a real stroke of luck, but actually, they more or less ignored each other as well.

I realized almost immediately that I had a big problem. They had taken my watch, but there was a clock visible from the cell, and I could see that the plane had been in the air for an hour. There were only two hours left before the bomb would go off, if we were right in what we had surmised, and no one would listen to me. Also, my bladder was so full it was throbbing painfully, but there was no way I could do anything about it. The street person was dozing contentedly on the toilet, and even if I were to muster the nerve to ask him to let me use it, I was afraid to put myself in so vulnerable a position with the others in the cell. I knew that I would have even less credibility when I was eventually questioned if I had wet pants, so I resolved to control myself.

Another half hour passed, and it was starting to hit me that time was running out. I knew that if I was there much longer, it would become involuntary, and I was going to wet my pants, but I didn't much care anymore. If that plane exploded and Astrid died, I didn't care what happened to me. For all practical purposes, my life would be over; I would have died with her, on that plane.

A female officer came into the reception area, carrying a folder which she handed to officer Farrell.

"Lady, look over here," called Eddie.

The female officer turned around.

Eddie pulled open his raincoat. "I'm buck naked!" he called gleefully.

The woman turned to the desk, picked something up and walked toward the cell, opening and closing a pair of blunt-edge scissors, the kind they give you in kindergarten. "Does Bobbitt mean anything to you?" she grinned at Eddie.

My three young cellmates grinned and, reflexively, brought their hands over their privates.

"What's that?" asked Eddie, still holding his coat open, but after a few seconds, he closed it and backed away.

"That's better," said the officer. "Now, you behave yourself until the 'bus' gets here."

Officer Farrell came back to the cell. "Goldblatt," he said, clutching the file that the female officer had delivered, "come with me."

He unlocked the door and I followed him down a corridor.

"Officer Farrell?" I said.

"What is it?" he asked, stopping for a second.

"Could you please help me? I desperately need to use the bathroom."

He said nothing, and I followed him through a maze of hallways, assuming that he didn't care one way or the other about my problem, but we came to a men's room, and he led me inside, standing silently by the door.

I wasn't crazy about being watched, but I had to go so badly that it didn't really matter. I stood in front of the urinal for what seemed like an eternity; it was taking me so long, I was sure he was going to get angry, but he just waited silently.

As much trouble as I was in, I thought of Artie. This time, in one of our contests, I would have won; no doubt about it. I could hear him in my head saying, "Well, you finally got me!" I know it was foolish, but for the first time that day, I had a glimmer of hope that things would be all right.

After we left the men's room, Officer Farrell led me through several more hallways. We passed through a lobby, and I think we were out of the jail, but I wasn't sure where we were or where we were headed. Finally, we came to a room, and he gestured for me to enter. Seated at a table were two men in suits and Inga. Thankfully, Jim Deckle was smarter than he usually acted.

Farrell handed the file to one of the men.

"Thank you, officer," he said.

Farrell nodded and went out, shutting the door behind him.

"Mitchell, are you all right?" asked Inga.

"Yes," I said softly, "but we're running out of time."

"Mr. Goldblatt, I'm agent Brown with the FBI," said the man to whom officer Farrell had handed the file. "Your wife's plane landed safely at Dulles Airport a while ago. All the passengers are off the aircraft, and it is being checked. If there really is a bomb on that plane, we will find the people responsible, but if this is your idea of a joke, you are going to be one sorry young man. We take terrorist threats very seriously."

"This is not a joke," I said, "and I don't remember making any type of threat. I was only trying to protect innocent people from getting hurt. Unless I've totally misinterpreted what I've seen and heard, there is a bomb on that plane in one or two suitcases, with my name on the tags, that my secretary was instructed to send to the airport."

"Yes, your friend Mr. Deckle talked to us. We also had a call from the Monroe County Sheriff's office about a woman named Beth Davidson at Businetex. The 911 center had received what they suspected was a crank call, but they passed the information on to us, on the chance that this was on the level. We sent a pair of agents out to interview her, and she managed to convince them that this was no prank. She provided us with a print-out of an email she said she read to you over a cell phone. I don't think your conclusions are unreasonable," concluded Agent Brown, "but if you fabricated that evidence, you can't begin to imagine how much trouble you're in."

"I didn't make it up," I said. "As long as those people are safely off that plane, you can do what you want to me; I don't really care. Where is my wife?"

"She's on her way to a hospital. Apparently, she became ill on the flight. The crew radioed for permission to land to get medical attention for her, so we directed them to a location where we had people in place to check out the plane. The flight crew seemed convinced that she was really ill, but if she's part of some bizarre scheme with you, she will be punished too."

"Now, just a minute," said Inga sternly.

"Mrs. Lindstrom, I'm letting you sit in as a favor to the sheriff, but you will not disrupt this session," ordered Brown.

Inga glared at him with those cold eyes but said no more.

A beeper sounded and the other agent stood and left the room.

"What's wrong with my wife?" I demanded.

"I don't know any of the details," replied Brown.

We sat in silence for what seemed like an eternity, until the other agent returned, opened the door and peeked in. Agent Brown rose and went out, shutting the door behind him.

"Thank you, Inga," I said when we were alone.

"I did not do anything special," she said. "I have met the sheriff on a few social occasions, and he happened to remember me. These people are much more impressed by the scope of my influence than they should be."

The two agents came back into the room. "The bomb squad found the suitcases Ms. Davidson described," said agent Brown. "The dogs reacted positively to them, and they were removed from the aircraft without incident. They will either be detonated or disarmed in a remote location, and we'll know more then about exactly what we are dealing with. We will want to question you extensively, but it appears that your warnings were sincere; we no longer consider you to be under arrest."

"Just like that," I said. Now, I was angry. "You didn't believe me, you treated me like a criminal; I think you owe me an apology. The individuals involved have probably killed before; I was only trying to save my wife and the others!"

"We understand that and we're grateful," said the agent. "Mr. Deckle has given us quite an earful about what the two of you have managed to piece together. Beth Davidson was able to confirm your story about the suitcases. Even as we speak, there are subpoenas being issued and an investigation is being launched. The people responsible will not escape punishment."

"Jim Deckle and Beth Davidson gave you written evidence; you have the bomb; what more do you need?" I asked.

"The evidence Mr. Deckle and Miss Davidson gave us is useless," said the agent. Then, in response to my puzzled look he explained, "It was illegally obtained. You broke into the email system."

"And thank God they did!" said Inga.

"Are we in trouble for that?" I asked.

He smiled slightly. "We have no real proof that you did anything wrong; no one actually told us how you obtained those messages; it's supposition on our parts, and we don't care to pursue the matter. We have warrants to search the email files of both individuals involved."

I gave a sarcastic laugh. "And you don't think they're smart enough to see that their messages are deleted before you get your hands on them? You're even more naive than I was."

"Mr. Deckle was very helpful in telling us exactly who to contact. Apparently, all messages sent or received can be retrieved from the system, even after they have been erased. Subpoenas are in the works, and we have taken steps to see to it that no one interferes with the system in the interim."

"I'd like to see my wife," I said.

"I would too," added Inga.

"We thought you might," said Agent Brown. "We took the liberty of making airline reservations for you; one of the sheriff's officers will take us to the airport. We'll be traveling with you as far as Dulles."

"Thank you," I said. "By the way, what happened to the others on the plane?"

"We would prefer to keep all of this quiet, until we have the evidence we need. Certainly, we didn't see any reason to alarm the passengers," said Agent Brown. "We had the plane land on a remote runway and everyone was bused to the terminal. They were told that it was necessary so the ambulance could have access. After the plane is thoroughly checked and serviced, and we are certain it is safe, we will send them on their way to St. Thomas."

"That isn't such a good idea," I said. "The rooms have been reserved, but there is no hospitality staff to meet them, and the activities they were promised have not been scheduled. They're expecting a trip where everything is arranged and paid for by Businetex, but they're going to find that they're on their own.'"

"So Mr. Deckle informed us," said the agent. "We took the liberty of instructing Beth Davidson to make the arrangements. We instructed her to spare no expense, and to have Businetex billed directly. I don't think she'll have troubling getting authorization, do you?"

I smiled slightly. Nelson and Stanton would have a fit but they wouldn't dare protest.

A sheriff's deputy opened the door. "We're ready, sir," he informed Agent Brown.

"We have to get to the airport if we are going to catch our flight," he said. "If you have any other questions, I'll try to answer them for you on the way."

We were ushered into an unmarked car in the garage below the building. I had many questions, but I didn't bother to ask them. I only wanted to know that Astrid was okay, and they wouldn't or couldn't tell me any more about what had happened to her.

Inga and I sat together on the plane. "Your Mr. Deckle is quite a character," she said with a twinkle in her eye.

"He's different," I admitted, "but after the way he came through for me today, I'll never say anything bad about him again."

"He was very helpful," agreed Inga. "He told me what was going on, where they had taken you, and he even advised that I try to get Astrid off that plane first. He did not think you would mind waiting in jail, as long as Astrid was safe."

"I never thought him capable of such insight," I said. I smiled slightly to myself, as I realized that Deckle's well-timed visit to the men's room was probably the biggest stroke of luck I'd had all day.

"Is something funny?" asked Inga.

"No, not really. Inga, did anyone tell you anything about what's wrong with Astrid?"

"No. She called me this morning, after her appointment with the doctor, and told me that she was going to surprise you in St. Thomas. I urged her to call you and tell you that she was going."

"That advice may have saved both of our lives, not to mention the lives of everyone else on that plane," I observed. "Did she tell you what the doctor said?"

"No," said Inga. "She said only that it is good news, that it is nothing serious. Apparently, he gave her a prescription to have filled, and he told her he was sure she would feel better within a week or two."

"Why did they have to land the plane and take her to the hospital?" I asked.

"Unless Mr. Deckle was mistaken, I assume you called her on that gadget she carries in her purse to tell her what you suspected," said Inga.

"I did get her on the cellular phone as they were taking off, but I wasn't sure she understood what I was saying."

"I think she figured it out and faked an illness, to get the plane down," said Inga. "I am sure she is fine and will be waiting for us when we land."

Someone was waiting for us at Dulles when we landed, but it wasn't Astrid. A man in a dark suit told agent Brown that he was there to take us to the hospital. We parted company, with Brown's assurances that he wanted to interview me extensively sometime in the near future. This wasn't quite the way I'd envisioned things going, and Inga and I rode to the hospital in nervous silence. When the information desk in the lobby told us that Astrid had been admitted, I was close to a state of panic. Inga and I virtually tore down the corridor looking for her room.

Astrid was sitting up in bed smiling, a tube from an IV bag next to the bed going into her arm. Maggie and Bobbie were sitting next to each other in chairs beside the bed. I could not have imagined a more bizarre scenario had I tried.

"What took you so long?" asked Astrid cheerily as we bounded into the room.

You have to remember that in one day, I had learned that I was working for a company run by murderers, and I had watched my wife take off on a plane with a bomb aboard. I had been arrested, handcuffed, accused of being a terrorist, thrown into jail with the dregs of society and briefly questioned by the FBI. I had then been spirited off to Washington where, I was told, my wife had been admitted to the hospital, but no one would tell me why. And it wasn't even dark yet.

I lunged for the side of the bed, took her in my arms and burst into tears. I didn't care who saw me.

"Let's give them a few minutes," said Bobbie, patting my back reassuringly as she stood to leave.

I had my face buried against Astrid's shoulder, and I didn't move.

"I will be right outside," said Inga apprehensively, as Maggie and Bobbie ushered her from the room.

Astrid was stroking my hair. "It's all right, Mitch," she said. "I'm really okay. They're keeping me overnight as a precaution, but the doctor promised that everything is fine. Please don't be upset."

"Why did they bring you here in the first place?" I choked.

"This is hardly the way I had envisioned telling you," said Astrid. "I had planned to surprise you with champagne, overlooking a tropical harbor during a magnificent sunset. I'm pregnant. I found out this morning. We're going to have a baby."

I sat up and looked at her to make sure that this wasn't a continuation of the bizarre joke that the day had been thus far. She reached out to wipe the tears from my cheeks and nodded.

"We've hardly been together since we decided to try; anyway, it would be too soon to tell," I protested.

"I'm two and a half months pregnant."

"How?" I asked. "I thought we were taking precautions."

"We were," she said nodding. "I'm sorry; it was my fault. When we went to New York for Artie's funeral, I forgot to pack my diaphragm; I got it out, but I left it on the counter in the bathroom. If I had told you, I knew we wouldn't have been together, and I thought you needed that; I wanted you too. I figured that once or twice wouldn't make any difference."

"But that was back in June," I protested. "It's been a long time."

"You know I'm not that regular," said Astrid. "I wasn't all that late, for me. Besides, the last time I got pregnant, it took a year."

"Why are you in the hospital?" I asked. "Is something wrong?"

"No, not really. What I thought was a urinary tract infection is pressure from my expanding uterus. The reason I've been feeling so awful is that I've had morning sickness.

While I was at the doctor's office waiting for him to see me, it started again. He gave me a prescription for the nausea, but I didn't take the time to get it filled, because I wanted to catch that plane."

I reached out to hug her again, and I saw her wince slightly when my arm touched her side.

"What's the matter?" I demanded, ready to call for a doctor.

"I retched so hard, they suspect that I may have cracked a rib," she said. "There's nothing to be done; they won't x-ray it because of the baby, but it will heal by itself. Since they taped it, the pain is much less."

"Is that the only reason you're here?" I asked, still concerned.

"I was throwing up in the terminal before we left and again on the plane. After you called and I figured out what you meant about Sven, I got a little nervous and I had diarrhea too. They say I was severely dehydrated. When the ambulance came, my blood pressure was very low. They did some tests when I got to the hospital, and they said that my electrolytes were off, and I needed fluids. They've been pumping me full of stuff since I got here, and now, I feel fine."

"Is the baby okay?" I asked.

"They think so. They want to do one more test, but I asked them to wait for you."

"May we come in?" asked Inga, knocking on the open door.

"Please," I said, beckoning to them.

"Mom?" said Astrid.

Inga went over and embraced Astrid. "Bobbie and Maggie told me the good news," said Inga. "Please do not be cross with them."

"I couldn't be," said Astrid. "They saved my life."

"We did nothing," protested Maggie.

"I was so frightened, I was absolutely useless. Both of you took such good care of me; I will never be able to adequately express my gratitude. Without the two of you, I wouldn't have made it through that flight," insisted Astrid.

"Thank you both," I said.

"I'm glad I was able to help," said Maggie.

Bobbie came over and embraced me. "Congratulations, Daddy!"

"Thanks," I said, kissing her on the cheek. "For everything."

"If the kid wants references, my three will vouch for you. Brandon wanted me to give you a message; he made me promise."

"What is it?" I asked.

"He said to tell you that he has a hot date as soon as he's through being grounded, but he still plans to keep his promise. Does that mean anything to you?"

I laughed. "Yes. Tell him that I may be cashing in sooner than he thinks."

Bobbie and Maggie convinced Inga to join them for a cup of coffee, and Astrid and I were alone again.

"Are you angry?" she asked.

"Angry about what?"

"We hadn't discussed starting a family two and a half months ago," she said. "I would never have decided something like that on my own; it really was an accident."

"Sweetheart, all our accidents should have such a fantastic outcome," I said, taking her in my arms again.

"You're okay about the baby?"

"I've never been happier," I assured her.

"You know," said Astrid, a slight smile across her face, "there's a good chance that this baby got started on Rifka's bathroom floor."

"It worked for Marilyn and Bert," I replied.

"You're kidding!"

"No," I said. "When they decided to try for a baby, they sneaked into Rifka's bathroom together and did it for old time's sake. It worked."

Astrid laughed happily. "Maybe we've started a family tradition."

Bobbie and Maggie had arranged for a flight back home. Neither of them had any desire to continue on to St. Thomas. I didn't quite know how to thank them for all they'd done.

"Actually, we should be the ones thanking you," laughed Bobbie. "Even in a bad novel, no one would ever believe that the two of us would end up being friends."

"We're glad we could help," added Maggie, "and actually, we owe you our lives. If you hadn't realized what was happening, we would all be floating in pieces, somewhere in the Atlantic."

"You try not to worry," added Bobbie as I put the two of them into a cab. "Everything is going to be fine with Astrid and the baby; I have a good feeling about this, and my good feelings are never wrong."

"You and Astrid are going to have a happy, healthy baby," added Maggie. "Both of you deserve nothing less."

When I returned to Astrid's room, she and Inga were engaged in earnest conversation.

"It wasn't the same as last time," Astrid was saying. "I never had morning sickness that time. This time, I've been green twenty-four hours a day. I wasn't all that late for me; pregnancy never crossed my mind."

"But you are happy about it?" Inga asked.

"Ecstatic," I answered for her as I joined them.

Astrid gestured for me to sit beside her on the bed. "Yes, Mom, I'm delighted. A little apprehensive but delighted nonetheless."

"There's no need to worry," I said, cradling her protectively in my arms. "Bobbie and Maggie are very confident that things will be fine, and they have assured me that they have a very good track record on those types of hunches."

"They were so wonderful," said Astrid. "I was no help at all. I was supposed to fake a miscarriage, to get them to land the plane, and before I could start, I got sick for real. The two of them took care of everything."

"We owe them a great deal," I agreed, "and I owe your mother just as much."

"Me?" asked Inga, surprised. "I have done nothing so special."

"She was great," I told Astrid. "She contacted the sheriff, she got the FBI off their duffs, she was ready to post bail for me; Inga, you are far too modest."

"No," said Inga quietly, "I know what it is like to be unjustly accused, and I was determined to make sure that it would not happen to you, if there was any way I could stop it."

"What do you mean, Mom?" asked Astrid. "When were you unjustly accused?"

"I am not sure this is the time or the place to speak of such things," said Inga.

"That's fairly promising," I said. "It could have been something that we did not need to know."

Inga smiled slightly. "I used to think that it was, but now I am not so sure. Many times in this life, things are not what they seem."

"I want to know," said Astrid.

"Are you sure that you are up to this?" asked her mother. "It will keep; it has for many years."

"Tell us now."

"If you'd like some privacy..." I began.

"No," said Inga. "Mitchell, you are my child too. After today, if I ever had any doubts of that, I never again will."

I took my wife's hand and settled back down.

"When Mr. Deckle called, I did not get all the details," began Inga. "He told me that Mitch had been arrested, because there was a bomb on the plane, that Astrid was on board, and that he was trying to stop it from taking off. I did not know whether he was some kind of nut or if what he said was true, but I realized that Mitch was probably in some kind of trouble, and I knew that I had to help, so I told him to come to the house. I thought if we spoke face to face, I would know how much to believe. The cat despises him, by the way. He hissed, spat and went under the sofa, and I could not coax him out, even with pickled herring. Mrs. Anderson promised to go over and take care of him later, after he had some time to settle down."

"That cat is an excellent judge of character," said Astrid, sounding more like Inga than I'd ever heard her sound.

"We all owe Jim Deckle a great deal," I said.

"Yes," agreed Inga, "and I told him and the FBI as much. Apparently, they decided that I was right; the last I saw of him, two agents were giving him the full VIP treatment."

I couldn't help but chuckle a bit to think of the most paranoid human I had ever met being fawned over by the FBI.

"While I was waiting," continued Inga, "I realized that if Mitchell had really been arrested, I would need money for his bail. Gus always kept a large sum of cash hidden in the house, in case of an emergency. I know that you two would not approve, but that was the way back home; your father never completely trusted the banks. I never looked at it after he died, but I knew where it was. I went to the hiding place and saw the metal box. When I opened it, the money was there and there were some other things inside."

"What other things?" asked Astrid.

Inga smiled. "There were all the birthday cards you ever gave your father, some of your school papers, some baby teeth and a lock of your hair from your first haircut."

"I never realized that Daddy was so sentimental," said Astrid.

"Nor did I," agreed Inga. "There was something else in that box too. There were several newspaper clippings. They were old and yellow, and I was astonished to discover that they were in Swedish. I started to read them and realized that they were clipped in Sweden many years ago."

"What were they about?" asked Astrid.

"They were accounts of my trial for murder," said Inga.

The blood drained from Astrid's face. "That's impossible," she said. "Who could you have murdered?"

"I did not murder anyone," said Inga. "I was unjustly accused of murdering my husband."

"That's crazy!" said Astrid. "Daddy died of a heart attack less than two years ago; no one thought that you killed him."

"My first husband," said Inga quietly.

"You were married before?" asked Astrid, wide-eyed.

"Maybe this isn't such a good idea," I said.

"No," protested Astrid. "I'm okay; I want to hear this."

"Yes," said Inga. "Before I met your father, I was married."

"Why didn't you ever tell me? Did Daddy know?" demanded my wife.

"It was a long time ago, Astrid," sighed Inga. "I did not think it had anything to do with who either of us was. I am still not sure that it does, but I have come to learn that the truth has a way of coming out, and the longer it is hidden, the more painful it is when it emerges."

"Did Daddy know?" repeated my wife.

"Yes," said Inga. "He knew that I was married before I met him, and he knew that I had been accused and found innocent of a crime. I never offered any of the particulars, and he did not ask, but when I found the articles, I discovered that he knew more than I realized. I did not know that it was important to him; I would have told him myself had I known."

"What happened, Inga?" I asked.

"When I was eighteen years old and living in the village where I grew up, I married a young man I had known for some time. Gunnar was a few years older than I, and we were very much in love. He was a laborer, and the nature of his work was such that sometimes, he went for periods without a job, but he was a good worker, and he always found something after a while.

"If Gunnar had any faults, the only one I knew of was that he had a bad temper but never toward me. With me, he was always kind and considerate. He was not a heavy drinker, but when he did drink, it seemed to affect him greatly; it brought his temper to the surface.

"One day, when Gunnar was between jobs, he left the house very early. I assumed that he had gone to look for work. Later that morning, I went to the market for some food. I had to shop very carefully; money was tight then, and I had barely enough for groceries. Our rent was due, and if Gunnar did not find work, I was not sure how we would pay the landlord.

"When I returned home, Gunnar was lying face down on the sofa. A table had been turned over, there was beer spilled, and there was a large kitchen knife on the floor. I assumed that Gunnar had been drinking and had passed out. I cleaned up the spill, put away the bottles, righted the table and washed the knife. I could not imagine what he could have been doing with the knife; it was all sticky and covered with a dark substance. When I washed it, I realized that it was blood.

"Quickly, I ran to see if Gunnar was hurt. When I turned him over, I found that the sofa was soaked in blood. It was coming from his stomach. I called for help but it was too late.

"But you weren't even there when it happened," said Astrid.

"No," agreed Inga, "but the authorities pieced things together differently from the way they had happened. People had seen me return home, and I did not call for help immediately, because I did not realize that he was hurt. I had tidied up the room, so they did not believe that there was a struggle. There was no sign that the door had been forced. The police concluded that I had come home and stabbed my husband as he slept."

"But what motive would you have had?" I asked.

"The prosecutors surmised that we were not getting along. That was untrue, but people who they spoke to told them about Gunnar's bad temper. We had been married for almost a year, and there was no baby. Gunnar and I had not tried to prevent having a baby; it just had not happened. They built a case that our marriage was unhappy, that I saw an opportunity to be rid of my husband, and that I used it."

"But you didn't do it!" protested Astrid. "Surely, a good lawyer..."

"My dear child," said Inga, patting her daughter's hand, "my parents were simple people. They ran a small dairy and earned a decent living, but they hardly had money for lawyers. They did what they could to help me, but things did not look promising. It was only by luck that the truth came out.

"During the trial, things were going badly. It was what they call circumstantial evidence, but it was very damning. Toward the middle of the trial, they called a man to testify. He was a tavern keeper in the town where we lived, and he was to tell about Gunnar having started fights in his place of business. While he was on the witness stand, this tavern keeper, Olaf Berqvist, broke down and confessed. He was the one who stabbed Gunnar."

"Why?" I asked.

"Gunnar had spent the morning looking for work. When he was unsuccessful, he stopped at the tavern for a drink. Apparently, on his way to use the toilet, he saw some money in an unlocked office and he took it. Mr. Berqvist missed the money and remembered seeing Gunnar near the office. He came to our home to confront my husband.

"Gunnar denied taking the money. Mr. Berqvist said that he was convinced that he had accused the wrong person. He apologized and Gunnar offered him some beer. When my husband returned from the kitchen, he had a bottle of beer in his hand, and his other hand was out of sight. When Mr. Berqvist reached for the beer, Gunnar lunged toward him with the knife.

"Gunnar was very well-muscled from the type of work he did, but Mr. Berqvist was a wrestler when he was younger, so they were equally matched, despite Gunnar having the advantage of youth. They struggled for the knife, knocking over the table in the process. Gunnar tripped over the leg and fell on the knife.

"If it was an accident, why didn't this man call the police and tell them what happened?" asked Astrid.

"He was afraid," said Inga. "When Gunnar fell on the knife, Berqvist did not realize how seriously he had been hurt. He stood up by himself and looked stunned as he pulled the knife out and threw it on the floor. Then, he started to lunge at Mr. Berqvist again and fell to the floor. Mr. Berqvist said that he went to him to try to help and discovered the money in Gunnar's pocket. Gunnar was unconscious, and he did not seem to be breathing. Mr.

Berqvist panicked. He put Gunnar on the sofa, took his money and left.

"A solid, upstanding citizen," said Astrid bitterly.

"I do not blame him," sighed Inga. "You have to understand that he, like my family, was a working man who had never had any dealings with the authorities. He was afraid. He thought that Gunnar was already dead; it may be that he was. He was certainly dead when I found him."

"That doesn't excuse what he did," insisted Astrid.

"I bear him no ill will," insisted Inga. "He said during the trial that he could not let someone as young and pretty as I was go to prison for what he had done. He had more of a conscience than many people we have both known."

"What happened after the trial?" I asked. "It's obvious that you were acquitted."

"Yes," said Inga. "It was also decided that Mr. Berqvist acted in self-defense. I think that was probably the right decision. My rent had gone unpaid while I was on trial, and so, I had been evicted. My belongings were put out on the street, and by the time I was released from custody, they were gone. I had nothing and nowhere to go. My family took me in but they were ashamed. Also, their business began to suffer."

"Why?" asked Astrid. "You were the victim."

"People did not see it that way. What everyone in the village remembered was that I had been arrested. These were simple, uneducated people. To their way of thinking, I had done something wrong, or I would not have been arrested by the police in the first place. I had an aunt who lived in Stockholm, and she offered to have me come to live in her home as her housekeeper. My family was grateful when I accepted, and I felt it was best to make a fresh start.

"While I was there, I was serving food at a church potluck supper, and I met your father. He started calling on me, and after some time, asked me to marry him. I told him that I had been married before, and my husband had died. He said that it did not matter to him. I told him that I had been tried for a crime and had been found innocent. He asked me if I had done it, and I told him that I had not. Again, he said that it did not matter. I asked him if he wanted to know the details, and he replied that he only wanted to hear them if I wished to tell. We never spoke of it again.

"Did you love your second husband?" asked Astrid.

"I loved your father very much, yes," said Inga. "If what you are really asking is if it was the same as it was with Gunnar, the answer is of course not. I was a bit older and a lot more mature; I was far less naive. I insisted that we have a courtship, during which we got to know each other, before I would respond to his proposal. Gustav Lindstrom was the kindest, most gentle, most honorable man I have ever had the privilege to know. We were very happy during our life together, and there is not a day that goes by that I do not mourn his passing."

"I guess what I'm really asking is if you settled for Daddy because you couldn't have what you wanted," said Astrid.

"Honey, that isn't fair," I protested, kissing the top of her head.

"It is a fair question," said Inga. "I did not feel the mad rush of passion for your father that I had experienced when I met Gunnar. I came to love him in a more subdued way during our courtship. When we stood before God and took our vows, I knew I was making promises that I could keep. I was not wrong; your father was a devoted husband, a wonderful father and a good man. He encouraged me to pursue my interests. I wanted to learn and he urged me to enroll in courses that interested me; he willingly paid my tuition. We may not have seemed to have very much in common, but we were content with each other the way we were and saw no need to try to change each other. That is not such a bad basis for a successful marriage.

"When you were going to marry Jeffrey, Astrid, I was opposed to it, because I sensed that you did not love him. Your father stopped me from interfering, reminding me that when we first met, I did not feel love for him the way he did for me. I accepted his advice because I had the utmost respect for him. Later, he admitted that he was wrong, that he saw nothing growing between the two of you to sustain a relationship, but he had not been wrong; that was a decision you had to reach on your own."

Astrid buried her face in my shoulder, and I hugged her to me.

"I have tired you," said Inga. "I should have waited."

"No, I'm fine," said Astrid. "It's just so much for me to take in. I've known you all my life and yet, I didn't know you at all."

"Astrid, I never told you because I felt it had nothing to do with who I am now. It was many years ago, in a far-off land, in a far-off life. I thought that if your father did not need to know, neither did you but today, I found out that he did need to know."

"Where did he get the clippings?" I asked.

"I have no idea," said Inga. "I suppose that secret died with him."

"I need some time to think about all of this," said Astrid.

"Of course," said Inga. "I called and reserved two rooms at a hotel not too far away. We should check in, Mitchell, so that Astrid can have some time to rest."

"No!" protested Astrid. "I don't want to be alone; I want Mitch to stay."

"I'm not going anywhere," I reassured my wife.

"Will you stay with me tonight?" she asked, clinging to me.

"Unless they throw me out," I agreed, tightening my arms around her.

"I will take a room with two beds," said Inga. "If you need somewhere to go, I will have a place for you."

She went to kiss her daughter, and Astrid sat there, wooden and unresponsive.

My heart went out to Inga. It couldn't have been easy for this very private woman to share the sordid details of her long-hidden past, and it seemed to me that she was being punished a second time for something she had not done.

I stood in the doorway, where Astrid could see me, to say good-bye to Inga. "You get some rest," I said gently. "It will be okay once she's had a little time."

"She is hurt that I took so long to tell her," said Inga, "and maybe a little angry too."

"She's been through a lot," I said. "So have you."

Inga took my face in both her hands and kissed me softly on the forehead. "You take care of each other," she said.

I put my arms around her and gave her a kiss on the cheek. I would never have dared to do that before, but tonight, she patted my back responsively. "I love you both," she said as she walked down the hallway.

Astrid stared silently after her mother for several moments. "Will you hold me?" she finally whispered.

I climbed onto the bed and took her into my arms. "Honey, nothing's different; this all happened over forty years ago."

"My whole relationship with my mother has been based on a lie," said Astrid miserably.

"It wasn't a lie," I protested. "It was an omission of an incident that your mother felt didn't involve you."

"Not too much different from what I did when I didn't tell you about Peter," said Astrid.

"I wasn't making comparisons."

"I, more than anyone, should understand her motivations," said Astrid, "but I think it's so sad that for all the years my parents were together, they were never able to talk about it."

"It isn't all Inga's fault," I said. "Your father could have told her that he knew. He could have told her about the clippings."

"He probably didn't want to embarrass her; I think she was ashamed, even though she was innocent."

"You may be right," I agreed. "I only hope that there is enough trust between us that nothing is too embarrassing for us to share."

Color rose in Astrid's cheeks. "Something happened today that I didn't tell you about."

"What?"

"This is really embarrassing," she said, the color spreading to the rest of her face. "I wet myself on the plane."

"Oh, honey," I said hugging her and laughing with relief. "I thought it was something really terrible; that's no big deal."

"It's never happened to me as an adult," she said. "I was scared and sick and before they taped my rib, it hurt just to move. I was too weak to stand up and, after a while, I was so uncomfortable that I didn't care any more."

"It's kind of funny, actually," I said. "I almost wet my pants in jail today."

I told her about the odd collection of humanity that was awaiting me when I was put into the holding cell. I also told her about my sense of Artie being with me in that men's room, and about how we had amused ourselves with peeing contests during our misspent youth. By the time I had finished, she was laughing along with me.

"I'm glad I told you," she said. "You made me feel better."

"You always make me feel better," I said, caressing her silky hair.

"You miss him so much," she sighed.

I knew she was talking about Artie. "Yes," I said, "and I regret that I never told him how much he meant to me when he was alive. I got around to asking him if he was gay, I criticized him for his religious beliefs, but I never said what was in my heart. I guess it wouldn't have been easy for me to tell him that I loved him, but I should have."

"And I should have told my mother that whatever happened in her life, even if she had been guilty of murder, that I love her very much."

"You can tell her later. She promised to call after she checks into the hotel.," I said. "I know she'll be greatly relieved."

"I do love her, you know," said my wife.

"I know," I said. "I love her too."

We melted contentedly into an embrace.

Two women and a man in a hospital coat, who I assumed was a doctor, pushed a machine next to Astrid's bed, forcing us to separate.

"You're looking much better," said the doctor.

"I'm a new woman," agreed Astrid. "Dr. Corrigan, this is my husband, Mitch."

"Nice to meet you," he said, extending his hand. "Your wife gave us a bit of a scare, but she's come around nicely."

"Is everything okay?" I asked.

"Everything looks fine," he said, "but there's one more test we would like to do."

"Let's go," agreed Astrid.

"This is the last test for today," said the doctor. "Promise."

"Do you want me to leave?" I asked.

"I want you to stay," said Astrid. "In fact, I want him to stay here with me tonight. Is that a problem?"

"Not for me," said the doctor.

"I promise, no hanky-panky," said Astrid.

"I wouldn't necessarily rule that out," said the doctor with a wink. Both the women with him giggled.

One of the women took a paddle from the machine and coated it with some type of jelly from a tube. Then, she lifted Astrid's gown and placed it on her stomach. The other flipped a switch and a screen, not unlike a computer terminal, lit. In the center of the screen was this area the seemed to throb. Other things around it were moving.

"There it is!" said the doctor, pointing to the area I was watching.

"What is it?" I asked.

"That's your baby," he laughed.

I could only stand there, transfixed with awe as he pointed out the head, the hands, the feet and some of the internal organs.

"Is everything okay?" asked Astrid nervously.

"I would estimate you to be about ten weeks along," said the doctor confidently, "and everything is just perfect."

I couldn't have put it better myself.

Epilogue

Over the past few months, I have had time to reflect upon the events of the past summer. It makes no more sense to me now than it did then. I thought that given some time, it would fade to the back of my consciousness but that has not happened. Of course, there was extensive news coverage in the Rochester area, but we didn't expect the national media to pick up the story the way they did. Reporters, even well-known ones, who I would have thought had better things to do would not let it die.

"I think you should talk to them, Mitch," said Astrid, after I had turned down yet another request for an interview.

"I don't want the attention," I protested. "I wish they would let me put it behind me."

"There's more chance of that after they get the story," she reasoned. "Once it's out there, it isn't news anymore."

"They're calling me a hero. Isn't that a joke?"

"Many of us agree with them," said my wife, "but if you don't, why don't you tell them in person why they are mistaken? I know you have something to say; maybe you'll get through to people, and possibly, prevent something like this from happening again."

Reluctantly, I agreed to be interviewed on the air by someone from NPR. I chose them because although I often listened, I doubted that many other people did.

The reporter, Ron Spring, was very solicitous when I answered my phone at the appointed hour. "Mr. Goldblatt, it's nice to speak with a real American hero."

"I'm not a hero," I protested, "and if we're going to do this, you'd better call me Mitch, Mr. Spring."

"I'm Ron, and I have to tell you that I am not alone in characterizing you as a hero. For those of you in the listening audience who have been living in a closet, Mitch Goldblatt is the man who stopped the Businetex corporation from bringing down a plane with one hundred fifty employees on it in an elaborate insurance fraud scheme."

"It was not the whole company," I interrupted. "There are many decent people who I was proud to work with at Businetex. This was a few bad eggs who happened to be at the top."

I smiled to myself at the bad metaphor and was grateful that he couldn't see me.

"Let's talk about those corporate criminals," said Spring. "According to my notes, Walter Nelson, a vice president, is under indictment for fraud and conspiracy to commit murder. Other charges may be pending."

"Yes."

"It is my understanding that he's cooperating with the authorities."

"So I've been told," I agreed.

"What do you know about this?" he persisted, obviously disappointed by my terse reply.

"I was told that when he learned that most likely, he would be indicted on federal charges that were punishable by the death penalty, he was anxious to make a deal with the prosecutors. He agreed to tell all he knew in exchange for a promise that the maximum penalty he could face would be life in prison."

"And has he told all that he knows? Has his account been truthful?"

"I wouldn't know," I replied. "You would have to ask him."

"Let's talk about what you do know. Have the authorities filled you in on any of the details?"

"According to what Walter Nelson told them, the original plan was to raise capital over a period of time by eliminating personnel that were considered superfluous."

"Simple minds, such as mine, would have thought of attrition, early retirement incentives or a layoff to achieve this objective," protested Spring.

"I agree," I said. "Layoffs are bad for morale, but most people are realistic about their necessity, and the stockholders generally react positively. However, all three of those options require a charge against profits, which hurts rather than helps immediate cash flow. Severance pay and benefit packages are more expensive than merely compensating survivors for unpaid vacation, and then, there was the little matter of the life insurance, payable to the company on the death of highly compensated employees."

"I understand that you declined to accept that coverage."

"I can't take credit for that much foresight," I said. "I thought it was innocent enough, but my wife was adamantly opposed. It was she who drafted and mailed the letter declining the offer; I only signed it at her urging."

"Then why were you a target?" wondered Spring.

"Initially, I wasn't," I replied. "I got in their way. The plan was diabolically simple. Employees were evaluated and, if they were deemed unnecessary, a fatal accident or illness was arranged. Once the J-6 printer was released to the market, it was decided that Bob McCann, my boss, had outlived his usefulness. When, in casual conversation, during a photo session for the newspaper, he mentioned a vacation to Cancun to George Stanton, the CEO of Businetex, the information was relayed to Walter Nelson, who arranged to be there at the same time. There were other incidents similar to this one throughout the company."

"The whole thing seems ludicrous," protested Spring. "Even eliminating several employees at once, they could not have generated enough capital to solve their widely reported cash flow problem."

"Exactly," I agreed, "so when it became apparent that the trickle of capital from the individual policies would not be sufficient to turn the company around quickly enough to save Stanton's job, they got greedy. They decided that if they put one hundred fifty employees on a plane and it was lost over the ocean, they would have the sympathy of the stockholders plus the cash they needed. After all, no one could fault them for purchasing flight insurance, when so many valued employees would be on board."

"This is so evil, it's frightening!" declared Ron Spring dramatically. "Let me read a quote from FBI spokesman George Merrill.

"The plan was so simple, they thought they could carry it out themselves; that was safer than bringing in outsiders, not to mention cheaper. The type of criminal expertise they required could have been expensive. In a ridiculous gesture of economy, they decided not to go to the expense of placing a hospitality team in St. Thomas to greet travelers they were certain would not arrive. Every aspect of their plan was so badly bungled and so amateurish, it is amazing it went on for as long as it did without detection, but the whole idea was so far-fetched that no one thought to look for such a connection between a series of apparently unrelated, if unusual, deaths."

"Do you care to comment on that?"

"No," I replied. "To be honest, I'd like to put all of this behind me."

Ron Spring was not yet ready to release his prey. "Let's talk about the emails, Mitch. You and a coworker..."-I heard him rusting papers-"...a Mr. James Deckle, hacked your way into the mailboxes of both Nelson and CEO Stanton."

"There were very few ground rules for this interview, and you are well aware that this subject is off-limits," I said curtly.

"I understand," he said knowingly. "We won't discuss how the emails were obtained, only their content. What were the 'loose ends?'"

I didn't want to discuss this. I felt sick when I learned that the "loose ends" referred to in the emails were Bobbie and Astrid. Their not too discreet inquiries had come to the attention of Walter Nelson, and he and Stanton had decided to eliminate them. They assumed that I was in on whatever they had learned, which made me a target as well. Maggie was truly an innocent victim; Jerry Fallow had insisted that she be included, and they decided it was easier to go along with that than to have him question why they were so adamant in their opposition.

"Look," I sighed, "this is really beside the point now. The guilty parties are behind bars, Businetex is struggling to survive, and I think the sooner all involved put this behind us, the better."

Spring sensed how close I was to declaring this interview, that I hadn't wanted to give in the first place, over, and he quickly changed directions.

"George Stanton, who is still proclaiming his innocence, gives Walter Nelson credit for the whole idea. Nelson insists he was only following orders from above. So far, Stanton has been charged with conspiracy and twenty-two counts of murder, and those are just the ones that can be proven. A federal grand jury is still considering further charges. Nelson is listed as a co-defendant in the murders with further charges pending. Who do you think is telling the truth?"

"I don't know," I admitted. "In my experience, both of them are probably lying. My best guess is that the truth lies somewhere in between."

"Fair enough," replied Spring. "I would like to add that thanks to James Deckle, and his intimate knowledge of the email system, the FBI was able to issue subpoenas for erased transmissions before Stanton and Nelson had the opportunity to get to the employees who could have obliterated those messages. The case is moving slowly, but the prosecutor wants to be certain that he will get a conviction before further formal charges are brought."

I knew that sooner or later, he was going to get to what was going to be the hardest part of this interview for me, the truth behind what happened to Artie.

"Mitch, you lost a good friend to this plot," said Spring.

"Artie Kornfeld; he was more than just my friend; he was a brother to me."

"Could you tell us what happened?"

I wanted to say no, to tell him that enough was enough, but I had come so far, I felt that I had to finish. "The hardest part of all of this, for me, was learning the truth behind what happened to Artie," I said.

"Why?" asked Ron Spring in a tone that suggested he was on the edge of his seat.

"I learned that he was never intended as a target," I replied.

I paused, hoping that he would accept that as my complete answer but the long silence that followed was deafening and I knew I would not get off so easy.

"He had allowed himself to be covered by the insurance, with Businetex as the beneficiary," I said slowly, "but it had been decided that he was needed for future projects. Jerry Fallow, on the other hand, was not only unnecessary, but he was the most highly paid employee in the department. What Walter Nelson did not know was that Artie shared Jerry's case of Gatorade when they played racquetball together. The bottle tainted with the Digoxin was meant for Jerry. Nelson was very specific about this."

"Why was that important?" mused Spring.

"For some reason, he felt that having murdered one innocent man while trying to murder another somehow helped his case. After Artie died, they were still determined to get Jerry, but they thought that using the same drug a second time was too risky. Therefore, they spiked one of the Gatorade bottles with alcohol after learning that Jerry never drank. They were hoping that, not realizing what he had consumed, he would get into his car, and no one would be too sympathetic about a drunken driver. Because they knew he had no real family and few, if any, friends, they didn't anticipate any great effort being made to clear his name."

"But you have cleared his name," said Spring.

"I hope so," I replied. "Jerry Fallow and I were not close friends, but no one deserves to have his reputation ruined unjustly."

"You have protested that you are not a hero, Mitch, but I think those of us who have heard what you say have concluded otherwise."

I could hear that he was about to wrap up the interview but I could not let it end there. I still had something important to say.

"May I comment on that?" I asked.

"Please, we'd like to hear what you have to say," replied Spring eagerly.

"I have been given a lot of credit for uncovering the plan in time to prevent those bombs from exploding on that charter, but in reality, much of what I did was stupid. Instead of running off to the airport with no real plan, other than to stop my wife from boarding that plane, I should have warned her much earlier, as soon as I suspected that something was not right, and I should have shared my concerns with the authorities. I don't know if I could have convinced them to take me seriously, but I am no detective, and neither are Astrid or Bobbie McCann. None of us had any business trying to get to the bottom of this alone. We never took the time to consider the kind of danger in which we placed ourselves. Certainly, I would have had a better shot at convincing people who could have put an end to all of this that something was amiss if I had gone to them earlier, rather than by approaching the airline agent at the gate, and telling her that there was a bomb on the plane. My defense is that I'd never had any experience with that type of situation, and I didn't know what to do. My only thought was to save my wife. I followed my instincts; what can I say? I'm not Indiana Jones or one of those action heroes. I'm just a regular guy whose only brush with the law before that day was a parking ticket."

"Thank you, Mitch," said Ron Spring. "I have been talking with Mitch Goldblatt, the everyman who became a hero by exposing the Businetex scandal."

I wondered if he had heard a word I'd said.

I had hoped that granting an interview would satisfy people's curiosity about what had transpired, but immediately afterward, interest increased. Apparently, NPR had a much wider audience than I thought. The post office brought bags of mail, and numerous gifts arrived at our door from all over the United States and Canada. We had to retain an attorney to arrange the return of anything valuable, and to set up a fund for the survivors for those gifts that we couldn't return. We were forced to take a new, unlisted phone number and to hire an answering service for the old one. I was overwhelmed, both by the unwanted attention and by the idea that so many people cared so much.

Gradually, interest tapered off. I was able to make a quick run to Wegmans for a quart of milk without being inundated by admiring well-wishers. Life returned to normal.

Now that some time has passed, I am more sad than angry. With the holidays approaching, the ghosts of those no longer with us are present more and more frequently. It is a time of greatly mixed emotions for me. On the one hand, I joyfully anticipate the birth of Astrid's and my child. On the other hand, I am sad and angry that Artie will not be a part of her life.

We know with relative certainty that our baby will be a girl. Astrid has had test after prenatal test, and the amniocentesis revealed the fetus to be female. The sonograms have no argument with that and so far, we have been assured and reassured that everything is absolutely perfect.

I get the feeling that Astrid is a little disappointed that it isn't a boy. "Is there some reason that you don't want a daughter?" I asked her as she frowned over the sonogram.

"No, as long as it's healthy, I don't care what it is, but I've heard that every man wants a son. I'll try harder next time."

"Come here," I said, holding my arms open for her.

She nestled against me. "I know I should be happy; they also say that every woman wants a daughter."

"I don't know about that," I confessed, "but I have to tell you, I could not be more delighted that the baby is a girl."

"Honestly?" she asked hopefully.

"Yes," I replied, nuzzling her hair. "When I was still a child, I began to notice how Marilyn looked at my father, and the expression on his face when he watched her. I don't think it was conscious on either of their parts, but to an observer, she was his princess, and he was her knight in shining armor, even when he was wearing old jeans and his favorite soft, faded flannel shirt as he cleaned out the garage. I remember feeling left out, like they were members of some secret club, and I didn't know the handshake. I decided right then that someday, I would have a daughter, and I too would know that feeling."

"So you would have been upset if it was a boy?"

"No," I replied, shaking my head. "I think I would like to have a son too; maybe even more than one of each, but if I only have this one child in my life, my longtime wish will have been fulfilled. We couldn't have done any better!"

Neither Astrid nor I will rest easy until our daughter is actually here with us, and we can count her ten perfect little fingers and ten perfect little toes, but we are trying to have a positive attitude. Astrid laughingly tells me that this pregnancy is so different from the last time, it's like it is her first.

About two weeks after Labor Day, the morning sickness disappeared as suddenly as it came, and she has been feeling wonderful ever since. She looks radiant and carries her well-rounded belly with pride. This baby is very active.

"I think that our daughter may break the gender barrier among NFL place kickers," laughed Astrid as we lingered lazily in bed on a Saturday morning.

She took my hand and placed it on her rounded belly. I felt three quick taps.

"I picture her more as a prima ballerina," I smiled, rubbing the spot where I'd last felt signs of a new life. "I have mental images of Margot Fontaine in *The Firebird*; Rifka took Marilyn and me to see the movie at the Little

Carnegie in Manhattan when I was still pretty small, but I have never forgotten the grace of that elegant woman."

"You don't want her to play football?" teased Astrid.

"Whatever our daughter becomes, if she does her best she will have lived up to our expectations for her," I replied.

We have decided that we will name our daughter after Artie.

"I think the name Arden is just different enough that he would have approved," said Astrid, caressing her belly lightly.

"I think he would like it because it will keep his memory vibrant for us," I said. "Artie would never want to be forgotten. Our daughter will remind people of what remains behind."

Her middle name will be Roberta, after her godmother. We hope that if there is some of Artie's genius combined with Bobbie's strength in her, she will be just about perfect to survive in this imperfect world.

Every day, Astrid and I sit and talk to Arden.

"Do you feel silly?" Astrid asked.

"About what?"

"About talking to a child who won't be here for another three months."

"I don't think it can ever be too soon for us to tell her how much we love her," I said. "She already seems so much a part of our lives that I can't help but feel that she cares what's going on."

"We already know her," agreed Astrid. "She should get to know us too, before she arrives."

I could not continue to work for Businetex after I returned from Washington, DC. I returned to the job long enough to arrange a vacation, and as soon as Astrid received the okay from her doctor, we were off to the Pacific Northwest.

"The place won't be the same without you here," said Beth, when I stopped by her desk to say good-bye. "What made you pick the Pacific Northwest for a vacation?"

"We have never seen that part of the country and have always wanted to," I explained.

What I didn't tell her was that one of the headhunters I had previously contacted had given me a lead on a job. While we vacationed, I interviewed with a small software company located outside of Seattle. They couldn't match my Businetex salary, but they were looking for creativity and innovation, and they offered me a share of the profits to sweeten the pot. They are very small, but my gut says they have what it takes to make it big.

My heart was saying to go for it, but I left it up to Astrid.

"Do you think we could be happy living here, so far from our families and everything familiar?" she wondered.

"I feel like it's time for a change," I replied. "Don't you?"

"Maybe," she mused.

She made a few inquiries, and made a social call to a former co-worker, who had relocated in downtown Seattle.

The result was that she was offered a fantastic opportunity. She is managing investment portfolios for corporate clients at a large brokerage firm in Seattle. Her salary is almost double what she was earning in Rochester, and there is room for her advancement.

"What's even better," she enthused as she related the terms of the offer to me, "is not only do they know about my pregnancy, but they have in-house day care for their employees. The CEO is a woman who has three children of her own, one of them still a toddler, so one of the principles the company strives for is to make child rearing and pursuing a career compatible activities."

We both felt that our ship had finally come in.

Perhaps the biggest surprise for us came from Inga.

"If you are moving to Seattle, I'm sure I will like it there too," she announced.

Astrid had resigned herself, unhappily, to being separated from her mother. "Are you sure that you're willing to move?" she asked. "You were adamantly opposed to coming to Connecticut and Seattle is much farther.

"I have come to realize that home is where my children live," declared Inga.

I suspected that the baby Astrid is carrying had more to do with it than we did, and I said as much.

"No," insisted Inga, "I am looking only to the present. Being near my grandchild is a bonus for the future."

She and Ole seem very happy in their airy garden apartment in a nearby suburb, and she has already joined the Lutheran church and found a part-time job in a small boutique near her home.

Rifka was not happy about our decision at all. She always thought of Rochester as the end of the earth but at least it was in New York.

"What's in Seattle that you can't find right here in New York?" she asked.

"I guess you'll find that out when you come to visit us," I replied.

Marilyn thinks that the move sounds like a great idea. "I've heard that Seattle is the new up and coming place," she enthused when we told her of her plans. "Long Island is becoming so congested, it would be nice to get away."

I think that she's secretly hoping that when they visit us, Bert will fall so in love with the area that he will want to relocate. Marilyn's lived with him for all these years, so I have to assume that she knows him better than I do, but my impression is that Bert is too much a creature of habit for so drastic a change.

We bought a home, a condo overlooking Puget Sound, a bit north of the city. I am ten minutes from my office; Astrid has more of a commute, but she doesn't mind. We shipped Sven out when we moved, and she assures me that she will enjoy the drive. I told you I would do anything for that woman.

Later today, we will pick up Bobbie and the kids at the airport. When we moved, she promised that they would stay close and, true to her word, her family is flying out to spend the holidays with us.

"I'm toying with the idea of moving west," Bobbie informed us when we called to give her our new phone number.

"Now?" I asked from my extension in our bedroom.

"Not right at the moment," she replied, "but when things are resolved, it's something I will consider. For now, I am of a single purpose in organizing the class action civil suit against Businetex that has been filed for the wrongful death of Bob and twenty-one others."

"But when the suit is settled you think you will come here?" asked Astrid hopefully from the kitchen phone.

"I think I would like to be closer to my brother, but I won't settle anyplace that's prone to earthquakes, which pretty much eliminates San Francisco."

"Seattle has them too," I informed her.

"Financially, Bob did right by me," she said. "I can more or less do as I please. I've applied to several graduate programs in archaeology, including one in Portland that sounds promising."

"Portland probably has earthquakes too," I said. "I think there's a fault that runs along the Pacific coast."

"I've never heard of a major earthquake in Portland," protested Astrid, "but you know that we prefer the University of Washington."

"The vote is split. I favor the program that sounds like it has the most to offer, Brett is on your side, Brandon has mixed feelings about leaving his girlfriend here, and Brittany doesn't care where we live, as long as there is a good bookstore nearby."

"Whatever you decide, I'm sure it will be right for all of you," said Astrid.

"Yes," I agreed, I added, "your instincts are beyond question.

"I'm not sure what's going to happen," said Bobbie. "The suit may be done sooner than anyone expected. Businetex, as a company, is foundering. They are not clear of criminal responsibility for the actions of their officers, and the financial burden of the lawsuits that have been and will be filed may be their death knell."

"I would hate to see them fail," I said. "The products they were producing were quality machines at a fair price, and a lot of good people will lose their jobs if the company goes under. On the other hand, it's hard to feel too much sympathy for a firm that puts profits ahead of common human decency."

In all fairness, I have no idea how deep the conspiracy ran. When I returned to work after my vacation, I was contacted by the new acting CEO, and assured that I was valued as an employee. When, in turn, I gave my notice, they offered me a generous raise and Jerry Fallow's old job if I would stay. I still declined.

Jim Deckle came to me before I left and asked me for a reference.

"After all that's gone on, I no longer feel secure working for Businetex," he explained.

Maybe both of us were rats deserting a sinking ship, but I felt his decision was justified, as was mine.

"You'll appreciate the irony of this," he continued "I'm applying for a position at Jerry Fallow's old company; it may even have been Fallow's old job."

"What did you tell him?" wondered Astrid, when I related his request.

"I gave him a glowing recommendation," I said. "I figured it was the least I could do; after all, he really came through for me when I needed his help. I said in my recommendation that if ever I were in a tight spot, Jim Deckle is one man I would want to have on my team. That is the absolute truth. He is strange, but he does have his unique talents. He also happens to be the only man I've ever met who claims to piss like a racehorse, but I omitted that detail."

Astrid laughed so hard the tears ran down her face. "They may have considered that to be an asset," she choked.

After thirty years of Fallow, Deckle should hardly be a challenge for them. He wrote to me in Seattle to tell me that he had gotten the job.

There is one thing I worry about all the time. I wake in the middle of the night in a cold sweat, my heart beating like a jackhammer. Astrid feels me bolting upright to a sitting position.

"Bad dream?" she always asks sympathetically.

"Always the same bad dream," I finally confide after awakening in that state three times in one night. "I worry about what kind of a world awaits our daughter. I wonder how a life can mean so little that it is expendable for money, no matter how many dollars are involved. None of us is blameless; we all take small liberties along the path of righteousness. Who, in the course of a lifetime, has not hoped to get away with some small transgression? My concern is when does the rogue become a felon, and where do we acquire the wisdom to know the difference?"

Astrid is philosophical. "The world is an imperfect place," she agrees, "but if we teach our children values, the world they take over will be a better place. All we can ask of ourselves is to be true to our principles, and hope that the many other good people will do the same."

I know that my daughter will have a guardian angel. Artie will be looking over her shoulder. Meanwhile, I will do the best I can as a parent and as a human being. Ultimately, I guess that is the most we can ask of ourselves.